DRAGONWÜLF AND THE DESTINY OF TYR

SALVATORE' DEBELLA

DRAGONWÜLF AND THE DESTINY OF TYR

iUniverse books may be ordered through booksellers or by contacting:

iUniverse
1663 Liberty Drive
Bloomington, IN 47403
www.iuniverse.com
844-349-9409

Illustrations by Angela Ort

ISBN: 978-1-6632-4735-3 (sc)
ISBN: 978-1-6632-4734-6 (e)

Library of Congress Control Number: 2022920413

Print information available on the last page.

iUniverse rev. date: 11/30/2022

For Karen Marie
The other half of my sky

ISLE OF KELDA

BEWARE THE
HARVESTER OF EYES

E UNDERSEA

WINTERSITE

HROTHGORN

LIFFS

REALM OF THE GHOUL GIANT

THE THRONE OF BONES

"If you are to believe that there are an infinite amount of universes with an infinite amount of possible variations on the laws of nature, then you are forced to admit that it is quite certain that in one of these parallel worlds, dragons exist." - Author: Lewis N. Roe

syn·chro·ny
/'siNGkrənē/
noun
noun: synchrony
Simultaneous action, development, or occurrence.
The state of operating or developing according to the same time scale as something else.

"Do you know Jacques Cousteau when they said on the radio
That he hears bells in random order, deep beneath the perfect water."
- Songwriters: Donald Roeser / J. Carroll
Perfect Water lyrics © Sony/ATV Music Publishing LLC

Contents

DR. JAMES WINTERFALL LETTER

Date: Dimension of Loki 1954 AD
Earth

Dear Professor Wilberforce,

Please permit me to introduce myself. I am Dr. James Winterfall, the grandson of the late Sir Robert Winterfall. As you may know, my grandfather disappeared in 1932, and his body was never discovered, even after a lengthy search. Strangely, the only things found were several thick vines of fresh wet seaweed in his office. It baffled the authorities at Scotland Yard.

I am writing to appeal to your once loyal disposition concerning my grandfather.

After leading several disastrous expeditions to try to locate the hidden mountains of what he referred to as the Hrothgorn Passage. Deep in the forest range of Norway, my grandfather believed a realm would have been found called Arom. Therein lived a sect of people of Norse-like tradition but unique in other ways. The people worshipped a little-known god called Roth'l Orca as well as Odin. The writings describe a being known as Ingegärd who caused great fear among the ancient people. This being was called "Witch Queen," but most likely she served the same purpose as Lucifer.

Sir Robert described these lands under the forests as "lands of perpetual winter." These lands are *under* the forests in a remote region of land and water. Some described them as the gateway to Middle Earth, a part of which some have also denied their existence. He came to believe these things after interviewing some of the area's indigenous people and discovering several antiquities, including a supposed lengthy narrative record on stone.

Sir Robert Winterfall had a supposed predisposition to chronic exaggeration and hyperbole. It was conjecture that the things he had written were either part of his imagination or at least opium-induced paranoia. He hoped to find a passage he claimed to have discovered in his early research as part of ancient stone carvings.

As you may be aware, he recorded that he could not locate the passage. I no longer believe that. I am sure that he encountered more there than he admitted after I discovered some odd artifacts in his mansion. He agonized over the ridicule he suffered at the hands of his colleagues. He was burdened with the nickname "The monster hunter" at the hands of nearly everyone he knew professionally. This name furthered his zeal to search for what may have existed and further damaged his scientific judgment.

Grandfather retreated into an odyssey of opium addiction and alcohol-induced insanity. His housekeeper reported she could hear him sobbing through the heavy doors of his study late into the evening. As an archaeologist and anthropologist, Sir Robert believed he had discovered another ancient civilization, which drove him mad that others ridiculed him

I have recently uncovered more of my grandfather's research that I had previously not seen, in addition to the original manuscripts from his excursions to the region in 1890-1894. While preparing the decaying Winterfall Manor for demolition earlier this year, I discovered these manuscripts tucked away in a false wall behind my grandfather's old study. He had hidden them sometime in the 1910s. I am fascinated by the intricate detail and accuracy of the records. Are these a flight of fancy? My feeling now is that my grandfather *did* locate this ancient civilization. I believe he may have entered the realm he sought. I know this is a bold statement on my part; however, the records are so detailed that it would have been nearly impossible to counterfeit such a thing. I include all I can find that he translated. Unfortunately, he went to his grave not having been taken seriously by his colleagues, but I have chosen you, Sir William, because of the trust he placed in you in your earlier days. Enclosed is a map of the realm and the history of the people of the hidden forest.

My grandfather described a civilization only accessible by a network of caverns and some entrances found at the base of some gigantic fir trees. He said there was a place called "The Portal of the Pines," which he claimed to have read about in his translations. He launched several sad attempts to navigate the confusing web of spider-like tunnels, including the last expedition where most of his party was lost in the caverns. He was sure of his belief that there was a way to locate archeological artifacts of the people, and due to his inability to find the realm, he was never able to publish his findings as accurate. I believe that his failure to prove the location of what he thought to be genuine is what caused his descent into madness and death.

In the writings are the histories of the forest people of Arom and their pact with a supposed evil King Drak'North, the son of Hrothgorn the Ruthless. According to legend, King Hrothgorn created soldiers from captured enslaved people, patterned their likenesses, and named them after himself. The people of the region collectively knew them as Hrothgorn. They were terrifying creatures that stood nearly four meters tall and had faces of evil that terrified even Kings.

Grandfather was not without his significant detractors. I remember an archeological summit where world-renowned Drs. Booth and Smithey ridiculed his work as "fantastical and ridiculous." The researchers mentioned above had a wager as to whether or not Sir Robert would attend a particular archeological summit that same year. When he arrived with his signature handlebar mustache and derby, they burst into laughter at such a sight. Ultimately, I suppose their mission was to embarrass my grandfather rather than examine his research.

I implore you, Sir William, as one of my Grandfathers' final students, that you might give this historical narrative another study.

I include the travel notes of Sir Robert's expedition guide, *Mr. J.W. Smithson,* who did not return from the expedition and whose later recovered artifacts. His narrative sheds some light on what happened during the last journey. The authorities never found his ship log.

As you may be aware, none of the men from the doomed expedition save my grandfather returned alive. The only thing discovered was the expedition ship the HMS *Longfellow,* which was found listing off the coast of Norway, completely soulless and drifting on the sea. Sir Robert was later rescued by the Norwegian Navy floating in the ocean on driftwood, quite dazed and almost starved to death, moaning some words about "sea monsters." He could not explain the fate of his crew, so he stood trial for negligent manslaughter in the deaths of his entire expedition in 1895. He was acquitted for lack of evidence by a British court. What happened to his men was never discovered. Sir Robert claims the men were lost at sea and others in the caverns. His foggy recollections did little to help the manslaughter case against him. I do not propose to try to envision what horrors my grandfather may have encountered on the North Sea; to my knowledge, he never wanted to describe them after his return. Please do not let that influence your study of this narrative. I implore you, Sir William, as I would be pleased to tilt the scales of public opinion in favor of the vindication of my grandfather.

Sincerely,
Dr. James D. Winterfall
On behalf of Dr. Robert Winterfall.

CHAPTER ONE

THE SMITHSON LETTER.

~~~

Date: Dimension of Frigg 1894 AD
Earth

*"Some of the horrors I have seen would send you screaming into the night,
so do not try to educate me about horror. Horror and I are old friends."*
-Excerpt from court transcripts during the
trial of Sir Robert Winterfall 1896.

O n 21 October 1894, we set sail on the HMS *Longfellow* from England across the North Sea to Norway. The *Longfellow* was a Blackwall Frigate from the 1850s. Sir Robert Winterfall chartered the ship and hired his crew for the voyage. He stubbornly refused to answer any questions from the men about their mission and became enraged when challenged. One of the crew said that Sir Robert had overheard a conversation in the galley. One of the men joked about little monsters and dwarves that Sir Robert saw in his "pipe dreams." Sir Robert smashed an ale bottle and threatened to slash a man across the face during a fistfight before retreating to his quarters. Nonetheless, there was the talk of treasure to be had, and none of the men was willing to give that up.

The trip across the North Sea was uneventful until the excursion reached one hundred twenty Kilometers from shore when it happened. A sailor from Dublin named MacTavish was on deck at the bow when a gray creature with skin like greased swine slithered his massive head onto the deck and snapped the poor man in his jagged jaws. There before our eyes was a sea serpent devouring one of our men! A damned sea serpent! Those who read this will think me mad, but I swear it was accurate on my mother's grave. The creature clapped its jaws like a bear trap around MacTavish's torso producing a horrible crunch and a muffled scream. The dread creature hissed and growled in madness as it shook this unfortunate soul from side to side, slamming him into the deck with violent force. MacTavish was already bloodied and dead before the monster dragged him into the sea. We were fired at the creature in all manner of chaos. It was a wonder we did not hit each other instead.

The men retreated below deck as they trembled in the cold. Sir Robert remained on deck with his rifle aimed at the sea.

"Come to me, you son of the devil," bellowed Sir Robert to the creature in the sea. As the rain slammed down and the lightning danced about him, Sir Robert screamed at the sea. He roared at the dark black waves until his voice was almost raw. "Show yourself to me, you vicious beast. I will shoot you between your eyes and hack off your head! I am right here. Do not hide from me." Sir Robert would have no revenge on the creature this day, so he leaned his rifle against the yardarm and began to sob and scream at the rain. If there were any doubt about the sanity of Sir Robert, we settled it immediately. He was raving mad.

Later, when we became aware of the fate of another ship, the HMS *Madagascar*, and her missing crew, it was only now that we knew what had happened to her. When Sir Robert stepped below deck, he addressed the men while drying his hair and face.

"I don't know what that was," he said, trembling. "All you men go back on deck and make sure you have a gun or a saber. If you see that slimy creature rear his head out of the water, harpoon it. I expect every man to be armed, stay above deck, and remain on guard."

"That's easy for you to say we got too much to lose. We got little ones at home waiting for us," argued crewman Jennings.

"I can't wait until we can spill his guts on the deck, and if you don't have the stomach for this, your shipmates will understand and drop you off at the Norwegian port," said Sir Robert.

"Do you say we are cowards because we don't want to end up like McTavish?" yelled a crewmember named Jennings.

"If you want to stay and venture into the forest of Arom with me, you will see things only imagined in flights of fancy or dreams of the opium plant.

Sir Robert explained," I believe your wildest riches are in store for you. I do not care for those things. I only wish to prove the existence of the civilization I know exists. Are you with me or against me, Jennings? Speak now!" He continued his tirade, "It is here, and I will find it if I have to go alone. It is too late for McTavish, but we did not lose him in vain. Can I count on you good men of stout heart to come with me?"

I only heard the sound of men moving toward their workstations.

"If I could send all of you home and do this myself, I would!" bellowed Sir Robert.

The journey continued for several more days in the storms as it reached the shores of Norway. The day was still cold and wet. The freezing pall in the air in Kristiansand was like ice hanging in the atmosphere like so many frozen diamonds. The deckhands offloaded the ship and bade farewell to the HMS Longfellow. Sir Robert procured four wagons for the provisions with entire teams of mules and fresh horses. The excursion into the forest from Kristiansand had begun.

The expedition transported the small band through mountainous passages covered with moss and fallen tree branches. There were rain deluges the men had never seen in England.

It was difficult for the horses to trudge through the mud and ice. The wagons cut deep ruts in the earth, and the team covered very little ground daily.

3

"Push on, men! There is gold and silver in these lands to the north," announced Sir Robert.

I think there was none. He used this as a dangling carrot for these simple men.

"There had better damn well be," I said aside. "These men will show you no mercy if there is no treasure to be had."

"There better be a treasure. I'm not freezing my ass off for nothing," said crewmember Jennings.

The team arrived at a thatched cabin in the middle of the forest, about one hundred Kilometers from the shore. It was tiny, and one could see through an opened door. Maybe one room and a parlor is all it was. A single candle illuminated the cottage, and a small fireplace puffed white smoke from the chimney. Sir Robert dismounted his horse and knocked on the door of the cabin.

A voice answered from within, "I must not have you at my door, and you do not know what is in store, leave now while you are able, and besides, my dinner is on the table."

"We mean you no harm. We merely wish to inquire as to our whereabouts, good Sir," said Sir Robert.

The voice again replied. "If you do not know of such simple things, how can I speak to you of ancient kings?"

Sir Robert demanded to speak to the cabin dweller. "Now see here, Sir, these are the things about which I must speak with you. Why do you speak in rhymes?"

One of the men shouted, "We'll take him by storm. We'll drag 'im out. We will!"

Sir Robert threatened, "I will shoot any man who makes the next move toward this cabin!"

Following a moment of silence from within, a small door opened and out stepped a *toad* no less than a meter tall. He was a giant by toad standards. He was indeed quite huge. There before us was a talking toad. Before you think me mad, I swear it was as I say. He was standing upright like a man, was dressed in overalls, and had a beard that grew to what we can only assume was his waistline. He was wearing shoes made of buckskins and brandished a cane made from an oak branch.

"We are not happy about our dinner being interrupted this way. We were having kidney pie tonight until you and your men caused us such a fright! Now I am quite sad, and sure it has gone cold."

"You say us and we… are there others with you in there?" asked Sir Robert.

"It is me that we are dining with this eve. Ask what you will so that you might leave," said the toad.

"What is your name?"

"Our name is not your business, but I will tell you nonetheless. My name is *Sebastian,* although it is none of your concern. Beyond the trees and across the meadow lies the thing you seek. You will find the door at the base of the largest tree there. It is the *Portal of the Pines.* Now go away and bother Sebastian no more," he said through the billow of his pipe smoke.

"What is and what lies inside the Portal of the Pines? Sir, tell us how you know what we seek," said Sir Robert in a voice increasing in urgency and volume.

"You seek what many have sought and not found. Ancient Kings and treasures abound. Beware of creatures that *stomp* the ground, they still live, and the widows mourn. Be gone with you, and Godspeed. Bless those who follow and those who lead," wished Sebastian. He entered his cabin and closed the door. The men stood mute and dumbfounded at what they heard and stared at the cabin door for eternity. Perhaps they were waiting for something further from the talking toad. They would be disappointed. He was burrowed in his cozy home, enjoying his kidney pie.

The band of treasure hunters and their leader followed Sebastian's directions and located precisely the Portal of the Pines. Hidden in the base of a tree trunk was the entrance to a great cavern. The toad in the cabin described it perfectly. The hole was large enough for a man to crawl on his hands and knees. The entrance lasted several meters, and the men could stand with some headroom. Each man entered in this fashion carrying a torch in one hand. The fiery plumes lit the inside of the wet cavern, so it glistened like ice. Because the mules could not make it into the small area, the men clumsily dragged the provisions through the caverns until they were deep enough to stand. Sir Robert began to laugh as if something was funny. The laugh unnerved my companions and me. "Why was he laughing?"

Many dark paths led in any direction imaginable, much like a "spider web." I think he was laughing because he had found that thing he had known was there all along.

I was not sure and felt uneasy from the start. A feeling of nausea in my stomach and beating in my heart greeted me that day as I entered the caverns. The darkness felt as though it led to evil, and there was something damnable about entreating entrance to any cavern passes. Icy sweat rolled down the back of my shirt as we crept further into the passage.

The cavern held no clues to the whereabouts of artifacts or any archeological evidence. Sir Robert claimed he just "felt they were there." He later claimed to have found some stone tablets with some writing on them, but I never saw them. Sir Robert sent each of the four men into a separate cave with provisions, and I went down the fifth passage with him. The walls were damp and weeping a cold mossy fluid. The floor of the cave was rocky, slippery, and uneven. The torches threw enough faint light down the passageway for about ten feet. As we crept into the darkness, we heard a muffled scream from another passage. Upon investigation, we discovered a large hole in the adjacent passageway.

One team member had fallen to his death there, as evidenced by the footprints. Terror overtook the other men and me, and we fled and left the provisions to scramble out of the catacomb. When we reached daylight, I felt like I might kiss the ground. The other three men refused to return to the catacombs, which resulted in a battle of words with Sir Robert. It was only with the treasure's promise that they would return to the cave as Sir Robert and I consulted the maps. We followed them shortly after to hear shrieks of terror and then silence. They were never to venture back out. I tremble to think what may have befallen them in that terrifying darkness, and I would never go back into the cave. Sir Robert and I hastily mounted horses, left the wagons, and retreated to the ship. He was sour and angry and refused to talk further.

10 September 1894

Sir Robert and I are the only souls left from the expedition, except for the ship crew. He spends his days aboard the HMS *Longfellow* babbling nonsense about Hrothgorn and evil kings that he purports to have translated from ancient writing he had found in the caverns. He had in his possession some stone tablets and paper with something recorded on them that I could not read, and he would not let me near them. Twelve of our companions died through what can only be called *misadventure* at the hands of Sir. Robert. I believe to all who read my words that an actual lunatic had been leading us. After being around him for so long, I have begun questioning my sanity. Last night as I lay trying to sleep, I swore I heard the sound of beating hooves on the ship's deck. When I got up to look, there was nothing there. The sea was driving me mad. There were no horses there, I think.

No weapons were left, or I might have considered running Sir Robert through with a long dagger or putting a slug in his head. Just when I thought I was safe, some robed figures of men on horses rose out of the surf and terrified me beyond words. That probably kept me from killing Sir Robert with my bare hands. They appeared on the deck of the ship and disappeared just as swiftly. I have no idea who they were or what they wanted. I had seen a sea serpent kill a man. I have seen a talking giant toad and robed figures returning from the deep.

The strangers from the sea made Sir Robert act even more paranoid. I fear he will sail us to our deaths if I do nothing. I fear for my life. If anyone reads these words, please send my love to my dear wife, Emma Mary, and two daughters if I fail to return.

J.W. Smithson Esq.

Author's note

Date: Dimension of Loki 1991 AD
Earth

None of the men from the doomed expedition returned alive. The only thing discovered was the ship the HMS *Longfellow*, which was found listing off the coast of Norway, completely soulless and drifting on the sea.

Sir Robert was later rescued by the Norwegian Navy floating in the sea on driftwood, quite dazed and almost starved to death, moaning some words about "sea monsters." He could not explain the fate of his crew, so he stood trial for negligent manslaughter in the deaths of his entire expedition in 1895. He was acquitted for lack of evidence by a British court. The court did not determine what happened to his men, but Sir Robert claims the expedition was being followed and cursed from the outset.

The following is my complete and unabridged translation of the records discovered by Sir Robert Winterfall in 1894 during his excursion to the region. One of my former students, Dr. James Winterfall, left them to me after his death in 1985.

I have taken artistic license and supplemented the narrative with attempted recreation of some dialogue to enhance the story's telling in a novel form. The facts of history remain intact. Current events were added by me later in 1990.

The Dimensions described in the title lines are a theory from Sir Robert Winterfall that proposed that all of the periods described took place simultaneously. Some modern Physicists refer to this as a "Multiverse" referring to Erwin Schrodinger's work. He called it "Superposition" in 1954. He believed that several different histories existed, and were not alternatives, but rather they were all synchronized. Sir Robert predated modern Theoretical Physics and had no access to Schrodinger or his work. Winterfall named his theory "Interdimensional Synchrony" (circa 1894).

The historical novel that follows should be considered a translation of the recorded events with embellishments for storytelling purposes.

Chapter Two

DIESEL AND DEATH

———Ⴡ———

Date: Dimension of Heimdall 32 BCE

"Now, in darkness, the world stops turning
Ashes where their bodies burning." –Black Sabbath

The Kingdom of the South was burning. *Biomechanical* horrors and hideous machinery tortured the terrified people of DragonBorne of Arom. None could escape, and there was no place to hide. The stench of blood, diesel, napalm, and metal permeated the city. The heart of the ancient city was lost in flames. Fiery stones fell from the sky in an orange-yellow display of ghastly death from above. Plumes of smoke billowed from the nostrils of the *Hrothgorn* as they plodded through the city, bringing death. The Hrothgorn were giant creatures covered in red skin. They wore breastplates directly over their bare chests. Several layers of metal sheets, which perfectly sit just under the shoulder plates, protected them from weapons. It covered everything on the fantastic beasts from the neck down and ended at the groin. They once were people of the kingdom who were peaceful farmers and craftsmen. They became Hrothgorn through the dark magic of the Witch Queen Ingegärd. The once-proud empire was glowing with a hue that was visible for miles. The corpses of the innocents began to pile like cordwood as they were gathered and sorted by the Hrothgorn. The ghoulish cannibals fought over the remains of the people. The attack was nearly over, and the Hrothgorn had murdered an entire city. The King of DragonBorne made the fatal mistake of refusing to pay the yearly tribute to the North King Armagorn. The city that once held busy streets of merchants and an ornate temple was now just splintered. Historically the streets were always crowded with peasants shopping at the farmers' markets. The quality of life was easy in DragonBorne. What was a township of a few residents grew into a large city with thousands of people. Now, after this abomination, the town was nearly decimated.

King Geir'wolf Tin'Old hid in his longhouse like a scared rabbit. He trembled at the thought of being killed in battle, so he hid from all possible danger and refused to protect his kingdom. He was a despicable human being who, by all rights, should never have been King of anything. He ascended to the throne ten years earlier upon the assassination of his mother, the Queen. The King had perfectly groomed white hair tightly pulled back. He was a handsome man while he was dressed in the armor of his people. He looked brave, but the armor hid his cowardice.

The Witch Queen Ingegärd watched the carnage from her vantage point in the sky.

"It is I, the Witch Queen of weapons and war. I will give you the tools of battle in the coming days! Bring my message of destruction and defeat of the weak. Show them my power and will, and I will make a place for you among the brave!" she bellowed over the roar of battle. She pointed a craggy, decrepit finger toward the forest floor. Her voice was a shriek and cut through the air like a sword. She floated above in a small, elegantly decorated boat in the air. She moved quickly from place to place, throwing thunder and lightning on the ground.

She was dressed in a gown of remarkable workmanship. It was a beautiful flowing white gown that might be seen at a ball. This extraordinary piece of clothing starkly contrasted with the hag that was wearing it.

She had discovered the portal that would give her passage between time dimensions. The Portal of the Pines is where Ingegärd brought weapons from the past and future with the knowledge to wield them.

Meanwhile, King Armagorn of the North sat easy and disturbingly relaxed on the gigantic Throne of Bones deep in the Kingdom of the Hrothgorn. He had no reason to hide. He was watching the carnage he ordered from atop Hrothgorn Mountain. The King had greasy, disgusting long hair almost entirely covering his face. His tunic was made of the finest Rhandobeast leather and fur draped over his shoulder. He was extraordinarily tall and of Hrothgorn descent, and his skin was scaly, scarred, and greasy red, especially on his face. He grew a rather large set of horns without trimming them. It seemed to give him a terrifying countenance. He witnessed the sadness and pain he had caused and did not care. He seemed ready to fly into a violent, bloody rage. Servants and officers of the court were busy going about their various concerns but attempted to avoid him. The dreaded King was eating something out of a large bowl. The contents would be sure to disgust even the most vigorous constitutions, but he slurped the contents as if it were liquid gold ignoring all decency and common manners.

"Get me another bowl! Cook, I want more," he twice repeated his demand as he belched.

"Another bowl for his majesty!" cried the courtier. A small Hrothgorn carried a large pot to the throne in the hope it would be able to satisfy the King.

"Majesty, your food," the cook said while bowing and holding his arms forth while trembling. He began to shake from terror.

Armagorn snatched the full pot while casting his partially filled bowl to the floor. "Get out of my sight now!" screamed the mighty glutton.

The cook was too eager to do just that as he scuttled away from the throne. The giant King slurped and sucked the putrid liquid from his evening dinner bowl. His tunic was stained by his attempt to stuff food in his mouth from his last meal.

King Armagorn was a nauseating tint of green covered with small scales. Gills on either side of his neck enabled him to swim long distances and breathe under the sea. He had several horns protruding from his skull on either side. A terrifying feature of the King's appearance was several large fangs at the corners of his serpent-like mouth. His tongue would flick in and out of his lips between bites of food.

Outside the walls of the Palace, a bloody attack by the Hroth- giant *Thunder-Blood* was underway. He was one of the last Hroth- giants in existence. The Hrothgorn soldiers were already gigantic, but a Hroth Giant is a sight to behold. They usually dress in some kind of armor and especially a helmet made from the most refined iron ore. His race of giants died in battle with neighboring towns and villages. Deafening claps of doom and perilous thunder accompanied the flashing of the enormous iron sky- buckhorns. Thunder-Blood barked out commands as he dragged his knuckles through the muddy dirt. Hrothgorn soldiers controlled the machines attacking the city. The biomechanical creatures took the shape of military tanks with open sides. Horizontal to one another were massive organs and body parts made of tissue, ligament, and muscle. The ghastly sight of a large *living and breathing machine* appeared to be the remains of butchered Hrothgorn squirming together with a sizeable beating heart in the center. Blood, combined with a foul fluid, flowed throughout the *creature-machine*. The stench of death coupled with diesel filled the air.

"Send the fiery rocks to the South lands! Let them taste our victory and our peril. Let DragonBorne taste despair in their mouths," bellowed Thunder-Blood from beneath a helmet that covered his pock-filled face. A skin disease scarred his face but also wormed its way into his twisted brain. The iron birds dropped fire from the sky. The sound of the fire-stones falling to the floor of the forest was enough to make the bravest soldier shudder with fear.

"They will make the human trash bend the knee," said the giant to his Hroth soldiers. "They have no defense from the fire rocks that hang under the iron birds like apples on a poisonous tree. Honor the carvings written upon them! We will have victory just as its creators wished!"

The iron bulls were filled with a vile diesel elixir given by the Witch Queen and were ready to roll over the helpless. The giant led the bull squadron.

"We will rain bloody hades on the people from the south. *Death* will come from above and below," said Thunder-Blood with a wry smile. As he spoke, his eye and the left side of his face twitched in a terrifying spasm. As he bellowed orders, he stuttered and shook.

The Hrothgorn soldiers continued their assault by foot. The marching feet echoed through the kingdom under the forest as the Hrothgorn soldiers began to chant.

King Geir'wolf of DragonBorne called his captains into the Long House. They sat on each side of an oaken table.

"Our scouts have informed us that King Armagorn is now on a second attack on our Kingdom. The weapons of Ingegärd are too powerful.

"We will move the sky arrows into place and kill those iron birds! By Odin, I swear it," said Thorleif Svartlingrsson. "We will bring them down in fire and death!"

"How will we halt the iron bulls that roll over whole armies? They are too powerful!" complained the guard's leader, "Some of them have already squashed countless brave men!"

"It crushed them? I know it is worthless to fight in that case … we will retreat behind the walls of our city. We must preserve the *monarchy* at all costs. It does not matter to me if it takes every man. I do not care if it kills everyone. I do not care if it kills *the entire Kingdom!* I will prevail, and I will survive. My army will preserve me!" The court member at the King's right hand attempted to hide a look of disdain.

"Sire, many brave warriors are blinded by snow and ice. They have nearly frozen guarding the gate," said Thorleif.

"*Let them freeze!* Keep them in place because they must protect the King. Armagorn will be nearing very soon, and we cannot leave the gates unattended," said the King. As he spoke, the Court Wizard Odious Forge entered the longhouse from the midst of the battle.

"Sire, it is urgent we must speak. There are signs in the cards and the stars," he said, out of breath. We are all marked to die! I see thousands of corpses more than we already suffer. I see my death in the cards. I fear the kingdom is beyond repair if we do not mount a counter-attack at once."

"Nonsense. We will retreat at once and live to fight another day," said the King.

"King Armagorn will destroy the city along with her people if we do not stand and fight!" reasoned an ever-angered wizard raising his voice. "It is not time to *retreat,* Sire. We must stand and fight!"

"Leave me at once. I will deal with you later," ordered the King. "The gall he has to raise his voice to a King! Thorleif, take this fool from my sight."

"Sire, we must do what is right. We must protect our people!" cried the wizard.

"Enough! Take him away at once!"

As Thorleif escorted him out of the longhouse, the wizard turned and faced the King.

"You are a coward as sure as I am not. You would use your people as a shield to protect yourself?" he spoke as he hung his head, realizing what he had just said in anger to the King.

The King bellowed, "Take him to the dungeon and chain him to the wall! Let us see who is a coward then!"

The wizard rebuked the King until he could no longer hear him. "You must not be the ruler of a Kingdom where you are responsible for people unless you believe there are things for which it is worth fighting and dying. Do you hear me, cowardly King? I do not fear you!

Thorleif grabbed the foolish wizard by his collar and dragged him away from the King and outside the great door.

"Shut up, you damned fool! Do you not know he must punish you now to make an example of you? He could even kill you. I have seen him do it for less."

Thorleif led him through the village roughly by his silvery robes adorned with stars. He dragged him into the forest and proceeded to release him. All the while, they were dodging flying rocks and hiding from Hrothgorn.

"Go and take your leave of me. I will tell the King you escaped into the noise of the battle. I am afraid you will feel his full wrath. You foolishly insulted the King in front of others. I would not do this, but I hate the King more than he knows. I refuse to be his puppet."

"No…, you cannot do a thing like that. The King will hold you responsible," reasoned Odious Forge. "I will not have you pay for my unfortunate words to the King."

"They were not unfortunate. You insulted his majesty in front of the court. The things you said are true," said Thorleif. "That is why I am showing you mercy, you old fool. Take my dagger and cut my arm so that blood runs over my coat. I will tell him you stabbed me trying to escape. Do not return. I warn you. If you return, I will kill you myself."

Forge did as Thorleif wished, and blood flowed over the tunic and coat of the kind man.

"I am sorry because I never wished to hurt you."

"I know…now *go* before you get both of us in trouble."

The wizard faded into the forest and trudged deeper and deeper until there was no light in his path. Thorleif the Younger returned to the Long House with his fabricated story as the Alchemist escaped the wrath of a deadly King.

CHAPTER THREE

THE LOST PRINCE OF DRAGONBORNE

———∽———

Date: Dimension of Heimdall (32 BCE)
Underforest Lands

*"There is but one soul who will have revenge
unto the beasts of destruction."*

A courier from the outskirts of the Kingdom ran to the royal court with an urgent message. "Sire… an emissary from Hrothgorn approaches and wishes to speak with his majesty," he said as he struggled to catch his breath.

"Receive him…but in captivity! We will see what Armagorn demands of us today," said King Geir'wolf in jest.

A large well-armored Hrothgorn was led slowly to the gates, where four of the King's men took him and shackled him hand and foot. They took his weapons and stood him before the King.

"How dare you bind and chain one of the royal guards to King Drak-North? I am a messenger today, and I come with my hands open to you in peace," said the indignant Hrothgorn. "This is how I get treated?"

"Peace? That is a farce! Speak Hrothgorn. Your time is already running out," said the King.

"I will remember your disrespect. I come with a message from the God-King Armagorn," said the Hroth soldier.

"Well...spit it out, beast! We grow weary of your King and his plagues on our people."

"Beasts? Listen to yourself. The way you speak shows your hatred."

"They look even worse in person, do they not? Their smell is worse than I imagined," said Thorleif to the King, ignoring the messengers' comments.

"Our God-King wishes to make peace with his new royal subjects. He wishes for you to throw down your arms, bend the knee, and worship him," said the messenger. "Then we might all live in peace."

"Oh, is that all?" said the King while laughing at the audacity of the Hrothgorn. "He does not want much, does he? We will bend the knee to him when we are dead and can no longer stand straight upon our legs." The court began to chuckle at the very impudence of this Hroth messenger.

"Laugh a good hearty laugh if you must, for it will be one of the last acts you do as living men," threatened the messenger. "Join our King to rule all forest realms... or die."

"Give this answer to your *god-king* with all expediency," said King Geir'wolf. "Tell him we are laughing at his threats."

"Very well, fool King! You have just sealed your fate as well as everyone in your kingdom. I will deliver your response to his Majesty and most high god," said the messenger. "Your jest will hang in your throat like dry bread crusts."

"Count yourself lucky I do not have you removed from my presence and separated from your sinews and joints and fed to the Rhandobeasts," said the King boastfully.

The messenger struggled to break free while spewing epithets, but he was later allowed to leave safely.

+ + ♦ ♦ ♦ + +

The ground and trees rumble as thunder as an army of thousands of Hrothgorn soldiers marched forward like hungry animals. A cadence of evil filled the air. Step after Step grew louder with the terrifying approach. The sound alone instilled fear into even the bravest of souls. The smell of leather tunics soaked with kerosene and the rattling of chainmail rise over the sound of the battle raging behind the beasts. The enemy could hear the creaking and straining of the bows and arrows coupled with weapon fire in fast succession over the war animals' growls and grunts. All of the other sounds all but drown out the iron bulls.

The Hrothgorn army and war animals are, as one, a well-oiled machine ready to take on and defeat its enemy.

Their soldiers filled the ranks, including archery, several defensives, and various flanking units. The army of Hrothgorn with iron bulls, fiery birds, and other weapons quickly invaded the quiet of the DragonBorne after the meeting with the emissary. The great birds of metal dumped fire on the land. As they passed back and forth, spewing death, the city's people panicked and desperately tried to escape the fire falling on them. The bulls rolled over tiny houses and bands of warriors in the way.

Thunder-Blood laughed as the city burned. "Let the fires of the power of Armagorn and Ingegärd burn bright!" he said.

The hollow bravado of the foolish King would soon be the undoing of the City in the coming hours. Double-headed square war hammers of King Geir'wolf will quickly be no match for the war machines provided by Ingegärd. The Kingdom was soon to be a memory left in the corridors of time. Survivors were just a few of the fortunate souls that were able to hide. Most of the residents were captured, killed, or eaten. The cannibalistic nature of the Hrothgorn struck fear in their enemies.

King Geir'wolf Tin'Old sat on his throne and buried his face in his hands. "What have I done?" he said to Thorleif as the young man stood baffled."I paid a great price this day. What have *I done to myself*? Armagorn must pay for this abomination!" As the monarch sat contemplating the day, he realized something had escaped his grasp. "The Prince is missing. I lost him during the battle. He must have slipped outside when I was looking away. *Find him!* Why are you waiting? You fools go now!" he bellowed to his court guards.

The entire court left the King in search of Prince Tin'Old, who was next in line for the throne of DragonBorne of Arom.

As King Geir'wolf and Thorleif contemplated their next move, four ghostly horsemen rode through the walls as if they were as thin as water.

"Stand and uncover your faces!" demanded Thorleif. The figures approached and kept their faces covered. From head to toe, their clothing was long tunics. They were marked with patterns of stars and multi-covered jewels and under the sleeves along the sides of the tunics were the hook and cross symbols. It represented the first god of the ancients. Beneath the tunics, the figures wore white blouses with long hanging sleeves. Their faces peered from beneath the hoods, which completely covered their heads. The figure in the lead drew his horse to a standstill and stretched his arms wide, pointing his gloved palms to the sky.

"Who are you in the name of Roth'l Orca?" asked the King. Thorleif drew his sword and held it toward one of the horses.

"Stay where you are," said Thorleif.

With his hands still pointed toward the sky, the lead figure waved with one hand and knocked Thorleif from his feet. He was thrown uninjured across the floor with one hand sweep.

"Silence! We do not come here for battle or to cause harm, but we are here to be a beacon of what is yet to come," said the robed equestrian.

"There is but one soul who will have revenge unto the beasts of destruction. We will some bright day lead and guide this brave one."

"Why did you not save us from the attack today? You could have done *something!* If you had, there would be no need for such a brave one," said the King.

"That was *your* place to do that, and you failed. You could not even be bothered to be a sentinel to the Prince and keep him safe and far from harm. How do you expect to be trusted with the Kingdom?" the Horseman asked. "No, you cannot be a watchman for your people, but we are here to lead one brave soul in the Kingdom to their destiny."

"Leave my sight, ghoul! I do not need ghostly apparitions and wraiths to rule my kingdom," ordered the King.

What you are doing is not ruling. You are hiding behind women and babies. You will pay for that kind of cowardice. You will see us again soon," said the rider.

"Are you threatening the King of DragonBorne? Such disrespect is punishable by death! Who is this brave soul of whom you speak? Tell me, I demand it," said the King.

"You have the authority to demand nothing," said the rider as all four faded into the walls and disappeared from view.

"It is *me of whom you speak*," said the King haughtily, yelling at the departing riders. "There are none more strong or brave than King Geir'wolf!" he said while pounding his chest." It must be evident to everyone. *Do you hear me?*" he screamed at the bare wall.

The search party returned to the Long House with a report that the Prince was still missing. They discovered one of the gold cloth stars from the tunic belonging to the wizard in the forest. Then the Rhandobeasts lost the scent of the Prince. The wizard had torn his robe, and his decorations fell off as he ran. The King did not see it that way.

He showed great anger. "Bring me the wizard! Find the Prince, and do not return until you have him. Go now. You are wasting time!

——————— ✦✦✦✦✦ ———————

In the meantime, the massacre survivors began to pick up the pieces. A few older men remained, some women and several children.

Several weeks had passed when a poor hunter knelt before King Tin'Old, trembling. All of the search parties were afraid to return, having found nothing.

"Sire…please have mercy on me…it is not my doing." The old man put his face on the marble throne room floor. "Please, sire… I have come to your presence with terrible news."

"Speak, old man! Do not force me to loosen your tongue! Speak!" said the King with an ever-loudening voice.

The old man quivered as he spoke. "Majesty, something…someone has been found in the woods during my hunt. It is a boy." The old man slowly opened his palm to the King, revealing what he held. The object was a bright yellow design of a hummingbird from the wizard's coat. I am afraid the boy is among the dead sire. He was holding this in his hand."

The men outside the throne room hurriedly brought the body to the King. It was that of a boy, but the Rhandobeasts had made identification impossible. The King was inconsolable. Those outside the palace walls could hear his screams of anguish.

"Bring the treacherous Prince slayer to me!" screamed the King in a mournful howl. Thorleif! Attend me at once! Execute all who will not help me find the prince. Leave this old man in the throne room. I want him to be honored and rewarded for his courage to come to me. Come back to me when you have finished!"

When they returned empty-handed, the King began to execute the search party. He went mad and killed everyone involved. He felt sympathy for Thorleif, who was "wounded" by the Wizard.

"I released the Wizard, sire," admitted Thorleif. "The wound was self-inflicted. I am responsible for the prince's death and my actions," said Thorleif hanging his head. One could only assume. He had seen people die for much less." I can no longer stay silent knowing people are dying because of me," he said sadly.

The King flew into a rage of screaming and tears. As he shook his head back and forth, tears and saliva flew from his ever-reddening face. He screamed for his attendants. "Take this infested rat away from me and bring his head to me later. He began to scream, repeating and howling the words, "the Wizard, Odious Forge. Bring him to me alive! I want him so that I might remove his head myself!" The mourning King was desperate for revenge and could scarcely catch his breath.

The fugitive magician could not hide long. The King's men captured the wizard after the execution of Thorleif. Forge received the sentence of death by beheading for the kidnapping and murder of the Prince. He placed his head on the block where many had already lost their lives. The King read the sentence while holding his sword at ready. "Odious- Forge of Arom, court Wizard, astrologer, and alchemist to the King, you are sentenced to death by beheading for the murder of Prince Falstuf Tin'Old. Do you have any last words?"

"Yes, I do," he said as he spat on the ground near the king. "A curse is upon you and your stinking family! I curse you with death-"

Thunk. The King's sword stilled the Wizard's words as Forges' head rolled into the basket.

"I have avenged the Prince," said the King, handing the bloody blade to his servant. "Clean this so it shines once again. If it does not, then throw yourself on it."

Not long after the Wizard's death, Prince Falstuf was found alive. The serpent Wormouth captured him, but when he discovered Falstuf was the Prince of DragonBorne of Arom, he hastily allowed him to escape. An elderly shoemaker from the village had found the Prince in the forest lost and injured and brought him to the King.

Two months later, a worried mother entered the court for help finding her young son, who had disappeared into the forest. He was lost two months before. Prince Tin'Old's foolishness and the King's fury had cost many lives. There will be a price to pay.

The lost Prince lives.

CHAPTER FOUR

INVENTIONS OF RARE NECROMANCY

—cᴠɔ—

Date: Dimension of Heimdall 32 BCE
Underforest Lands

"I am single-minded. I vow that revenge will be mine."

King Armagorn surveyed his destruction of DragonBorne. "Where was King Tin'Old? Why was he allowing the taking of his kingdom?" The Hrothgorn had taken all of the best from the city. There was nothing left to steal and destroy. Where was the King's anger? Coward! Come out and face me," Armagorn shouted at the palace. "I will spill your guts to show your people you have none! What challenge is an enemy that will not fight?"

Even an evil creature such as King Armagorn could not respect the military *ineptitude of a coward*. The tanks had done their worst of death and pain as they rolled over the city, leaving destruction in their path.

"There will come a time when I will invade the stone throne and cut Tin'Old's heart from his body. Until then, I will enslave all I see before me," said Armagorn in an ominous tone. I want to hear the sounds of bodies hitting the forest floor like bags of mud. The sound is music to my ears!"

The father of Odious-Forge the Wizard, Eldon Void, sat perched on the edge of his seat at his large oaken feasting table. He was a man of money and power, accustomed to getting what he wanted. He mourned the death of his son as most other fathers in his position would. The bright orange fire in the fireplace burned brightly and threw a flickering intensity over the face of Void. He considered the magic of his family. The Void magic comes from death. The family was careful to gather newly deceased individuals who have retained all of their memories that have not yet flowed into the grave. When a life ends, the person's knowledge and energy flow to a member of the Void family. This energy is how it was with Odious-Forge. Those with the most potent lives in older generations yield tremendous energy to produce magic. The family became accustomed to death and the power within the spirit.

"T'Par! Attend me at once! He motioned to his servant to come from the adjacent hallway.

"Yes, my lord," T'Par said while attempting an awkward bow.

"Bring me the book," Void ordered. "The answer lies in the book."

"What answer, sir?"

"There may be hope for my son found in the pages," he said. The servant knew well that the king had beheaded the wizard, and he could not see how there was hope for him. Nevertheless, he scuttled to the library to find *the book.*

"In the name of Odin, I swear I will find a way to redeem you, my son," he vowed, throwing his voice into the face of the fire.

When T'Par returned with the book, Void swept the dust and cobwebs away from the cover of "*The Inventions of Rare Necromancy.*" The much-consulted book had been in the family for centuries.

"I cannot practice the dark art of Necromancy, but I believe I can find someone who will oblige me," said Void to his servant. "We need only to search the pages, and soon Odious will return to me."

"Surely he must be in Niflheim by now, sir," reasoned T'Par.

"The dark world of the dead will be one spirit short today, I swear. The witch queen Hel is denied!"

Odious-Forge had already been buried, but Eldon Void had not been notified, so he could not attend his son's grave. He was presented with his son's head as proof of the execution. Void put the grisly artifact in a small golden chest in his main room. "Those who have harmed my family will pay," he said. "We shall see what goes unpunished."

"Sire, the wizard's family may want retribution for his execution," said the King's first attendant later that day.

The King leaned forward on his ornate throne to emphasize his following words. "*I am not in fear of Eldon Void or anyone else.* Do you understand me? He was my former advisor many years ago. He will be loyal," said King Tin'Old. "Make sure to surround me with protection. We must preserve the monarchy."

"Our information shows Void seeking knowledge from the gods and wisdom from the ages," said an advisor to the throne.

"Just keep an eye on him."

In the days following, Void sought wisdom from the gods and chose a course of action against the assembled forces of King Tin'Old. He sought answers from dreams, prophets, and even directly from Rothl'Orca (*the Whale God of the Sea*). "I must make the King pay," he said. He knelt in his long black gown and cloak and rested his head on his makeshift altar to his god.

When Odious-Forge was beheaded, he was buried in a pauper's grave in a potter's field in the city of the dead. Void's search led him to the woman of Arom, who claimed that she could see the ghost of his son if it rose from the city of the dead.

"Old woman, name the thing you desire, and it will be yours. I only ask that you let me speak to my son from the city of the dead," implored Eldon Void.

"My name is Isadora of Arom... not... old woman. I only want a position in the household of Void in your service as long as I live."

"It is yours. Are you certain it was Odious- Forge?" asked Void.

"We will summon him. Place your hands on the table with me," said Isadora. "Odious- Forge, I command you to come to us. I invoke the spell of rare Necromancy," she said while stretching her twig-like arms on the tabletop. The witch's body began to tremble and twitch. "The pain is too great. Take this spell from me! *Romus vernomus promalus* Necromanus!" She started to speak in the voice of a man.

"*Why do you do such a thing to try to bring me back from my death slumber? You have disturbed me!" said the voice. "Why would you allow this hag to disturb me? How could you do this, Father?"* asked Odious.

The voice of the ghost at first frightened the witch of Arom. "I fear I have unleashed a power that will be strong in the spirit of revenge. I feel his vengeance. Get me away from this evil!" screamed Isadora.

Odious- Forge's ghost berated his father for disobeying the gods. "You have opened a portal to a world we should not see," he said barely above a whisper. "The passage is now open, and it will not close. You do not know what you have done. I have seen a vision. I predict King Tin 'Old's downfall. He will be dead before the sun sets," he said. "I will have my revenge...tonight!"

"I care not for Tin'Old. I hope he dies a painful death. That is not the reason why I am doing this thing. I want you restored to me!" said Eldon to his son. "Bring him to me, and I will grant any wish you desire," said Void to the old woman.

"We must have a Necromancer to be able to return your son from the dead! I will do this for you, but I cannot be responsible for what evil we unleash with my spell," said the old woman. "I have seen the Necromancers slash and tear at the skin of the living. I have seen them strangle people to death. That, my dear Wizard, is all on your conscious."

"That is nonsense, old woman. I am not afraid," boasted Void.

The witch howled a loud cry in fear when she sought the Necromancer's spirit. She recited a spell that was not audible. She moved her lips with an unknown tongue.

"Speak to me in many voices and tongues!" said Isadora.

The form of a Necromancer rose from the floor after the spell by the witch of Arom. It was bluish in color and maintained only a faint shape of a man. It floated like a cloud high above the floor near the ceiling.

"I am here for a short time," the Necromancer whispered as he rose from the floor. *"I must be brief."* His face was covered and well hidden. As he rose from the ceiling, his appearance terrified both the old woman and the father.

"King Tin'Old will perish as foretold by the wizard from beyond. King Armagorn will defeat the King of Arom this day," he said.

"I have had enough of this! Show me my son, old woman! I will pay you handsomely," said Eldon rudely.

The Necromancer pointed his boney finger in the direction of the City of the Dead and spoke, "Odious Forge Void of DragonBorne... come forth from the dark and foggy world of the spirits of the dead."

An apparition appeared before their eyes. The ghostly form materialized into that of a wizard, complete with robes and other decorations. The figure was missing its head.

"This is what you must do, Eldon Void, and cannot be left to others. You must place your son's head on his neck," said the Necromancer in a ghoulish voice.

"Are you mad?" asked a shocked Void.

"Do as I command!" said the Necromancer through clenched teeth as he bared his sharp claws.

This terrified Void as he reached into the gold box and produced the head. The edges of the neck were jagged and torn. The King was a novice executioner. The wizard took a deep breath and moved his head as his father placed it on his shoulders. A rush of blood filled the head, changing it from s gray-green to a pinkish hue.

"What in the name of the witch queen?" asked a confused Odious-Forge. "Why have you brought me back?"

The father embraced his son and held on tight.

"I will see to it that vengeance is ours on this day. I have brought you forth because *no one* takes what is mine. Not my riches or glory and certainly not my son."

The next day, Tin'Old's army is defeated as prophesied. The Hrothgorn wounded the King, and he tried to commit suicide by falling on his sword to avoid suffering. He could not make himself do it because of his cowardice and asked a young soldier to give him the coup de grâce. Through a spell cast by the wizard, the face and form of the soldier turned terrifyingly into the shape and form of Odious-Forge, who gladly murdered the King with no mercy.

"I will kill all of the descendants of King Tin'Old," he screamed through his clenched teeth as he ran King Tin'Old through with his sword. "Die coward... die! I am single-minded. I vow that revenge will be mine." Exhausted Odious sat down with bloody hands and the sword across his lap. He looked down at the dead King, and a terrifying smile crossed his face, turning to chilling laughter. Revenge would have a bloody holiday.

CHAPTER FIVE

THE GIRL AND THE HUMMINGBIRD

———•———

Date: Dimension of Odin 100 AD
Underforest Lands

*"My father is a foolish old man who has numbly
mistaken your beauty for skill and intelligence."*

O ver a hundred years passed from the time of the destruction of DragonBorne. King Falstuf Ragnon Tin'Old, *the lost prince,* grew old and carried on the traditions of his father, Geir'wolf Tin'Old. Nearing his twilight years, a young servant girl named Valorii Thurield tended to his shoes, food, and many other royal concerns. She had no interest in any things political. She was there to serve the King. He loved the girl as one of his children. As she prepared the King's bath, his son Falstuf Tin'Old the younger entreated entrance to his father's chambers. The Prince was unkempt, foul-smelling, and exceedingly obese.

Valorii greeted the Prince, "Good evening, your grace," she sheepishly said with a clumsy curtsy. Valorii was terrified of the younger Tin'Old because she had witnessed his brutality and horrible treatment of servants and his wife. Tin'Old grabbed the young woman around her waist and clumsily pulled her close to him.

"Please … to call me *your grace* seems too proper. It suggests so much distance between us." He leaned forward while squeezing Valorii around the waist and whispered in her ear." If you give yourself to me later in my chambers and I will make you my mine, and you will have all you desire. *Do you realize I can give you whatever you want?*" he said in a growling whisper

Valorii looked upon the disgusting blob of a man, and her facial expression indeed gave her away. The young girl was very proper and innocent of the ways of the kingdom.

"Your grace- I must return to the King at once- he requires me now."

"You will take leave of me when I desire it and not before," he growled. He took Valorii in his arms and kissed her full on her mouth. She pulled away and hastily wiped her mouth with her sleeve in a vain attempt to hide her disgust with him.

"Your grace, I cannot do what you wish me to do…." she said. She found the Prince quite revolting. *What a disgusting pig,* she thought.

"Do you find me repulsive? Why do you wipe your face so? Does my wealth stick in your throat and disgust you? I am sorry that you find my silver and gold so sickening," he said, " If you will stay with me, you would no longer have to serve the King."

"No, your grace, I just cannot-" she said, choking back an upset stomach.

"That seems *unlikely* because of your *unseemly* upbringing," he said with a disgusted look while narrowing his eyes.

"I beg you your grace-"Valorii said, struggling for the correct words. She wondered where her imaginary handsome prince had gone. It certainly was not this filthy swine. His stench was sure to make her vomit very soon.

"If it were for me to decide, you would be in the gardens pulling weeds and in the kitchen with your hands raw from dishwater where you belong. My father is a foolish old man who has numbly mistaken your beauty for skill and intelligence. Even your face shows your low upbringing and your stupidity. I offer you a place in my chamber, and you treat it as if I am offering you a place in my hound's quarters."

"I am sorry. Your grace for"-

"Be silent field harlot… and get away from me!" he ordered as he threw a water basin across the stone floor. "I will see my father now. You make me sick. Now clean up this mess."

He would look just right on a spit over a roaring fire with an apple in his mouth, thought Valorii.

Tin'Old the younger entered the royal bed-chamber to find his father seated on his ornate bed, staring into the hall with great concern.

"Good evening Majesty and my most honored Father," he said with a half-hearted bow.

"I know well of your cruelty to my kingdom's people. Save the hogwash for someone more foolish than me, young man. How dare you treat that young woman that way?" he scolded his son.

"You are aware that she is just field trash," said the prince.

"If you were not my son, I would have your head for that. You will *not* touch that girl in any way. She has done nothing to you. That is a decree from your King!" said the King loudly.

"As you wish, Sire, said the prince sarcastically.

"Have you not bathed recently? You smell like a dung heap. It is quite disgusting, you know."

"Your nightly visits to certain farm widows are disgusting to most of us within the palace. Do you suppose we do not know of your perversions, *father?*"

"You are an insolent usurper. I know you are aware of *that* fact," the old man reminded his son.

"I know you no longer have control of your senses."

"I am as strong as a Rhandobeast! Do not challenge me again!" After gathering his thoughts, the King asked, "Now, to what do I owe the honor of this visit? What do you want?" he growled, growing closer to calling the palace guards.

The younger Prince Tin'Old withered away from his father and continued. "As you may know, your *grace,* there are rumors of Hrothgorn soldiers of the North venturing into our lands when it is not the season of the tribute. There are also rumors of danger to his Majesty."

The elder Tin'Old smiled a crooked smile. "It pains me how you say *your grace* in a certain tone when addressing me. It makes me think that you do not feel my rightful place is on the throne."

"I am and always have been at your service, father. I am shocked you would see me that way." The prince was not convincing. Neither man believed it.

"Why do I need to fear this supposed danger?" the King asked his son.

"We hear mumblings and murmuring in our travels. The people are restless and may be ready for a change. That is all we hear. Forgive me, Majesty. I am just a *faithful* messenger of the whisperings that fall on our ears. My heart is always with you."

"I am sure that the idea of stealing the throne would break your dry little black heart. It is good your mother could not see what a treacherous little ingrate you have become," the old man lamented. "Tell me of these dangers you have heard?" he asked, knowing that his son knew more than he would say.

"Some men of the south wish to avenge their family members. I do not know who they are. I recommend a special detachment of guards posted outside your door as a safeguard. The young woman to whom you are attached cannot have access to you unrestricted. We can no longer trust her."

"Nonsense. I will not hear of it. Valorii Thuireld is like a daughter to the throne and me. She remains."

"As you wish, Father, my only concern is that she may spoil the King's stately domain with her *common and ordinary* conduct," he said with a wry smile.

The King pulled his hand away sharply as the Prince made a fake attempt to kiss his ring.

"I would just as soon have you kiss my arse," said the King. "Leave me! It is time for my night meal and bath. It is time for you to climb back under your slimy rock from where you came."

The son retreated from the royal chamber. His father knew in his heart that he would soon be the next to sit on the Throne of Stone. As he left the palace, he saw the King's guard Tor'Vold.

"Do not let him leave the palace, or it will mean your head. I will place it alongside Valorii Thurield's head."

"Yes… your grace," Tor'Vold answered as he trembled. The Prince would be true to his word.

The King shouted to an open door as his son left."Your heart will perfectly match the stone in the throne room."

Valorii entered the chamber and brought the King to the bath. She began to anoint his head with aromatic oils and soaps.

"Do not fear my son, my dear. He is not as intelligent as he supposes. He does not fool me with his feigning of lack of political aspirations."

"Yes, your Majesty…" Her mind began to wander back to another time. She thought about a terrible time. Many years ago, the Hrothgorn descended on the peaceful township where her family lived. Valorii's memories of the tribute were as clear as if they had occurred yesterday. She witnessed some of her neighbors' captivity to satisfy the tribute's pact. The prisoners were used to forge swords, hammers, and war axes. The Hrothorn forced the captives to fashion clothing for the giant Hrothgorn soldiers and fit them with armor. The Hrothgorn guards would put to death workers if the swords or armor were not to the liking of King Drak-North. Some of Hrothgorn were cannibals. Valorii shivered in fear.

After she brushed the King's hair, she returned home. It was a quiet night at the end of the fall harvest, and all was peaceful as the residents of Olde Turknorse made busy preparations for the next day. Valorii played in the meadow with her elder sister Ine'Ath while their mother, Ek'roin Thuireld, cleaned up from the evening meal. The field was full of tall grass and willows. There were beautiful trees to climb and horseshoe rabbits to chase. Valorii closed her eyes in the tall grass and flowers *and daydreamed that she was flying.* She imagined she had learned to fly and that she had wings to soar over the valley. She closed her eyes in the meadow and imagined she would fly over her troubles and away from all the hardships her family had to endure. When she dreamed, she soared. The sound of birds in the air sounded like flutes and pipes from a minstrel's band. She daydreamed with such intensity that she could almost smell the colors of the fields.

She wondered if she was a bird that wanted to be a girl or a girl that wanted to be a bird. "No matter," she thought. *Someday I will soar over the clouds, even if only in my dreams.* Valorii caught a glimpse of one of the flying machines that came from the portal of the pines. It roared like a wild Rhandobeast and was as elegant as a hummingbird as it floated above the forest floor. She thought the gods must want us to fly for some reason to bless us with a gift like that.

Continued...

The Girl and The Hummingbird

PART TWO

The blistering sound of raw thunder started slowly and built to a tumultuous roar within a few seconds. It was the marching of the army of the Hrothgorn into the realm of the Kingdom of Arom. The village of Turknorse was built near an extensive mountain range. Its majestic forests were the home of the people for many centuries. It also afforded good protection from the outside. That was not to be true for the coming of the Hrothgorn.

A regiment of hundreds of Hrothgorn soldiers marching to a ghoulish cadence of death appeared in the clearing of trees. They chanted as they stomped their way closer. The sound of the terrifying chant was as if it had come from the throat of a giant chimney. The sound choked out a phosphorus belch throughout the land of the forest under the trees. *"Hroth thrash Gorn Ama Gorn! Hroth thrash Gorn Ama Gorn!"* The translation is, "We will do our King's will." The Hrothgorn took away all that the townspeople knew forever within a short period.

Valorii Thuireld and her sister ran to the house to find their mother already starting to bar the doors and drown out the lights.

"They are coming for the tribute! They are almost here!" cried out Valorii to her family.

King Tin'old never forewarned about the coming of the tribute. The townspeople filled the streets, retreating to their homes and taking cover in cottages and stables.

"The Hrothgorn are here," an old woman screamed. "Run as fast as you can and bring King Tin'Old, and he will save us,"

A Ghoul-Giant appeared in a clearing. His head was protruding from the hatch of a heavy tank as it crush-rolled into the village, flattening the wooden cottages with their thatched roofs. Fire-Fang discovered this monstrosity of a machine as he visited the Portal of the Pines. The strange tank commander bellowed to his warriors.

"Stand fast, you cowardly rats! The first one of you that runs away from this hunt will feel the hungry end of my sword!" General Fire-Fang barked orders to the army of Hrothgorn as they descended upon the kingdom of Arom."Take as many of these human trash piles as you can carry. Put the live ones in your nets. They will make acceptable workers! Pile the dead ones on the trucks." He waved his clawed hands in the direction of the vehicles. The filthy gray Russian army trucks belched a Deisel stench into the fresh air of Old Turknorse.

"There will be a hearty feast tonight, my Hrothgorn brothers! Work well, and you will eat well, Work badly, and I will kill you myself," promised the Ghoul General. "March fools… March! Do all of these things at the pleasure of King Drak-North! He will reward those who deserve it and kill those who do not," bellowed Fire-Fang.

The soldiers had trudged from the Kingdom of the South under the lash of Fire-Fang. They finally reached the crest of the hill at the outskirts of Turknorse, and the townspeople beheld the ghastly sight. The Hrothgorn were over four meters tall and wore crudely forged armor from foot to neck. Their uniforms were an armored version of an ancient uniform. Their covered heads left a terrifying view of the beasts' eyes through their helmets. Their faces were dark tar red with no hair, with several small horns on the top of their massive skulls. The soldiers cut two to three large horns resembling a ram's horn to a stump. When they stomped the ground, it shook like an earthquake. As they marched, they chanted, causing a disturbing cacophony of noise.

Horrible shrieks of anger and pain interrupted the chants.

"Hroth thrash Gorn Ama Gorn! Hroth, Hroth, thrash Gorn, Ama Gorn!"

As the people scrambled through the streets, the Hrothgorn reached down, wrenched the hair of fleeing townspeople, and picked them up by their scalps. They flung them back over their shoulders into giant nets mounted on their backs. They stacked the townspeople as an angler carried fish in a creel.

Fire-Fang bellowed an order. "Save the fat ones for me! Extra rations for the Hroth soldier who brings me one!"

As the roar of the tumult became unbearable, the extreme carnage continued. An iron bull (tank) with a turret ready to fire topped the hill. The only sound anyone could hear was the grinding of the massive engine. The tracks of the tanks rolled over the homes of the people of Turknorse. The Hrothgorn rode with half of their bodies sticking out of the turrets because there was not enough room for them inside. From behind the tree line, several Hroth soldiers began to fire rifles in the direction of the town.

The Constable of Arom ran panicked into the streets, shouting a warning. "Everyone to the sewers and jump down the holes... the beasts are too large to get in there! Run before it is too late!"

"It is already too late...for you!" bellowed a random Hrothgorn as he picked the Constable up by his long white hair and slammed him into the cobblestone street. He lay there quivering in death as a truck rolled through the city.

Two Hrothgorn approached the Thuireld home and kicked in the front door. One snatched Valorii's mother, Ek'roin, into his net, followed by her sister Ine'Ath. Valorii had hidden in the bread locker where she used to play hide and seek. A squinted-eyed Hrothgorn looked from left to right. Smoke poured from his nostrils as he smelled human flesh. He bellowed, "Mahratta Drak ona me Gorn." (Hrothgorn will do the will of Drak-North). Valorii trembled but did not move. To avoid being discovered, she dared not breathe. The Hrothgorn soldier turned around with Valorii's sister and their mother trapped in the net shrieking and went to the window. They were gone. There would be no way to find them or to discover what had become of them, and she began to weep. The Hrothgorn completed their horrible task and marched outside of the village. They faded into the distance, and the residents of Arom could still hear chanting. Valorii was unable to move from her spot. *Where is my King when we need him to help us? He is a mighty and strong King and will make the Hrothgorn pay for this!* she thought.

Tin'Old had locked himself in the throne room and hid like a rabbit from a wolf. There would be no help from him today.

After darkness fell, Valorii emerged from her hiding place to hear the weeping of children and the sobs of her neighbors. A foul stench of kerosene, diesel smoke, and death hung over the city. The Hrothgorn had taken or killed nearly five hundred of her fellow townspeople. Legends say that since the Hrothgorn massacre, the township of Olde Turknorse has remained silent and *unrepaired*. The people chose not to move on and stayed frozen in time. It was said of Turknorse, "hate had made it immortal in its sorrow." Valorii found solace in her service to King Tin'Old as his maidservant, so she carefully made her way to the palace. She wanted to know why he did not send soldiers to help her family in their time of need. She was sure there was an answer, but she trusted him in all he did.

"I am sure that he fought valiantly to save the people of Turknorse from the Hrothgorn," said Valorii to a remaining neighbor. "He probably fought so bravely that he could not come to our aid. The Hrothgorn were not supposed to collect another tribute until the following year. I thought we were safe."

Valorii ran into the dark of night to tell the King of Arom what had happened. As she arrived at the Palace, she noticed a large gathering of people in the front. She ducked around to the servant's quarters' entrance and slipped inside.

Falstuf Tin'Old, the lost Prince, could not have known these would be the last hours of his reign on the earth. After eating in his private resting room, he fell into a deep slumber.

King Tin 'Old's chamber was deep inside the mountain range that had been his people's home for many centuries. They fought wars and did great deeds unsung until this time. Their stories were likely inside the mind of the old King as he slumbered. The final minutes of his life flew away on wings in the weak twilight hours.

Six hooded riders with six hundred and ninety-nine pounds of iron horses under their control cranked hard on the throttle as they blazed toward the Palace. The sky was full of rain as they glided through the thick black morning-night toward the outskirts of the Kingdom of Arom. The spirit of revenge was a travel companion as they rode toward the King's city on their machines known by their most common name, "Rat cycles." The figures roared into the grounds of the Palace, plowing through a detachment of the Royal guard. They powered down and dismounted. The floating, gliding visitors of doom hurried through the corridors, drew daggers, and commenced their horrible work. They hacked and stabbed the helpless old King until sounds emitted from his throat like a dying animal. Prince Tin'Old the Younger skulked in the shadows outside the throne room doors with a hood pulled over his face. As he lifted the hood from his head, the twisted face of Odious-Forge the magician appeared for a few seconds.

"Damn you, Villains! Damn you to the fires of Hades!" the King screamed in anguish.

The masked assassins thrust their daggers into the side of Old King Tin'Old as he smacked his head to the floor of the Stone Palace. Four masked figures had entered the stone palace with help from inside. Their soft-bottomed biker boots made no sound on the hard marble floor of the throne room. The assassins grasped the daggers with the hands of farmers, blacksmiths, and stonemasons. As King Tin'Old writhed on the cold marble, the ruthless killers continued to stab him until his expression was a crimson mask. He opened his eyes to see the figure of another biker leaning down before his face. His eyes were fixed on the ghoulish killer's eyes, and the biker's face transformed for a few seconds. It was the face of *Odious Forge*, the killer of Kings. He had done as he promised.

"I wanted you to know it was me who did this, and you will die now as your father did many years ago…at my hand. I wanted you to see my face and to know that my curse endures. You did this to me! I will have my day!" said Forge. "So goes the *Lost Prince!*" he said. He thrust the dagger into the King's bloody chest and disappeared into dust as if he had never been there.

The Stone Palace guards were not in place and *seemed* unaware of the next room's horror. The King shrieked while trembling, "You have already slain me; I am all but dead already. Be gone with you!"

"I don't even care if he doesn't pay us. I would have done this for *no* money," said one of the biker assassins laughing as he retreated. Prince Tin'Old skulked around the corner, spying from behind the shadows.

The four ran to the grand main hall and disappeared into the visitor's crowd. As the great King lay dying, they roared away. Prince Tin'Old skulked around the corner, spying from behind the shadows.

Valorii stumbled into the throne room and knelt near the King. Tin'Old drew her close, smearing his life's blood on her pure white dress. "Come closer, my child." He drew his last breath and said, "I have been a foolish coward…do not let history judge me harshly. Do not let it end this way. Please tell the people I fought bravely in my last moments. There is something you should know ..."

"What are you saying, majesty? I do not know what you are trying to tell me," Valorii asked the King as he spoke his last words. The answer would go unspoken for all time and eternity. She knew the King did not fight when his people needed him, and he never left the palace during the massacre. She slowly let the King's head rest on the floor in eternal stillness. King Tin'Old then passed into the Realm of the great Kings, where the gods would pass judgment for his deeds. Spies in the grand Stone Palace slithered a retreat to Drak-North to return and report. As Valorii held the dying King in her arms, she thought of the people of Turknorse and the dreadful price paid that day. She loved the King and had no other purpose before but to serve his grace, but she could not forgive him. She ran into the courtyard, her fine apparel covered in the blood of the King, and fell to her knees. Valorii had lost her family, and Tin'Old, the Lost Prince, had been murdered. The rain began to fall in the Kingdom. She wondered if it would ever stop. The Palace of Stone held the forever-locked secrets in its corridors. She walked out of the front gates of the palace and vowed never to return, for she knew well who was now the King of Arom.

Many days passed after the death of the King, and *Valorii Thuireld* roamed the countryside in search of a kind soul to supply food and shelter. She found solace and comfort in kind strangers who fed her and kept her warm on the cold nights in the forest. She wandered into the forest deep and did not mean to step so far into the forest realm. She lay at the base of a mighty fir tree and closed her eyes. She could hear the quiet call of the forest birds and the sweet sprinkle of rain on the canopy of trees above. The rain touched the base of the forest and splashed on the bed of pine needles and fir branches. There were faint whispers in the trees of the tree sprites.

"Who is she?" "From whence does she come?"

One of the grand old tree spirits who had been there for centuries looking out from the fir trees whispered, "This is my forest realm, and if she wants to sleep on my floor, then she shall have a sweet sleep."

The rain fell on Valorii's hair as she slept the sleep of a princess in a new palace of trees. Dreams entered her head as she slumbered. She saw her mother's face smiling in their little cabin as she made bread and cakes with the children. She felt peace enter her as she dreamt of eating sweet cakes and playing with the pet rabbit that she had named after the King. Mother had told her it was acceptable to keep the name, but if any of the King's men came to the cabin on the farm, the rabbit's name was *cottontail*.

"No need to aggravate his grace," said Mother.

She heard beautiful music from the harp as she slumbered. She thought of good things and smiled deep within her soul. It was the first relief since losing her family and the assassination.

A sound from the treetops woke Valorii from her sleep.

"Oh, my... who are you?" Valorii asked, startled.

"I am a tree spirit. Have you not seen and heard us before?" she answered.

"I have... I have heard of you before but have never seen you," Valorii answered, looking shocked and surprised.

"I live in the trees with all the other spirits in the forest and the woodland creatures. I am the protector of the forest realm."

"I did not mean to disturb you-?"

"You were in the forest asleep on our pine needles, interrupting the sanctity of the forest. You mean not to disturb us. Why does that surprise you? You did not pay a tribute or even ask permission, yet you have slept peacefully here," scolded the tree spirit. "Now you will pay!"

Valorii covered her head with her hands, waiting to be struck by the tree spirit any second.

"Oh, leave her alone, you big oaf! How often do you have to be warned about being mean to visitors?" said another tree spirit. "We apologize for him, my dear. He is quite the bully. We are honored by your presence," said the more diminutive tree spirit.

The other tree spirits echoed throughout the forest in agreement. "You are our friend and a guest of this forest realm, you may stay a night, or you may stay forever." "Is there anything we may do for you, Valorii Thuireld, daughter of Ek'roin of Arom?" asked the tree sprite.

"But how did you know who I am?"

"We possess all manner of white magic. We can help you, but there can be no malice in your heart," said the tree spirit.

I most definitely have malice in my heart! The Hrothgorn have stolen my family and murdered my King as he rested. My blood boils at the thought of the evil done to my loved ones and me."

"That is not malice, young one, that is righteous pain, and the gods will make rightful retribution yours in time. Seek a place called The Portal of the Pines."

"I know the things found at the pines portal were considered gifts from the Witch Queen. The items were usually tools of war and destruction. Why should I seek such a thing?" said Valorii.

"In due time, you will require them," said the tree spirit.

"I am a person of peace just as was my King, The great Tin'Old. Is that prophesied from the spirits of the forest?" asked Valorii.

"You may call it to prophesy if you wish, but we much prefer to call it a promise. Prophesies are such silly nonsense. We can tell you to *study* the ground as you walk, and there you will find a great discovery, a friend from the Portal of the Pines."

"I am to find a friend… on the ground? I do not understand. You speak in…."

"Keep your eyes on the ground until you return to us."

The woodland spirits guided Valorii through the forest realm until she came to a safe place in the land of Arom near the edge of Lake Shem.

"We leave you now, but we will always be close by," said the tree spirit.

"Wait… do you have a name?" asked Valorii. "How will I know if you are in my presence?"

"My name is Alerian'i'. We will be with you anywhere in the realm where there are trees until wings deliver justice to the world. Be at peace Valorii Thuireld."

Chapter Six

VICTOR VOROBYEV

∽

Date: Dimension of Loki 1969 AD
Earth

"Oh, my God, this is gonna hurt."

I n another part of the world, on October 31, 1969, riding a modern steel horse was a man named Viktor Vorobyev. He was dressed in black leather tasseled chaps. His helmet was a German World War One issue with the spike on top. He was unshaven and dirty from his time on the road. He realized that the case of monkey butt he developed was not going away unless he stopped for a couple of days.

Suddenly from a side road, four dark hooded figures on horseback started chasing the biker, and he could not escape. The faster he rode his bike, the quicker the horses charged behind him. They called to him over the *roar* of the engine.

They're only on horses! How can they be keeping up" he thought. The leader shouted as the horses pulled along the highway's left lane next to him.

"We speak for the *souls* of those you have murdered," said one low, rumbling voice. "We moan for those you have thrown into early graves, but we wish to redeem you."

"Who the hell are you? Leave me alone!" the biker begged. He knew what they spoke of, and he knew it was true. Viktor Vorobyev had killed a man in a fight in Vegas last year. He beat him and left him to die. His temper was the reason others had also died at his hands. Viktor looked over his shoulder; the rest of the horses had gained ground, almost touching the soft tail of the bike.

"Know this, Viktor Vorobyev! There will come a time when we will see you face to face," the horseman spoke as if in a tunnel. "Reckoning will come soon."

The sound of pounding hooves on the pavement stopped suddenly. Viktor pulled his ride over to the shoulder, and they were finally gone. He was shaking inside from cold and fear. The memories of the *murder* crept into his brain. He could still smell the blood and hear the pleading of his last victim.

He shouldn't have been shootin' off his damn mouth, he thought. *He would still be alive.* He tried to calm himself and find a reason for this visitation. *I guess it could have been bad mushrooms.* Viktor rode on into the night.

There had not been a cop around all night. That *is* some good luck. He cranked hard on the throttle with six hundred and ninety-nine pounds of American steel under his control. He was proud of his bike, although some might call it junk or a "rat bike." Those happen to be motorcycles held together with spare parts, twine, and prayer. The sky was crying big fat tears as he sliced through the thick black morning-night toward the outskirts of Memphis. The biker could feel the spirit of Elvis as he rode toward the King's city. He was soaked through to his pants but at least that dirty city would get a drink of water from the storm. He was hauling ass on his Fat Boy alongside a freight train charging along the highway. It sounded like a ghost train as the cars screamed and groaned down the tracks.

The big rusty Tennessee freighter wanted to challenge Viktor to a race. He took that challenge and lost miserably.

There they were again ahead in the fog blocking the highway. The four horsemen! He squashed the brake and slowed but not enough. He prepared for the impact with the horses. *Oh, my God, this is gonna hurt.*

Cloudy thoughts entered and exited his brain, passing each other on the way out. The huge Harley slid into the horses and riders, throwing plumes of sparks as it slid along the highway. They disappeared entirely into *nothingness* before the impact. He stared into the darkness for what seemed like minutes but was just a few seconds. He gathered himself, righted his damaged motorcycle, and rode on. It wobbled a little, but that's to be expected after all...he dropped it.

The heavy early morning fog made it nearly impossible for the biker to see the road ahead, so he was riding blind. The musty air hit Viktor's face like a dirty washrag. All he could do was suck the Mississippi river air into his lungs. *Air that you can wear*, he thought.

The highway took a ribbon of turns when Viktor saw a rider on horseback riding at full speed in the middle of the highway. The rider took a sharp left turn down into a ravine. I gotta know who these guys are, thought Viktor.

"Who is that down there?" a Tennessee Highway Patrol officer had pulled in behind him and peered into the ravine.

"Stand right where you are, and don't move," he ordered. "What are you doing here?"

"You would not believe me if I told you,"

"Keep your hands where I can see them. What's your name, son?" the officer asked.

"Viktor Vorobyev," he said as he spoke in a typical southern Texas accent. *I can't believe I told him my real name*, he thought. *Dumbass.*

"Bull-crap, what's your real name, boy?" the cop asked as he spat a stream of tobacco juice.

"Dude, that is my name," he answered. "My parents were Ukrainian immigrants."

"We reported that someone had seen a guy on a horse on the highway here. Know anything about that?" the officer asked.

"See, that's the part you would not believe. The dude is gone. He is just gone. I can't figure out where he could have gone."

"I'm coming down there and patting you down for my safety and yours. Keep your hands on top of your head. Don't move." the cop ordered. Viktor projected a false calm until the officer got to him.

According to his badge, the cop was Officer Toby Johnson, and he could not have known how much danger was in front of him. The authorities wanted Vorobyev in three states for an assortment of crimes, including strong-arm robbery, attempted murder of a police officer, and forgery. Not *really* bad stuff, according to Viktor. Most people have a career or at least a job, but Viktor had a career in crime. A career of evil. As Officer Johnson got close enough, Viktor took a big swing at him. He connected with the right side of his jaw, and the officer spun around and fell to the ground.

Dammit, now I'm gonna have to kill a cop, he thought, reaching for his piece. He had a Canick 55 in his leathers, so he yanked it out unceremoniously. He pressed the pistol against the temple of the terrified cop who was regaining consciousness. He pushed so hard that *it might drive the barrel through his stupid skull. I can get out of here with some pressure on the trigger.*

"You can't just shoot me!" Officer Johnson struggled to speak through the blood coming from his nose. "You're not going to get away with this. Them boys'll hunt you down and kill you. Don't even expect a trial. These boys here will waste ya," he said, struggling for his sidearm.

Viktor squeezed the trigger.

Click... Misfire. The cop took the opportunity given to him by providence, or just plain dumb luck, and tackled Viktor and threw him to his back. The gun flew from Viktor's sweaty palms and landed in the dirt. The cop pulled his service revolver and pointed it directly at the biker. The wiley criminal kicked the legs of the officer, causing him to fall backward and lose his gun. Johnson stood back up, threw himself over the burly man, and dug his fingernails into his face. The cop took the open opportunity and grabbed his second pistol from his belt.

Viktor grabbed Johnson in a chokehold and forced him into the dirt. He did not see the veteran cop recover his second service revolver. As far as Viktor was concerned, he only had one.

"I... would...let... you go, but it's too late for that. You couldn't just get in your car and mind your own business!" said Viktor as he struggled to catch his breath.

"Shoot a cop? Shoot a cop?" Johnson repeated. "I should kill you right now!" He reached up through the pain of the chokehold and placed the gun under Viktor's chin. "One move, and I blow your damn head off. I am dead ass, serious boy," said Johnson. Viktor had no idea how Johnson had gotten a gun in the struggle.

As Viktor tried to escape, the last thing the biker felt was a sharp pain across the back of his head and chin and an earth-shattering *boom*. When he awoke, his eyes were trying to adjust to something. The pain in his skull was harsh and soul-crushing. He could focus and then lose it. As he regained consciousness, he saw a nightmare before him. He tried to scream. As it rose from within him, almost like a howl, he realized he could barely breathe.

"What the hell is this? How did-?" he screamed.

A glowing figure appeared with a large flowing robe adorned with stars, planets, and a hummingbird design. Officer Johnson was gone.

Viktor found himself under the surf of some body of water far away from Memphis. He heard bells ringing in his head as he floated quickly to the surface and came face to face with a stranger in robes. "Oh my God, what the hell?" The figure hoisted him roughly out of the water by his wet clothing. "What are you going to do to me?" he begged. "Where am I?"

"No...it is 'when' are you? Listen carefully to what I have to say, Viktor Vorobyev. *You are a dead man.* You have now ceased to be. You are in another time but yet the same time."

"What are you talking about"?

Soon you will meet others from *their* times. You are a corpse. The authority of your law mortally wounded you in the head."

"I feel ok now, though. Just lemme' go. I don't know what you're trying to pull here, but I ain't any fool. You gotta be yankin' me whoever you are," said Viktor.

"No, I assure you that you are dead. The officer 'blew your head off,' as you would say."

He was terrified and apprehensive as he reached to touch his face, and it was not there. His head was not there. Viktor began to panic and scream. "How can I scream if I don't have my head?" A scream fell out of his spirit like a phantom.

"I am the messenger of The Destiny of Tyr, and I come on behalf of *the others*. I have tasks for you," said the messenger.

"What do you want me to do? The Destiny of what? I would do anything to undo the last few minutes. Why would you want something from me?"

"That will be revealed to you at a later time. Come with us on our quest or remain here and be another useless bag of guts—just another corpse. Live forever with us or remain dead. It is your choice," bargained the robed figure.

"Why do you want me? It don't make sense...I'm ain't nobody!" pleaded Viktor.

"Not true, Viktor. You are a creative and cunning murderer and criminal. We have need of you."

"You got me. That's just damn weird! Tell me what to do."

CHAPTER SEVEN

WOLFCLAW AND THE HALL
OF THE ANCIENTS

❧

Date: Dimension of Odin 140 AD
Underforest Lands

*"If I do not speak, all of our dead will speak
for me from their lonely graves."*

I t was now during the age of the third King Tin'Old, son of the lost Prince and grandson of Gier'Wolf Tin'Old of DragonBorne. The grizzled old man struggled to slog through the deep freezing snow in the realm of the forest. *My feet are freezing. He thought my face is cold, but mostly I am freezing my ass off.* The wild grain mead caused him to be unsteady on his feet and muddled his already confused thoughts. *I will reach the hall only a few more steps to the city's outskirts.* As he looked behind him in the snow, he could see a long trail of bloody footprints. He had a wound that he had sustained but did not know from where it had come.

Many years had passed since the massacre at Arom. The old man's mind wandered and dreamt in the cold air and wind. He found himself fading fast in the snow and ice. His thoughts transported him to an earlier time when the heroic did not seem impossible. *Another daydream.*

Why can I not go for more than an hour without one? Thought the old man. He thought about a time long ago and stopped in his tracks. The memories filled his head with wild visions of his past adventures. The old warrior fell face-first into the snow. The warrior reviewed his life.

100 years previous, in the city of Halfthor, Wolfclaw dreams…

The massive scaled creature spat acid fire on all the men around him, but Warwok Wolfclaw Thur'Gold held his ground in the face of undeniable doom. The Jörmungandr boasted of his invincibility.

"I cannot be defeated. I am unflinching. Lay down and die, for you are already a dead man," the sea snake hissed.

"You may be invincible, the great serpent, but you are a faint-hearted fool. What you do is cowardly. You feast while all around you starve. You destroy villages and take food from the mouths of children," bellowed the brave warrior.

"Silence!" You are nothing more than a court jester! Fool! You are doomed! How will you save yourself? Will you wield swords, shields, or hammers? They are simply tools of the weak," the monster sea snake hissed.

"None of those are my real weapons," replied Wolfclaw. "My weapon is that I do not like to lose."

The men to Wolfclaw's flank screamed in bloody, fiery death, but he pushed forward toward the ghoulish monster. His armor was searing his chest as the acid fire consumed it. The Jörmungandr shrieked in a high-pitched refrain as the men danced like ghoulish marionettes in a chilling ballet of death on the deck of *The Ice-Piercer*.

"You have breathed your last fire of death unto this people." With a piercing war cry, the ancient warrior thrust his sword into the face of the Jörmungandr. The blade pierced above the nose and between its eyes and exited the back of the beast's head. It quivered violently and fell to the deck of the ship. An enormous pool of blood formed on the deck at the warrior's feet as the creature's head lifelessly draped over the vessel's side.

Today the people of the villages are safe from the Jörmungandr and its lust for death, thought the confused old man.

Wolfclaw Thur'Gold was jolted from his daydream to reality by a clap of thunder and picked his weary body from the snow. *They are just the dreams of an old man who was still face-first in the snow. It was another useless daydream from an old drunken warrior.* He was not waging a fierce encounter against a massive serpent. Standing up was the only heroic deed Wolfclaw was able to do. Heroic feats and victories in battle were behind countless doors in the corridors of his memory. All this remembrance and he still froze his feet in the harsh, heavy snow while he trudged toward the Hall of the Ancients. He saw the outline of the Longhouse just visible through the icy curtain of snow. He knew he must regain his senses.

The warrior arrived and threw open the enormous oaken doors of the Great Hall of the Ancients. The old man covered in furs burst through the open doors with an explosion usually reserved for battle.

"Avast, ye sleepy, lazy bastards!" the old pirate bellowed. "This is not the time for slumber!" he said, startling the hall's men. "Hide your gold and silver!"

The men in the hall began to laugh with their old comrade, except for the Grand Chair.

"See here, Warwok Thur'Gold! There will be order in these proceedings!" said The Grand Chair Arkule' as he rose to his feet. "There *will* be order."

"The elderly warrior carried his heavy two-handed broad sword over his shoulder as if he was charging into battle. He had arrived in the middle of the weekly meeting of the elders and took his place rather noisily in his rightful seat at the great table in the Longhouse.

Wolfclaw was an imposing man with gray hair and blazing brown eyes accented by bushy white eyebrows. In contrast, his skin was tough and leathery from many war-worn years outside in the sun, snow, and rain.

"Welcome, old friend!" said Svæin, the Elder.

There was no response from Wolfclaw. His icy cold stare exuded emotions of many years. He glared menacingly at the council members in silence while he tried to hold his enthusiasm upon seeing his old friends once again.

"So what are ye waiting for? Fetch me some drink, bring me a poultice, and bind my wounds. I still have a seat in the council, do I not?" asked Wolfclaw.

"So what are *we* waiting for? A ridiculous buggy-eyed old man?" asked a traveling young warrior named Halfdan. "I have heard his stories are as much cow patty as can be found in the pasture. I am supposed to learn something from the likes of him?"

"Quiet, you shameless fool!" snapped Svæin." The hall erupted with laughter.

"These great halls were filled with men who used to care about the realm. The hall contained many men who knew honor, integrity, and bravery. Where did they go? I seek to destroy the pact of Tin'Old and relieve King Drak-North of his head. Are there any brave souls left among the cowards here that will join me on this noble quest? We must destroy the King of darkness and all of his works. We must have vengeance for Turknorse!"

It was a surprising sudden declaration met with more laughter.

"You must be out of your damned mind," shouted one of the elders. "You drunk old fool, just who do you think you are calling cowards?

"You are a fine array of men," said Wolfclaw.

"How dare you interrupt the sanctity of the Hall of the Elders with such a ridiculous request?" asked Fältskog the Ready. It was never straightforward what or why he was ready. Something was frightening about him. It could be his temper that could explode at any moment, or more likely, his reputation. People usually hated him but were afraid to say it.

"It is an outrageous idea that an *old man* such as *you* would even be thinking such a thought. It has been years since Turknorse. Why now?" Fältskog expected a story or a boast of some kind this day but not a call to war.

"What are you afraid of?" asked Wolfclaw fighting back the urge to vomit. "I know what it is. You are afraid of a piece of parchment! You fear the pact of Tin'Old. When he signed the treaty with Drak-North and agreed to let the Hrothgorn take people from among us rather than war, you all became sheep! Brave warriors of the past are afraid of paper. Oh no, here comes some paper! Hide you warriors of the great hall! The paper monster is among us."

"We fear nothing! You are a shadow of what you once were," reasoned Elder Fältskog.

"Hold fast your tongue! You may jest all you like, you rogue vagabond. Wolfclaw was fighting fierce battles while you were still yet broiling in your father's loins," admonished Svæin.

"King Tin'Old the First surrendered the freedom of all his people, and King Drak-North took the best from our land," said Wolfclaw. He had often wondered how the cowardly Tin'Old could sleep at night knowing what upon he had agreed. "His majesty was a spineless *mongrel.*"

"Silence," ordered Arkule'. The Grand Ancient One was seated in the most oversized chair at the head of the house and presided over all the state's intricate affairs. "This matter is settled and has been visited and studied earlier. After *your* failed campaign to rescue Lady Thur'Gold, I cannot allow you to try again."

"You cannot allow it? Why do you believe you can stop me? You all know her capture occurred during the tribute season, and I have done all I can to find her," said Wolfclaw. "I know she is alive, and I must try again."

"That is when you fell into the Mead barrels, and still you have not returned," said Fältskog.

"I am sure that there is a reason that I have not beaten you to death yet, but I do not remember after all these years," said Wolfclaw as he became increasingly impatient with Fältskog.

"The Kingdom lost fifty good men during that expedition. I have already given my answer, and that is… no," said Arkule'. "It was settled previously. There is further pressing business to come before the council today."

"Was it settled… really?" innocently asked Wolfclaw." What *pressing* business do you have at this time that is more important than destroying the scourge of the realm? We are the victims of a massacre.

They must pay for their deeds. Is yours the pressing business of *mead*? Is it the critical business of *women*? For what reasons do you lose sleep?"

Arkule' replied, "You know well by the name of Rothl'Orca that mead and pursuit of women are not the concern of the council or its purpose!"

Wolfclaw continued, "Hrothorn are torturing family members of some of these men in this great hall. I know my Aspeth is among them, and I will rake the earth to find her. Yet Drak-North *still* sits on the Throne of Bones. What are we as a council going to do about it? Answer me now! Do not wait to frame it in diplomacy! The time of cowards has passed!" said Wolfclaw slamming his fist to the heavy oak table.

"I demand order in the hall. I will hear no more," Arkule 'said in a thundering voice. "I made my ruling days ago when you came to me in private, and then I admonished you never to speak of an *army to march against Drak-North*. Look at yourself. You are half frozen and covered in blood. You appear as though you are soon to die. I will have you removed from the fellowship of the Hall for insurrection, but I would rather you seek the help of the shaman and the shield maidens to carry you hence."

The old warrior stood and drew his heavy sword, which rang with a metallic sound echoing the brave battles in its history. He raised the great blade over his head with one hand. "Insurrection, shaman, and shield maidens? I was content with a debate until you used those words. Damn you to the fires of Hades! You will not dare threaten the elder statesman of this hall!"

"I will hear no more from you. I will see to it you are banished," said Arkule'.

"Banish me from these corridors, do it now!" his voice wavered and cracked. "Silence me, and do not fear that I will no longer speak. If I do not speak, all our dead will speak *for* me from their lonely graves." The sword began to shake under the fatigue of his tired arm. He roughly returned the blade to the sheath and calmly caught his breath. "I am not afraid of what we must do. I have no fear of the wrath of Drak-North or Tin' Old the Younger. I have faced demons with just a sword. I escaped the *Harvester of Eyes* after he plucked the eyes from my comrades. *Monsters* and I have been locked in battle since I was young. After those nightmares, I fear nothing."

"The matter is closed, and there will be no more discussion of this," ordered The Grand Chair.

There was a quiet in the hall that it had not seen in a long time.

"See, young man, Wolfclaw can strike fear with just his voice," said Svæin to Halfdan. "He did all the things he said he did."

"Seems like the hot wind to me." Halfdan was an imposing figure much taller than Svæin. He dressed in a leather tunic, sheep's wool trousers, and large fur-toed boots. He was a comical site next to the very short and stout Svæin.

"Young one- do not"-said an interrupted Svæin.

"No, it is well. Do not take the boy to task, my old friend," said Wolfclaw. "I understand that my stories are tough to believe. Sometimes they make me wonder if I was there. I think I was and have the scars to prove it."

Wolfclaw *lived* the tales he told. He was telling the truth if he claimed to have killed a Rhandobeast with his hands. It was an accurate tale if he said he made love to the Queen of the forest realm when he was a young man.

"You should do well to listen to his every word, shut your gob, and learn something. I earned my seat many years ago in the hall. He was here years before me," said Svæin.

"I am sorry, but I am from the surface lands above, and I do not know of this man. I do not even know *your* history," said Halfdan.

Svæin did not seem to accept this explanation. "Just try not to get in the way today."

The council returned to the usual loud conversation, boasting, games, and arguments. This behavior was considered a regular day in the long house.

Halfdan had been seated in the hall at the invitation of Svæin in the hope that the young man would learn to humble himself. The young warrior seemed taken aback by Wolfclaw, as he could not reconcile the appearance of a broken old man in furs with a mighty warrior from the past.

"Look at him! He seems unable to fight a simple house cat rather than do the heroic deeds you say he did. What is that stuck in his face? It seems an odd decoration," said Halfdan.

"Keep your voice down," admonished Svæin quietly. "He was and still is called Wolfclaw by some of the ancients. If you care to listen, they still tell stories around campfires about how he killed a she-wolf with his bare hands. The battle left one of the wolf's claws buried in his face. It is a real wolf claw in his face, and he never took it out."

"You know when time passes and memories fade, past deeds get exaggerated? I do not believe in tall tales," said Halfdan skeptically.

Wolfclaw stood, stripped his sleeve, and presented his arm to any challenger in the hall who might be brave enough to lock arms with him.

"Which one of you wants to go first? If I lose, I go alone. If I win, and I will, you will come with me into battle."

Svæin pulled off his coat to show a vast, rough oaken-like arm. His gray-brown, long hair covered part of his scarred and weathered face. His piercing green eyes could see through any lies or deception.

A terrible explosion of flame left a scar on his forehead, running down the tip of his nose and ending on his chin. He was barrel-chested and covered with a red beard nearly to his chest. His green eyes blazed with the promise of and the support of every one of his ancestors. A fight with him was "a fight with all his kin."

Svæin placed his massive elbow on the table and boasted loudly.

"I can and will show the back of your hand to the tabletop." The two elder statesmen clapped their hands together as great clouds of thunder.

"A wager! A wager!" shouted Fältskog. "We must make this interesting!" Each man throws ten Gromels in the ring and picks a champion." Fältskog missed the point of the match.

The hall erupted in cheers and laughter as each ancient made his wager.

Wolfclaw's voice thundered across the table to Svæin, "If I win, you must come with me."

"Now, why would I do a thing like that? I mean, what is in this for me?" asked Svæin in a teasing manner.

"Honor and glory are your rewards," was the response.

"I cannot buy my worldly goods with honor and glory. I have tried, but the storekeeper will not give me flour and oil for my honor," said Svæin in a sarcastic tone.

"Worldly goods cannot show you the ring of the great hammers, and I know that you fear nothing. I also know that you have no remorse in laying waste to a skull with a hammer or ax," replied Wolfclaw.

"You have judged me wisely, but I have no thirst for the battle today. However, I will tell you what I will do. I will agree to tear off your arm and send it home to your family in a bag," bellowed burly Svæin. Stop wasting time. Your defeat has come."

Fältskog squeezed the two great hands together as they strained and sweated in anticipation of the battle.

"If I vanquish your mighty arm, you will come with me!" demanded Wolfclaw again. "You will make bloody terrible war with me! We have worn callouses on our old arses in this hall. I grow weary of sitting. It is time we stood up and fought our enemies, and I cannot let my age decide the battle for me."

"We will see as the match unfolds," replied Svæin, not wishing to lose face in front of the men in the great hall.

The battle began with the straining of ligaments and stretching of muscles. The purple engorged blood vessels in the combatant's foreheads were bulging and straining to carry blood to the brains of these great gladiators. Svæin spewed an epithet of his creation, but it was more of a groan heard throughout the hall. *"Blorthe!"* The wrestle was even. Their arms quivered and glistened, but neither gave heed. The hall echoed with the loud cheers of the men and the pouring of honey wine mead. The flagons were filled, emptied, filled, and emptied again. The men called out the name of their champion as they roared approval at the match.

Svæin blustered in the face of his adversary, "I will separate you from your head and make your children cry!"

"Impressive," admitted Wolfclaw. "I have no children. Perhaps I could borrow some so they could weep your supposed tears of despair for me. You will still come with me on my quest and carry my arm *and* head on your horse as we ring hammers together, and if I must go to war torn from my joints, I am going."

Svæin groaned and shook, his arm quivering like a giant tree in a storm. His face grew red, and the blood vessels on his forehead looked like they would burst. Both men were locked in battle.

Svæin let out a mighty grunt as his arm slammed into the tabletop. Wolflaw had beaten him. Svæin collapsed to the table like a mighty tree as the men scooped up their winnings.

"Be in the Inn of the Weary Traveler in the early eve ready to travel," said Wolfclaw, half grinning to a defeated Svæin.

"I was comin' with ye anyway, laddie," said Svæin. "All ya had to do was ask. In the meantime, mate, you go clean up. You look like shite."

CHAPTER EIGHT

THE GHOST RIDERS

~~~

Date: Dimension of Odin 124 AD
Underforest Lands

Well, outside in the cold distance
A wildcat did growl
Two riders were approaching
And the wind began to howl -Bob Dylan

"How do you and I, as *old* men propose to defeat an enemy like Drak-North?" asked Svæin. "We have pain in our sinews and joints, and we fall asleep in council meetings. Not to mention, the dark king has weapons we do not have."

"That is absolute nonsense! It sounds like some magic trick to me," said Arkule'. Let us not tempt the gods, old or new. There is nothing to be found at the base of that pine tree. It is all witchcraft!"

"Witchcraft, my arse!" said Wolfclaw, "It sounds like the dark king has some friends on the surface. Beware of these weapons, my companions. The Hroth have iron horses that shoot fire from their heads and fire sticks that hurl burning metal," warned Wolfclaw. "Do not take this lightly. What other reason do you have for those things other than surface men?"

"Every time I go to the Portal of the Pines, I come back empty-handed. It is not worth the trip to the great forest, and the Hrothgorn guards it well," said Svæin. "Besides, fighting Rhandobeasts and giant forest snakes is not what I do anymore."

"Drak-North is pure evil, and some say he has powers of the underworld on his side," said Halfdan.

Wolfclaw pointed at Svæin and the men in the hall. "I will only say this to you, brave men. We will crush the face of evil when it appears, or it will return more powerful with a bloodthirsty vengeance. He will surely want more if we give the monster blood to drink."

"I will come with you and fight. I feel your cause is just, and I want to go with you on your quest because I thirst for a fight, and I wish to spill some Hrothgorn blood," said Halfdan.

"Sit down, fool. These men are not impressed by your swagger,"- Svæin was interrupted.

"Do not confuse my willingness to fight with my trust in you. I believe you will be among the first of the dead," said Halfdan in a patronizing tone.

"Hold fast your tongue, young man," snapped Svæin.

"Let this young one's actions speak for him, and we will see," said Wolfclaw.

As they spoke, powerful pounding hooves of mighty beasts approached. Four cloaked figures on horseback appeared through the walls and moved in a ghostly glide toward the men.

"Uncover your faces and reveal them to us! I demand it in the name of Rothl'Orca!" said Wolfclaw. "Begone with ye spooky bastards!"

Several of the men drew their swords and moved toward the strangers. Fältskog stepped out first, swung his mighty sword from right to left across the belly of the horse, and landed it on *nothingness*. The heavy sword, which had seen many battles and had cut through flesh and bone, quickly fell through the figure as water. Fältskog gave a bloody war cry as he ran the figure through. The cloaked personage raised his hands again, facing the Elders.

"Surely such a mighty sword would have killed anyone be it a stranger, specter, or demon," said Wolfclaw.

"I have seen these robed figures before. I recognize them. Many years ago in the Village of A'zore," said Svæin in a surprised voice. "One of these strangers set me free and saved my life!"

The figure spoke barely above a whisper and only with the cloak covering his face.

"It is good to know that you are well, brave Svæin. We knew the time would come when we would meet you again.

"But who are you? I never had a chance to find out," asked Svæin, stumbling over his words.

"We are speakers of the truth. We have witnessed the laying of waste to Kings and Ladies. We have seen it all. Our home is in darkness, and we move in the shadows. The souls of the dead heroes howl and moan from their graves. The people of Arom lived lives of quiet tranquility hidden from the chaos of the rest of the world until there were wars, death, and suffering of the innocents. The souls of great heroes still howl!" said the mysterious visitor.

"Why do they in their graves speak? Surely they speak nothing. What do the dead have to say?" inquired Arkule'. "Whatever they had to say should have been spoken in life."

Suddenly the robed equestrian's skin peeled away from his body. He threw his robe open and revealed his skeleton covered in spider webs and dust.

"What do the dead have to say?" he said in an ultra booming voice. "We are the keepers of the truth. We control the plague that will soon be upon us. Most of all, we cry for justice, old one!" said the horseman as his steed shifted his weight from left to right and seemed more agitated. "We mourn for what was and what could *not* be. We seek justice and balance in the universe. We represent conquest, war, famine, and death!"

Fältskog cried out, "What? You speak in mysteries. Be gone with you specter, what trickery is this? Are you wraiths or witches? What manner of unnatural talk is this? Is this a trick?"

The figure continued in a barely audible voice,

"The only trickery is within your minds and souls as you believe there is never a cause for which to fight and die. We are not wraiths in appearance or deed. We are not witches. We are not ghouls, but we are the very opposite. We have come to speak to the brave as it also appears... cowardly men."

Arkule 'replied in anger, "See here... ghost or demon or whatever in the name of Hades you may be. We were warriors, all of us, and now we are diplomats. We have all stood for justice and heard the hammers ringing on our enemies' skulls. Do not propose to lecture us on bravery. You have tasked us enough!"

"This is your only task, and it is right before you. You must *avenge* the innocents. This is what you must do," replied the cloaked stranger.

"Be off with you fools! You speak nonsense," said Arkule.'

"Fools as we may be, we will see your faces again soon to discover who among you will answer the call of the ring of the hammer. Know this O'-wise one! You will see haunted forests, magical spells, and unknown creatures. Before you complete your quest, you will see darkness fall upon the land, and many of you will die. One day, one wise soul will arise to bring light to the kingdom and make light the dark places. One will come to bring war, justice, and order on swift wings," the hooded figure promised. "You must bring this to pass!" The four mysterious strangers turned and melted into the walls in a mask of darkness. The sound of the pounding hooves of horses faded into the distance.

"Why do they ride ghost horses if they are not ghosts?" asked Fältskog. "Surely they did not ride through walls."

"How could this be?" asked Halfdan. "Surely, these shadowy figures were your deception. You had this arranged with a troupe of actors. The timing of this is suspect," he said, accusing Wolfclaw.

"*I trust* them because I owe them a debt I cannot repay. Listen to them!" admonished Svæin.

"I know they speak of what I have been trying to make this council understand. I also saw them as a young man in the Kingdom of The DragonBorne. We have heard the prophets speak," explained Wolfclaw.

"So these are prophecies now? Why is it that when a mysterious person or figure says something mystifying, it is always a prophecy?" asked a suspicious Halfdan.

"You tried to form an army in one morning. It seems a bit too convenient if you ask me. I think you are full of shite," said Fältskog. "Halfdan is half right! Somehow, you had your hand in the appearance of these strangers," he said.

"They speak the truth, but I do not know what they ask of us," said Wolfclaw.

"Maybe they are Dragon Masters," observed Svæin. "Whoever these horsemen may be, I believe them."

"Everyone knows they were all killed in the last age by General Fire-Fang," said Fältskog. "You are too easily fooled."

"Who in the name of Rothl'Orca is Fire-Fang?" asked Halfdan. The name of Fire-Fang drew fear from some of the men in the hall because they knew him well.

"He was a ghoul-giant from the caves of Arom and was feared by the entire Kingdom of King Tin'Old the First. He came down from the caves to feast on flesh and returned under cover of night," replied Svæin. "He was a god from the ancient age of the old gods. They had left hastily and abandoned Fire-Fang to rule civilization. He chose evil as revenge against the old gods.

"Tin 'Old's army had waited for him on many occasions only to be left with mangled bodies on the ground. King Drak-North had captured Fire-Fang and used him to build the Palace of Bones with the bones of his victims," said Wolfclaw. "He commanded the army of the Hrothgorn in the massacre."

"He resides in the Palace of Bones. His bones will line the hallways, and his skull will be on a pike!" said Fältskog. He has caused too much pain and death in the last age and this one. All of that has come from the Palace of Bones."

"Drak'North built the Palace with bones, so it will also collapse with *fire*. Hades always gets its due," said Wolfclaw reminding his comrades of the duty before them. "Wraiths, equestrians, ghosts, or demons, whoever they are, have only given me more fuel for the fire. Why are so many cowards in a place for the brave and the chosen?" asked the old man as he considered the other old men in the great hall. Where are your spines? Did Drak-North take those as tribute also?"

"You do not speak for us. *You do not speak* for the ancients in the hall," Arkule ' snarled."Why do you keep arguing this?"

A voice from the back of the hall came like a clap of thunder.

"I will come with you and do the will of the gods for the good of the people!" It was the voice of the mead server, a slight man named Olaf, son of Gandar. He dressed in an apron, a brown shirt, and laborer's trousers. He was thin and not very tall. He had never raised a sword, but Wolfclaw could see his heart because of his willingness to fight. Olaf removed his apron hastily and flung it to the ground.

"I will litter the ground with Hrothgorn dead as I have with my apron, and I will feed their bodies to the birds," he promised with a trembling voice. "If I can do this, you so-called warriors should be ashamed of your weakness."

"Come with us, good Olaf, and you will be a terrifying sight to both the Hrothgorn and Drak-North," said Wolfclaw. "They will tremble in their boots and lament they had not stayed home." Are there any among you that choose to dwell with the gods this day and stand with brave Olaf? Speak now, for the matter will be closed, and you will have sealed your fates and the fates of your loved ones," Wolfclaw admonished.

Fältskog bellowed from the rear of the mead table,

"Who are you to decide to war against the Hrothgorn and Drak-North, and what chance does an old man have against his immense evil?"

"We cannot ignore tyranny, or our apathy will feed it like a hungry beast," Wolfclaw answered with the knowledge that Fältskog was probably right. "I am going to see if I might trade some trinkets for the fire swords of the hill people."

"Drak-North has those 'rifles' also! We cannot march against the bullets of the fire swords!" Fältskog said in a fearful tone."After all, he has two iron bulls that roll over houses."

"That is not the damned point. Drak-North tis the Devil himself surrounded by all of his demons," rifles or tanks, I am not afraid!" said Svæin.

Wolfclaw's reply was swift and to the point, "If he is the devil, then let us who are good show him the *door to Hades*. Again, I ask who is with me on this quest for justice and vengeance. Who will stand and fight with me?"

None would stand with the ancient pirate.

"This is not my fight! I am merely passing through and wish not to get involved in combat with the demon- king. I do not need that kind of trouble," reasoned a visiting elder. "I believe you would lead these men to their certain slaughter."

"I leave you at once with a promise that your cowardice will live forever. Your bodies will rot in the ground, and the souls of those who fight will speak from the grave and cause you to vomit from shame." At this point in his rant, Wolfclaw became nauseated from drink and began to falter." Our hammers will ring in great Valhalla, and the only ringing you will hear is the tolling of the death bell for your souls, and you will only know the rotting *stench* of cowardice all your days."

"I told you he was an old drunk," said Halfdan.

"Are you quite done? You are the most long-winded booze-sack in the kingdom of Arom. Be off with you," shouted Fältskog as his voice echoed in the great hall.

Arkule' raised his hand from the Grand chair and spoke.

"Peace, brave men, and good elders. Wolfclaw Warwok Thur'Gold the brave, you do not have our permission for such a quest. You will surely be defeated because Lord Drak-North's power is dark and great. We do not believe the words of the hooded strangers. We *do not* give you our permission. If King Tin'Old the Younger inquires about you, we will *not* protect you in your insurrection! We also will not offer any information to Tin'Old. Let him hear what he will from the whisperers of Arom."

Wolfclaw, Halfdan, and humble Olaf then took leave with a handful of the younger men from the hall. Svæin went on ahead to prepare for the morning.

"At least we know Arkule' will not tell the King about this," said Olaf.

"For now, but do not take this for granted," said Wolfclaw.

"I know so very little about our brave elders in the Hall," said Olaf to Wolfclaw. "Will you tell me about the legend of Svæin, the Elder? The Ancients told me you are one of the only people in the kingdom that knows him."

"Let us walk and talk, and I will tell you a tale fit for a King."

CHAPTER NINE

THE BLACKSMITH'S TALE

Date: Dimension of Odin 24 BCE
Underforest Lands

*"For you, the tables turned full circle now
And all those people you call friends
See who defends you when you're down again."- Asia*

A century before, he was defeated in the great arm wrestle in the Hall of the Ancients, and his part in Warshield lived young Svæin, son of Ben'Tar, the Elder. His training was as a blacksmith and a maker of swords in Asgorn near the city of Arom. An expert in swords would greatly assist Warshield and its mission. Svæin was often tormented by local boys when he was a child. It was at that time that he developed a horrible temper. He was explosive in his dealings with others. One day, he saw some local soldiers and warriors who preached power, kingdom, and glory. They claim to conquer all within their grasp. One such warrior named Margoth had business in the shop one day."

"How is your brave father in his battles abroad?" he asked.

"I do not know his whereabouts, but I hear this question from others. Let me ask *you* a question. You have often asked about the brave

Ben'Tar, but have you asked about the well-being of his son who stands before you? I am in no way a partaker of the glories or horrors of war. I simply have no use for it."

"Take care. Someday you should be so honored to carry the boots of the war dead, as the Valkyrie carry them to Valhalla in honor and glory," replied the warrior.

"I do not care for such things. I do not care for glory. Fighting against an unbeatable foe is a fool's errand. I only wish to be left alone. I will never fight in a war; anyone who does is a fool."

"Be careful, or someone might close your mouth for you," said the warrior. Svæin recognized him as one of his former tormentors.

"Is there a sword here I have prepared for you? If there is one, please take it and go, 'snapped Svæin."

"You do have a sword here for me," replied Margoth. "But I have just decided I do not want your disrespectful, bad curse on my sword. I would not want such a tool of bravery fashioned by a coward."

"My father was away making war and had no time for his family. My mother cried herself to sleep every night. Ben'Tar can rot in Hades, as far as I am concerned. Please take your sword and go now."

"I no longer want you to create my weapon of war," replied Margoth.

"I have much time and expense invested in your sword. I made it to your specifications. You must take it!"

"I do not care. I cannot touch a sword touched by a coward."

"What am I supposed to do with a sword made just for you? I have *gold* invested in this sword."

"You may dispose of it by shoving it in your arse," replied an insulted Margoth.

"Damn you and your war! Damn you and your honor and glory!" said Svæin.

Margoth reached across the workbench and punched Svæin squarely in the face knocking him to the floor.

The act of violence enraged the young Svæin, who reached for a hot coal poker resting in the fire and swung it furiously in the warrior's direction. Margoth drew his heavy sword and cut a deep slash in the face of Svæin, causing a sizeable bloody gaping wound on the side of his face.

"Let this wound be a reminder to you. When you reach to touch your face, remember that is the reward for thinking you could match my steel with a hot poker." Margoth threw Svæin into the black tar dirt of the shop floor with his foot. 'Stay down, fool, until I am out of sight," he ordered.

Svæin covered his crimson face with his dirty gloves and screamed in anger. Later that evening, he lied to his wife, E'lory, and told her he was in the path of a sharp piece of metal as it jumped from the fire in an explosion inside the furnace. He remembered something his father had said. ' Lies have many colors, all found in the artist's palette of life. Let them see your one true color, and they will know your truth.' He felt dreadful for lying to the only person who deserved the truth. "Do not be full of fear, E'lory. This would not have happened if I had only a minute before the blast to pray to our god Rothl'Orca. The god of protection would not have us harmed."

"No matter, I will clean your face with cool water and bind it. My kiss will heal it for you," she said, kissing his wound.

Later that evening, Svæin stared at the ceiling in his bed, trying to make sleep come, but none came. He wanted to return and defeat the warrior who had confronted him but was fearful. "Am I a coward? Why did I just stay on the ground?" he said.

The next day, Svæin was working in the blacksmith shop when Margoth the warrior returned. His gait was uneven, and he spoke with a drunken tongue.

"Blacksmith, what say you about my boots?" Svæin knew Margoth had returned with more torment in mind.

"What about your boots? I am not a cobbler."

"They are filthy and in need of cleaning. I do not need a cobbler. I saw a *bootlicker* here today," the warrior said with a self-indulgent grin.

"Why *must* you do this, was yesterday *not* enough for you? You wounded me, and now you wish for more?"

Margoth drew his sword roughly, "My boots are dirty, and you have a tongue that speaks disrespectfully of the brave, especially your father. He must hang his head in shame to have a son so meek and cowardly. I cannot let this go. Use that cowardly tongue to lick my boots!"

Svæin prayed fervently, "O, great Rothl'Orca god of the whales and the sea. Help me to know the right thing to do."

The warrior rushed Svæin and put his face so close he could feel his hot breath on his lips. He grabbed the blacksmith by his tunic and brought him closer. "Lick my boots! Clean them from the grime of the brave battle I have fought and won. Eat the slime under the soles that you might taste of the victories over Hrothgorn the Ruthless," he said with a growl through his clenched teeth. He pushed Svæin to his knees, forcing his face to the boots. The massive warrior laughed at his prey with a hearty sadistic laugh. "Lick, you fool!"

As the scene unfolded, E'lory entered the blacksmith shop and witnessed the horrible scene. "Leave him alone, you monster! He has done nothing to deserve this," she screamed as she grabbed the warrior by his armor and tunic. Margoth threw her to the dirty floor with one sweep of his arm.

"Unhand me, woman. He has no honor, so he crawls on his belly like a beast."

"My husband is an honorable man and is braver than *two* of you!" cried E'lory.

Svæin was embarrassed for his wife to see him like this. "Run, my lady. Run. Get yourself from my shop right now!"

Margoth was enjoying the anguish of Svæin and the humiliation of E'lory. Something rose in the spirit of Svæin as he faced the grit of the floor. A roar appeared in his ears like a great waterfall. He trembled within his soul and could feel the shaking inside his chest. His temper rose in him like a tempest raging. Margoth had humiliated him in front of his wife. He reached down to his boot flap and procured the long leather knife he used for boot-making in his spare time. Red heat covered Svæin's eyes with rage.

"This is the last time anyone will torment me. It ends here!" he raged. With one smooth and terrifying lunge upward, he drove the knife into the belly of the warrior. He could feel the steel slip into the flesh, and the warrior's eyes widened with surprise. Svæin pulled the blade from left to right. Blood splattered in a downward direction as the warrior grabbed his mid-section, attempting a scream. Margoth dropped his sword and clutched his open belly with both hands in a futile attempt to staunch the blood flow. He crumbled to the floor, leaning on the wall as his life ebbed away. The warrior was fading away.

"You have killed me because I made folly of you? Are you out of your dammed mind?"

"We must go now! Run home and get our girls, and I will get a handcart for our things. We must hide,'" said Svæin hastily.

"What have you done? You did not have to kill him! We will explain this to the constable, and he will understand what has happened," she said desperately.

"Do as I say! They will not understand, and I will hang as a murderer. Go now!" Elory went to gather her daughters, packed a handcart, and struck out into the unknown.

The family of Svæin traveled for many days in the wilderness with all of their worldly possessions. They arrived in a clearing of trees where the small peaceful village of A'zore stood. There were rows of thatched-roof cottages surrounding a small lake. A quiet and serene feeling filled the town that the family of Svæin had not felt for many months on the run. They were starving and depleting their provisions. The family was greeted at the village gate by Lothor of A'zore. He was dressed in furs from head to toe and wore leather boots. He carried no weapons but had a filet knife on his belt to cook and prepare the lake's catch of the day.

"Why would a man, a woman, and two children be out here alone?" asked the elder.

"We need shelter and food," said Svæin. He was careful to speak softly and partially cover his face so as not to be recognized as the murderer of the warrior in Asgorn.

"We do not have many worldly goods, but Rothl'Orca and Odin will provide all our needs. You are welcome to share all we have," Lothor replied. "The service and worship have already begun. If you hurry, you can be part of it. Then we will see to your needs. What is your name, traveler?"

"Bjorn of the Hill People," Svæin replied, cleverly changing his name on the spot.

The family of Svæin entered the hall where the service was already in progress. There was a small circle of people at the altar with raised hands as they chanted in worship to Rothl'Orca.

O great Whale god of the sea and land, hear our prayer that we might be attended to day and night and be kept safe from harm. O' protect us from the wrath of Hrothgorn the Ruthless.

As the family entered, they were subjected to stares and questioning looks. However, as time went on, they became part of the village of A'zore.

Svæin continued his craft as a blacksmith and even opened a small shop at the south end of town near the mouth of the lake where it met the mighty river of Arom. They grew strong and content in the village, and Svæin went unrecognized until many years had passed.

———— ·◆◆◆◆·· ————

The constable of Arom was traveling through the village of A'zore when his horse lost his shoe and became lame. He sought out the blacksmith shop for new shoes. When he arrived at the shop, he came face to face with a memory he had thought long since gone.

"Are you Svæin … the blacksmith?"

"You have me mistaken for another man, dear sir. My name is *Bjorn of the hill people*," answered Svæin nervously.

"How it is that one who has done murder can live in peace? I am sure I recognize a cutthroat when I see one, *Bjorn of the hill people*. I can even smell the lies on you! You are older and fatter, but Svæin even so. I am also familiar with the mourning of the children of the warrior of Arom that you murdered, *Bjorn of the hill people*," said the Constable with a sarcastic tone.

"Sir, I must ask you to"-

"Ask me nothing cutthroat! Stand in place!" The constable of Arom called for the men of A'zore, who put Svæin in chains and led him to the dungeon within the great hall of the people.

"Svæin of Arom, I have finally found you right under our noses after all these years. I will see you hang for killing Margoth, a hero of the people. I will stay in A'zore until then."

As was expected, Svæin was found guilty by the elders of A'zore and sentenced to die. He was locked in a cell to await his execution. The people of A'zore waited for all of the children of Margoth to arrive. Many weeks passed while Svæin languished in a dungeon cell. By this time, he had given up hope of being freed. No one had come to his aid. He was fed rations that were not large enough for a rabbit. E'lory and his children one day visited him.

"My heart pain is too much to bear. Please do not find your way to me again. I could not stand to see my precious girls in such a filthy rotten place. I am to hang in seven more sets of the sun." He was able to see the gallows from his cell.

The prisoner in the cell adjacent to Svæin taunted his fellow condemned souls. He screeched from behind his bars.

"I have heard stories about the hangmen being paid extra by the family of the murdered person to make the rope too short," he began to laugh cruelly. "That short rope will make your head pop off like a bottle of wine." He laughed with horrible glee. "It will roll down the street like an ox-cart wheel, and you can see where your head is bouncing if ya keep yer eyes open."

"Shut up, you vicious piece of filth," yelled Svæin. The other prisoners only reacted with laughter. The taunting frightened Svæin beyond measure as he sank to the damp floor of his cell and buried his head in his hands. More frightening was the prospect of a Norse blood eagle about which he had heard rumors. The rumor flying through the prison was there would be a trade of the hanging for the blood eagle. He had seen it done as a young man to a mutineer from a ship. The pirate begged for his life as his ribs were cut and spread wide like an eagle's wings. Svæin remembered the terrifying shrieks begging for death. Just as he drifted to sleep, a man's voice awakened him.

"Are you Svæin the blacksmith?"

"Yes, who-?" Svæin said from his sleepy fog.

"I am Margoth, the younger son of Margoth the warrior. I was ten years of age when you murdered my father."

Svæin covered his face with his palms and turned away from the young man trembling.

"Why are you in front of my cell…right now?"

"I could order the men who hold you to turn you over to me as is my right as the surviving son of the slain. I could kill you in your cell with a crossbow. I have thought of that many times."

"Do what you must. I no longer fear death. I have repeatedly looked over my shoulder in the last many years. Let it end," begged Svæin.

"I could watch you hang or suffer the blood eagle," said the young man. "I want to see the tool of the people of A'zore. It is called the guillotine. It will take your head off faster than a swordsman will. I will not believe it will happen until I see you begging for mercy. I traveled a great distance to see this and to hear the sound of your sobs."

Svæin stood to his feet and sobbed, releasing years of guilt and pain he had stopped up within him.

"Now I have seen the murderer of my father face to face. I will be at your execution next week and find great joy in it. I will revel in your suffering." The young man turned to leave, and as he walked away, he said, "I will spare the lives of your wife and family by allowing them to leave A'zore." Margoth the Younger left Svæin to his guilt and pain.

The next day as the sun rose over the great forest, melting some of the newly fallen snow, the sound of women screaming awakened Svæin from his sleep. He climbed atop his bed to peer out the window at the top of his cell to see people running through the streets.

Svæin saw people with fluid-filled blisters and bloody bruises all over their bodies. *How could this thing have happened overnight?* He had only seen this another time, and it was the plague. The village people he saw in the past survived no longer than a day or two with the sickness. Svæin became desperate to hear from his wife and children.

"Someone, please tell me if my family is safe! Please have mercy on me and let me hear from them!" he begged inside his cell. There did not seem to be anyone left in the prison yard in the outer rooms.

The dungeon seemed abandoned. Svæin prayed aloud to his god. "Rothl'Orca, I know you can deliver my family and me from this sickness. Take us far away! I have been a faithful servant of you, O' whale god." He begged and prayed and begged some more. His prayers fell on the ears of a deaf god. He languished in his cell for several more days without food or water. He could only hear the sounds of silence in what was a busy village.

On the day of his predestined execution, dressed in a hood and robe, a man unknown to Svæin opened his cell and set him free.

"Save yourself and run while there is still time. You are free. Go far from this place."

"What about the townspeople? Where are they?" he said, noticing the streets were empty.

"They lay dead in their homes from the sickness. You are the lone survivor as your cell protected you from illness."

"But my family, why-..." as he spoke, the figure moved gracefully toward the rock wall in front of him. "Come back...who are you?' he asked. Your dressing gown is bizarre."

"My name is Jarvis Nightwish, and if I told you from where I came, you would not believe me."

"Why do you set me free? I am a murderer and a scoundrel."

"It is something I have to do to level the universe."

"I do not understand, kind stranger. I do not know u-nee-verse," explained Svæin. "Thank you, and I will never forget this. I must find my family!"

"Go... run to them and do not speak of me to others. There will come a time in which we will have need of you. It is not today." As he spoke, he faded into the wall and disappeared.

"Svæin ran to his family and home and discovered the ghastly scene. He shook within himself as he ran from the village. Near the outskirts of town, he fell to his knees and looked toward the sky. With raised fists, he railed at his useless and indifferent god."

"In the name of all that is sacred from this day until eternity Rothl'Orca, you and I are now mortal enemies. I hate all of your incarnations, and I swear by Odin that I will fight against you all the

days of my life! Rot in Hades! I will ruin your name for all my days."
Svæin fell to his face and into the soft dirt of the forest.

The broken soul wandered alone for many months in the forests
of Arom, trying to find a place where he belonged. He feared the
authorities would hunt him down for the warrior's death. He was
unaware that everyone who would condemn him was already months
in their graves. He would not learn this until much later.

Many years later, in a clearing before the great mountains, Svæin
saw three large men beating a man and robbing him. The men beat
and punched the defenseless man until he fell unconscious. One of the
men drew his dagger, held the young man by his hair, and was poised
to cut his throat. Svæin felt he must do something. He remembered
being tormented by Margoth and many others and did not wish for
this young man to suffer as he had."

The robbers boasted, "Now stay down and do not try to get up.
Try to move, and we will kill you. I will bleed you like a stuck pig! You
are no match for the highwaymen of Arom."

"Face *me* if you want a contest. You can cut my throat instead if
you think you can," shouted Svæin to the men gathering all the courage
he could.

"Ah, who do we have here? Someone who wants to die today." The
men drew their daggers, and Svæin drew his sword.

"Ya may not be a match for my sword, young laddies," he warned.
"It has a mind of its own, and someone is liable to get hurt." He mustered
all the courage he could summon even though he was trembling with
fear.

The three men surrounded Svæin with their daggers in hand. He
circled with his sword and pointed at them. "Now leave him alone and
move along. You have what you want now. Leave him."

"I think we will leave him when we finish with you. What makes
you so brave, *man of the road?*"

"I cannot abide a bully. Leave now, and I promise I will let you
live," Svæin threatened with a lump in his throat.

"That is funny and would make for a good time if we were laughing.
We are not laughing." The men lunged at him at the same time. He

spun in a circle with his sword outstretched before him hacking open two of the highwaymen with one mighty swing. The third man ran into the forest to escape. Svæin stood alone with the young man on the ground, having saved his life. He approached him and turned him over to his back. The sight astounded him. It was Margoth the younger, and he was regaining consciousness.

"I should have known you were with those highwaymen. You are of the same scum. I thought you had surely died in the plague at A'zore."

"I just saved your life, ya daft fool. They were about to cut your throat while you lay there. I think they were keen to cut your head clean off! I had no idea who you were until now." The two men looked at each other, wondering how the other had survived the plague.

"I lost my wife and my two girls. I had no place to go and have been wandering," said Svæin.

"Suppose you did save my life as you say. What difference should that make? I still want to see you die for killing my father."

"Your father was a tormenter who tried to force me to lick his boots and gave me this scar on my face. He was cruel. You must have known this about him."

The beaten and tired man was quiet at first and then answered.

"He beat my mother and was cruel to my sister and me, but he was a warrior, and I was proud of that. You killed a warrior, and you must die." Margoth drew his side dagger and attacked Svæin. The two men wrestled for control of the blade while rolling in the dirt and pine needles of the forest floor. Margoth bested Svæin and pinned him to the ground. He moved his dagger to the blacksmith's face to make the final cut. Svæin reached up with one chubby hand and knocked the young man out with one blow.

Svæin attended to the wounds inflicted on Margoth the younger. He bound him and made him as comfortable as possible. He went to the river and brought back water to quench his thirst.

As Margoth lay in the snow on the forest floor, he began to speak after a long pause. "I suppose I will hate you for all of my days. You have saved my life, it seems. Why did you not slay me when you had the chance? You could have easily killed me."

"I do not have a desire for your blood. There is only killing when there is no other way possible. Someone spared me from a horrible fate in A'zore." Tears welled up in his eyes. "I wish that I had died also. The pain has been too much to bear. I am alone and wander, trying to escape those who would pursue me."

"Where do we go from here? I have no desire to kill you now. I have lived for your death for many years. I do not know what to do now. Revenge has been such a part of my life," lamented Margoth.

"Come with me. We will go to my father, Ben'Tar, fighting in the North against Hrothgorn the Ruthless. I want to ask him to train me in matters of warfare. Come with me and learn," said Svæin.

It is said that the two men became brothers as they fought side by side in many battles. There was never a more valiant warrior than Margoth the Younger. He fell alongside Ben'Tar and entered the Hall of Valhalla at the battle of Murkey Bay. Svæin carried on having his brother and father's spirit with him. Therefore, as you see, he was never alone again.

CHAPTER TEN

JARVIS NIGHTWISH

Date: Dimension of Thor 2396AD
Saturn Moon Enceladus Colony

We are the priests of the temples of syrinx
All the gifts of life are held within these walls
-Geddy Lee / Alex Lifeson / Neil Peart

S everal worlds away from Arom, as Wolfclaw and the ancient
ones formed their army, a man wandered the streets of a strange
moon in the cosmos.

The chill rose from his torso and crept down to his fingertips. The
rainy frost landed lightly on his face and ears. He used to smile, but
there was no use any longer. Most of the people he had known died in
the war with the ice giants. The people expected invasion would come
from outside this world. No one could have foreseen the appearance of
the ice giants. The old gods must have released them from bondage.
Why anyone was left alive was a mystery. Jarvis Nightwish was one
of the last Disruptors of the Temple of The House of Eternity on the
Saturn moon Enceladus. He no longer had a *scuttle* to get from his
meager home to the Temple, causing him to walk in the cold rain. The
scuttle could only carry two but was convenient for short trips.

Ominous black buildings line the street and appear to lean threateningly toward those who would travel the city of Enceladus. A city of many cultures had become a religious landscape of fear and coercion because of the great ice war. The former population was nearly ten million. Now there are barely one million people. Nightwish walked into the hard concrete streets of the city. He met a dark figure with a shining steel blade on the dank, wet road. The soon-to-be robber was unaware that he was confronting a very talented executioner.

"Put your damn hands up, or I'll gut you like a fish. Don't try me because I'll do it!" the man with the overcoat and heavy beard demanded. "Reach into your pants and give me all of the credits you have on you."

"Are you sure this is the way you want this to play out, my friend?" asked Nightwish. "We have been through too much with the war and all. How about I just let you go, and we forget all this?"

"Are you deaf or just stupid? Give me your credits!" the robber demanded.

"One more chance, friend!" said Nightwish.

The robber lunged forward, leading with his razor-sharp blade while Nightwish pulled his disruptor weapon from his coat and vaporized the robber. The disruptor caused the man's skin to disappear as if burnt, followed by his skeleton, which disintegrated similarly. The only human thing left was the echo of a shriek and an odor of burnt flesh.

Nightwish was angry as he muttered, "I warned ya, dumb bastard. I hate doing that." His blood pressure rose, and his pulse increased as he balled his fist, clenching it in frustration.

The temple awaited him and his services. Xemias would hold him responsible. He began to run through the streets. It was in the distance gleaming with its spires in the sky. It emitted a bluish light visible for kilometers. As he approached, Nightwish heard the sounds of chanting from within. He was late for the opening exercises. The old Gods were back when the people least expected them, and it was time for worship.

I will not petition the gods for more than I am entitled. They decide my fate. I will not seek my place in the world; it is not my station to do so. The people within the temple repeated the prayers of the day.

As Nightwish entered the Temple, one of the High Priests, The Diviner of Ice, greeted him

"I beg your forgiveness, O' holy one," said the officer as he dropped to one knee. "A highwayman detained me on the road to the Temple."

"It is unfortunate that happened... but now the matter at hand. A flock member must pay for their sin," said the High Priest. "That is your position here now. Brother Okazik has been relieved of his duty, and I have chosen you to administer the correction."

"Thank you for the trust placed in me, holy one. I feel I am not worthy. If I may be so bold as to ask, how am I to be sure the member is guilty?"

"That is for the Supreme Seer to decide after consulting Xemias. Keep in mind that there are no innocents here, only sinners. They are all guilty of something."

Nightwish wondered what the moon was like before the wars and the return of the old gods. He was just a child, and the memories were foggy at best. Xemiasism is an ancient religion with a single god Xemias. The belief system in this Jupiterian religion teaches intolerance toward imperfection and sin. These teachings are passed to the people by way of the temple. Xemiasism's instructions come from the ancient ones after the society was all but destroyed by Ice-Giants. Failure to adhere to the tenets of the Xemian Temple is death by disruption.

The high priest took Nightwish by the hand and led him to the great hall of the Temple of the Eternities. The Priest and the officer of security stood before the congregation of thousands. A powerful silence took over in the sanctuary.

"Brother Nightwish has been chosen by *Xemias* and must be treated accordingly. Every member expects a transgression-free life and worship, and there are no exceptions. If we let a person's sin stand, there would be others to come that would do the same," said the High Priest pointing at a man in the third rank of seats. "*He* must come before the judgment of our Supreme Seer, the representative of Xemias in the flesh."

The priest put his face to the altar, gazed into the holy seer stones, and muttered a few prayers to an unseen deity. He arose and pronounced judgment.

"Member *E 336,* you have been found guilty of heresy by the Diviner of Ice and the Seer. Your sentence is correction with the disruptor.

The man began to cry and scream.

"I have a name! I am not E 336! My name is Emerson Scully, and I was a soldier in the war against the Ice giants! I just asked questions! Use my name! I am not afraid."

"Take him at once to the chamber to face the disruptor," ordered the high priest. Scully was screaming as Nightywish led him down the corridor.

"Don't make this harder than it needs to be, my friend. We are doing this to save the purity of our people," the new head of security said. "Keep moving and try not to scare everyone. There are children in the great hall. Think of them."

Scully stood with his back to the wall when the two reached the chamber. "Do I get to speak last words now?" he asked.

"I never do this, but I'm in a good mood today. Make it quick."

"Insanity has found its way to King and Country. Madness has entered the sacred Temple of Eternity," the condemned man said.

"I will not have you blaspheme our Holy Seer," said Nightwish.

"Please let me speak. I beg you. After the Great War, we were all stranded out here, unable to return to everyday life. They tell us what to think and do and are given numbers for names. It has been so long since anyone has called me Emerson. I had a wife and children once. The Ice Giants killed them all. I only ask you to call me by my name… once…please

Nightwish grew tired or possibly just bored, so he touched the disruptor tip to Scully's arm. "Goodbye, Emerson," he said as the poor man's skin burnt away, exposing all that was within, he shrieked with all of the air he had left in the last few seconds. "See… Wigmir! " he screamed as he faded away.

Nightwish had no idea what the man meant by see Wigmir. He did not care either. Scully was talking nonsense anyway, and the Disruptor would be needed in the Temple again later.

◦◦◦◦◦◦

Nightwish snapped his eyes open like the shutters on his windows. He had been dreaming in color this time but could not remember what he dreamt. He was just terrified. *I will never sleep again if that is going to happen all the time,* he thought. He looked to his left, and there she was with the morning moon-dark lighting her face with a soft glow. He met Alice Vigil some weeks ago and hid her in his apartment. He enjoyed losing himself in her charms and beauty each night after the services at the Temple.

"Good morning, beautiful, said Nightwish.

"Says you it's a good morning. Misogynistic jerk," Alice said as she shook the sleep from her eyes. "Holy crap, you're sweaty. Hit the showers. Do something about your breath also."

Jarvis stood up and dropped his boxers, causing instant nudity. He looked at Alice with a side glance that suggested a lack of innocence.

"No… that is not going to happen this morning. You know I have to be at the office by eight. I have several patients already this morning. Everything from runny noses to the ice flu," she said.

He laughed as he climbed into the shower. A few quiet moments went by before anyone spoke. "Have you ever heard of anything or anyone named Wigmir?" he asked.

"No, why?" she snapped back.

"No reason, I just heard it …somewhere. Just forget it." As Jarvis finished his shower and began to get dressed, the Temple bells began to ring, catching him unaware.

"Come on! We need to run to be on time. I did not realize we were so late. My scuttle has bad air pumps, so we have to walk or run!"

"No, you jackass, you walk or run. I'm taking a cab."

The wall screens began to crackle with life.

"Nightwish… Jarvis Nightwish. I know that you hear me and see me. This is your five-minute alarm. We trust you will not be late again," ordered the High Priest through the overhead speaker.

I must keep reminding myself that I am a killer and could kill him if I wanted, thought Jarvis. *He did not realize how close he came a few times… Moron.* "Yes, O' holy one, I will be there directly," he said aloud.

"Be prepared. We have three for the disruptor today. Is that a woman in your room Jarvis? I am sure I do not need to remind you of the edicts against relations without the consent of the Temple!"

"No, holy one, it is not as it appears," Jarvis lied.

Alice glared in the direction of the speaker and then at Nightwish. "I am not coming back tonight, Jarvis."

"Why, baby? Aren't we having fun?" he asked.

No, we are not. You make me *sick*. You do not need me. You have the disruptor to keep you warm at night. You pretty much suck as a man," she said as she slammed the door, never to return.

She knew who I was before we got together, and now she is surprised?" thought Jarvis.

There was a time when the idea of killing someone or something would have been a ghastly thought, but now Jarvis treated it routinely. The Ice Giant war changed everything. They showed no mercy. Therefore Nightwish would show none. A few days previously, he was to disrupt a member of the temple when the woman began to beg for her life. *I hate when they do that,* thought Nightwish.

"Please, sir, I have children! If you let me go, I will do anything you want. I mean it," cried the woman.

"That's how you got here in the first place! Stop begging. It's unbecoming."

He showed the woman no mercy.

On his way to the temple, four dark figures ambushed Nightwish. They stood in his path and became startled. The decoration on their robes were symbols of the planets and stars. The leader reached out and landed a heavy scepter on Jarvis' head, knocking him out.

When he regained consciousness Jarvis' eyes were trying to adjust to something. The pain in his cranium was harsh and soul-crushing, He could focus, and then he would lose it. As he regained consciousness, he saw the nightmare before him. He was strapped to a hospital gurney with his hands and feet bound. He looked up to see four robed figures. The first thing Jarvis could do was try to scream. As it rose from within him, he realized he was bound and barely able to breathe. *What the hell is this? How did this happen?* He thought. "What are you going to do to me?" asked Jarvis as he looked to his right and saw a disruptor. "Oh my God," he said in a haunting voice.

"You should have thought of that before you chose executioner as your vocation."

"Oh please, God help me," Jarvis pleaded. "What if I leave? You let me go just like that, and you'll never see me again as long as you live," pleaded Jarvis.

"I cannot do it. I will deal out the same amount of mercy you gave to Mr. Scully and the woman in the temple, you vicious monster," the second figure said as he reached for his disruptor.

"I promise you will never see me again," said Jarvis.

"I must do this. I am curious to see what *you* have to offer to save your life," said the stranger.

"I have money and some vintage wristwatches at my house. You can have them."

"Is it money that you think we demand of you?"

"Yes?" asked a confused Jarvis.

"That's because you are shallow and ignorant," the stranger said mockingly. He moved toward Jarvis with a disruptor in full motion.

"Wait. Wait! Wait! Can you not wait a damned minute? Don't be in such a hurry. Am I not deserving of mercy?"

The robed figure thought for a moment. "No."

I do not understand your purpose."

"I'm not offering you mercy, and I never told you that you were getting any," reasoned the figure.

"You can kill me, but I am not like Scully, the coward. I will not beg for my life. You can own my death but never possess my life," cried Jarvis in a desperate panic.

The disruptor the figure had been holding touched Jarvis on his head. He disintegrated while emitting a shriek of desperation.

"I was growing weary of his babbling," said the robed one. "He will be a fine addition to our collection. He has no remorse for evil deeds, and in truth, he justifies them. Observe what he has done in the past few hours. He has executed a robber. He has executed a member of his sect and accepted a position to continue the same."

"He is perfect," said another robed figure.

CHAPTER ELEVEN

WARSHIELD BEGINS

—◦○◦—

Date: Dimension of Odin 124 AD
The Hall of the Ancients Ancient Norway

Then will he strip his sleeve and show his scars,
And say, "These wounds I had on Crispin's day."-Henry V

Meanwhile, Wolfclaw spoke to those who had joined him under the forest floor of ancient Norway

"I want to begin by making something clear." Wolfclaw's voice filled the Inn of the Weary Traveler. "I am not a good man. I do not *care* that I am not a good man. I can only tolerate most people for a short period. Most people can kiss my arse," he said in jest as the other men laughed uncomfortably. "Do not follow me into battle because you like me or I am agreeable to you."

"That will not be too much of a problem," said Svæin.

"I have fought in the north wars, and I usually run *to* a fight because I am a warrior," he boasted. "I thirst for the ring of the hammer and ax. I yearn for the sound of crossing swords and hunger for its rich sound,"

"You are not a god. You are just a man. You are made of flesh and bone and can die like the rest of us," said Halfdan."

"Yes, I can, but it will take much more steel to achieve that than the average warrior has in his sheath, "said Svæin with a chuckle. Out of the corner of his eye, he saw Fältskog the Elder slip into the Inn, trying to be quiet and not seen. Being stealthy was not his best attribute.

"I am *not* righteous, my fellow ancients…but my quest *is* … and it is one you can trust." Wolfclaw became tearful, and his brave voice shook with the lament, "No fight was *personal* to me at all until the Hrothgorn came for our people for tribute according to the pact of Tin'Old. They are vile cowards. All must pay who made this damned pact with Drak-North. I vow to spend my remaining days searching for the one who demands the tribute. I mean to stand hard and fast on the neck of Drak-North. I depended upon our King Tin'Old to make these things right, but he is as cowardly as his father."

"What of the Hrothgorn?" inquired Svæin. " Have you seen them?" he asked, pointing to Halfdan.

"No, I have not. I am from beneath the Southern realm," Halfdan replied.

"The ghouls of Drak-North sharpen their blades by day so they can hunt and slay by night," said Svæin. "The Hrothgorn are terrifying creatures nearly three to four meters tall. They have gigantic feet and clawed hands. Their bodies are mostly covered by reddish skin. There are usually three to four horns protruding from the face of the Hrothgorn."

"Their faces strike fear in those who would look upon them. Two holes are gaping where a nose should be. A glistening film covered the entire body in a disgusting slime covering," Olaf added in an animated manner using his hands for effect.

"Do not worry though," said Fältskog surprising the men at the Inn. "If you do not see them, you will smell them. Once you smell them, you will not forget that vile stench. It is a little like rotting corpses and wet cattle. They are a terrible and awesome sight and cause men to freeze in their boots and a cold sweat to run down their backs."

"Good of you to join us, mate!" said Wolfclaw.

"I am *not* here to join you. In truth, I am sent by Arkule' to return and report."

"You are a spy? I will not worry about you. Tell me a good reason why I should not leave you for dead right here?" threatened Wolfclaw. If you knew how much spies enrage me, you would"-

"I suppose you will not kill me because you are a good man."

The men in the small group began to laugh.

"So you think I am a good man, do you?" said the old man. Do not let that soothe you into thinking I am harmless. I am like a sleeping Rhandobeast. I look harmless but do not put me to the test."

In the distance, a Hrothgorn howled a moaning cry of the Hroth.

Wolfclaw became fearful as he thought about the Hrothgorn. He would never let anyone know that fact. He thought, *We are old men, and this work is best suited for men with young blood and stout hearts.*

"Are you not afraid of the giants that roam the land of Hrothgorn to the North?" Fältskog questioned pointing to Wolfclaw. "Many families have been killed or taken into slavery by the Hrothgorn and Drak-North. We do not wish to make it worse or that they may kill the people already kept in the work camps. We all lost loved ones in the pact with King Tin'Old." Do we want to lose more?"

"I knew I should have killed you when I had the chance. No matter. Let us prepare. Our *destiny* waits," said Wolfclaw as Fältskog skulked back into the darkness.

The daily meetings in the Hall carried on as usual. The elders smoked, they drank their ale, and they shared ideas. They were also very restless as the words of Old Wolfclaw rang through some of their ears.

The Grand Chair Arkule' said, "Can a mere man defeat a demon and all of his devils? It is best if we do not challenge him. Let us leave this alone."

Fältskog addressed the hall some days later. "It seems those of us who battled soaked in our blood and the blood of foes would understand what it is to battle an enemy that seems unconquerable."

"We are statesmen, and we are teachers. We are soldiers, and lastly, we are subjects of King Tin'Old, and I would not advise that we would forfeit our learning and force ourselves into a battle we will not win. It is pure suicide. I can hear no more of it," said Arkule.'

"The passion of old Wolfclaw was convincing, but I do not believe his quest is one that he will have won at the day's end. He does not have a personal blessing. He cannot have the permission of the high council," reasoned an Elder.

"His Majesty has forbidden such a thing, and the matter is closed!" ordered Arkule.

"Are we pleased with our lazy seats here, or would we like to be seated with the gods someday? Are we indeed cowardly so that we would allow the eldest among us to fight in our place and get our seats in Valhalla? Our seats in the council are poisoned with the blood of all who will die at the hands of Drak-North. I am ashamed to be a man of the realm today," Fältskog said quietly,

One of the men challenged him, "If you be so ashamed, why were you so against this before?"

"Shut your gob! No one gets glory before me. *No one steals honor from me.* I will have my seat in Valhalla," yelled Fältskog drawing a stern glare from Arkule'. "The next man that challenges me will feel my steel."

"Peace to all our members here… there is no need for violence. We will go to our homes and think upon this thing," said Arkule'. "This contention offers us only more questions but no answers."

Wolfclaw could not sleep that evening. He slept, woke, and slept again. He dreamed terrible dreams until his pillow began to feel wet and cold.

"I must put myself in this fight that is not mine, but now it is…" He finally fell asleep, and his dreams came to him like bloody messengers in the night. He saw visions of men, women, and children under the lash of the Hrothgorn. They were forging swords and armor in which the Hrothgorn would do battle. He heard children crying as the Hrothgorn lashed them with leathery whips and chains. Surely, he could help them today. He dreamed he could rush out of doors in his nightclothes, storm the realm of the Hrothgorn, and rescue the poor children. *Foolish, foolish heart,* he thought within his dreams. He talked to himself—*you old fool. Go back to your lazy slumber.* He saw the women with their blistered hands and scared backs sewing tunics for the Hrothgorn soldiers. They seemed to whisper to him in the darkness of the night. *The soft voice I hear from the dark has now become a plea.*

Several nights later, as the small band prepared camp past the city limits and the corn and strawberry fields grew lighter, some visitors surprised them.

"Stand down. Who goes in the shadows there?" shouted Wolfclaw. Out of the darkness stepped Fältskog and fifty good men from the hall of the ancients. Wolfclaw was shocked and surprised at seeing these old men in his presence.

"It is my fellow stinking cowards and me, as you have rightly called us, who stand before you. Although we do stink, it is *not* because we are cowards," said Fältskog amidst laughter from his men. All the men embraced in fellowship, welcoming the new members of a growing small army.

"What about Arkule', asked Svæin. "Surely, he must be furious."

"Yes, he was. He turned his back to us when we left and acted as if he did not see us. I suppose he has protected himself and the remaining elders," said Fältskog.

The change of heart from the Hall of the Ancients moved Wolfclaw. He said in a humble tone, "Today, you have come to put on more fuel for the funeral pyre of the Hrothgorn. It will burn all the more bright and hot for King Drak-North."

"How are we to proceed in gaining the head of the Dark Lord Drak-North? Do we procure it while he is sleeping? Do we hire someone to take it for us? Do we simply hack it off while he sits upon his throne?" asked a curious Olaf.

"Nay," explained Wolfclaw. We will harvest his head bravely in an overwhelming battle. We will take it from him while his eyes glare upon us. I want him to watch me cut his head off."

One of the ancient ones approached Wolfclaw. "I am Odious-Forge, and I want to offer my experience as a reader of the stars, user of magic and alchemy to help you in your quest. Unfortunately, my magic is failing," admitted the Alchemist. "It is my age."

"What good is a magician without magic?" asked Wolfclaw.

"I am an alchemist. I know my potions can help the quest. Please let me go with you. Almost everyone in the realm has forgotten me, and I want to help you. I believe Drak-North can be defeated. He is not a god. *We can kill him.*"

"What is your Alchemy, and why should I believe something so... unbelievable"?" asked Wolfclaw.

"He's a witch! Get him away from here, or his evil will cause our destruction!" said Olaf. "Nothing good can come from this."

"Keep your voice down. We do not want to cause panic in the ranks," said Svæin.

"*I am not a witch.* I can explain my alchemy by understanding the power of my seer stones or runes. They have magical powers, but I do not. I can sometimes predict the future, or I might protect a person from misfortune," explained Odious-Forge. "I can change the qualities of some objects. They can also do curses and spells. That is what brings me here today."

"Show us your powers, Sorcerer. I wait to be impressed...," said Wolfclaw skeptically.

Odious- Forge reached into his large bag, carrying candles, bells, chemicals, and other objects of his trade as an alchemist. He opened the large pocket in his spacious bag and produced, to horrified onlookers, the petrified and severed head of a horse. Several of the men jumped away from the Alchemist in fear. "See here, whatever your name is, this is not-..." said Fältskog. "The old and new gods will want retribution for this needless and horrible act."

Forge took the head and carried it to the forest edge, and there he found a large oak that was dead. Using a spike and hammer from his bag, he spiked the head to the tree with three steel spikes. He faced directly north and spoke these words.

"I have set up a cursed tree in the forest. I curse King Drak-North with all the possible curses I can conjure. I send the same to Fire-Fang, the ghoul-giant using this tree. I curse him with a painful death that would be fitting for a ghoul. I seal these spells with the sacrifice of the noble horse." The wind started to blow almost gale force at once. The small band of the fellowship began to try to take cover. Wolfclaw and Valorii stayed in place and witnessed an unbelievable sight. Odious- Forge was holding a stone up to the tree. The horse's head began to breathe hot breath from its dead nostrils. Suddenly the horse began to neigh. One neigh and then another until he remained again dead for eternity.

"Sorcery! What man can do this?" said Wolfclaw. He thought for a time, looking into the faces of his companions. He appeared stunned but also seemed impressed by the curse's power. "This is not a man you would wish to be angry with you," said Wolfclaw to Svæin. "Now we have more arms for the attack."

"Do you have a sword, and if you do, can you wield it?"

"No, I do not. I am an Alchemist, Wizard, and an Astronomer. I do not need a sword."

"Yes, you do, and you will learn to wield it if you are to come with us." Wolfclaw handed a broadsword to the small man, and he was barely able to hold it up. "No matter, sorcerer…you will soon learn to strike fear in the Hrothgorn with it."

"We will defeat him from above and below. Welcome to the fellowship. It is indeed good to have one so knowledgeable amongst our tiny army," said Svæin.

The men marched to the armory of Rylin, where they helped themselves to swords, battle axes, and hammers that had lain dormant for many years. The cowardice of King Tin'Old, the Elder, reflected on every inch of dust on the weapons of war. The guard of the armory, a seasoned soldier named Al'Dor, was caught unaware and quickly decided to join the fellowship of Wolfclaw. After carefully considering the options presented to him by Svæin and his sword, he became part of the company. Fältskog chose a heavy mace and Wolfclaw chose a battle-ax and sword. Most of the other men took swords even though they were not well practiced in the art of sword combat. Svæin, Wolfclaw, and Fältskog were the greatest warriors and would lead the others and train them in the ways of war.

"I do not wish to remind you of bad news, but what of King Tin'Old the Younger?" asked Olaf.

Wolfclaw laughed, "The less *Tinny* the Younger knows, the better off we will be."

"Surely he would have your head," Olaf asked. "I am trying to understand why you are not afraid."

All were silent to hear his answer.

"Let me tell you this, The King and his Father were ignorant to the screams of the enslaved people and our loved ones and turned a blind eye. I would pray for that same blind eye to turn toward our quest."

Within the armory, there were sounds of steel ringing and clanging, along with the sounds of brave men singing songs of victory. *"Victory onward to victory, we will free the captives and vanquish our foe. Onward to victory, onward we go."*

Wolfclaw stood still and stared into the distance as if seeing some invisible ghost on the horizon. His eyes filled with tears of sorrow. "One hour," he said. "One damned hour. My dear Aspeth was alone for just one hour. I left her alone so that I could hunt something small for supper. As soon as I had sunk an arrow into some fresh rabbit, I returned. There were deep muddy Hrothgorn tracks in the village. They led to our home, where the monsters smashed everything to bits. There is no doubt she put up a great fight. My Aspeth has been dragged away; I do not know where. I only know I must do all in my power and *your* power to find her and rescue her. Many of you feel the pain of a missing loved one."

"Why do you wish to search for her after all this time has passed?" asked Fältskog. "It seems you should have gone to find her as soon as the Hrothgorn took her. I hope we will not have another failed campaign and lose more men."

"I did desperately try to find her ...several times," snapped Wolfclaw with his fists clenched. Fältskog came very close to a punch in the face provided by the eldest warrior in the realm. "I went to the edge of all of the forests and could no longer track the Hrothgorn that took her. I was desperate to find her. I brought my dilemma to King Tin'Old the Younger. All I got from him was his sympathy. He hid behind the law of the tribute season. I never stopped trying to find where Drak'North held her. I know we will find our lost people if we can locate the Hrothgorn camp."

"What if we do not find them, and what if the power of the Hrothgorn and Drak-North is too strong, and we are defeated?" questioned Fältskog.

Wolfclaw answered with all the wisdom he could muster, "If there is one thing I have learned throughout my life as a highwayman and warrior, it is that when we confront truly evil men, they wither like weeds in a garden. They do not wish to confront something or someone that will stand up to them. Truly evil men *are* bullies. They victimize the weak and run from the strong. We will be strong *for* the weak, and we *will* prevail."

The men continued to cover themselves with armor and chainmail. Some chose strong bows, and some chose crossbows and bolts.

"We will bring all we can carry, for our army will grow as we move along," said Wolfclaw hopefully. "Tinny will be angry when he sees what we have purloined," laughed Wolfclaw.

The small army marched to the outskirts of the forest and disappeared into its branches and darkness. As they disappeared into the woods, young Halfdan asked," What makes you so sure that we can defeat Drak-North, and who are *you* to know this?"

"My history has served me well as well as my kinsman in battle," replied Wolfclaw proudly. "We will be known from this day as *Warshield*! I know we will win the day because our cause is righteous and good."

Outside the armory skulking in the darkness, trying not to be seen, was a young woman who followed Warshield into the Southlands.

Later near the campfire, Svæin sat quietly with Wolfclaw.

"Do you have something you would like to say to me, old friend?" asked Wolfclaw.

"Yes, I do…When you vanquished the enemy in our past battles together, what did you think while it happened?"

"Why would you ask something like that… in the name of Hades?" Wolfclaw asked. "I was thinking about getting the battle won and making it back to my family in one piece. What did you think I was thinking?"

"I want to know. It seemed like you liked it. You know the killing part of it.," said Svæin. "Aren't you afraid Rothl'Orca will be angry with you for some of the things you did?"

"I have no use for gods, old or new. If there were real, they would come to help us. The enemies also believed in their gods, but they did not come to help them. I have no need for gods. The enemy needed more help than we did," Wolfclaw said with a chuckle. "I captured a prisoner many years ago, robbing and killing innocent townsfolk. I sentenced him to die by the sword. He begged and cried to his gods to save and have mercy on him. He started crying like a baby. He started begging his god to save him. I told him he could have one night to pray, and if his god saved him from my sword, I would let him go. Would you like to wager a guess as to who did not come to his aid? Worthless gods!" exclaimed Wolfclaw. "He was surprised...I was not."

"That does not prove mean a thing," said Svæin. "It may be the gods were busy."

"Yes, my friend... busy not exi*sting,*" answered Wolfclaw. He was jolted for a moment as a moment of familiarity struck him. He thought, *have I heard this exact conversation before? It sounds as though I have already been here.*

"I just want to know why you seemed to like killing sometimes in battle."

"*I did,* and I will tell you why," Wolfclaw answered. "Vengeance is what makes *war* worthwhile. I believe that the universe is always balanced. Everything happens for a reason. When one thing happens, something else happens to make up for it. Therefore, when we kill King Drak'North, we will do the universe a favor because now it is evened up. Do not ever ask me to feel guilt about our success in battle. I have no problem being a Knight of the universe... an agent of balance."

"Do you believe in Valhalla?" asked Svæin.

"I do not have use for that, "answered Wolfclaw. That is just something that the elders used to control us. Why are you worried about all this?"

"The Elders said that is where we all go when we die bravely."

"They are full of shite. You know that. What are you going to do? Float around up there in your battle clothes and blow the buckhorn? No, give me a mead flagon when I die and lean me in the corner somewhere."

"Well, I believe it.," said Svæin.

"That, my friend is because you are a simpleton," said Wolfclaw. "But you are a simpleton with a great heart and much bravery!"

"You recovered well, Wolf. You just avoided a painful punch in the face."

Chapter Twelve

TOR'BJORN THE COBBLER

—◦◦◦—

Date: Dimension of Odin (125 AD)
Underforest

"This is our fight from which you cannot run. It will follow you like a hungry wolf for all of your days."- Wolfclaw Thur'Gold

Winterhawk with white tail feathers and a proudly pointed beak circled Warshield as they continued their walk into the forest. Wolfclaw and his men drew deeper and deeper into the hidden realm, where there lived a man named Tor'Bjorn. He dwelled quietly with his wife and three small children in the peaceful region of Shem in the Forest of Arom. Tor'Bjorn was a cobbler and was responsible for shoes and boots on the feet of the people of the Forest of Arom. This simple cobbler went about daily business without a thought to the outside world.

His customers heard him say, "The world is not my business unless the world wears shoes. That is my business. I deal in shoes, boots, slippers, and manly combat wear. I would be a much better person for not having anything to do with the world otherwise. If you do not have shoe or boot business with me, then you have no business with me."

Tor'Bjorn lived in a simple home in a small village outside Lake Shem. After work, he would fish from the shores for Copple fish, a tasty delicacy of the pan fish variety for the people of Arom. His family would then sleep with bellies full of Copple Fish and pleasant dreams of waving wheat and meadows near their home. All was well. He had heard distant rumblings of some of the bad things in Olde Turknorse and other places concerning giants that stomped throughout the land. He had *no use* for such stories as nothing had ever happened in his humble home. While fishing for Copple Fish, Wolfclaw's small army approached Tor'Bjorn's lakeside dock.

"Ho there!" Wolfclaw heartily greeted Tor'Bjorn. "My name is Warwok Wolfclaw Thur'Gold, and these are my fellow weary travelers. We require some Copple Fish tonight. Any chance you might know where there is some?"

"This is supper for my family, and although you might be good fellows, I need to look after and think of my own. Now, if you gentlemen would excuse me, the night grows dark, and I need to make my way to the house."

In a voice as dark as the black dirt of Lake Shem and drawing his sword, Wolfclaw spoke.

"What is your name, little man?"

The cobbler became fearful and stumbled over his words. "My name is Tor'Bjorn, son of Sul'lia, maker of boots and all things footwear. "Are you going to kill me or rob me? I am afraid I have nothing for you to steal."

Wolfclaw and Svæin began to laugh deep laughs from under their large bellies. "No, good sir, we have that simple question for you. What has six legs, three swords, and enough courage to destroy the kingdom of darkness?" asked Wolfclaw.

"The answer is *us,* young man…it is *us,*"said Svæin. It is not a good riddle, but Wolfclaw is not very good at those things."

"Stop talking in riddles, old men. I lose my patience with you. Do you mean to rob me or kill me with your jovial laughter? If you do plan to kill me, please get on with it. You are exhausting me.."

Olaf sat down on a rock next to the dock and spoke to Tor'Bjorn. "Please excuse my companions. They still have a fair amount of pirate in them. These men seek to avenge the deaths of thousands and free many from the bondage of slavery under the brutal and horrific King Drak-North. They mean you no harm. We wish to ask you to join us. I have agreed to come with them because I want to give all I have to help."

Tor'Bjorn looked confused at the men. "You want me to believe that a small band of old men and a boy can defeat the army of darkness and the devil himself? You are indeed brave and hearty but foolish, and I have no wish to die alongside you and your tiny army."

"We are small today, but as the great storm, we will be a furious tempest for the enemy to tame," said Wolfclaw.

Olaf promised an oath as if to the gods in person, "I swear to you by all that is sacred that before the sun sets many more times, I will hoist the bloody head of King Drak-North on a spike over my head. All will know the name of Olaf, son of Gandor!"

Wolfclaw interrupted, "what do you think about my companion? I know what he lacks in strength and size; he makes up for in courage and the ability to terrify our enemies with words and phrases. He would already be in his grave if we could defeat Drak-North with flowery words. We brought Olaf to strike fear in the Hrothgorn as we approached them. Do you think it will work?" he laughed heartily. "What say you, brave Tor'Bjorn, maker of all boots, will you join us?"

The cobbler replied in subdued tones, "I cannot because I have *too much* to lose. People depend on me. My wife and little ones depend on me, and there is too much to give up for your worthwhile yet misguided quest. I wish you Godspeed and victory. Now be off with you."

Wolfclaw captured Tor'Bjorn with a cold stare, "this is *our* fight from which *you* cannot run. It will follow *you* like a hungry wolf for all of your days. I am afraid *your* guilt will surpass the pain of knowing you did nothing."

"This does not affect me. I only care about Copple fish tonight. That is *unjust* to hold me responsible for something that has nothing to do with me," he retorted. "I do not need anything else; that is all I have to say on the matter."

Svæin announced, "No matter, shoemaker, tonight we dine. We fight later."

"You do not hear me, sir. Be off with you and leave me alone!"

Wolfclaw took the net from the shoreline and cast it into Lake Shem. He pulled in a great pile of Copple Fish. There was so much that it took four men to pull in the net. The feast was hearty as the men ate Copple Fish and told stories of their exploits in war. Fältskog was the loudest of the merry band.

"There was the time in the land of the north when a hungry Rhandobeast attacked some brave souls and me. The mighty animal killed my compatriots, but the great Fältskog of the Northlands conquered the beast. I grabbed him by the scruff of the neck and opened his throat. I ate him for dinner that night and still wear his teeth around my neck." Fältskog pulled out the gnarled, sharp fangs of the Rhandobeast from around his neck to show the rest of the men.

"In a bloody pig's eye, you did that," cried out Halfdan. "You are full of shite."

The men groaned in disbelief as they drank their ale and spun tales, each larger than the previous.

Tor'Bjorn grew even more uncomfortable with every story and every boast. He reminded the men, "I should be going to the house. My wife will be worried."

Wolfclaw slapped him hard on the back, "stay brave, shoemaker and drink heartily with us. We have only just tapped this keg."

Tor'Bjorn felt an icy chill run down his back as he looked at the impromptu fish feast. "It's getting cold; I must be getting back to the house." He turned for home, putting his angler's cap on and slinging his burlap fish bag over his shoulder. These men had ruined his peaceful day with what seemed like things that could never happen. The thought of a gray-bearded old man taking the head of the evil King Drak-North was laughable. There was Copple Fish to catch and new boots to make. He needed to repair shoes and play with his children. *War* was for someone else.

Several weeks went by, and many Copple Fish went into the pan. As was inevitable, the thundering and stench of King Drak-North's soldiers interrupted Shem's peaceful village. The kerosene trucks roared, and the Hroth soldiers stomped a path to the town. The Hrothgorn shook Lake Shem and struck fear into the people's hearts. Tor'Bjorn began to run. He was shocked by the suddenness of the attack. He would not make it to his house before a Hroth soldier captured him in his back net.

"Silence, you human scum!" bellowed General Fire-Fang over the shrieks and begging of his prey as he trudged away from Lake Shem. Tor'Bjorn friends and neighbors screamed for mercy. The horses made of steel fired flaming rocks out of their heads. The fire sticks threw metal pieces in succession. *Rat-a-tat-tat- rat-a –tat.*

"Work fast, you worthless piles of mule dung! We will be rewarded by the King when we return with his bounty. Move you cockroaches!" shrieked Fire-Fang. The Hroth army moved out as quickly as they had appeared. They traveled to the Kingdom of Hrothgorn with their terrified prisoners for many days.

"I must escape. The old man was right. There is no way for me to hide from this." said Tor'Bjorn to no one. He finally fell asleep from exhaustion and began to dream. He dreamed he was in his boat in the waters of Lake Shem, where he could do some fishing; in his dream, he remembered something. He remembered something that might work. Something beautiful, something extraordinary, something deadly, and he smiled a devious and lethal smile as he awoke. He remembered he had a sizeable razor-sharp filet knife in his fishing creel. Tor'Bjorn reached around his left side to his Copple bag and located his knife, and with a deadly scream, he forced it to the hilt into the back of his Hrothgorn captor just to the left of his greasy spine. The creature straightened up and shrieked in searing pain and agony. He turned to his side and fell as if a mighty oak crashed to the ground. If the mammoth beast fell on his back Tor'Bjorn and the massive weight of the Hrothgorn soldier would crush the others.

Tor'Bjorn could free himself and the others from the net and run into the forest with all his strength. The remaining Hrothgorn were alarmed by the noise and ran to their comrade's aid as Tor'Bjorn entered the forest. He ran through the trees deeper and deeper into the forest as he heard his captors scream and moan in anger and frustration.

A booming shriek of "Gorn, me hath Gorn!" rang throughout the forest like a terrifying symphony. "Gorn, me hath, Gorn!" they screamed in waves of vengeance. The translation is "gods avenge us."

Tor'Bjorn could feel the temperature of the forest dropping the further he ran into the woods. Soon he could see his breath in front of him, and he could see the frost on the bark of the trees. Presently the howling screams of the Hrothgorn fell silent, and he found himself seated on a log deep in the forest. He buried his face in his hands and began to weep quietly. He fell into a deep sleep beneath the pines.

The tree spirits watched him awaken.

"Who are you? I can hear you but cannot see you," interrupted Tor'Bjorn.

"We are the tree spirits and will be with you wherever there are trees. We will offer you companionship as you travel. All you need to do is call on us as you stand in the forest ."

"What could you possibly do to help me? Ya cannot even move," said the cobbler.

"True… we cannot, but we have ancient wisdom that surpasses even the wisest among you," said the spirit. "Trust us."

The tree spirit was interrupted by a sound in front of Tor'Bjorn. He raised his eyes to see a robed figure appear suddenly before his face. The figure was on a heavy motorcycle that roared a terrifying rumble throughout the forest. He wore a long black cloak from head to toe, and his face was not visible.

"Why were you sleeping in the forest?" asked the figure.

"I am not certain. How long have I slumbered? What is your name, and what do you want from me?"

"You have slept for many days and nights. I am merely a Horseman. I ride a steel horse. I tell the truth to everyone that will listen."

"I must admit you are frightening in your robes and jewels."

"Do not be afraid of *me*, be fearful of what is about to begin among the people of the forests. Fear is a weapon, and when wielded in righteous hands, it becomes courage. When in the wrong hands, it becomes hate. Are ya courageous, Tor'Bjorn, or are ye full of cowardice?"

"I am not fearful of any man," snapped Tor'Bjorn.

"You are wrong. A man who refuses to protect his family is a coward."

"The fight has come to me, and I have no choice. I could not protect my family from Fire-Fang," said Tor'Bjorn "I was no match for the sudden violence and death that happened at Lake Shem, but I can *fight* to find my family. Make no mistake about it, horseman! I will find them!"

"Good ...now use all that anger to go and find your family, do not waste any more time! You can redeem yourself," warned the steel horseman. The figure faded into the forest's darkness, and Old Wolfclaw Thur'Gold appeared with his sword drawn.

"How long have you been standing there? Did you see the man on the steel horse?" asked Tor'Bjorn.

"Long enough to know you are supposed to be with us. What is a steel horse?" asked Wolfclaw.

"Forget I said anything. I was probably dreaming."

"No matter! Come with me, Tor'Bjorn; together, we shall fly to the moon and stars and drop war upon the ground! Are you afraid?"

Tor'Bjorn lowered his face. "I am not fearful but full of anger toward the Hrothgorn. I cannot contain myself. I want to find my family, but I feel overwhelmed and do not know where to go. Tell me what I must do." asked Tor'Bjorn with a determined look. "I am your servant. It seems Rothl'Orca has shown me to you."

"The whale god had nothing to do with it. This is your decision to make and yours alone. Do not blame a god."

As the men hurried from the outskirts of the forest, they shuffled into an area where trees formed a giant tunnel. Moss hung from the gray-green trees as water from the melting ice dripped down them. As they hacked their way through it, they could hear a low rumble, almost like a growl.

"What ...sound...is ...that?" inquired Tor'Bjorn.

"Push on," admonished Wolfclaw. The rumble became louder, and an odor in the air appeared. It was much like rotting flesh mixed with moss. As the tunnel grew deeper, the smell increased to a vomitus level.

"Ughh," groaned the men as they climbed down. Just as the smell and sound became unbearable, two large red eyes appeared on the path ahead. As the fog cleared, the men could make out the figure of a serpent head. An enormous snake lay before them.

"And where might ye be going, wrinkly old fools?" the snake inquired in a raspy voice. "You do not think you can just walk across my forestland. You smell like rotten men, you do. You are already no good, so you must be up to no good business. Well, are you?"

"We are forming an army. We need passage to the outside, and I do hope we are not intruding on your supper time?" asked Wolfclaw politely.

"Ordinarily, you old ragged creatures would *be* my supper, he said with a flipping forked tongue. I am not sure why but I like you and already have a better dinner. Therefore, I will let you pass."

Wolfclaw promised, "We thank you, great one," in an attempt to flatter the snake. The men quickly tried to walk a wide path around their scaly host.

"Yes, I like you… and I do not know why. Let me think…My name is Wormouth, and this is my home. Please see that I am not bothered again…but not so fast. Why are you forming an army?"

Wolfclaw stood on a stump of an old fallen pine so the great snake could better see him because the men seemed tiny to the giant serpent. "We are on a quest to rescue captives and kill as many Hrothgorn as possible."

The snake laughed at the thought, "How can you leathery old fools…, defeat the lord of pure evil? I suppose I should just kill you all now and save you the suffering later. You have no idea of the task you are about to undertake," he said with his flipping tongue. "I would be doing you a favor."

"We wish you would reconsider killing us," replied Svæin. "We would rather die fighting if that is all the same to you. If *they* kill us, we will take as many of those bastards as we can. We want to be polite because we are in your home. Let me ask this of you, O' great one of the forest. Will you come with us and fight King Drak-North, brave Wormouth!"

"Me? A snake? You do not understand my real nature." Wormouth was surprised by the compliment just paid to him. "I am flattered to know you think I could be a warrior. I trap people who dare to cross my path and *eat them*. I capture woodland creatures and *eat them*. I do not know what a fair fight is. I would spoil your companionship with my disdain for what is good and right, and I would likely end up eating some or all of you. It may sound strange to your ears, but I do not deserve your fellowship," said Wormouth ashamedly.

Wolfclaw reminded Wormouth of the truth. "All of us have done things of which we cannot be proud, but we can all do what is *right now*. I would pay a ransom to see the look on King Drak-North's face as he saw us approach with Wormouth leading the way."

"I have done too much in the past. Much has happened. It is too late for me. I am not about to start feeling guilty now," said Wormouth.

"You must go now, all of you! It is too late for me, but perhaps if you hurry, you may be able to fulfill your quest. I do not want it said that I let you pass with no fee. A tribute or a gift is what I need. Yes, I must have a tribute, and then I will let you pass by me," Wormouth demanded of the men. "You did not think it would be that easy, did you? It must be an object of worth, something not seen in the sky or on the earth. It must be special so that others will covet it. The thing that I need is no bauble or trinket. Surprise me with a great gift!" hissed the serpent.

Tor'Bjorn reached into his Copple fish bag and retrieved one of his shiny filet knives. "This is a tribute unto you, o' great serpent! I have used this to kill a giant or wound him badly."

The snake's eyes lit up like fire and let out an overbearing squeal. "This will do, yes, this will do very nicely. Go on your way. When you see other serpents on your path, please tell them Wormouth has given you a safe passage."

"They will not believe us... I promise you," said Svæin.

"They will believe you, or they will face *me*. Be gone with you… and may gods be with you to mark the way."

"Good day, the great serpent of the forest!" Svæin replied. The men cut through the branches slowly as they moved forward. When they were a safe distance from Wormouth, they began to run as fast as they could without looking back.

They traveled for many days past the foggy mountains and the blue lakes. They walked to the furthest reaches of the Kingdom of Arom.

Wolfclaw proudly proclaimed, "Here amid this land, the people will tell tales in storybooks about brave Svæin, the arm wrestling champion, and brave ancient one. Old ones will clank ale flagons to toast Olaf, the tender of the bar, and his bravery in the face of doom. They will spin great tales about brave Tor'Bjorn, the angler who saved the fellowship with a Copple fish knife! All praise the bravery of Tor'Bjorn. All hail Tor'Bjorn the brave.

"Do you think people will make up songs about us?" asked Tor'Bjorn.

"We mean all that we say…someday people will sing of your bravery. I know it," said Wolfclaw.

Meanwhile, the mysterious young woman stayed just out of sight as she continued to follow Warshield.

Her time would come.

At this exact moment, in the dark and dank throne room of the merciless King Drak-North, there were also echoes and chants of the Hrothgorn praising *him*. The Hrothgorn roared and chanted praises to their old gods. Artifacts of the great conquering of King Drak-North filled the great throne room, all in the name of Ingegärd.

Drak-North turned to his servant B'jor.

"These were skulls of my enemies that peer from within the walls of this palace."

Thousands of ghastly, defeated stares protruded from the black-wet walls of the cavern. Drak-North continued his bragging. "These are the spoils of battle. I reaped weapons, jewels, and gold from the vanquished!"

King Drak-North sat high upon a throne made of the bones of his enemies, and his feet rested upon the remains of skeletons covered with the pelts of the great Rhandobeast.

"I killed this beast with my bare hands in a fight to the death."

Most of his Kingdom did not know who he was or from where he had come. Drak-North sat uneasily on his throne of bones. He wore furs and chainmail over his massive torso. Two giant horns protruded from the front of his head, giving the appearance of most other Hrothgorn, but Drak-North was different. One arm, the left one, was severed at his shoulder. He had a deep, transverse scar running the entire length of his face. His left ear was gone, and there glared back at the world, a ghastly hole for all to see. A bolted work of metal attached to his head around the eye orbit and covered his eye. His voice was like wet gravel, presumably from prolonged screaming for some unknown reason. His giant hand rested on a femur bone of a great Rhandobeast as he used it for a walking stick. He had a pronounced limp when he walked, making it impossible for him to walk long distances. Enslaved people carried him everywhere on a massive carriage of ivory with five men on each handle of the carriage.

"Drak mun Gorn!" bellowed Lord Drak-North. In Hrothgorn, it meant, "Do my will!"

King Drak-North's hand of the King and General of the Military, Fire- Fang threw a peasant at his majesty's feet. "Your grace, this man was caught in the act of thieving food from a street vendor in the city of the King."

"P-Please... show mercy to...me," begged the old man. "The people are starving, and I could not see... another way. My family..."

Drak-North interrupted the man. "Do not try to justify your crime. Kiss my hand, pledge yourself as my servant, and worship me as a god."

"I cannot serve two masters, your majesty, as I already serve the Lord of the people of the Sun."

King Drak-North was furious. "The people of the Sun do not know whom they worship. They await a god to come that will never appear, yet they still wait for Him. They worship a shadow. *I am your god* here in the world under the forests and mountains. Worship me!"

"I cannot, your majesty, you are my King, but you are not my god."

"Take this pitiful old fool away and remove his hand slowly. You dare to deny I am a god?"

The old man began to cry and shake. "You may take my hands, but I will still tell people of the God of the Sun. I swear it."

Drak-North raised one arm as if to make a royal decree.

"Leave his hands. Impale him on a spike in the gardens for all to see. Make sure he stays alive for three days. I want to see if the God of the people of the sun saves him. This should be interesting."

The old man shrieked through the corridors of the throne of bones while Drak-North ordered his evening meal. As the King ate his royal dinner, the fellowship that sought to destroy him became more significant in number as they moved about the countryside. They came by the hundreds. Simple country folk, shepherds, laborers, and soldiers of fortune all came to help with the cause. Warshield was now a sizable fighting force. The lord of the Throne of Bones may have overplayed his hand. Still, Drak-North ate his dinner in peace while prisoners suffered under the lash.

CHAPTER THIRTEEN

WHACKING SALLY-BOY

———ᔕᘉ———

Date: Dimension of Loki 1987 AD

"Death comes sweeping through the hallway like a lady's dress. Death comes driving down the highway in its Sunday best!"- Blue Oyster Cult

I n another part of the world in another time, another killer struggled with his job. Luciano Cantore' stayed awake at night staring at the same stars Jarvis Nightwish would see hundreds of years later. The Destiny of Tyr lurked in the shadows to observe Luciano Cantore, a mid-level Mafioso enforcer.

"C'mon. Why you draggin' your ass tonight?" prodded Johnny. "Gotta do what the boss says,"

"Shut up. You know we been up all night," said Luciano. "Sometimes I think that *you* think this is like a *Mafia* movie. Like the Godfather or something."

Johnny laughed. "Let's make him an offer he can't refuse," he said while pulling his cheeks away from his teeth.

Luciano yelled at his partner. "I'm glad you find all this so funny. This is my brother we are talking about lighting up. What am I supposed to tell Ma?"

"You don't tell your Ma nothin'. You keep your freakin' mouth shut," Johnny warned. "Now hurry up; we gotta go."

Luciano and his partner, Johnny Fellini, walked quickly away from the fleabag hotel where they had been waiting for the final word on what to do with Sally. Boss Joe Genovese would be furious if he knew that Luci was having second thoughts.

"Put one right behind his ear," was Fat Joey's order. "No muss, no fuss. Just whack him and walk away." It was going to happen. This was the worst part of the job. You could not trust anyone. Not even your own family. All the boss told the crew was that Sally had been seen meeting with a known FBI agent for some reason. There was a rumor that Sally had whacked a guy from the Calabrese crew. Nobody knew if that was true. Luciano knew in his heart that it was true. This is just something you never do.

You do not ever do that. I am surprised I didn't notice the stink all over Sally boy him when I saw him at Ma's dinner last Sunday, thought Luciano.

Luciano and Johnny were middle-level enforcers and would never say no to what they had been ordered to do. Luciano was about twenty-five years old and had been on the Genovese crew for four years already. He liked the life and thought regular people who led everyday lives were dopes. Luciano just wanted to live the good life and be left alone. He could make in a day what it took regular dogface boys to make in a month. He knew he was too good to sweep floors and cook burgers. Two things he did not like were canned marinara sauce and the Carlini family. Both were sorry substitutes for the real thing. The Carlinis were Italians from New York, but they had no honor, no trustworthiness, and no code of behavior. They were Mob *trash* with no class. They were the kind of goombas that wore warm-up suits to a wedding. They were into cocaine traffic and cheap street drugs. *The Godfather* was right. It caused people to lose their souls. The Genovese family would have none of that in their family.

He had another problem. He had been waking up screaming with nightmares. They sometimes say that wise guys do not get help with their heads because they might talk, but he had trouble figuring out what part of him was mob Luciano and regular guy Luciano. He would lie awake in a cold sweat and think of what he had to do and what he had already done.

Luciano was the son of Vincent Cantore, Fat Joey's number-two guy. He was in the inner circle. There were rumors that Luciano would be made at a young age because he was Vincent's son. They even called him *Junior*. He remembered his last job with Johnny Fellini and how his partner seemed to enjoy the torture of Nino Marbolini. They called him "Marbles." Johnny made Nino, who was usually a tough guy and an enforcer, scream for his Mother. After they whacked the poor bastard, they had to chop him up and *disappear him*. Marbles is now in several garbage bags in more than a few different landfills throughout New York State. Luciano shuddered and shook at the thought of Johnny doing this to his brother. The hitmen walked to the warehouse district, where they were supposed to meet Sal.

"Are ya cold?" Johnny asked.

"Mind your own friggin' business," Luciano snapped back. "What are you worried about my temperature for?"

"Alright, don't get your jockeys in a wad. I was just sayin'," said Johnny.

Luciano's mind started to race like a lunatic searching for a hiding place. *What if I ran away and hid him? I could warn Sally that way. Maybe we both could escape to Mexico. There were plenty of fine women and lots of booze there. There is no way anybody could find us there. We could sit on the beach and drink the umbrella drinks and watch the Senoritas bounce up and down the beach.* Luciano had some idea what he might tell their Mother. He would lie to her and say that Sally ran off with one of the strippers from the Jersey Club. She would not like it, but it was better than the truth. Still, he had a terrible feeling in the pit of his stomach.

"You're not gonna make me whack him on my own, are ya?"

"Ya gotta do something this time, the boss says," Johnny said in a threatening voice.

"Shut the hell up! I'm ok. We gotta do what we gotta do." His Saturday night special's smooth hardness was pressed against his chest.

He could feel it inside his coat pocket. *Somebody* was going to get wasted. Luciano made a pact with the Genovese mob and swore he would never break the code, but Sally Boy was family. This was not right to tell him to do this.

The pair got into Johnny's big car. Luciano's mind melted back to more leisurely days on Grandpa Leo's farm in the Adirondacks. He could almost smell the pine trees and the aroma of baked goods. He used to walk in the snow with Sally Boy, who would open their mouths skyward and eat snowflakes. He was sure that since that day, he had never had a meal that tasted as good as those snowflakes. An ambulance passed with its sirens blaring violently, snapping Luciano out of his memory trip. The radio blared out a local rock station like a violent, ironic punch in the head,

"Do you believe in heaven?" asked Luciano.

"I don't have much use for that stuff, " Johnny answered. That is just something that the Catholics use to control us. What are you all worried about that for?"

"It's just that Father Kelly said that's where we all go when we die,"

"He's full of crap. You know that. What are you gonna do? Float around up there in a pink dress and play the harp? Nope when I die, give me a beer to go and lean me in the corner somewhere."

"Well, I believe it.," said Luciano.

"That's because you're a dumbass," said Johnny.

Luciano gathered up his best tough-guy act and asked, "Alright, where are we gonna find Sally?"

"Big Joey says our boy is hiding near the old elephant tents at the fairgrounds."

Boss wants to see us first, though," answered Johnny.

Luciano thought, *What if I jump out of the car when Johnny slows down? Nah, probably a bad idea.* He held the butt of the gun under his coat and seethed beneath the surface.

Johnny was vicious, and it showed on his face. One tooth in the front was capped with a stained piece of ivory. Grease seemed to drip from every inch of his head in a futile attempt to keep his hair in place.

Luciano thought, *what kind of clown wears a suit to a job?* After all, his reputation was as a ruthless enforcer. Johnny could break a working man's thumb for being late with the vig and then eat a steak.

Why do these stupid bastards borrow money when they know they can't pay it back? Luciano thought. It did not matter that a working person would not be able to pay the sharks after that. It was almost a death sentence. When Nino Marbles got whacked, Johnny was particularly vicious. Luciano wanted to shoot him and get it done, but Johnny thought it was not good enough. He cut him from ear to ear in a "Sicilian Necktie." While he bled and gurgled, Johnny beat him with a Louisville slugger in areas of his body that would not cause death. He was laughing like a damn fool as if somebody had told him a funny joke. His laugh cut through the air like a knife. He looked like some evil clown that you see in the comics. The hair stood up on Luciano's neck. He had done jobs before, but Johnny scared him bad. Marbles had it coming, but Johnny had way too much fun. This was a friggin' profession, like any other job. They were soldiers, and soldiers do not fool around with a mission. They get it done and move on. When it was over, Nino's eyes silently begged for death to come quickly. Luciano felt somewhat sorry for him and put a slug behind his left ear. He did not feel *too* sorry for him, though. After all, he took Big Joey's money and ran with it. Nobody does that. Screw him.

Back at the Jersey Club, Joe Genovese waited. The Jersey Club was a topless place in South Jersey famous for mediocre-looking women and even worse booze. That was way back when and now it was a run-down meeting place for Joe and his crew, a haven for trench coat perverts and aging dancers. Joe was fat and usually dressed in a jogging suit. *Like that fat bastard ever gets any exercise*, his patrons often said. He sat at the front of the bar like friggin' Jabba the Hut stuffing his fat face with chicken wings. He always had grease on his hands, even when he was not eating. When he drew a breath, he would gasp, and you could see the other people in the room getting angry because he was sucking all of the air out of the room. There was no question that Joe was a slob. He was also the boss of the largest crime family in Jersey. Joey owned almost all the strip joints, which were a little more than covers for hookers and twenty-dollar lap dances. He also had his big fat hand in Local 246 and any other union he could control. Tonight though, he waited. He waited for revenge and quickly reminded everyone around him at any time that *vendetta* was an Italian word. Vengeance was a dish served best with pasta. One of the main rules was broken, and someone would pay with his life.

Joey's cigar formed an ironic halo smoke ring around his balding head as he waited. "Hey, bartender!" he bellowed. "Did ya know that there are two kinds of people in the world? - Italians and people that wish that they were Italian!" Joe was the only one in the room full of people of Polish descent that thought his joke was funny, but they laughed out of courtesy but most likely fear.

Most nights at the Jersey Club involved Big Joey buying rounds for the neighborhood drunks with ass grooves worn in each barstool. All eyes were on the aging Sheila, who was Joey's favorite. If he only knew that the FBI had talked with her last week, he would have her killed. They were sniffing around about some job the crew did in upstate New York a few years ago. Tony Paulo made the mistake of clipping a New York State Highway Patrol Officer that got in too deep and knew too much. Joey would have left him alone, but he just kept pushing. They all do that. They figured Sheila knew something. Today she would try to entertain her boss in a pitiful attempt at being sexy. Her skimpy outfit smelled of stale perfume and cigarettes. She was one of these women with fingertip bruises on her thighs that had not seen the sun in years. Even when she was working, her skin always had that same smell. She was used up. Joey liked her anyway and paid her well.

Luciano and Johnny came in the back door.

"Hey, boys!" bellowed Joey. "Did ya get lost? I was about ready to send the cops out for ya. Now listen," he spoke softly and closely, "I want Sally to feel pain, I want him to pay big, and then I want him dead. You get it?"

"Yeah, we get it, don't we, Luci?" said Johnny.

"Yeah, we're all good, boss, he said in his most convincing voice.

"I know you can do this thing, Luci," nudged Fat Joey. "Go and get a beer, Junior. I wanna talk to talk to Johnny." After Luciano was out of earshot, he said, "Is this thing ready to go, Johnny boy?" he asked.

"Yeah, boss, you can count on me."

"Is this family thing gonna be an issue?" said Joey with a concerned tone.

"*I'll* make sure it doesn't come up," said Johnny.

"I can't have him in my crew, Johnny. Just clip him and bring me his ear."

"Whatever you say, Boss. It's just that his ear seems kinda rough," answered a dutiful Johnny.

"Go get Luciano and get the hell out of here. You're stinkin' the joint up," said Fat Joey. Ironic.

Luciano and Johnny slid quietly back in the car with no plates and headed toward the fairground.

He contemplated death as he never had before. *Was it like ceasing to exist? Was it just blackness or darkness forever, or was Father Kelly right? Was Sunday school right? Were Joseph, Mary, and the baby Jesus there waiting? Maybe the wise men came from the east on camels like the Christmas scenes?" Wise guys, wise men, what was the friggin difference now?* Luciano came bearing a gun, death, and bullets, not frankincense and myrrh. Screw Father Kelly.

The car hurtled toward its destination, and Luciano broke the silence. "Hey, Johnny boy, when we whacked Marbles, what were you thinkin'?"

"Why the hell would a guy ask something like that?" Johnny asked. "I was thinkin' about getting the job done and makin' it back to macaroni with my family. What did you think I was thinking?"

"I just wanna know. It seemed like you kinda liked it," said Luciano. "Aren't you afraid God will get sore at you for some of the things you did?"

"There ain't a God. If there were, he would show up and just give us the high five or something like that. I did a job a few years ago, some mook on the dock I was supposed to clip. I brought him to one of the shipping containers, and he started crying like a baby. He started begging God to save him. I told him he could have twenty minutes to pray, and if God saved him, I would let him go. Guess who didn't show up?"

"Have we talked about this before? I know we have. Didn't you tell me about God not showing up? Anyways that doesn't mean nuthin' Johnny," said Luciano. "Maybe he was just busy."

"I just wanna know if you enjoyed any of the jobs you did," asked Luciano

"I did, and I'll tell you why," Johnny answered. "Revenge is what makes the world go around." I believe that the universe is always balanced. "Everything happens for a reason. When one thing happens, something else happens to make up for it." My girlfriend called it Carmine, or Karma something like that. Have you heard of that? So when we whacked Nino Marbles, we did the universe a favor cause now it ain't got to even it up. Don't ever ask me to feel guilty about our jobs, junior. I got no problem with being hired out by the universe."

The fairgrounds came up faster than Luciano wanted it to. They parked outside the old elephant tent, pulled up the huge canvas flap, and went inside.

"Sally Boy!" Johnny called out.

"I was waiting for ya?" said Sal softly

"Come on out, Sally, you know what we got to do?" said Johnny.

Sal Cantore' appeared out of the shadows. He was wearing a trench coat and smoking a skinny cigarette that smelled like cigars.

"Luciano, this doesn't make you feel bad?" asked Sally.

"Yeah, but there's nothing that can be done now? It is like a giant boulder rolling through the universe, you hit me, and I hit you. You gotta pay for what you did. It is not up to me, Sally Boy. If it were, I would let you walk away. The universe says I gotta do this. I would be breaking the law otherwise.

"You sure you want it this way?" asked Sally.

"Dammit, stop screwing with me. You know Johnny and me gotta whack you! You have done enough of these jobs to know this. You are not stupid. Now come into the light where we can see you." Johnny remained quiet during this whole time, which Luciano thought was unusual. He was not smiling or laughing.

"Come on out, Sally Boy," said Johnny.

Sal stepped out into the clearing of the tent where the three-ring circus used to be. In a terrifying and perfect split second, Johnny pulled his nine millimeter and pointed it squarely at Luciano's' temple.

"What the - Johnny, wha- what is this?" He just realized that the Carlinis paid off his brother and partner. It had to be. There was no other explanation for it. "Your life won't be worth anything! You pieces of crap got your nerve! You're both dead!" bellowed Luciano.

"Maybe so, Luci, but you're gonna be there first!" From under his trench coat, Sally Boy pulled out his piece and pointed it at Luciano's forehead.

"Oh God, no! You ...set me up," Luciano cried out.

"God ain't got nothin' to do with this at all, junior," said Sally. A click from the front, and a deafening bang exploded through the fairgrounds. Time stood still. Luciano could see the nine-millimeter slug rocketing toward his forehead."

Time caught up with Luciano, and the bullet from Sally's gun crashed through his forehead and another one through the temple from Johnny.

Maybe now the Universe is even.

Screw the universe.

As soon as the bullet entered his brain, Luciano woke up floating in the surf of some sea, somewhere covered in seaweed. He heard bells ringing underwater so much that they had awakened him.

"How the hell did I get here?" he said. As he opened his eyes and focused, he came face to face with a robed figure standing in the surf. "What happened? Who are you? What am I doing here?"

"You are dead," said the figure stating the obvious. You have departed the year 1986 AD Earth and have a bullet in your brain. We find it difficult to believe that, given your lifestyle, you did not see this coming."

"No shit! Really? Where am I then?" Luciano said indignantly. "Get me back where I'm supposed to be! My boys will be lookin' for me. I can promise you that. What are you dressed as? Which crew sent you?"

"Again, you are dead; your brother did this to you. They do not want you in their company any longer. I am called the Destiny of Tyr. and I have a proposition for you."

"What's that word mean?" asked Luciano. "You know the proper-position word?"

"Proposition. It means we have a *deal* for you."

"Ok, let's hear it. I ain't got all day," said Luciano.

"You do have all day. You have all day tomorrow and forever. You have an eternity," said the figure. "You are rather strained in your understanding of things."

"Are you calling me dumb because-?" "I ain't straining."

"We have someone we would like you to meet."

CHAPTER FOURTEEN

THE DARK KING DRAK'NORTH

———ൟ———

Date: Dimension of Odin (125 AD)
Underforest Land

*"I will make weak the strong, I will make poor the
rich, and I will make dead the living."*

I n another part of the world, as the Mafia dispatched one of their
own, a small ancient army trudged the fresh snow on day fifteen
of their trek to the Northlands. This was no small feat for men of
advancing age. It was no small feat for the mysterious woman following
Warshield.

"Who do you think she is, Wolf?" asked Svæin.

"Who? - What *she...* are you talking about?" asked Wolfclaw

"You know the young woman following us since we left. I cannot
figure it out. I wonder what she wants from us. She thinks we cannot
see her either. She has been following us since the Arom forest. Want
me to go grab her up?" asked Svæin.

My eager friend, let us wait until she shows herself."

"I know who she is," offered Olaf. "I know her story and why she
is following us."

"Well, who is she? Do we need to drag it out of you?" said Svæin.

Olaf explained, "She was a poor ordinary young girl raised amongst the Southern people of Arom. She was from a farm family who used to labor in the fields by day and in the court of King Tin'Old the Elder by night. After she sowed her seeds and harvested them daily, she would trade her leather tunic for fine adorning and apparel so she could appear before the king at night. She handled his temporal needs. She brought his meals and cleaned his face after he was done. She brushed his long beard after he slept and after his meals. She was considered a trusted member of the royal household. The young woman tended to the finery of the kitchen and the making of the king's bed-chamber. In return for her loyalty, the King allowed her to ride the royal horses in the same meadow where she played with her sister as a small child," said Olaf.

"What is her blasted name, man? Speak up!" demanded Svæin.

"I remember her face, but I cannot remember her name. People who had been servants for generations raised her. She was born to a family cursed with mostly short lifespans and little hope. I think I remember her father died when she was yet an infant. He suffered an accident with the Oxen cart in the field. I think she follows Warshield because of some sense of duty to her King, perhaps?"

"No matter, if she draws that giant sword she has on her back, then capture her and bring me the sword," said Wolfclaw. "I honestly do not know how she can even lift it," he said with a chuckle.

"Hurry boy, ye lag, and the Hrothgorn will get you and feed ya to Drak-North himself!" said Svæin to young Halfdan.

"I do not know anything about this King Drak-North because I am from the surface realms. We are to find and kill someone I know nothing about," said Halfdan. "Can you tell me anything about him?"

"I can try to tell you the history of King Drak-North as I know it," said Svæin.

"I am all ears and at your service," said the young warrior.

"The Dark Lord Drak-North fancied himself a god," explained Svæin. "He knew he was and when he came to power. There was no cause for him to believe otherwise. When he came to power, he convinced himself and others there was something miraculous about his birth, survival, and quick rise to power. He was the King of the Northlands in the days of King Tin'Old and still is."

"Was he always an evil King?" asked Halfdan. "No one is all evil all the time."

"This one is, young man. If ya sliced him open, evil would spill out instead of guts," said Svæin exaggerating to the best of his ability. "He was ruthless and sadistic and used the race of the creatures called the Hrothgorn to kill his enemies at will." Svæin lowered his voice to a thick baritone as if imitating Drak-North.

"*I am chosen by the gods to sit on this throne.* As Drak'North, the King sat on the massive throne of bones, he recited the exact words, *I am selected by Roth'l Orca! The Witch Queen Ingegärd has chosen me to crush her enemies and roll over the realm like a plow into the soil. I am invincible. I am a god. No man can stop me.* Drak-North was overheard by a defector in his court. His words have been written and remembered by generations," explained Svæin. "This is the story I have been told over the years."

"Drak-North was the helpless child of an unholy union of a Hrothgorn soldier and a farm maiden named Aliradi from the mountain people of Arom. The Hrothgorn pillaged the village for whatever they could steal, including young women and girls for workers or wives. One Hrothgorn soldier snatched the young girl Aliradi from her family and brought her back to his filthy camp. She fought and clawed at an attempt at freedom but could not escape. He forced her into being his unwilling mate among the filth and squalor of the Hrothgorn. She gave birth to a child whom the Hrothgorn named Drak-North."

"She had a child with one of those...monsters?" asked Halfdan. That means they-"

"As I said... she was *unwilling.* Are you not listening? It is hard enough to talk while I am walking. Are you sure you want me to continue?" asked Svæin. "Aliradi found some comfort in some of the other women of the forest who had been taken prisoner also. They helped each other in the day-to-day Hrothgorn duties to help ease the burden even slightly. Her child grew strong in the eighth year of his life. One day as she was preparing food, the Hrothgorn soldiers were drinking large flagons of ale and telling stories of great conquest. As they laughed like thunder and boasted, the more, they drank. As the night wore on, to Aliraldi's surprise, every single Hrothgorn fell asleep at the campsite, "explained Svæin.

"Did she escape?" asked an impatient Halfdan.

"I was going to tell you, ya daft bastard. Ya did not give me a chance. Now be quiet, and let me talk. She *did* escape and ran frantically to the forest carrying her child. She ran until her lungs were burning with a deep passion for freedom. For days, she wandered about in the deep forest range of the realm of Hrothgorn, "said Svæin. That is the entire tale as I know it."

Fältskog had been listening from three paces behind the pair. "That was the sorriest storytelling I've ever heard," he said.

"See if you can do better!" snapped Svæin.

"I will. I know most of the story because it was told to me by the elders in the village when I was a young man."

"By all means...finish the tale. I would like to hear it myself," said Svæin.

"This is how it was told to me by Elder Halfthor, son of Halden of Turknorse." Fältskog became animated as he began to narrate the history of Drak-North.

"On the seventh day, Aliradi came to a clearing in the wood where there stood a group of warriors from the Kingdom of Tin'Old.

'Where are you going, young woman?' the leader asked.

'Oh, you have startled me ... I have escaped the Hrothgorn with my child, and I seek safety. Can you help me?' replied Aliradi.

'Is your child a Hrothgorn?' inquired the fur-covered leader of the warriors.

'Yes, he is. It is no fault of his, and I have to protect him with my life.'

The soldiers began to surround the young mother and her child.

'We were told there was a Hrothgorn child in the forest. Hrothgorn children grow up to be Hrothgorn adults. They grow to be demons. Now move away from the child,' ordered the leader of the men.

Aliradi trembled with fear and anger.

'He is just a child, and there will be no such thing, I swear! He has a Hrothgorn name given to him by the soldiers, but I refuse to say it. I call him *Airohem,* after my Grandfather. When I think of his Hrothgorn name, it makes me sick and makes me want to vomit where I stand.'

The soldier explained, 'I know he is just a child, but I am telling you that he must be stopped for the good of everyone everywhere. It must be done to erase the Hrothgorn in our society. They bring disease and evil, and our King will not tolerate such lawlessness. It will be difficult to have the power to stop them if they all try to come to the lands of the south in great numbers. They must be stopped before that happens. Give us the child, young woman, and save the realm from his type of creature,' ordered the leader of the soldiers.

'You *will* not harm him! I would sooner *die* than give him to you!' cried Aliraldi.

The child hid behind his mother's skirts and tried to protect himself by disappearing under the folds of cloth.

Aliradi screamed and tried to run from a group of warriors. 'You will not hurt my child. Be gone with you, madmen.'

The child tried to run into the forest, and his mother lunged to try to catch him. The leader sent a crossbow bolt in the direction of the child. The bolt sliced through the air and buried itself in the young woman's chest. The child made it to the tree line and ran back into the forest amidst a volley of arrows. Airohem ran deep into the forest realm, and tears streamed down his face.

He wandered for days in circles, unable to find his way. Every tree looked the same; sometimes, he recognized his last footprints in the snow. He fed himself berries from the trees and various nuts he could glean from the forest floor. He was wrapped in a cloak for warmth. Aliradi had removed it and covered her child tightly before the soldiers intervened. He slept on the forest floor, protected by the forest creatures and the fairies of the night that stood watch close by.

Although the roving beasts of the night were set to stalk and the Rhandobeasts were bound to ravage, Airohem was safe from harm. With their fangs dripping with the blood of the kill, the wolves hungered for fresh blood, but they found no prey in the child. An old woman awakened him one morning, bending over his face.

'Child are you sleeping or are you dead?' she asked.

'I am…alive, who… are you?' he asked.

'I am Ensel Andréa of the forest. My home is not far from here. Please let me take you there, feed you, and get you warm.'

Airohem agreed and followed Ensel to her home. He slept in the feather bed of the cottage for what seemed days until she was rested well enough to sit in a chair next to the bed.

Ensel Andréa brought him toast, honey, and some tea. 'Tell me why you are out here in the forest. You are a Hrothgorn child and nearly frozen to death?'

'I am afraid I do not remember everything. I just know that I escaped from some soldiers, and they… *killed my mother*. She was trying to protect me,' cried the young boy. "I will never forget the leader of the soldiers. His face was different. I do not know why.'

'I will see to it that you are safe from harm. I am sorry about your mother, dear one.'

Airohem shook as the old woman spoke, 'I am not sure how far we are from the soldiers. They do not seem to be following us," she said. 'No need to worry, little one.'

Ensel Andréa became a grandmother to Airohem and took him in as one of her own. He helped cook meals and helped the old woman to the best of his ability. It was said they made a home together that was free of fear and was filled with laughter and goodness throughout the days of Ensel Andréa. The two would sit in the front parlor of the cottage lit by candlelight and talk. They played with face cards well into the evening.

'I knew the gods would send me someone in my last days. I have been alone too long and have spent too many nights worrying and staring into the darkness only to know with a surety there was no one looking back,' the old woman lamented. 'My husband died many years ago for his love of the vine's fruit. He loved his drink more than he loved me. We never had children, and his selfishness left me alone. Your presence here, my dear, gives me hope.'

Seven winters of snow and ice passed in the little cottage, and the makeshift family was exceedingly happy. By this time, Airohem was nearly fifteen years of age and in strength of body and will. Ensel Andréa had taught him to hunt and fish, as shown to her by her husband. The boy always kept the home full of Copple fish and deer.

One day as Airohem was in the forest in search of a rabbit, he stumbled upon the dreaded Wormouth, the serpent guardian of the woods. The boy smelled the beast and tried to turn and run for the safety of the cottage. He attempted to scream for his grandmother, but Wormouth clamped him in his jaws and brought him back to his cave in the woods. The boy screamed until his throat was torn and raw. Wormouth kept him in his cave while the old woman frantically tried to find him. Ensel was inconsolable and would not sleep or eat until her precious Airohem was found.

Days turned into weeks and weeks into months; there was no sign of him. It was said that the old woman died of a broken heart because her grandchild was never found. It was revealed later that Wormouth had planned to eat the child, but he was discovered by some Hrothgorn soldiers. The leader of the Hrothgorn group seized Wormouth around his throat. The giant snake creature hissed, cursed, and howled, baring his fangs to the soldiers but was defeated and left for dead in his cave. They made a mistake by not making sure he was dead.

"Damn you to hades, filthy creatures," he hissed. "Someday, you will be paid back for your thievery!"

The soldiers took Airohem back to the North to be with his people and reclaim his name. The snake had so tortured him that he was missing his left arm and eye. The inside and outside of his body were scarred. The Hrothgorn taught him of their ways. The goodness and mercy taught by his mother and Ensel Andréa were lost on the training battlegrounds of the Hrothgorn village. He no longer cried for his mother and the kind-hearted Ensel Andréa. He swore revenge on the soldiers that so cruelly killed his mother. As time went on, he had all but forgotten his name given to him by her. Her face faded from his memory. What was left of his poor heart was forever broken. He became a soldier in the army of the Hrothgorn, and now his broken heart was filled with war, pain, hate, and destruction. He became Drak-North, son of Dorn.

He said, 'I will make *weak* the strong, I will make *poor* the rich, and I will make *dead* the living.'

"This is the entire story that I know," said Fältskog. "I probably did not happen exactly like that, but the elders were good at storytelling and remembering."

CHAPTER FIFTEEN

A HROTHGORN TALE

———✦———

Date: Dimension of Heimdall 60 BCE
The Kingdom of Hrothgorn

In those days, the King of the Hrothgorn was an old Hroth named Armagorn. He had been King of the Hrothgorn for many years and was ruthless to his subjects in the North. King Armagorn sat on the Throne of Bones, ruling the lands of the North and destroying his enemies. He did not venture out of the Northlands. King Armagorn thought it was not valuable to attack the Southlands because he viewed war as expensive.

By this time, Drak-North grew to over three meters tall and tried to compensate for the injuries inflicted by Wormouth by increasing his cruelty and brutality. He was overheard bragging."

"The South is full of riches and prisoners for the taking. King Armagorn is a coward and a fool. Why should we take crumbs doled out to us by the King when we can have all we want for the taking?"

By this time, Drak-North had many followers in the Hrothgorn army. He stood on a large rock on the outskirts of the forest and spoke to the soldiers."

'The day is upon us, brothers. We can no longer be satisfied with the rubbish King Armagorn throws us as if we are beggars!' said Drak-North.

The Hrothgorn in attendance roared. "Gutta Mort Gorn."(We are all one). Drak-North spoke as if dragon fire were flying from his mouth.

"I have one arm, as you can see. I have one eye and many scars. As well as one ear. My voice sounds as if it were coming from a wounded Rhandobeast. Despite all these things, I am still willing and able to lead the Hrothgorn Kingdom better than our so-called King Armagorn. I will kill him with my only arm. I will see him writhe in pain and die like a dog with my only good eye. I will hear him scream and lament his last moment with my only ear. Death to Armagorn!" he barked in his gravel-like voice.

The Hrothgorn were stirred into a twisted frenzy and began to beat the ground with their massive feet. One thousand Hrothgorn pounding their feet on the forest floor made such a quake that it could be heard in the surrounding towns. Shopkeepers and cottage dwellers closed windows and doors in the villages below the forest as if they were aware of the bloodshed.

Drak-North swore an oath. "Tomorrow, we march and carry death to King Armagorn!"

Armagorn the King sat high on the Throne of Bones. He was poised as if he was ready to retreat any second. Armagorn was more considerable in stature than most others of his race were. He was large around as well as nearly four meters long. To his right sat a large Rhandobeast with a chained leash and a large riveted collar around his neck. The Rhandobeast had a face that was long like a wolf's but also had tusks. His fangs protruded from the giant bottom jaw. His coat was like that of a bear containing several layers of black flaxen fur. Armagorn spewed epithets from his mouth as any other man would spit saliva. To his left was BáulfR, of the forests of the far north. He was taken prisoner during the tribute but showed great promise to Armagorn as a protector and fighter for the Hrothgorn. He was from the people of Børger, who were great and proud native people from kilometers beneath the forests of the north. They once roamed proudly, but the Hrothgorn hunted them nearly to extinction. They kept the proud warriors' skulls for trophies and took their women as their own. BáulfR was one of the last of his race, once proud and great in number. They now survived in numbers of less than one thousand.

"I am uneasy, my servant," Armagorn said softly.

"What is your reason for this, your majesty?"

"The kingdom is too quiet, and the soldiers stir in their barracks in the forest pines. Never in my time as your King have my people fallen so silent. I am old but not so old, I think, as I cannot read the simple writing on the wall," said the King lamenting.

"What do you mean, your majesty?"

"The writing that says my time is at hand. What know you of this, my young servant?"

BáulfR remained silent and stared at the front of the great throne room.

"You say nothing? Have you no voice to soothe your King? You have no remedy for my sorrow?" As he spoke these words, there was a harrowing commotion in the courtyard of the Palace of Bones. The sound of the pounding of feet and the screaming of death- pain broke the silence.

"Guards! Guards! Attend me!" he screamed.

There were no guards, for they had broken their covenants with King Armagorn. The great throne room door was rammed in with great force. Armagorn released his Rhandobeast, who charged the door. The beast roared at the commotion on the inside. As the door burst open, Drak-North stormed the room with his Hrothgorn. One of the Hrothgorn soldiers cut the throat of the Rhandobeast and finished him with a spear. The beast cried out and writhed on the throne room floor as he thrashed about in a massive pool of blood.

Drak-North drew his dagger and approached the King. " Your reign ends this moment, and a new realm begins!" he announced as he sank his blade into his King's chest.

"Filthy Serpent! You will always be a Filthy Serpent, and the Hrothgorn will always know you are!" cried the King.

Drak-North taunted the dying King, "I may always be a filthy serpent, but *you will always be a dead King.*" He laughed at the dying man as he watched the old Hroth choke on his blood.

The dying Monarch vomited blood as he coughed his last breath. The Hrothgorn soldiers celebrated as they pulled the King's body from the throne room and threw it down the grand stairwell.

The soldiers knelt before their new King and worshipped him.

"All hail King of the Northlands and King of the Hrothgorn King Drak-North!" They were not taking any chances of incurring the new King's wrath.

BáulfR, who had survived the attack, knelt before the throne and kissed the new King's feet.

"I am at your service, Sire!" he groveled.

"Well done, BáulfR, well done. Without your service, we could not have known his doings. Leave me and attend to your quarters. Your reward awaits you there. You will be handsomely treated by my soldiers."

"Thank you and the gods for your kindness, your grace,"

Drak-North nodded to his conspirators subtly. As BáulfR walked from the assassination scene and its brutality, he walked toward his quarters in the main hallway. He saw two Hrothgorn soldiers with their swords drawn looking in his direction. His face grew ghostly white as all of the blood rushed to his feet. There was a cold splash in his stomach as he was hit by the reality of the situation. He ran into one of the side hallways and out into the courtyard in a full run. He could make it to the trees because of his small size and speed. He disappeared into the forest, and soon BáulfR learned of the betrayal of Drak-North not a moment too soon.

For the next several weeks, King Drak-North executed hundreds of Hrothgorn soldiers and civilians who opposed him. Thus began the reign of the evil dark lord Drak-North. He used the bones of the killed Rhandobeast to add size to the Throne of Bones and to fashion a walking stick from the femur of the beast. He announced to the people of the North, "All who oppose me will die."

Meanwhile, as the grip of Drak-North became as hard as iron, BáulfR ran through the forest, always ever looking over his shoulder, heading southward.

Chapter Sixteen

MORAK THE UNDER-SEA

———— ༀ ————

Date: Dimension of Odin 125 AD

"I wrote a love song on the bottom of the sea."

The fellowship of Wolfclaw and Warshield grew in number as the brave ancients crossed the rugged terrain. The number of brave souls was nearly five hundred good and stout men. It had been many years since the ancients felt the heaviness of a pack and sword. The pain and heaviness were already working their way to Wolfclaw's feet and back up to his head. He could not let his new companions see what was happening. Svæin was younger than him by at least seventy years.

Wolfclaw thought for a moment. *"I am one hundred and ninety years of age, making Svæin one hundred and twenty. I cannot show him weakness,"* Young Olaf, son of Gandor, was having difficulty keeping up with the ancients, causing them much satisfaction.

Svæin blustered, " Too much for ya, boy? We can slow down for you if you like!"

"Never you mind me, sir. I can handle my own business! I can keep up, and I will kill my fair share of Hrothgorn devils when I get a chance!"

Wolfclaw laughed, " If you have the same stuff in your heart that you do in your mouth, then I feel sorry for those poor bastards."

The men all laughed at their companion but believed in their hearts that he was able to do what he said. Olaf had never wielded a sword, but Wolfclaw hoped he would watch the elders and learn from them.

"Watch and learn, boy, and you will be fearsome very soon," promised Fältskog as Wolfclaw listened to the exchange. " You cannot learn it overnight, but stay close to me and do what I do, son…do ya promise me you will not go off and get yourself killed?"

"I would prefer not to have things end that way," said Olaf.

"Good… very well. Continue with your duties as our cook. If we cannot eat, we cannot fight," reasoned Fältskog.

The fellowship approached the banks and shores of the great dark undersea of Morak. The water was many meters deep, right off the shore. It was a dark black deep color that did not yield any of its secrets to the world.

Wolfclaw stood on the shore of the Morak UnderSea. Many memories came to him as he cast his gaze on the waters. "The army can go through the mountain pass beyond the great meadow. We will bring the provisions for Warshield on a boat across the UnderSea."

"That will take a very long time for the army to go through the pass, are you sure?" asked Svæin.

"Yes, we will meet those good souls on the north bank of Morak. We need a diversion to draw Drak-North away from our provisions. You know, my friend…many things lie in the deep that were not known to men and were never to be revealed. Many of the skyships of those who had gone before had tried to cross the great waters of the undersea. They never reached the other side and lay on their broken bellies under the sea."

"I heard about some of the great longboats that could not stay in the sky because there was very little room between the bottom of the forest floor and the water's surface. The ships were forced to touch down in the water to cross," said Svæin.

Even the most experienced seamen were terrified of the UnderSea and what was held in the darkness.

"Cowardly bastards," said Svæin." Exactly where do you suppose we will get a boat out here?"

As the fellowship peered into the blackness of the waters, they knew they must find a way to cross, or the quest would fail and finish there.

"We must build a longboat," said Wolfclaw stating the obvious. "Does anyone in the fellowship have boat-making skills?" Wolfclaw's request was met with deafening silence. " I thought as much. We will camp here on the undersea banks, and perhaps we will see more clearly in the morning. We will cross these waters if we have to swim. Perhaps we will all let Olaf, son of Gandor, carry us on his mighty backside to the other shore!" he said, laughing with the other men.

"I would carry all of you brave ones on my arse across the waters one at a time if I must," said Olaf with firmness in his voice.

"Let us wait until the morning and see what awaits us then," assured Wolfclaw.

Dawn came early for the brave souls in the wilderness alone. The cold of the night became the cold of the morning. The men gathered their axes and began harvesting gigantic pines for their ship.

Wolfclaw offered a fervent prayer. *"Father Pine,* we thank you for the kind offering of your wood for our ship. We will use it wisely, and we will waste none. We will only use the ship for purposes that would make the gods proud of our quest. May it's keel kiss the sea."

The men cut green pine because it was more flexible and would stay green in the water for many years. The smell of freshly cut timber filled the air with hope and wonder of what was yet to come. The sound of axes planing the fresh wood filled the forest. Pine pitch filled the nostrils of the men so much that some of them could taste it. Wedges split entire trunks of trees. They could be hewn in half following the grain of the wood. This gave the wood incredible strength.

Wolfclaw thought. *I hope I remember how to build a ship. I have seen it done in my years as a pirate..., but my mind was on pillaging and raiding rather than creating anything.*

The boat began to take shape as the days passed, and the strakes were put into position. The ship's builders used tar and pelts from the

Rhandobeast to make the hull watertight. The men did all the long boatbuilding with axes, hammers, and a few other tools. Using wooden dowels rather than a nail was employed to hold the strakes to the keel. The planks are overlapped until the ship takes shape. The men riveted the planks to the next using the wooden spikes. The longboat quickly took shape over the next three weeks and was ready to bear the hearty souls across the UnderSea of Morak. There would be no sail, so there would need to be holes for oars. There was room for twenty-five oars on each side of the longboat.

Days turned into weeks, and the ship was shaped like a sculptor's clay. As sure as she was a newborn babe, the longboat slid the rail down to the water and took to the water as a bird took flight.

"We will call her *The Albatross* because she reminds me of a seabird," said Wolfclaw. The men boarded her and began the journey across the sea.

The UnderSea of Morak was violently tossing and turning like an old man in bed. The water was black, dark, and deep. Creatures untold were beneath the surface and as far as thousands of meters below. The UnderSea of Morak divided the Northlands and the Southlands of the Subterranean Kingdoms. If there was any hope of getting to the realm of Drak-North, the fellowship must traverse the sea. The black sea threw the ship back and forth, causing it to roll violently against the dark waves. *"Pull. Pull. Pull. Pull."* The command was given by Wolfclaw to his men as they pulled the oars toward their mighty chests. The sound of the men grunting with abandon filled the sea as they pulled the oars. The ship quickly moved away from the land, leaving it in the distance.

" The Albatross will fly across the sea; she will," affirmed Svæin.

" I knew we could make her seaworthy, sir," said Olaf.

"I had no idea what sea –dogs I had in my fellowship," quipped Wolfclaw. " I feel lucky to have such salty beasties alongside me!"

"Aye, sir," said some of the men answered. They were a well-organized force set on the destruction of Drak-North far across the sea.

"These old men know nothing of being on the sea," complained Halfdan. "Wolfclaw is going to get us all killed. I cannot believe I came aboard such a useless tub," he complained to Olaf.

"I trust him with my life," said Olaf.

"You are a fool then."

"Take an oar, shut up, and go to the aft and row," ordered Svæin. I would give real money if he just stopped talking," Svæin said aside to Wolfclaw.

"Row to the dream men. Row to our glory. Row to our history-making quest. Row to our *destiny*," said Wolfclaw. "Keep your penny meant for the ferryman. We will ferry ourselves to Valhalla if need be. We will ferry ourselves to hades if needs be, but the ferrymen get no pennies today!"

As the rowing continued, the fellowship sang an ancient song in time with the strokes of the oars. "*The Tempest will be tossed, and sailors will be lost. Ride the waves as long ago, trust our lady the Albatross. Mother, sea, keep our horizon in sight. Show the way. Bring us to the end of the world, If we die today. Let us look over the edge and see the dragons and wraiths. A death dive over the edge for we who are valiant awaits.*"

Fältskog stood to watch at the bow of the longboat. As they drew further into the sea. The sky grew dark and cloudy, making it hard to navigate by the stars. Several of the men pushed the homemade anchor overboard. Fältskog used his flint to spark the tobacco in his pipe. He sat quietly like a man in a cathedral, smoking. He was startled by an apparition suddenly appearing at his side, seated on the opposite side of the bow.

"Where did you come from, beastie? Who are you?" he said as he drew his dagger. The apparition raised his face. He was what was left of an old sea captain. His face was covered with a snow-white beard that continued to his chest. He wore a captain's hat made of brass with the insignia of his ship. It is that of the long-since lost *Fjordcutter*. She went down in a storm some sixty years before.

"Are you the Captain of the Fjordcutter?" asked Olaf.

"That was in my time as a mortal. She was more important to me than anything or anyone else. My crew of scurvy wretches tied me to the main mast and let me die. They cast me overboard after leaving me to rot. The ship went down very soon and brought me to the murky depths. I hope the fish ate them all!" The Captain produced a match and a pipe. His hands were almost bones with no skin, and his teeth were barely covered with his lips. He spoke softly and slowly. His voice sounded as if it was coming from inside a dark chest of hidden belongings. Olaf backed away from the apparition.

"No need for ye to fear me, young man. I canna no hurt you any more than I can lift your anchor."

"Wolfclaw! Do you see this?" yelled Fältskog.

Wolfclaw made his way to the bow of the boat. "Why on earth are ya doin' so much yellin'? Of course, I see him, ya daft bastard."

"Are you the Captain of this fine ship, good sir?" asked the ghost captain.

"Yes, I am. I trust you are not here to hitch a ride to the North, are you?" asked Wolfclaw.

"I stand as a sentry of the UnderSea of Morak. My name is *Drek'ar.* Do not try to cross this water. It is filled with dangers that you know not of. I am here to warn all who try to cross. This is the spot where the Fjordcutter sunk to the depths."

"We are hearty souls who have no fear. We mean to cross. We are a family of warriors!"

"I had a family once… I lost everyone I knew when I was forced to sleep forever in the mud at the bottom of the sea. My corpse is still there somewhere in the slop of the deep. The cutthroats tied me to the mast on the deck of my ship, and then something grabbed me and brought me to the deep. I held my breath as long as I could, but soon I sucked seawater into my chest, and the world became black as night. The bells rang in random order deep in the murky depths. I heard bells. That terrified me more than any sea monster that slithered the sea floor. I have seen the future. Death calls to you… how do you answer?"

" I answer as I always have. I am a highwayman. I am a pirate. I am a robber. I am a diplomat. I am a statesman. I am ancient. Most of all, I am a soldier. I will run them through with a sword all who dare to oppose me. *Bring death to me,* and I will snatch his bloody tongue from his head."

The men heard this and raised a rousing cheer above the sound of the beating waves.

"Do not underestimate the power of death. He is protected by the power of evil, and he takes no guests or prisoners," warned the old sea captain.

"I do appreciate the warning, my good soul. We will be diligent in our journey across the sea."

"I will leave you now, but before I go, I wish for you to take my spyglass. If you insist on crossing these waters, you will need it. If you peer through the glass, it will guide you where you need to go, and you may see the danger ahead. It was touched by a sorcerer on my last visit to the north. It is used to see through the dark and even under the black of the sea. It no longer has all of its' magic. You can see far ahead, though," said the Sea Captain.

"It just so happens we have our very own Alchemist aboard, and we will see his magic bring the glass to life," said Wolfclaw.

Very soon, you will meet a man of mercy who will help you in your quest. We all share a common enemy…evil. This man will help you. He will show you mercy just as he showed me many years ago."

"Who is he? What is his name?" asked Wolfclaw.

"You will know him. Beware the isle of Kelda." The apparition faded into the sea as he spoke.

"What did he say about the isle of Kelda? I did not hear that," asked Fältskog.

"Beware… does not tell us much. We must move faster as time is not our friend today," ordered Wolfclaw.

The Albatross continued to toss as driftwood in the surf. Olaf was slumped over the side, vomiting violently.

"I feel sorry for ya, my boy, I do. I did this kind of thing to myself back in my mead days," boasted Svæin." Get it all out. We need you on the oar arms."

The journey was three days old, and the fellowship began to run out of rowing power. The sea was as calm now and serene as a lake. The men took this time to rest and try to return to full energy. Odious-Forge conjured all of the power of his sorcery into the spyglass left by the Sea Captain.

"Let this glass see all there is to sea from life to death and death to life. Let it breathe as a man draws breath! Let it have power from this time until it serves no purpose," Odious- Forge conjured. The glass glowed a beautiful yellow hue and seemed to quiver in its sheath.

Wolfclaw put the glass to his eyes, and they were opened to the wondrous spectacle. He saw to the bottom of the depths and deep into the forest floor. He could see what was behind and what was in front of the Albatross. Before passing the glass to Svæin, Wolfclaw spoke loudly for all to hear, " Just below the surface, I can see a dark shadow below... It is moving from starboard to port and back again! The damn thing is nearly as long as the boat!"

"Men be on guard. Something looms below," Svæin warned at the top of his voice.

In an instant, a massive head was raised out of the sea. The face was hideous, with large needle-shaped fangs and two walleyes. Gills slapped against the side of the creature's scaly head, and water dripped from his fangs. A loud hiss emitted from his gray, wet face as he opened his giant mouth. The men scrambled and fell over each other, trying to escape the massive jaws. The sound of steel being drawn from many scabbards was heard over the hissing sound. The beast snapped his jaws closed on young Halfdan, who was in the boat's aft section. He closed his massive jaws as the man tried to scream and was cut short in death. The creature returned to the deep with his prey.

"Damn you, Wolfclaw. He was just a boy! How many of us will die?" asked a frustrated Fältskog. " I will hold to my bargain, but how many of us will be killed by Hrothgorn or eaten by sea creatures? I wish I had never left the Hall. How do we fight such a thing as that?" Fältskog hung his head in defeat.

The remaining men on the boat trembled where they stood in the cold.

"I do not know what is to come. Even if we die or live. I do not know if we will win the day. I do not know if we will even make it to the other side of the UnderSea. I do know for sure some things. I know we have a righteous cause and what we do is good and right. I know evil cannot win forever, and it must be defeated. I know we cannot leave things the way they are. That is no life to live. Let us move forward. If you see the shadow under the water again, spear it as soon as you see it. Do not give the ghoul a chance to surface."

The men stared at the still black waters, and the creature never gave them the satisfaction of revenge.

Fältskog screamed into the sky.

"You heartless devil… Come and take me; I will stick in your throat like a dry bone from a Rhandobeast. Come and choke on me. I am here waiting…."

<hr />

Several more days passed, and Fältskog saw land in the old sea captain's spyglass. It was still several days away, but it gave the crew hope they would make landfall soon. Fältskog peered into the sky with the magic spyglass. He saw Ingegärd looking back at him. He handed the glass to Wolfclaw, who also peered into the face of the evil Witch Queen.

"She is as ugly as Hades. I never imagined. I wonder what manner of evil awaits us onshore. The glass has told us Ingegärd is aware of what we do," noted Wolfclaw.

"She is an unsightly thing to behold, is she not?" asked Svæin. " She *is* a sea hag."

"She can change into whatever form she chooses… so beware. She can also appear quite beautiful."

The Isle of Kelda loomed over the horizon. Creatures unseen await the fellowship on the mysterious island. At least according to the stories, Svæin was spinning for young Olaf.

"Oh yes, my boy, there are monsters and demons on the Isle of Kelda that can eat ya whole and just let out a burp. One creature had a bear's head and a warrior's body. He ate a whole boatload of explorers at one sitting… at least that is what I heard."

" I think you are too much in drink and not enough in truth… elder," Olaf replied.

"You do not believe me? How many battles have you seen? Svæin inquired, aggravated in tone. "Have you ever been over the mountains? I do not think so." He stripped his sleeve to show his battle scars which ran the length of his arm. "I did not get these lying around the house or sitting at the Hall of the Ancients. I have *earned* storytelling rights."

"I do have the experience to know a tall tale when I hear it," said Olaf.

" What if I just crack you on your head …?"

"Wait," blurted Wolfclaw. "There is the Isle of Kelda as I gaze on the horizon."

The crew made ready to run the Albatross onto the beach leading to the island. The fellowship readied to make camp there to devise further plans to grow an army of brave souls.

CHAPTER SEVENTEEN

THE HARVESTER OF EYES

—ᥩᎴ—

Date: Dimension of Odin (125AD)

"I can see all you know and all that you are. You cannot lie."

S ome years before Warshield, another boatload of soldiers arrived at the Isle of Kelda. They were nearly starved to death and fatigued from marching. The island was a welcome oasis.

"This is as good a place as anywhere else. We will make camp here and try to find provisions. Look for a village, said their leader.

"I see the light from across the island. It might be a village, sir," said a soldier.

"Very good. Take three men and go there at once. Find out what is there and come back and report it," said the Captain.

The boat Captain became concerned later when the group of four sent out to scout did not return.

"After we camp here, we will all find our comrades."

The group ventured into the forest as the sun rose the following day. As they approached a clearing, they were flanked by men in armor with bows and spears.

"Come with us. Our leader wishes to speak with you," said the group leader. "We were ordered to kill all of you if you refuse."

"Die trying ya silver bastards!" said a soldier.

"He means to speak with you. Come with us," said the leader.

The men were led through the clearing. In their path was a large fortress not visible from the other side of the forest. It was made of gray granite and shone like a beacon in the dusky morning. The drawbridge was lowered, and a man of large stature walked outflanked by four men, two on each side. The man was older, graying, and wore a flowing robe with a tunic and trousers. A long gray beard flowed over his chest, and he walked with a large walking stick. His face was gaunt and pale, indicating walks outside were very few. There were holes where his eyes were giving him a hollower look. He was flanked by his men, perhaps for protection, but more likely, it was so they could lead a blind man where he should go.

"Welcome to the Isle of Kelda, my island," he said. 'It was unfortunate that you were not invited."

"We needed provisions and rest, and then we would be on our way," said the Captain. "Where are our four comrades?"

"They are inside and quite comfortable," said the strange blind man as his guides showed them across the bridge into the fortress.

"My name is Hansel Gru'el, and I am the owner and inhabitant of this island," he said. "Come and see your comrades."

As the men entered the great room, they were met with a horrific sight. All four men sat in chairs around a table with bloody bandages around their foreheads. There was a large amount of bleeding from soaked bandages.

"What in the name of Rothl'Orca, has happened to you?" asked the Captain.

The man seated closest said in a panicked scream, "He tore our eyes out!"

"Explain yourself, old man! I will order my men to kill you immediately. We may die, but we will fight!"

Gru'el's men outnumbered the soldiers and disarmed them immediately.

"Let me show you what I can do," said Gru'el. He reached into a glass case he carried and took out an eyeball freshly snatched from one of the scouts. He stuffed the eyeball into his eye orbit.

"In the name of... what manner of sorcery is this?" said one of the men.

"I have been called 'The Harvester of Eyes' in the past, among many other things. I do not much like the name, but it is descriptive. I snatch the eyeballs of anyone I please. After I stuff them into my blank eye sockets, I can read the mind of their former owner. I can see the things they saw and think their thoughts. I have a large collection of eyes that I have ...harvested."

One of the men, Harold of Arom, stood bewildered at the Harvester of Eyes and his pure matter-of-fact evil. He let his guard down when Gru'el reached out in lightning-fast lunges and ripped his left eye from the socket. He screamed in agony as the harvester stuffed the freshly harvested eye into the hole. The Captain and his men were being held back from killing Gru'el by his bodyguards.

"Bandage him and make him comfortable," said Gru'el to his men. "Now, I will show our unwelcome visitors what we can do."

The men strained to get loose from the guards. "I will remove your stinking head as soon as I am free!" bellowed the Captain. "That man deserved none of that."

The Harvester went into a trance-like state. "I can see through the eye and know all things. I have your consciousness." He opened his mouth, and the voice of the soldier Harold came forth.

"You have no right to invade the private part of my mind that only I know. I am a soldier. It is my place to do my King's and Captain's will," said the voice.

"This is absurd! I will not stand for this," said Harold as he attempted to staunch the bleeding.

"Our Captain is leading us into death. I just know it. We should never have stopped here for camp. The first chance I get, I will kill this Gru'el person with my bare hands.

I ...hear...a prophecy...or a promise. I must share it! A time will come when a Daughter becomes Queen of all the land. The Kingdom will exist in harmony," said Harold.

Gru'el removed the eye from his skull and placed it in a pouch tied to his belt.

"You and your men are free to go your own way. You can tarry; I will have my men make you suffer the pain of death... or *you may go*. The choice is yours," said the Harvester.

The band of wounded men trudged their way to the ship through the snow and ice. They attended to their injured and newly blind.

They would not forget the Harvester of Eyes, Hansel Gru'el.

<hr />

Many years later, As the men of the army of Wolfclaw disembarked on the Island of Kelda the Albatross, they were met at the tree line by a tall man in a dark cloak that went nearly to his feet. He was old and very frail-looking. His gaze was as ice as he had no eyeballs glaring back from empty holes. His lips were bluish from the cold, and his face was albino white. He walked with a cane made from a tree branch and was surrounded by several companions dressed in armor and armed with swords.

"Stop where you stand this instant," he ordered. The Island of Kelda is mine... and you will have no part of it without payment first."

"What payment do you require, old man?" asked Wolfclaw. "We have traveled far and only wish to make camp here a short time. We seek to free our people from an evil slaver and to deliver the world from Drak-North and his power of evil."

" Not a problem of mine and is of no concern to me. I require payment."

" We have no gold *old man*. I am Wolfclaw Thur'Gold, and this is my company of brave men. We do not wish to war with the Island of Kelda but *will* if we are forced. Let us camp and replenish our provisions, and we will be on our way."

" I do not take kindly to threats in my home, *old man*. I could have my men descend upon you and leave you for dead, and the shores of Kelda will be your graves."

"Order them, so I am certain you do not recognize me. But you and I have unfinished business. Your death. *Surely* you must recognize me from the battle of Murkey Bay all those many years ago."

"You know this ghoulish old fool?" asked Svæin.

" I do, my friend. This so-called man is known as 'The Harvester of Eyes.' He rips the eyes from the heads of his victims and places them in the gaping holes of his head."

"In the name of the gods... why?" asked Olaf.

"He peers through the eyes of the former owners, and he can see what they have seen and knows what they know. He sees everything they have seen. He collects all knowledge from the eyes he snatches. He is said to be cursed," said Wolfclaw.

"That is not the name that I wish to be known. I am not cursed, and I am not a ghoul. I consider it a gift," said Gru'el.

"There are four of my companions from the battle of Murkey Bay that would disagree with you strongly. They no longer see the world and can only dream of the past and imagine seeing their loved ones. For this today, you will die."

The fellowship and Warshield drew their swords as the Harvester's men drew theirs. Swords clashed, and shields crashed into one another. The Harvester's men were quickly dispatched, leaving the old blind man alone amongst his dead bodyguards.

"What have you done?" he asked. " You have invaded my home and killed my men, and *I am* a ghoul? I wonder if that same finger of shame can be pointed at you?"

"My companions at the battle of Murkey Bay had their eyeballs snatched from their heads by you in a bloody display of torture. Lecture me no more, you demon! By the power of the Hall of the Ancients in the name of his majesty Tin'Old the Younger, I sentence you to death." Svæin grabbed the old man and bent him over a log on the beach for Wolfclaw to behead him with his sword.

"Wait... I have something you will want first!" cried the old man. Wolfclaw lowered his sword." I will give it to you if you spare my life."

"Is this a trick, you pitiful old fool? You must pay for the crimes you committed against the kingdom and my men, and you will pay with your head," said Wolclaw firmly. "There are very few things that would keep me from removing your head."

"You want this thing I have...spare me, and I will give it to you."

Wolfclaw thought better of the offer, but curiosity overcame him, and he relented. "What is this thing you have, and why do I want it? No tricks."

"I have the left eye of a *certain* King of the North. I have the eyeball of Drak-North himself. I received it from Wormouth, the serpent who tortured the young boy King. He gave it to me as barter in exchange for passage through the island. I have peered through the eye and have seen the madness of Drak-North. I will do the same for you. The eye still knows the mind of its former master. It calls to him."

Wolfclaw shook his head in agreement ... and amazement.

Sometime later, in the lodge of Harvester of Eyes, Wolfclaw and the fellowship stood before a glass box surrounded by silver inlay. Inside the box was the left eyeball of Darak'North, the evil King of the Northlands. The Harvester of Eyes reached into the box to retrieve the eyeball. It was gray and submerged in a yellow fluid for preservation. The old man held the eye up to the fellowship. "I will now tell you what I see, and when I have finished, you will leave me in peace and spare my life."

"If you give us what we need, you have my word," swore Wolfclaw.

"Your honor is like so many useless island lava rocks to me, but I have no choice," reasoned the Harvester.

The old man placed the eye in the gaping bare spot in his eye socket and began to speak. His voice changed into a low, *grave* tone that was not his own. It was the voice of King Drak-North.

"Who has my eye?" I can see you Hansel Gru'el! Bring it back to me now, and I will not put you to death."

The voice changed to that of the old man once again. " I see through the eyes of a boy...Airohim." The old man smiled and then cried in the voice of a young boy.

" I see Ansel Andrea and... mother. I must get home to my mother. *Wormouth... beast of Hades.* I must have his head. He must pay. I see one man riding an iron horse. I see another wearing a long robe and carrying a weapon. I see yet another...I cannot see his face, but he wears all black."

The Harvester, who caused much pain to others, was feeling the pain of the life of King Drak-North.

"I wander lost with no way to return home. These Hroth look like me, but they are not good," said the voice of Airohim.

"I see what Drak-North has seen. I know what he perceives, said the Harvester.

"I do not care for his miserable and putrid life. Drak-North can kiss my arse. Tell us where he has imprisoned all the enslaved people he has taken as tribute," ordered Wolfclaw.

"I see a large colony of workers at the cliffs of Athgor. There are many women and children among them. They work making garments, and the men forge armor," said Gru'el

"How is the Throne of Bones fortified?" asked Wolfclaw.

"I see it is guarded by one hundred Hrothgorn soldiers, and the throne is protected by a Rhandobeast."

The voice became the raspy voice of Drak-North once again.

"I still see you, Wolfclaw Thur'Gold of Arom. I can barely see your face. You fool no one hiding in a cloak. I know who you are, and I will be waiting for you. I will see all of your stinking bodies on spikes at the entrance of the Throne of Bones. I will drink mead from your skulls.

Have you ever seen a man flayed Hansel Gru'el? It is not a sight you will be able to forget. I promise you that you will beg for your life and weep like a motherless child," threatened Drak-North.

"Can you see where he is now?" asked Wolfclaw.

"Please, I do not wish to be in his presence any longer," pleaded Gru'el.

"Report what you see, or I will separate you from your head."

"He moves about the region but stays mainly in the Throne of Bones," reported the Harvester.

The voice of Drak-North once again emitted from The Harvester's mouth.

"Harvester of Eyes, Hansel Gru'el, I know you wear my eye. For what reason do you do this? You are companions of those who seek me and seek to destroy me. If you help these rogues, I will flay you along with them. I have Hroth on the path to the Island of Kelda as we speak...."

The old man reached into his left eye orbit and pulled the eye of King Drak-North from the hole.

"I can no longer bear the evil in my head. His mind is filled with terrifying and dark images. I can no longer stand it! Please... I have seen too much. He has shown me his evil! I kept the eye as folly, but now I will cast the damn'ed thing into the UnderSea of Morak. Bring me with you before you go to the sea. I no longer want to live here as I am. I have seen too much suffering, much of it I have caused. Drak-North and I see all. It is too much the same."

Wolfclaw looked at the old man with searing eyes. " This is not of your choosing. There are things we do not get to choose, but we can choose freedom, and we can choose to fight. This is our choice. For the rest of your life, you will feel the pain your victims feel. You are left to think about your deeds alone." The old man fell to his knees and pressed his face into the sand.

"Kill me, I beg you. Do not leave me here alone with what I know. At least take me with you ...take me with you, I beg you," pleaded the whimpering man.

Warshield later told of how they could hear the old man howl and moan in pain as they left him on their way back to the UnderSea of Morak. They would not forget The Harvester of Eyes.

The Destiny of Tyr would not forget him either. Gru'el's ghastly gift was too valuable to ignore.

Five figures entered the Isle of Kelda as they waded from the surf.

"We are the Destiny of Tyr, and we are entreating entrance to your island to speak with you," said one ghostly figure.

"I cannot see you, but I can sense there are five beings in front of me," said Gru'el. "What do you require of me? Make it fast. I have very little patience."

"There are four of us and a future man known as Luciano. We require his skills as well as yours. We need *your* unique skill. Luciano kills without question; we know you will do the same. We require you to come with us immediately and without delay," said the Destiny.

"What will happen if I do not wish to come with you?"

"We will insist."

"In that event...seize them," said Gru'el to his two remaining bodyguards. "Bind them all, and I will have their eyes."

One of the members of the Destiny reached out with a disruptor, touched each of the guards slightly, and watched them disintegrate in unbelievable pain almost simultaneously. They had received this weapon from Jarvis Nightwish. Four bodyguards lie in smoldering ashes leaving the Harvester of Eyes alone.

"What have you done? What have you done in the name of the old and new gods?" Gru'el said, trying to make sense of it all.

"Now, you will join us on our quest or suffer the same fate."

"You have me...do what you will," said a dejected Gru'el.

The entire group waded into the surf and disappeared beneath the waves.

CHAPTER EIGHTEEN

THE HOLY FOREST OF ER'OSQUE

—◦∞◦—

Date: Dimension of Odin (125 AD)

"I am you, and I know the evil you plan."

As the Winterhawk traveled above in circles in the sky, Wolfclaw grew curious about its presence.

"Odious- Forge, what do you know about the Winterhawk? He seems to follow us."

"The mighty bird represents life, death, and the soul. Many Aromite myths have linked the Winterhawk to the arrival of life or death. With their power of flight, these winged creatures were seen as carriers or symbols of the human soul, or as the soul itself, flying heavenward after a person has died."

"Well, he is giving me the shakes. It seems like he is always there," said Wolfclaw.

"The Ancients in the Hall believe the soul, once freed from the body, takes the form of the Winterhawk."

"If he gets close enough, I am putting an arrow in his breast meat," said Wolfclaw jokingly.

151

The people along the path of the marching army believed the fellowship's quest was true and pure. Some even joined the fight on the spot.

One member of the army was not pleased with the journey. Fältskog of the Hall of the Ancients was freezing his toes.

"We are on a fool's errand and cannot win this fight. We are all bound to die, yet Wolfclaw takes us deeper into the forest," Fältskog told a warrior by his side. "We are all nearly starving from the rations we have been given. A Rhandobeast would cook up very nicely in a stew kettle."

"A fire would give us away, sir," the warrior answered.

Fältskog stared him down. "Idiot. The first chance I get, I will kill a Rhandobeast, and we will eat heartily. Let Wolfclaw get his own Rhando." The warrior wandered away quite disgusted with Fältskog.

The roar of a Harley Davidson echoed through the forest, and the biker rode to Fältskog and dismounted.

"A steel horse?" asked Fältskog." I have never seen one of those creatures. I have only heard of these."

"My name is Viktor. I have come to talk to you."

"What? I am of no consequence. Why would you be interested in me?"

"I know a criminal when I see one. I am one myself. I am wanted by authorities in my world for thievery and other crimes. I even tried to kill an officer of the law. You are too humble. Admit your crimes."

"See here now- I do not know you. How can you say such-?"

"*You are planning something.* I do not know what it is. Maybe you could tell me," said Viktor.

"I honestly do not know what you want to hear me say," said Fältskog. "Who are you, and why should I talk to you?"

"I am sent by those who see the *past and the future as the same.* I do not know why or how I am here. I am supposed to be a protector of the realm," Viktor said, leaning in and lowering his voice to a near whisper." I sense you are about to do something that will hinder the cause of your leader," said Viktor.

In an instant, Fältskog drew his sword. "Take your leave of me at once. Get on that steel horse and ride into the forest!" Viktor sat on his Harley, and it roared to life.

"I will leave you with this. I am watching you at all times. What you do or do not do here matters very much. I know *about* you because I *am* you. The difference is that I hold hope for tomorrow. It seems you have given up."

"No, I have not given up, but tomorrow's hope is a broken promise made today by those who were disappointed yesterday," said Viktor as he rode away into the thick forest.

King Drak-North prepared his battle plan for the inevitable approach of Warshield. The forest of Er'Osque lay before them. The dark trees covered with snow drooped lazily like old men in the winter of their lives. The snow was packed deeply as the men plodded through it. Silver ice hung from the trees like jewels glistening with the light shining from the moon through the forest floor above. The wind howled like ghosts in a wintery cathedral with icy stained glass windows. Wolfclaw reached down to feel his long beard, now caked with icy crystals that crackled and crunched through his gloved fingers. He could feel the ice creep up to his nose from his beard, causing him to smell the winter crisp through his mustache. The highwayman and pirate who cared for no one now shifted his thoughts to others.

The beauty of the underground forest and the unknown are unequaled to anything on the surface world. I fear someday, it may all be gone, and there will be no one to let the rest of the world know we were all here. We cannot fail in our quest, for our people will be forgotten.

The peasants living in the mountain region Rothl'Orca told many tales of lore that were passed down from generation to generation through the ages of time. Many legends persisted in the time of King Tin'Old and Drak-North. One of the peasants told a story to the passing soldiers about a mysterious Rhandobeast that prowled the forest looking for souls and blood to steal. It was enormous for a Rhandobeast and was covered in white fur. The beasts are usually brown or black. It was said the white Rhandobeast could suck out the souls of men and their blood and bones, leaving a husk where a man once stood. Svæin the Elder regaled his young companion with tales of husks of men and missing souls.

"Olaf, my boy, you should have seen it! A whole army of men lying flat as potato pancakes, bein' as they had all their blood sucked out, not to mention their bones."

"Why do you tell such tales Svæin? If you are trying to scare a man, it is not working," said the young man.

"I must keep you young ones on your toes. Just remember this white beasty has pink eyes, and they say if you look into his eyes, that is when you die."

"I will let you fight all the white Rhando-beasties then, my good Svæin!" announced Olaf as the men laughed through the snow showers.

The army approached what seemed an impenetrable area of the forest that was so dense they needed to cut a path with swords and axes. The military made small work of the forest pass, and they stood in the middle of the trees in little time. They surrounded the men like a cathedral with leaning gods staring down at their subjects. Odious-Forge hurried excitedly up from the rear, all the while calling for Wolfclaw. He found the fellowship at the front of the militia.

"This is the holy forest of Er'Osque. I know it from my charts and its position to the stars."

Wolfclaw, not to appear too disinterested, said," Thank you, my good man, but what does this mean to us and our quest, and what makes this sorry dirty piece of ground holy?"

"This is where our forefathers made sacrifice unto Rothl'Orca. We cannot venture into its realm without sacrifice. It is needed to appease the *angry* gods," said Odious-Forge.

"So why should I care about that? Angry gods or good gods are all the same to me. If you ask me, we should be angry at all of the gods' terrible jobs. Angry gods indeed! Why should I care what they think?" said Wolfclaw.

"You do not understand. There must be a sacrifice…a human sacrifice. It is required by the old gods, and that is what I am trying to tell you," reasoned the Alchemist. "It is their land and their realm in this forest. It belongs to none other. We must turn back now...or surely we will not live to see the other side of Er'Osque!"

Wolfclaw was quite aggravated at the Alchemist. "It is superstition Odious- Forge and nothing more. If the gods want this piece of shite for ground, they may bloody well have it. We must move forward before nightfall, and the winter storms hit. The old and new gods can rot in Hades. I have no use for them."

"Please do not make light of them. They will smite unbelievers in their sight," pleaded Odious-Forge.

"Let them smite me! Damn them! They sat *idle* while good people died. They sat *idle* while Aspeth and the others were taken by the Hrothgorn. They sat *idle* while bad things happened all around them, and they did nothing! Nothing! What good is a god that does nothing?" Rothl'Orca can go to hades. They are the ones who deserve a smiting."

"I beg of you -" said Odious- Forge.

"Let us move forward now. No more discussion of this" said Wolfclaw.

"You do not need an Alchemist. You need a man-servant," said Odious-Forge as he moved toward the rear of the formation. "I do not want to be near you when the gods smite you."

He lowered his face and moved to the back of the formation like one who had been defeated.

The sight they beheld in the next clearing was terrifying and caused a collective gasp and swells of arguments about what they had seen. Arranged in a ghastly semicircle hanging from the trees dead center in front of the fellowship were the carcasses of seven frozen solid horses. Their intact bodies hung from their necks from jagged black tree branches. They glistened in the light from above, and the ice gave a silvery glow to the snow below. They swung in the gusts of wind, and the groan of rope fibers was all that could be heard. Smaller objects to the left of the fellowship were attached to the trees. Staring with open eyes were the corpses of seven men. They were spiked to the trees with one spike through the chest and one through the head. Blood had been drained some time ago, as the corpses were ghostly white. The faces of the unfortunate victims looked as if they had been trapped by surprise. This sacrifice had not been recent.

"The poor souls look like they have been here for a long time," said Svæin.

"We know only too well of the brutality of the Hrothgorn. It looks like someone has already made the sacrifice. Pass the word to Odious-Forge so he can behold the *mercies* of his beloved gods. Does anyone need more proof that the gods do not care? We will push through to the edge of Er'Osque," ordered Wolfclaw.

"Take down these men and bury them. We can at least do this service for them. Bring the horses for meat!" ordered Svæin

Fältskog had been watching this from his place in the ranks. "This is black magic, and the gods are angry. We must give ourselves unto them and ask for mercy!" he said as he approached Svæin.

"Come to your senses. We must move on to face our foe and look him in the eyes," reasoned Svæin. "We must let nothing sway us from the task we must finish!"

Fältskog was not easily convinced. "Warshield is in danger. Can you not see it?"

Some men had begun a fearful retreat to the outer line of trees by this time. Small groups of soldiers poured into the clearing as if a great floodgate had opened. The sound of panic and the clanging of swords against armor as the men ran were heard. The army ran more rapidly as they passed the tree line where the sacrificial corpses were nailed.

"Stop, you fools. Stand your ground," ordered Wolfclaw. The sky darkened, and the soldiers' sound was overpowered by roaring, rushing fire and thunder. The land shook, and the trees were uprooted from the ground. The soldiers tried to run but could not stand because the earth around them was quaking. The rain of fire had begun in the holy forest of Er'osque. In the center of the tumult, the Witch Queen appeared as a giant dragon as she emerged from the clouds and hovered above the ground in winged form, gray from head to claws. She landed among the men in the center of the clearing as hundreds ran from her. The dragon emitted a roar from the forest floor and a stream of orange fire ten meters or so in length. She had captured five dragons some centuries before and had stolen their fire for her own. She fire-roasted alive nearly one hundred soldiers of Warshield near her landing spot. The shrieks of dying men in fiery death could be heard as well as screams from the dragon

The dragon screeched from her fiery throat, " the pitiful souls of *Warshield* will pay for your disobedience." She sprayed another fiery stream of death at the soldiers as they ran away to the horizon line. "All will bow to me and my servant Drak-North! You did not bow to me, and you did not do my will. Drak-North has a reason for his hate, yet he remains my servant. He has done my will. You will know of his reasons soon."

Screams of dying men as they burned and victory cries from the dragon were too much for some of the simple farmers. They scattered like sheep into the woods in the surrounding areas and dropped their weapons where they stood.

"Bow unto and serve me, and I will spare your pathetic lives! You will be in my service forever, but I will protect you. I will see to it that you have anything you wish," the dragon whispered as fire flew from her fanged jaws. The great tail of the scaly creature swung from side to side, clearing all the trees in its path. Each monstrous shriek was accompanied by fire and phosphorous belches of violence and doom.

Warshield sprinted for the tree line, followed closely by the hideous dragon. Her fire torrent burst into an explosive orange-yellow ball right behind the fellowship illuminating the sacred forest in the light of her hate and destruction.

"You cannot run from your destiny Wolfclaw Thur'Gold. *I* am your destiny. Give yourself to *me,* and I will let the others live," promised the dragon. She opened her jaws to display several rows of jagged and curved teeth with razor-sharp points. "I will rip and tear at your flesh and the flesh of your kinsmen. Man flesh tastes the same to me, but I hunger for yours tonight. You seek to destroy my masterpiece King Drak-North, and for that, too, you must pay with your life."

The dragon slapped her jaws closed at the feet of the soldiers, causing a snapping sound that was heard throughout the clearing. A rank of crossbow sharpshooters sank several cross bolts in the monster's flesh, causing her blood to run to the ground in a stream. She turned to face the crossbows and enveloped them in dragon fire. A second rank at the command of Wolfclaw fired a barrage of bolts at the dragon's head, causing her to falter.

"Hit her again hard! I am not impressed by your power. I do not believe you are a superior being. Come and get me if you want me. I am here. I am not moved by your play-acting," said Wolfclaw in a challenging tone.

This caused another angry shriek from an insulted Ingegärd.

Another shower of bolts from another rank pelted the monster. The archers fired at will at the dragon and caused her to fall just short of the tree line. The fellowship and most of Warshield disappeared into the trees. More volleys came from inside the tree line. Svæin grabbed a steel lance nearly two meters in length and ran up her tail and around the back of the dragon as she was in the horizontal position, being wounded by bolts and arrows. Svæin struggled up the dorsal fin to the creature's head and planted a boot on either side of the spine at the neck. Svæin raised the lance above his head and drove it through the scaly skull of the dragon. A terrific crunch followed a horrific scream as blood flew from the wound. Svæin twisted the lance into the brain of the monster.

"Let us see you walk away from this!" thundered Svæin as he drove the spike deeper, killing the dragon.

"Stop, you fool! I will do anything you wish!" she begged. It was likely a trap for a less seasoned warrior.

Svæin was having none of it. "You will do anything? Good! I want you to die!"

The beast collapsed dead on the forest floor and sent Svæin tumbling across the snow.

A ghostly apparition appeared in the form of a woman, white and floating, wearing a flowing gown made of sheer material that rose above the dead dragon.

The voice of the mighty whale- god Roth'l Orca dropped from the heavens like steel. Ingegärd, "you have tortured my subjects long enough! Return to me at once! I will make you as lonely as the *former god* Fire-Fang.

"You have only seen this incarnation of me... human rubbish. There will be more. Do not think you have defeated me; you have just lived to fight another day. You will bend to my will," promised Ingegärd as she returned to her elder brother.

She laughed and screamed into the sky as she rose and disappeared.

"Why do you let her have so much power and strength?" Wolfclaw bellowed at the sky with no response from Rothl'Orca. "You can help us. I know you can! Why did we have to kill the monster ourselves? Where are you?"

There was no answer.

"I warned you of the wrath of Roth'l Orca," said Odious-Forge. "Why do you want me here if you will not listen?"

"He can rot as far as I am concerned," said Wolfclaw.

CHAPTER NINETEEN

PIRATES OF THE SKY REALM
SANTIAGO OLD-TURAS

———— ⟶⟵ ————

Date: Dimension of Odin (125 AD)
Caribbean Sea/Pirate Realm

"Swift retribution on wings of pain and death."

The Destiny of Tyr held their council meeting on a pirate ship in the Caribbean somewhere in the annals of time.

"We must talk of our mission amongst ourselves," said Avat'or. He seemed to be the leader of The Destiny. Our newest members must not be kept in the dark any longer."

"Yeah, tell us! This is ridiculous that youse guys rescued us and then kept us as prisoners. Why are you doin' this?" asked Luciano Cantore. "At least my crew and the boss told us what our jobs were."

"All I know is as long as I can keep my bike, I'm ok," said Viktor. These dudes here saved me. I didn't have a head or nuthin'. I ain't angry at them."

"I do not understand your primitive talk. It puzzles me. What is a 'dude and ain't'?" asked Nightwish.

"It just means *I'm not,* answered Cantore before Viktor could speak. You got a problem with English. A dude is just a guy…you know a dude. You look like a jackass in that long gown."

"I will not be addressed as such from the likes of you! You will-"said Nightwish abruptly.

"Enough nonsense!" interrupted Avat'or. We must be about our business."

"What exactly is our business?" asked Cantore.

"*Death*," said Avat'or.

At the same time, another Spanish Gallion floated from the sky as the army of Wolfclaw marched. The sails billowed from every direction like a heavenly lionfish. The grand old airship was called the *North Hundrun*. There was a row of cannons ready for thunder at any time. The great ship flew through the clouds and over the horizon. She was well captained by Santiago Old-Turas, an experienced Spanish Galleon pirate. His crew was known as the notorious "Pillagers of the Thunderstorm."

When Captain Old-Turas was a sailor's apprentice, he voyaged from the outermost edge of the land of the South to the realm of the North and the kingdom of Drak-North in search of treasure. The crew found gold on the side of the mountains. Bright shining slabs of what they thought was pure gold were protruding from the wet sides of the sheer cliffs. Among the seasoned crew who sailed with him, many cutthroats did not wish to share the newfound wealth with any other person. The Captain, Drekar, was also to be left out. Their eyes shone with the black of night and the greed of the devil himself.

On their journey back to the Southlands, the filthy sky dogs mutinied and imprisoned their captain, tying him to the mainmast and torturing him for their vile amusement. They refused to feed him or give him a drink. They reveled in grand parties around the mast in view of Captain Drekar as he wasted away from hunger and thirst. His body became burnt and devoid of water as his lips cracked and his throat became parched and raw from thirst. Young Santiago Old-Turas mopped the deck and did not take part in the torture of his Captain. His eyes met the pleading eyes of the dying Captain.

"I know there is nothing you can do, Santiago, do not feel bad on my account," said a weak Drekar. He likely knew that the boy had nothing to do with this betrayal.

"If I could have stopped them, I would have Cap. I swear it on my mother. I didn't know what they were planning," pleaded Santiago as he began to cry.

"Let it be to your credit when you reach the bright shores, boy."

"When the crew falls asleep, I will bring you a drink of water," promised the young man.

Later that night, the old Captain began to beg for more water when it was given to him. Santiago thought, "No *man will ever hear me weep like a child, no matter what happens to me.*"

He whispered to the broken man, "I will try to set you free tomorrow."

In the awful heat of the summer sun, the captain did not survive long. The next day just a few days after the mutiny, the old captain died from hunger and dehydration. One of the men, a cutthroat named Hag'Gar, proclaimed himself the new captain.

"I got no sorrow for this dead captain and even less for the sons of bitches that done his bidding for him," announced the new Captain. Hag'Gar was greedy, filthy, and ruthless. He left the body of the old captain tied to the mast as a message to all who might challenge him. Santiago tried to keep away from Hag'Gar as much as he could and never to make eye contact with him at any time. That ended one afternoon after a drunken binge Hag'Gar ordered the boy to kiss his ruby ring as a sign of his loyalty. He refused and remembered the words of his old captain. A man lives no more than his fair share of days. He said, "I will not pledge loyalty to one with so little honor."

The false Captain Hag'Gar seethed with rage that he should be challenged by a boy in front of his men.

"Take this puny sky rat on deck and tie him to the mast with his captain!"

The first mate who liked the boy brought him to the mast and loosely tied him there. He whispered, "you act like it is so tight you cannot breathe. Do you hear me?" The boy did what he was told. Over the next few hours, a storm started to draw up speed and power over the ship. The wind blew the rain, so it cut through skin like knives. The lightning danced a dance of death over the ship, and the thunder tossed the ship as it roared through the sky. All the men hid below the deck in bunks clutching their night pillows.

The ship was dashed against the massive oaks as it was thrown across the sky. A giant gash tore the ship's belly. When it finally came to a rest on the forest floor near Rylin in the Southlands, Santiago was still tied to the mast with his dead Captain. Because mercy was shown to him by the first mate, he could free himself from his bonds. He had outlived all of the scurvy dogs that had no honor. "I hope their corpses rot," he said. He had much wisdom and anger beyond his tender years.

As the years wore on, Santiago became somewhat of a local storyteller, but the sky's call was in his blood, and he became a sailor on the North Hundrun, where he later became its Captain. He became hardened at the sights he had seen. Mercy is for the weak, he taught his men. Then one day, he met a dark figure with a shining steel blade in the dank, wet street. The soon-to-be robber was unaware that he was confronting a ruthless pirate captain with a short supply of mercy.

"Put your damn hands up, or I'll gut you like a fish. Don't try me because I will do it!" the robber demanded.

"Reach into your pants and give me all the silver you have on you."

"Are you sure this is how you want this to play out, my friend?" asked Santiago. "How about I let you go, and we forget all this?" The interaction made Santiago shiver with uncomfortable recognition. *This has happened before. I cannot remember where.*

"Are you deaf or just stupid? Give me your silver!" the robber demanded.

"One more chance, friend!" said Santiago. "Do you know who I am?"

The robber lunged forward, leading with his razor-sharp blade while the crafty Pirate pulled his dagger from his coat and viciously stabbed the robber through the heart.

Santiago was angry as he muttered, "I warned ya. Ya, dumb bastard. You made me do that." *I will never show mercy again in this life*, he thought. His mind began to wander to an odd place. I know this has happened before...somewhere else I do not remember."

Many years later, the villagers of Watershire began to run for the protection of their homes. They had never seen a site like the North Hundrun. The ship floated like a balloon traveler to the floor of the forest. Several crew members in brown leathers and furs threw eight anchors from all sides of the boat. The anchors landed on the forest floor with a hard thud and grabbed their hooks into the soft ground of the pine-covered earth.

The Pillagers of the Thunderstorm were mooring their ship like a heavenly Zeppelin and were preparing to land. The people of Watershire who could not reach their homes fell to their knees as if they had seen gods and angels. The massive ship had sails, which reached the sky on three separate moors, and wooden slats held it together like a giant oaken barrel. There were many portholes and cannon ports on the port and starboard sides of the ship. The people had never seen such a ship as this in the air. It was a terrifying sight that day. The moment seemed lost in the noise and fury of the landing as the ship scraped into the forest floor and ground to a halt. The heaven-ship hummed with busy sounds from within its hulking hull.

The Captain had bellowed his orders to K'Gar, the Boatswain who was in charge of a ship's anchors, cordage, colors, deck crew, and boats and would be in charge of the rigging while the ship was in the dock.

"All hands on deck. Call the Boson's Mates," ordered the Captain. The ship stood ready for the departure of the Captain. A massive gangplank emerged from the Starboard side of the Clipper ship, and from there, a prominent figure dressed from head to foot in brown bear fur that included the head of the great beast. His hair was braided in tight braids at the ends, which held lit candles that smoked while he walked. The sound of his massive boots planting themselves on the hollow gangplank sounded as if giants were walking the earth. A sound caused the villagers to tremble where they stood. Just as the captain had made his way down from the ship, he was followed by eight crewmembers who, with drawn swords, sought to protect him.

"Bring me the Mayor of this city! I wish to confer with him," Old-Turas ordered.

The townspeople had already begun to run in various directions in a loud cacophony of shrieks, men yelling orders to one another and trampling on the ground. As the crowd thinned, a small yet brave man stood, Balder-Brownstone the Elder, the Constable.

"I seek drink and food for a tired Captain and his men!" demanded the Captain. "I seek these things as well as answers to questions. Do these well, and I will spare your people," promised the Captain. "Do not suppose I have mercy... because I have none!"

Balder-Brownstone pointed the way to the Inn of Rylin at the edge of the village. "There, you will find food and drink for your men. All you had to do was ask. There is no need to threaten violence against these people. What is it you seek? If it is riches, we have none. We survive by working the land. You may all of the potatoes you wish."

Potatoes? You jest." The Captain answered, "I want to find a coward that hides among you. Do not try to cover him, for I will scratch out the souls of your people to uncover this disease from among you! We are from beyond the realm of your world under the forest. We are pirates, but I do not prefer such a man's moniker. I prefer to call us highwaymen of the air," Old- Turas rationalized. "I seek one of my men who started a mutiny and murdered several of my men before he escaped. I will find him; I will boil his skin from his bones and cause the lamenting of his wife and children. I will have him and will not relent because I have already sought him throughout the universe."

At the Inn of Rylin, Captain Old-Turas and his men ate heartily and drank their fill. They threw plates and bottles against the mason work of the great fireplace as they ate and drank. The villagers scrambled to their homes to hide from the loud and violent crew.

"Lift the beer high, brothers!" said one of the crew. "Today, we avenge our leader, our brother!"

Captain Old-Turas had his arm wrapped around the neck of the Constable, pulling him close like an old friend.

"Now, my good man, please don't make my journey any harder than it has been already today. I do not wish to remove your skin today, as it is arduous work. Be a good man and tell me what I need to know, so my men and I can be about our business!" he said with a drunk voice.

Balder-Brownstone the Elder shook, and sweat ran from his brow into his eyes, stinging them. His lip quivered as he replied, "I... I do not know of this *Warlock* you asked me about."

The dread Captain hissed, "*Warwok,* you damned fool. Warwok Thur'Gold is the name he was given. He calls himself Wolfclaw. He fancies himself as somewhat of a wolf killer. He has a bloody Wolf-Claw in his face! He uses many names, but I will call him ... bloody corpse. That *is* his new name, bloody corpse!" laughed Old –Turas as his men laughed with him

"I do not know him, begged the Constable, but I do remember a report of a man who left here with some other mysterious ones on a journey several weeks ago. He was seen with one of the ancients named... Svæin. I know not where they went. Now leave us, I beg you."

The Captain roared, "I will leave no one alive until I find Wolfclaw! I will burn all the houses and the shops until he is delivered unto me. Now my men and I will return to our ship and await this man's delivery. Do not put me to the test, Constable. What kind of ridiculous name is Constable? Remember, my revenge will be the weeping of his children, and I will kill anyone to hear its sweet music. Bring him to me alive. He must be alive. I must be the one to kill him myself in my way. The scoundrel Wolfclaw is no good to me dead, and I will *make dead* whosoever kills him."

Old Turas threw Constable Balder-Brownstone to the floor and departed to the North Hundrun. Constable stumbled to his feet and ran into the streets of Watershire, seeking wisdom as to his next move. He fell once again to the dirty street to pray.

"Who is this cutthroat Wolfclaw, and what will his treachery cost?" As he raised his face from the dust, a figure of a horse and rider stood before him. "Who are you? You startled me."

"Vengeance... is like standing at the foot of a mountain during a rock slide. The boulders will return upon him with such great force that it will squash that same life he would take from another," spoke the horseman. "The person seeking redress for his trespassers is crushed along with his enemy."

"Who are you again? Why do you speak of Vengeance?" asked the Constable.

"The Captain of the great ship seeks *revenge*. The man he ventures to find seeks *vengeance* as well. The kingdoms of Arom and Hrothgorn will burn vigorously. I am no one with whom you need to be concerned, and yet I am everyone," answered the Horseman. "Tell the Captain of the great ship that he will find his prey in the lands near the mountain of Esgarth to the north, where he seeks to destroy King Drak-North."

"Oh Specter, please tell me the little ones of Watershire will be safe!" begged Balder-Brownstone.

"No one is safe as long as there burn the fires of hate and war, but… *mercy* will touch the old man's heart this night."

The equestrian bowed his head in silence and faded into the forest.

After a long night, balder-Brownstone closed his eyes later that evening and drifted off to sleep. "Sleep is the protector of dreamers and the savior of fools," Brownstone was heard to say in days already gone. "Slumber is the only time when the world's responsibility cannot touch the dreamer. In sleep, we are free of Hrothgorn and the world's cares," he had told his wife many times. Watershire was safe for the night. Captain Old-Turas would return in the morning and expect an answer. Perhaps the man sought by Old-Turas was where the Horseman said he would be. Perhaps that would keep the good souls of Watershire safe.

Morning sang its early song as the unwelcome sun appeared over the land and brightened the town of Watershire. Balder-Brownstone woke to discover the great clipper had not departed in the search for the mutineer. The North- Hundrun was still floating above the village while great ship chains clanked and rattled their song. Captain Old-Turas stood defiantly on the bow of the ship. As he was lowered to the ground, he gathered himself and approached Balder-Brownstone.

He stood defiantly before the Constable. "You know I mean what I say about returning me the despicable Wolfclaw Thur'Gold. I know you are aware of the power of my crew. They would live and die by my order," he said menacingly while folding his hands across his chest.

Trembling in the morning, cold Balder-Brownstone answered in a meager voice. "We are poor villagers and would easily be destroyed by you and your crew. As the Constable of the village, Captain, I would ask for mercy."

Old- Turas seemed disappointed, "Someone who folds so easily is not a good opponent in battle or even card games. You are a pitiful coward. You did nothing for your village or your people. You disgust me, you spineless fool."

"We have been at the mercy of the Hrothgorn and have lost family to King Drak-North. Losing more good people to his murderous rampage is almost unbearable for us. We can no longer fight. I was told the man you were seeking and some other old men were in our village. He was trying to obtain more men for a raid on the North. He wishes to kill King Drak-North. He is marching toward Esgarth. It is a suicide mission and a fool's errand in which no one in Watershire took part."

Old- Turas chuckled, "Now that we can agree. Now I know what direction Wolfclaw roamed. We know where to rake for his measly pelt. I will now be heading north. I should kill you for being a weak fool and putting your people in harm's way. The people of Watershire deserve a better man. I promise the gods I shall return and put you in your grave if you lie." He bellowed a command to an unknown sailor, "Prepare to shove off and set the sails to the Northwind. Pull the anchor and chains, and we will ride the wind!" He grabbed the rope ladder as his men pulled him into the sky to perch upon his ship once again. The vessel groaned like an old man rising from a chair and began to move slowly at first, and then gaining speed, it entered the upper currents and flew swiftly to the north.

Captain old-Turas stood on the deck of his ship and spoke with K'Gar. "I don't suppose that old fool even was aware of how close he came to a pirate's execution."

Later that evening, the cold night air came creeping in from the empty sky above as Captain Old-Turas lie in his bunk in his meager quarters. It was minimal space for the captain of a ship and afforded little escape from his discomfort. *No man ever flies from this place*, he thought in his near-sleep state. *I would drift and drift until I had no enemies.* He knew well he had terrified the little constable man with his idle yet terrifying threats, but he could not let anyone think he was less than a bloodthirsty murdering robber down on the main street of the sea. He remembered the mutiny so many years ago and the sound of the pitiful captain crying and begging for water. Warwok Thur'Gold could not go unpunished for his attempt at his revolt. They had been good friends, but this man had no honor. Captain Old-Turas fell asleep at last.

Chapter Twenty

THE SWORD OF KILMISTER

—⚬—

Date: Dimension of Odin (125 AD)

"I am a man trapped in steel."

Wolfclaw spoke bravely and with conviction to his comrades. "Brave men of my own company, hear me. Today is the day we will march into the land of the north. We will seek out the Hrothgorn, and we will slay them. If you see Hrothgorn, you will kill them. No questions or prisoners will be taken. We will split their throats while they sleep and snatch their heads from their wretched bodies with no mercy.

"Today is the day we will always remember as we took a stand against Drak-North and his cruelty. Today is the day we will march and speak for those who cannot speak for themselves. In the company of good Wolfclaw, Olaf son of Gandor, and Tor'Bjorn the brave, we can no more be defeated than an army of ten thousand!" echoed Svæin.

The men wildly cheered as they raised their swords and hammers.

"We are in the company of stout-hearted men. My heart is always with you, good and brave men," Tor'Bjorn said from the front of the ranks.

Wolfclaw drew closer to the men and lowered his voice as if to give instruction. "Listen well, my friends; remember, stealth is our friend. We will plod softly into the realm of Drak-North and the Hrothgorn and destroy them not only with our weapons but will defeat them with our spirits."

"Aye, and the spirits of our fathers who rest in the bosom of Valhalla," affirmed Svæin.

Wolfclaw smashed his great hammer on a stone below where he stood until it sang a war song. Wolfclaw became solemn. "But brave men of Arom hear me... I have grave counsel today, brave warriors. There will come a time in our realm when men have no honor, for it has escaped them. There will come a time when men have no bravery, honesty, or integrity. All of these things will be left in the past. It is entrusted to our fellowship and us to see this does not come to pass in our lifetimes."

"Bag of wind," muttered Fältskog to his shield bearer. "He is just going to get all of us killed." He was almost overheard by the men before him.

Later the rain fell sideways, and the flooded ground was like a moving river. The men marched and sang. They labored up the hills and slipped down the other side. The furs they wore were either wolf pelts or bearskins. The water fell off the fur just as it had the original owners and kept the men dry within their coats. As night drew closer, the army made a camp for the night. Later on, Wolfclaw and Svæin sat around the meager fire they had prepared and discussed what was to come.

Tor'Bjorn said matter-of-factly. "The Hrothgorn are in the tens of thousands, and we number a meager five hundred. Why are we trying to do this when help is so scarce? We do not have enough men for this."

"We all have lost something dear to us. The stinking Hrothgorn came in the middle of the night sometimes. They took away all that we knew," said Wolfclaw with a surety in his voice. "Let us go to them and take it back!"

"We believe you to be on a righteous quest, and we will follow you and fight," said Tor'Bjorn. "But why now? Should we not wait for more men?"

"We battle a foe called Indifference, and that is the friend of our enemy. As I speak to you, the Hrothgorn armies have already wrought great swords to wield for the battle ahead. The Mayors of our villages have refused to join in the fight. The people refuse to help because they do not wish to invite the wrath of Drak-North. I am ridiculed in every town for trying to raise an army to destroy the Hrothgorn and King Drak-North. They call us fools and chase us from their villages."

Tor'Bjorn appeared to choke up, "What if we die? Do not confuse my fear with an unwillingness to fight. I will fight. My wife and daughter are out there, but it seems too much for me."

If we die, my brave man, we will bring scores of the Hrothgorn with us. They will shriek to their deaths as we strike bloody blow after blow to their leathery necks."

As the evening grew colder and darkness surrounded the camp, the men settled in for an early start in the morning. Wolfclaw and Svæin warmed themselves by the fireside and kept watch by night.

The men were visited in the small hours of the morning by a dark figure on horseback from within the forest.

As he drew closer, he spoke, "Wolfclaw, you are being sought by Captain Old-Turas of the Airship the North-Hundrun. He wishes to slay you."

Wolfclaw let out an uncomfortable belly laugh. "You certainly are a terrifying sight, and I admit it is enough to put me off my dinner. I know that you do not mean us harm, or we would already be dead. I laugh at Old-Turas and his pot belly getting near enough to bother me!

Before you disappear again could you tell us why you and your fellow horsemen were pinned to the pines in the Holy Forest?" asked Svæin. "I mean, we see you a great deal for men crucified on trees...."

The visitor spoke in a spirit of abrupt impatience. "Be silent and do not make light of this. That was the *sacrifice* we were required to make to continue our work here. The old and new gods will not be mocked. What you see now are our spirit bodies."

"That was a terrible requirement ordered by gods," said Wolfclaw in jest. "Perhaps someone else was afoot there?"

"It was the gods. We swear it."

"I know someone who has experience spiking horses to trees," said Wolfclaw as he wondered if Odious Forge had been in the forest before the army.

"That is not the matter at hand! You will align yourself with the person of Captain Old-Turas before the sun sets twice more. Heed me."

Wolfclaw appeared puzzled and insulted, "I am a fool? Only a real fool would need an enemy to help him?" he said.

The figure faded into the darkness.

"Damn them. I hate when they do that," complained Wolfclaw. "Nonetheless, we must prepare. Svæin, the Elder Counselor in the Hall of the Ancients, you are my second in command, and the men will answer to you if I fall to the sword or hammer. Olaf, son of Gandor, now will be a soldier in the left flank that will take the Hrothgorn from the forest of Lake Shem."

"I am not a skilled fighter, but I know I can do this," said Olaf.

"I know, young man, that is why you will be surrounded by others that can protect you. I cannot keep an eye on you," said Wolfclaw.

Tor'Bjorn will go with the men to the right flank and take the Hrothgorn by surprise and fear by way of the mountains of the Kings," ordered Wolfclaw."I need a member of the fellowship with each part of Warshield.

"Make ready the swords, hammers, shields, and fire rocks! We will march to the lands of the North," shouted Svæin.

As Warshield marched, they passed by mountain ranges capped with snow. The sky was the color of white haze as it fell upon the land. The sound of the rattling of chain- mail rang through the forests. The men chanted their approach to the lands of the north. Many of the men had the faces of their mothers, sisters, and wives in their memories as they marched on. The Hrothgorn took them as a tribute. The voice of vengeance fell easy from the tongues of the men of Warshield. Day turned into night and again into daylight.

The leaders approached a clearing near the edge of the forest of Arom. The woman that had been following for these many weeks finally showed herself. She was dressed in fur and held a giant sword that seemed to give her little trouble wielding.

"Lassie, how did you catch up to us? We thought we lost ya' at the UnderSea?" asked Svæin. He was as puzzled as the rest of the men.

"It is not safe out here where there are Hrothgorn about," said Wolfclaw. "Now is the time to explain. Why are you following Warshield and the fellowship?"

"I want to join your quest. The Hrothgorn have taken my family at the Massacre of Turknorse, and they have killed our King. Let me join your quest, for I am filled with the boiling blood of vengeance!" pleaded the woman.

"I am sorry about your family, but as for the King, he got what was coming to him. He may have been your King, but he was not mine," said Wolfclaw.

"I agree," said Fältskog. "This is no place for a woman. You are but just a petite flower."

This caused the young woman to draw her sword in a flash. "I have a sword, and I can wield it."

The men witnessed a glint of steel as the sharp blade cut through the air slicing the top of the eagle feather in Fältskog's cap. Fältskog had no time to react before her sword was again at her side. "As you can see, I have been taught to fight well with it," boasted the woman. "Petite flower, my arse."

"Who are you that you can handle a sword in such a way?" asked Wolfclaw.

"My name is Valorii Thuireld, daughter of Ek'roin, and *I am not a houseplant* that must be protected by the likes of you. I can and will fight my own battles."

"We cannot be responsible or protect you in the forest," said Fältskog, all the while backing away from Valorii with trepidation.

"We are agreed then? This is no place for her, and it will slow our march into the lair of King Drak-North," said Svæin.

Like a flash of lightning, Valorii hurled a large throwing blade, so it sailed right past Svæin's left ear and buried itself in the tree next to him.

"Damn you to Hades! You could have killed me," protested Svæin. "I felt the damned wind blowing from it. This cannot stand Wolfclaw"-

"Wait, wait...I see something in your eyes the same found in the eyes of these good men," said Wolfclaw as he addressed Valorii. "I am ruled by common sense to send you home, but... I see the courage in you."

Valorii spoke in a firm voice, "I will carry myself, my supplies, and my sword as well as any man I swear by Old King Tin' Old's memory."

Elder Svæin shouted, "It is by *his name* that we must fight an enemy who became too strong. King Tin'Old bears that burden even unto his grave."

"He lived in fear of the Hrothgorn and entered into the pact as a way to keep them from destroying our people and our way of life," said Valorii.

"He was a damnable coward," said Wolfclaw.

"Nevertheless, I will help avenge him and our people."

"We will make camp here and decide in the morning, men make ready for our stay! You... *who are not a petite flower* make ready your place to sleep," ordered Wolfclaw.

Later that night, as the tents grew darker and the night was at its blackest, Valorii Thuireld approached the tent of Old Wolfclaw.

"I hear you approaching! Prepare to identify yourself or die!" Wolfclaw bellowed.

"It is I Valorii Thuireld. I have come to meet with you as asked."

She walked out of the darkness, took a seat on the stump inside, and began to tell Wolfclaw about herself.

After the King was murdered, she wandered into the forest realm alone. She met the spirits residing there. Some days later, she heard a voice call to her from the woods. It started softly at first, so it could scarcely be heard.

The voice said, *"Find me... save me."* The voice grew louder yet again.

The voice said, "Help me avenge my loved ones."

"Where from do you speak?" asked Valorii of the voice.

The voice was a low, coarse man's voice. "Find me here beneath this rock."

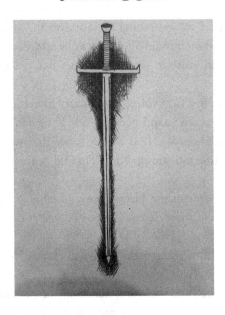

She saw a large stone in the woods several yards away. She took a tree branch and used it as a lever to turn the rock over. It was complicated and cumbersome. The large gray stone overturned with a thud, and a sword stood before her eyes. A sword! It vibrated as it spoke. It was exquisite in artistry and over a meter in length. She picked up the broad sword and beheld its beauty. It was so heavy she could scarcely lift it.

"Let me hold it and feel its weight," said Wolfclaw, almost like an order. "This is a sword of Hrothgorn workmanship. The Hrothgorn smithy would run the glowing hot blades through the skin, muscle, and sinew of the slaves to cool the blades and forge a razor edge of exquisite sharpness. After the blade was forged and the edge perfected, the Hrothgorn practiced the horrible finished product by dismembering the poor souls at their joints with one deadly swipe at each limb. The finished sword was a blood-red blade that cost the lives of innocent screaming people," explained Wolfclaw.

"The Hrothgorn claim the souls of those enslaved people were contained in some swords. Death came so slowly to them while in torture that the sword engulfed the soul of the unfortunate person before it reached above the dead body," added Valorii.

"This is a well-forged sword, well suited for battle, and so I am also," said Valorii.

The sword vibrated in Wolfclaw's hands, startling him. Suddenly it began to speak as Valorii grabbed it from his hands. "Oh, I did not have a chance to explain," she said as she stumbled for the right words.

The sword spoke in a metallic ringing voice, "I am Kilmister, and I speak to you as one of the first souls to whom I have spoken in many years. I was in the service of the Hrothgorn. My soul is enslaved still by this sword. I am now a sword and no longer a man."

Wolfclaw shook his soul, "How can this be so?"

"Please do not let your fear scare you away from me. I need your help. I was in the service of the Hrothgorn when they dragged me from my bed in the middle of the night," pleaded the sword. "I was frightened and did not know what they wanted to do with me." As the sword vibrated with a metallic voice, he explained. "I was brought to the foundry where the Hrothgorn had already started a raging fire. They pounded steel into a sword blade. Hot hammers pounded the steel into terrifying swords of war. My flesh was burnt and cut through as I screamed unto my death. The red flaming steel ran through my muscles and ligaments until I fell dead and dreamt of heaven and reuniting with my god. It was not to be," lamented Kilmister. "My very soul was trapped in the sword as it cooled. I was dropped from a horse many years later as one of Drak 'North's monsters rode through the forest and have been lying here in the dust, rain, and snow all of these years."

I told him I would help him," Valorii explained to Old Wolfclaw. "I had no need or want to be a warrior of any kind. I hated war and all it stands for. After all, that is how I lost my mother and sister. I thirst for *revenge* with a bloody passion. Not war. War seems to imply there will be fighting on both sides. There will only be the death I bring to them. When Kilmister offered to teach me to wield the sword, I wanted no part of it. I could scarcely lift it, much less … kill with it. I promised to help and carry him, and that is all. We walked through the great forest alone for several days surviving on berries and roots. I drank the water in the cool mountain streams beneath the forest floor."

Wolfclaw sat on the edge of his bunk and pulled his boots off. "I can see this is going to take more time than I had thought," he said, laughing.

"I don't mean to impose, but I implore you to hear me in full,"

"Please go on, by all means...."

Chapter Twenty-One

TRAPPED IN STEEL AND FORGED IN PAIN

～∽～

Date: Dimension of Odin (124 AD)
Told by Valorii Thurield

"As I rose from the mountain stream, there stood three men on the other side of the stream. I called them to unfold their identity to me. They laughed and refused as they began to walk through the water swiftly toward me. I felt a chill down my back, and the hair stood on my arms."

'Good morning, young lady!' One of the men yelled, coming toward me.

'We mean ya no harm,' said another. 'You do look a little soft, and ya might do for a little bit of fun for us this morning,' said a third man.

"Get away from me!" I begged them to leave me alone. One of the men reached out, grabbed me by my tunic, and tore it open in the front, exposing my breast.

'O' look what we got here! More fun than I thought, mates!' squealed the second man."

"Kilmister spoke softly from my side," Valorii explained. "He spoke with a voice very softly, and I could feel the vibration of the sword with each word."

'Do as I say, young one, do nothing more or nothing less,' he instructed. 'Lift me out of the sheath. Wield my handle with both hands and hold it before you.'

'She's got a bloody sword!' the men laughed. 'It's as big as you are! Put it down and make it easy on yourself, lassie. This thing is going to happen if you like it or not. You may as well like it,' the second man said as he snorted like a pig. 'Ya better put that away, or ya might get hurt on the thing!'

"Get away from me, you disgusting slobs!" warned Valorii. "I will make a deal with you. If you walk away right now, I will not kill you."

The men laughed at such an idea. 'You will not kill us? Thank you very much for your mercy.'

Kilmister spoke again, 'Thrust me into the chest of the biggest man there and push me deep. Do it. Do it! Do it now!' he ordered.

"I lunged forward and buried the sword straight into the chest of the largest man there, the man who tore my tunic. The surprised look on his face was almost something a court jester would find very funny, and if I had not been so scared, I would have thought so. As I pulled the sword from him, he fell backward in the dirt."

'Swipe from left to right with both hands striking the next man who comes to you,' instructed the sword. 'Make a sure swing so that it finds its mark.'

"One of the other men, furious at the attack on his companion, grabbed me around the throat. I pulled back and stepped a few paces. I swung from left to right, completely missed, and was thrown to the ground. The first man rushed at me and stood with one foot on my hand so I could not reach the sword that lay in the dirt."

'Come on... let us nail her to a tree and let the birds have dinner tonight,' said one of the men, his voice trembling with anger.

"The other man grabbed me by the hair and dragged me through the dirt on my back."

'Just kill her and let us be gone,' said the first man.

'I want her to die, but I want to do it slowly,' he said to his companion under his breath.

"I do not know to this day how he did it, and he cannot tell me, but as I was being dragged toward my certain death… I'm sorry, am I just going on and on?" Valorii inquired of Wolfclaw, who had a contorted and concerned look on his face by this time.

'Oh no… please tell me … do not leave me in such suspense,' Wolfclaw blurted out.

Valorii continued her tale. "I do not know how he did such a feat, but Kilmister jumped up from the dirt and flew into my hand. My captor became startled and jumped back. I stood to my feet and heard my sword tell me,"

'Now! Left to right… with all of your might.'

"With all the strength left, I swung the sword in a straight line, even with my elbows. I closed my eyes and felt some resistance in my swing, but it finished on my right side. I opened my eyes to see my adversary standing before me with his throat open and gushing blood. I had sliced it clean and simple from shoulder to shoulder. His bleeding body fell to the forest floor with a disgusting thud like the sound of a bag of fish guts."

"The third man wanted no part in this attack and began to run into the woods screaming something to the effect that I was a sorceress or a witch. The days and weeks that followed the sword taught me to wield it and be an unmatched warrior. The sword taught me all I had to know, and he and I are on the same quest."

Wolfclaw stood in his tent and thought deeply about what he had heard. "Valorii, daughter of Ek'roin, just because you have managed to find a talking sword and can use it does not mean you have either the strength or the reason to join my army in my quest. You may stay for two days, but after that, you must go on your way, I do not have the time or inclination to deal with a woman and her frailties, and I cannot care for you during my quest," he blustered.

"I do not need to be cared for like a child. You have allowed a mere boy to join your ranks, yet you will not yield to allow me to join?" asked Valorii. "Let might fight for you! I will carry my weight!"

After some silent thought, Wolfclaw relented."After that time, you *must* go your own way." In truth, Wolfclaw already knew that Valorii

Thuireld was something exceptional but was not going to tell her that. Wolfclaw found Valorii a post at the rear of the army. Kilmister was at her side as always. He had never left her side since she discovered him in the dirt of the forest.

"I am a man trapped in this damned sword! I want to break free, hold her, touch her sweet skin, and run my fingers through her red hair. I would bleed and die to love her. She was as the night and just as mysterious."

Valorii marched vigorously and with a surety of her mission. As her gaze moved to the left, she noticed a twinkle in one of the branches of the trees. She must have imagined this. After all, she was exhausted from the grueling march. Then she saw it again. This time it looked like a hummingbird in flight. There indeed, were no hummingbirds in winter.

A voice floated over the ghostly wind. "Fear not, Lady Thuireld, for we are with you." Valorii drew her sword, causing it to make a sharp ringing sound.

"Who is with me? Show yourself at once and show me your empty hands!"

"We do not come with sword or mace, but we are armed with the power of the forests." It is us, the tree spirits, and the forest spirits."

Valorii lowered her sword and smiled. "I thought you were a dream." Tears came to her eyes. "I am not Lady Thuireld. Just a simple Valorii will do.

"We were always here every step of your journey and never left you as we promised.

You were never alone. Go on with your journey, and we will be with you no matter what happens," said the tree spirit in a twinkle of light

"How can I know what will become of us," Valorii asked.

The tree spirit answered, "The future is not for us to promise. We cannot know what is to come. We can only promise to be here in spirit and voice."

Valorii felt peace in her spirit. She grasped the sword Kilmister tightly and moved slowly, one boot in front of the other.

Her sword spoke reassuringly, "Fear not, my dear one, I have been dead for over a century. Believe me, death is too much about nothing."

Valorii laughed through her shivering.

———— ✦✦✦✦✦ ————

In another part of the realm, in the Stone Palace, King Tin'Old the Younger was summoning his steward. "Boy!" He bellowed. "Boy, where are you hiding this time? If you don't come here this instant, I shall thrash you within an inch of your being!"

"Y-y-yes, your majesty." The poor young man replied. The boy was dressed in a servant's smock and a simple hat. His name was unknown because the king had never used it and did not care to know it. King Tin'Old the Younger was a fat King who let his greed and gluttony spill into the outside world. One would only need to look upon his swollen countenance to see what was in his heart. The king had survived an assassination attempt several years earlier when a farmer who had lost his wife to the Hrothgorn stabbed him in his vast stomach. It was said black, greasy fat leaked out of the wound for days afterward. Handmaidens to the King still talk about the horrible, vile smell of the rotting fat in the king's belly. The young king was indeed horrific and despicable inside and out.

"Boy, bring me a Lamprey pie and a flagon of wine at once!" As the young man disappeared from view, King Tin'Old turned to his advisor and trusted hand, Tor'Vold. "Do you read?" he inquired.

"No, your Majesty, I find it quite distracting and destructive to my imagination. I was never able to fit such a folly into my life," replied Tor'Vold.

"Pity, I find it a great diversion from the day's cares. If I read enough pages, the day sweeps by me, and I have very little with which to deal." If I am well-fed and well-read, my day is very peaceful. Today is not one of those days, Tor'Vold, and do you know why?" asked the King in a raised voice.

"No, your Grace, I do not know," came the answer with hesitation.

Tor'Volds' King already knew the answer. He struggled to his feet and bellowed," Here is some reading with which to fill your eyes.

It is a letter from one of my loyalists from the Hall of the Ancients. I must hear you read it. Perhaps it will not destroy your imagination too much!"

Tor'Vold began to read, your *grace it has come to our attention that the elder named Warwok "Wolfclaw Thur'Gold and a large group of the old men have attempted to put together an army and are marching to the North to the Throne of Bones. They intend to kill King Drak-North.*

Tin'Old threw his letter opener and a wine glass at Tor'Vold, smashing them across his head.

"This is something you should have known. Stop them! Stop them now! If they reach the walls of the Palace of Bones, all of Hades will rain down upon us! We cannot defend this city or the entire realm against Drak-North. Our peace will be broken, so a few wrinkly old fools will feel young again. It is a foolish thing for old men to break the pact. Take two thousand men at once and march double time until you catch up to them. When you do, slaughter the entire army of stupid old fossils. They must not reach the Throne of Bones! We will pray now to Rothl'Orca for his great wisdom and guidance to make war on these traitors. If you fail, fall on your sword before you return!"

"I will prevail in our quest, your grace!" promised Tor'Vold.

"The King shrieked, "Why are you still talking, and why are you still here, you fool? Make haste to the Hall of the Ancients. Go and bring me the grand ancient one called Arkule' to answer for his act of treason at once. I will not be trifled with. Go... now," the King bellowed as water and sweat flew from his fattened jaws.

CHAPTER TWENTY-TWO

THE CATHEDRAL OF THE UNKNOWN GODS

———— ⟲ ————

Date: Dimension of Odin (125 AD)

"Sometimes all that is needed is a good punch in the face."

The next day, the fellowship made their way along a mountain pass below the forest floor. Svæin the Elder ventured into a wooded area to fetch nuts and berries. As he came out of the forest, a giant spider the size of a warrior's shield descended from the trees above and settled on him. The creature was black and had two sharp fangs the size of spikes coming from his opened maw. He made a screeching and hissing sound that terrified all who heard it. The colossal beast sunk both of his fangs into his shoulders before he could react. Valorii spotted the arachnid from the entrance of the bank of trees. She drew her sword before anyone else noticed and charged at the beast in a full run driving the sword into the face of the creature, killing it instantly. It fell to the ground and emitted a white milky substance and an ear-piercing shriek. Svæin sunk to the ground and became deathly white. He was not dead, but he seemed as much.

Valorii attended to Svæin for the next several nights as the fellowship marched on. He recovered slowly and well enough to walk, but he owed his life to Valorii's bravery and quick sword work.

Some days later, Wolfclaw and Warshield trudged through the snow and ice, deep under the great forest, climbing over tree branches covered with moss. The toads croaked a welcome to the band of soldiers thrown together with farmers, sheepherders, and servants. The armor was of ancient design and faded with tarnish but covered the chests of these brave men well. Valorii Thuireld carried Kilmister close to her side and followed in the company's rear ranks.

Wolfclaw dropped to the back of the formation and spoke with her. "Valorii Thuireld, the brave-hearted. I fear you have fallen behind and cannot keep up as you promised."

She replied, "There is no need to worry. I can carry myself and my sword. You need not be concerned."

Wolfclaw smiled. "I'm just poking fun at you!!" he admitted to her. "I am just a foolish old man, after all. I am thankful to you for helping Svæin. He is a lightweight and needs all the help he can get," he said.

"Do I hear my name thrown about up there?" asked Svæin.

The men marching with Wolfclaw laughed a collective laugh.

"We have come far from the lands of the South. We have frozen our toes in the dead of winter and have done so with no complaints. We have all sworn our allegiance to you and the fellowship of Wolfclaw. You said you are foolish, but I do not believe you are foolish. What more do we need to say that has not already been said? Our quest is righteous, and we will take the realm of Drak-North by storm."

Wolfclaw was impressed with Valorii's bravery as he was also shamefully impressed by her red hair and porcelain skin. He coughed and managed a humble reply.

"We are not alone in the forest. We have the bravery, honor, and glory of those who came before us. They walk with us. Although we cannot see them, they are here with us. A mighty army marches with us. You have the strength of the Hrothgorn and my heart and trust."

She looked into his eyes, and they stopped for a moment. Wolfclaw spoke, shaking his head, "I fear you remind me of someone I once knew.

Your youth and determination have given me the strength to go on." He turned from her and returned to the front, bellowing orders, "March ye man of valor! We have a short distance over the mountain pass, and we shall taste victory! Each man will have his purse filled with gold from the spoils of Drak-North!" Wolfclaw said when he knew there was probably no gold to be found. Notwithstanding, they continued his mighty trudge to battle.

Over the next great hill, the band spotted the points of a great cathedral made of stone and covered with thick moss. There were many boulders of gigantic proportions strewn about the cathedral grounds as if they had been used in a board game played by giants.

Tor'Bjorn asked, "Who were the builders of such a heavenly vessel?"

Svæin replied knowingly," This is the Cathedral of the Unknown Gods spoken of in stories told in the Hall of the Ancients. Here was kept the wisdom of the ages. We do not know of the builders or the keepers of the knowledge."

Wolfclaw and his band approached the entrance.

"Perhaps we should bypass this place, good Wolfclaw," Olaf said. " It has stood here undisturbed for all this time. Who are we to awaken this giant from her slumber?"

Wolfclaw climbed the massive stone stairs onto the cathedral's great door, followed by his original fellowship. The door was oaken with wrought iron straps binding and had a giant ring handle with five oversized hinges attaching it to the stonewall. He pushed with all his might, but the great door did not move. It took the strength of all four men to open the door to a long dark hall before them. Svæin thrust a flame into the darkness as they entered.

"Are there any souls within here that might hear my voice?" bellowed Wolfclaw. The echo returned empty.

The men crept deeper into the hall. As they came to the end of the massive corridor, they reached the great dome of the cathedral. It was as tall as a mountain and covered with paintings in the fresco of the realm's gods. Odious-Forge fell to his knees and worshipfully spoke, "O gods of the realm, hear us!"

Wolfclaw laughed, "arise, you fool, the gods are not here. They are here!" he said, pointing to his chest. As soon as he spoke, a cloaked figure appeared.

The figure spoke directly through the arm of his cloak as if hiding his face in the darkness. "Hear me, for my time is brief. I am the caretaker of this edifice."

"Is this your realm?" asked Wolfclaw trembling.

"It is ours and has been since there was *nothingness*. We have been and will always be called by a name that is not known. We speak to you today because your quest has brought you to us and led you along this path. We haunt this old cathedral as if we were specters, but we are not. Our spirits are always to be with you. You will find an enchanted battle ax and hammer in the great hall. They are the ax and hammer of Artonimous, the ancient god of victory! Use them well, and they will serve you well on your quest."

Wolfclaw inquired, puzzled, "How will a magic ax and hammer serve us? I mean, I can guess why but...."

"Know this, O' wise ancient Wolfclaw, there is one who will come and lead the way for all to follow. They will be able to wield the ax and hammer."

"Who... is it to be? How will we know?" asked Wolfclaw.

The figure retreated into the darkness and was gone as Svæin tried to follow with his torch. Tor'Bjorn asked with a confused look, "How will we know who shall wield these weapons?"

Wolfclaw answered directly, "I will, I am the leader of this great army, and I will hold these weapons as we go into battle. Our cause is good and righteous, and we will win the day. All our enemies will lie at the feet of the Axe and hammer of Artonimous."

Valorii Thuireld watched from the doors of the great hall. She gripped her sword Kilmister the living sword, and held it close to her side.

The sword spoke in a low vibration only to her, "I am honored to have you carry me for this great cause. I would lay down my life for you because you have been kind to me."

Valorii replied, "I will for you also, my friend. I also make a solemn vow that I will do all in my power to have your life's blood restored to you. I do not know how but I will."

As the Fellowship of Wolfclaw moved from the old cathedral, a lightning storm started to form, and a deluge of rain began to overtake the band of brave souls. They traveled slowly and cursed the rain as they moved toward the lands of the north. The mountain's peak at first seemed as though it was touchable but seemed to get further away as they slogged on. Wolfclaw wondered what they would do when they arrived in the presence of the enemy. The task was easy, defeating someone with a hearty arm wrestle or a game of wits, but what would they do against the evil demigod Drak-North? His very name struck fear in all who spoke it.

Somewhere deep in the realm of the forest, two Hrothgorn soldiers stopped their march into the woods for food and rest. They had killed and eaten a deer and part of a rotting Rhandobeast and were enjoying a fattened rest. Spies had informed them of the army of men heading to the north. They were sent by the word of Drak-North to return and report the movement of the fellowship of Wolfclaw. (All this was spoken in the Hroth language) "The Rhandobeast was not very fresh, but it was my favorite," said the first Hrothgorn.

"I prefer *human* man-flesh, but they fight for their miserable lives and are hard to catch, not worth all the fuss. I admit I have reached into my bag for man flesh on occasion," bragged the second Hrothgorn.

His companion boasted, "I captured some South men during the tribute season and threw a fisherman in my bag. He stabbed me like a fattened hog he did. He escaped after he stabbed me in the back and cut my bag open. I will find him someday, and he will be a feast for me!"

The first Hroth reminded his companion, "We must not sway from our task. We are to find and stop the fellowship of Wolfclaw and report to King Drak-North!" As they spoke, a small man running through the forest stumbled upon the Hrothgorn. He was dressed in a tunic usually reserved for a soldier. He appeared to be a deserter from Warshield.

"And *what* do we have here?" said the Hrothgorn as he grinned.

"Are *you* a soldier?" asked his companion. "We think you are runnin' away you are!"

"Ah, what we have here… is more dinner for us, my friend!" The first monster said, speaking in Hroth. "He will be a tasty morsel for us!"

The little man ran, and immediately the giant Hrothgorn captured him. "Please, I beg of you, let me go. I did not mean to interrupt your dinner! Please let me go!"

The hungry Hrothgorn drooled and slurped his disgusting lips, "We need to tear him in half so we can both have some! You have to share today. You were already warned about bein' greedy with yer food."

"If you don't shut your gob, I will eat you instead." Do you want him raw or cooked?" he asked.

The little man squirmed, "I know something that you want to know, and if you let me go, I will tell you," he bargained.

"No deal!" the Hrothgorn snarled.

"This is so good you will want to know this. Let me go, and I will tell you, you have my word. It is about a certain hammer and battle-ax." The Hrothgorn snapped to attention as if in military formation.

"We will set you free if you tell us what you know. No tricks."

The little man bargained, "I must have your promise to let me live."

"Tell me now, or we *will* kill you*!*"

"The fellowship of Wolfclaw is one day's march ahead, and they have been given the hammer and ax of Artonimous to wield!"

The first Hrothgorn stopped to think, "We must find a way to take the hammer and ax for ourselves! Drak-North will reward us! Throw this man morsel in the pot!"

The man screamed, "We had an agreement!"

The Hrothgorn replied, staring into the pitiful little man's eyes, "Did ya not know? Hrothgorn always lies."

<hr>

Warshield continued in the thunderstorm, slogging one step at a time while their tools and weapons rattled on their belts, breaking the sound of the storm. By this time, they had grown to nearly five hundred men, mostly farmers, shepherds, and shop owners. All wanted to put an end to the tyranny of Drak-North. The small army did not have the consent of King Tin'Old the Younger. The army of the King was still and idle. They protected the castle and the cowardly King within its walls. Wolfclaw knew what he was doing was insurrection and would surely be punished for treason. As the tiny army reached the top of the next hill, they caught sight of a giant pirate Galleon- ship descending from the sky.

"Old -Turas!" he yelled. "Damn! Old-Turas is coming. He finally caught up with me, and his timing could not be worse."

The ship from the heavens descended slowly and hovered somewhat above the ground. An anchor was dropped to the ground with a great crash as it smashed through the trees.

Old-Turas bellowed from on deck, "I see a dead man walking! Ha! What a sight to see a corpse just walking in the forest."As he celebrated with sinister laughter, a small detachment of pirates rappelled from the ship to the ground. "Seize him!" ordered the Captain. "Seize that dead man."

Wolfclaw drew his sword and swung it at the pirates as they approached him. Svæin and Olaf drew swords and surrounded Old-Turas.

"I cannot be taken now. There is too much at stake." Wolfclaw was captured in an overhead net before his army could battle with the pirates. Old-Turas' crew scurried back up the ropes to safety. Wolfclaw's army threw spears and fired arrows at the ship, but they were of no effect. Svæin threw his spear with all his might and sunk it into the belly of the boat as it floated away.

Sometime later that night, Wolfclaw opened his eyes, staring up from the floor of the North-Hundrun. Dirty water was running under the back of his head and into his ear. He could feel the warmth of his blood running from his forehead to the left side of his head. "What in the bloody name of *Hades* did they do to me?" As he opened his eyes and through the blood and sweat, he could make out the figure and the face of Captain Old- Turas.

"So mate, I see we meet again. It's so funny that you thought you could get away from me. Your old Captain and your old friend." Old-Turas raised his walking cane over his head and let it land with a smack on Wolfclaw's head.

"As much as I would expect from someone so weak and frail." taunted Wolfclaw.

"Laugh on, dead man, laugh on. I feel that the only laughter that you will hear is my laughter as I throw your corpse from the ship." retorted Turas. " I want to know one thing before I kill you. Why did you mutiny on the North- Hundrun? It was not for gold, for you know we have none. We do not have women aboard, so it's not for that. Why?" Turas' men roughly helped Wolfclaw to a chair. "Leave me now, boys, while old Wolfie and I have a man to Wolf talk."

Wolfclaw's head spun in confusion and anger from being pulled from his army and quest. His face was that of a crimson mask.

"I am a pirate, you know that," affirmed Old-Turas. "I have no morals, so it is not that I object to what you did on those grounds. We have all done worse than that before. We all have danced in the ruins of cathedrals and schools to pillage what we could. A few trinkets here and there." reasoned an angry Turas. "The main reason I have to kill you is that you made me look bad in front of my men. That is all. You made me look like a fool, so I will have to dispatch you in a very unpleasant way. Before I remove your head and throw you overboard, what do you have to say?" Old-Turas motioned for a man in the main hallway. "Bring this horse's ass a bottle of our best ale. I cannot kill a thirsty man. I am not a monster."

Wolfclaw began to whisper. " Gold."

Turas repeated the word back... "That is your answer, you insane old fool?"

Wolfclaw more loudly whispered in a barely audible voice, "Yes, it is. Gold, silver, rubies, and diamonds. All this you will have and more if I am victorious in my quest to rescue the prisoners of the South from Drak-North."

The face of Old-Turas changed from anger to shock. " *You lie, old man*. I promise you if you want to die faster...."

"You know what I am saying is true. Think about it in your heart, and you know it is true. Drak-North has stolen all of the wealth of the North and the South. Where is it? Of course, it must be returned to the people after a finder's fee. We can do it with my Warshield and the North Hundrun as part of a massive army."

"Well, what if I decide to kill you anyway, throw your corpse overboard, and get the gold myself?" asked Turas.

"Aye, you would have a tough time getting to him without an army. Just a handful of scurvy, bowlegged pirates and thieves will overthrow an evil king?" reasoned Wolfclaw logically.

The two men stared intently at each other for an eternity, and then the stalemate was broken.

Old- Turas slapped Wolfclaw on the back and laughed heartily. " I could never stay mad at ya too long, you old pirate! It's settled, then. We get the gold only after we make Drak-North pay for his deadly rule or… if I find it before you do!" he laughed halfheartedly. "Untie this old pirate at once," he motioned to one of his men.

"There is just one thing before we begin," matter-of-factly mentioned Wolfclaw.

"What would that be, old boy?"

With all the strength he could summon, Wolfclaw doubled his fist and punched the old pirate captain squarely in the face.

Chapter Twenty-Three

THE BATTLE OF HARVEST MOON

—cʌɔ—

Date: Dimension of Odin 125 AD

"Pain is an evil brother to me."

The days were growing shorter, and evil was blowing in from the North. Warshield was growing closer to the Realm of the Hrothgorn. Monsters roamed the realm as the Throne of Bones loomed ominously over the warriors. The moon was high in the sky and lit the canopy above the forest ceiling. As the army drew closer to the light, they saw what appeared to be a cave in the distance. As they approached the mouth of the cave, they saw a red glow from within.

Svæin ordered a halt to the force behind him. "Dammit! This would have to happen when Wolfclaw is not in our company this night. I am kicking his arse when he returns. He got himself captured before we had a chance to fight. Stand fast, brave souls, until I see what this is before us." He thrust a torch forward, and a massive toothy array greeted him.

"I knew it. I knew it was too quiet in there!" observed Svæin. As soon as the light hit the sight, they drew their swords. The sound of hundreds of pieces of steel being dragged from their scabbards rang through the forest. Two gleaming red eyes were at the top of what appeared to be a massive skull of a snake long since dead.

"Let us run the beast through with our steel!" Svæin demanded.

"Stand fast, fool! The monster has been dead for a century," answered Valorii.

As the men circled the calcified yet massive head with its gaping maw, they heard a clap of thunder escape from the mouth. There were stalactites meeting stalagmites in a solid mass from top to bottom jaw throughout the face of this long-dead beast. A flash of light and clap of thunder shattered the men's ears just like so much glass. Svæin and Valorii stood in front of the teeth many meters higher than a person. A voice came from within.

"You are in the realm of the Hrothgorn, and there is now no turning back."

The voice was a low rumble. The rumble became louder and increased to a deafening roar as hundreds of Hrothgorn feet ran full unto Warshield. The battle cry of the Hrothgorn in unison was terrifying to behold. It resembled a low moan that turned into a scream. It shook the trees of the forest. Swords clashed, and metal sounded like a great battle. Wolfclaw's forces fired crossbow bolts that landed in the chests of the Hrothgorn demon soldiers.

"Fire at will," bellowed Svæin. "Send these bastards to Hades. Let them taste our resolve."

The sword of Kilmister came to life in Valorii Thuireld's sheath.

"Trust me, lady! I will lead you into battle. Wield me unto our victory!" The sword swiped a death blow to Hrothgorn from left to right. Lady Thuireld controlled the sword with all the skill and strength of any of the ancients in the army.

She fiercely fought and screamed her victory cry. "The day is ours, Kilmister!"

Hrothgorn soldiers poured from the mouth of the dead beast with weapons raised and the roar of war in their lungs. The Hrothgorn activated their massive catapults from behind the giant dead dragon skull.

"Let them taste fire today!" screamed the Hrothgorn officers. The Hrothgorn had filled giant barrels with oil and set them ablaze as they were catapulted. The first volley flew like a great rumble through the air, lighting up the heavens. It landed with a fiery explosion of red and yellow. The soldiers of Wolfclaw scattered like sheep. Several more flaming barrels flew past the front lines and landed, missing their targets in the rear of the battle. The battlefield was ablaze with orange fire. Olaf, son of Gandor, ran to the front of the formation leading his flank into the fight. The ax he bore was heavy and was a burden for him to handle. He raised the ax and landed it with all his might on a Hrothgorn soldier's head. It split like a gourd as he fell to the earth like a mighty oak. Olaf had surprised himself with such a mighty victory. He could not wait for Wolfclaw to be returned to them so he could boast of this victory. As each Fierce Hrothgorn emerged from the monster's head, they were felled by a crossbow bolt of a long ax to the chest. Lady Thuireld and her sword ran victoriously through each Hrothgorn that dared stand before them.

The bodies of the Hrothgorn continued to pile as trees at the entrance to the monster cave. Tor'Bjorn had been missing from the assault, and Svæin could not find him during the melee.

"Where are ye, my boy?" bellowed Svæin. "I hope he had not run to the forest like the rest of the farmers and sheepherders," Svæin said.

As it came to be known, the Battle of the Harvest Moon raged on nearly all night. The sun cleared the trees, and the darkness flew away. Then it began to lightly rain. The rain fell on the hundreds of corpses of Hrothgorn as their empty stares glared into the sky above. Among the pile of bloody Hrothgorn corpses lay the bodies of many of the Ancients from the hall. They had taken Hrothgorn arrows and several rounds from M16 A1 rifles that Warshield called "fire sticks."

Valorii stood over them and began to tear up. "We will finish what we have begun here, boys, I swear to the gods above. I promise you, good Men of the Hall of Ancients, I will avenge you."

Svæin raised his voice above all of the noise at Harvest Moon and addressed his army,

"We have slain hundreds of Hrothgorn demons this night, and I pray these devils are being dragged to Hades as we speak. Victory is ours this night but do not be fooled by this because these Hrothgorn are a small group of sentries guarding the realm. We have a greater task to face. Let our brave friends not have been slain in vain." Warshield marched on until night camp and much-needed recovery.

Valorii sat down on a large stone and laid her sword across her lap. "You have done well, my teacher."

"The apprentice has surpassed the teacher on this day, lady," said her sword proudly.

Eight soldiers of the fellowship approached the front with a Hrothgorn soldier in chains. Two men on either side of the beast were attempting to restrain him. They dragged him through the battlefield as he howled and fought them. "We have taken this one alive. What should we do with him?" they asked.

"Why should we keep him as a prisoner?" asked a puzzled Svæin, "You should have left him on the battlefield as another corpse for the Hrothgorn to count." Svæin faced the chained prisoner and proclaimed, "Hrothgorn soldier, you have been captured by the forces of Wolfclaw. Will you come with us and fight for our cause, or do I kill you right now?"

In his Hroth tongue, he replied, "Kill me here, for it would be a disgrace to return to my people as the only Hrothgorn of King Drak-North's guard to be kept alive. I would be thought a traitor! I would not be in your presence among the stink of your people."

Svæin smiled at Valorii, "Well, I speak low Hrothgornian, and that is twice I have been told I stink in not very many months. Perhaps I should look into it."

"Kill me and suffer me no longer your presence!" demanded the Hrothgorn.

"On your feet or your knees, it is the prisoner's choice," demanded Svæin.

"I want to stand," decided the prisoner.

Svæin paused for a moment, and then it sunk in. "Well, now we have a problem, a big problem. I can in no way take off your head with you standing. I would need a stool or a ladder, which would not look well for either of us. You will come with us, and I promise to kill you later."

The Hroth prisoner let out an angry groan as he was led away.

Olaf reminded Svæin, "They will be looking for him, you know."

Svæin sat down on a large rock and replied, "I hope so; that way, the fight will come to us. Be on the ready brave Olaf."

Later that evening, Valorii Thuireld sat sharpening the blade of Kilmister as she softly sang a madrigal tune of her people.

"There is a lady who waits in the meadow, in the cool and calm of the evening shade. She waits for her prince to come home from war with trinkets, baubles, stories, and lore...

"What an absolute bucket of crap that is," she thought." I do not need a prince or useless trinkets. A warrior requires a sword, a hammer, and the willingness to split skulls."

As she softly sang, Olaf approached her."Olaf, son of Gandor, you handle an ax very well." He seemed embarrassed by the comment, as he was not accustomed to being honored in such a manner.

"Thank you. Watching you kill those rotten ghouls gave us the strength to continue."

"Why do I deserve these compliments? What do you want from me?" asked Valorii.

"I have questions... for you or..your sword," said Olaf pensively.

"Ask what you will. He has much knowledge to share," said Valorii knowing her sword would not disappoint.

Kilmister began to vibrate with a low tone. "Ask me what you wish to know. I am at your service."

"Tell me about your time as a man. I want to know about who you are," inquired Olaf.

The ancient sword spoke from the blade that had felled many soldiers, both Hroth and man.

"It was so long ago in the ripples of time I can scarcely remember what it was like to be wrapped in skin. I know that I once felt love, and I once felt the touch of a woman. I remember well what it was like to have children fall into your lap and how it felt to have a breeze for a time in your face." Kilmister said softly with remembrance. "I know well what it was like to feel pain also. The Odyssey of pain is an evil brother to me," he lamented. "I am no longer afraid now that I have a friend."

Olaf spoke sheepishly, "We have lost some of our brave Ancients, and as ashamed as I am to admit it, I am a little afraid."

Kilmister paused for a moment to gather his thoughts and then spoke. "I was tortured at the hands of Hrothgorn, and my pain was so unbearable I entered another world. I was surrounded by walls, and there was no escape. Then the pain ended, my body became weightless, and all happiness left my soul. I began to mourn and weep when my soul entered the Hrothgorn sword, and I became a prisoner in the steel blade. My soul is still trapped in this sword, and I yearn for the day when I can be loosed from my bonds. I pass the time in song and poetry in my spirit. These simple songs' fleeting happiness has allowed me to forget I am trapped eternally.

"Ay, as long as there be a slave that dies. As long as there are sweet maidens that cry. I will be loosed from my lonely prison in time. I will fight for both maiden and slave in kind. Only then will I truly be free, and my spirit may fly."

The funeral pyre for the brave ancients burned an orange ring into the night sky. Valhalla celebrates the brave dead on this day of the harvest moon. Ingegärd rained dragon fire and lightning upon the earth to show her disgust for the Hrothgorn dead. She rained fire on the burning corpses that started to stink of tar and smoke. They rose from the dead out of the mud to become new Hrothgorn. They trudged a muddy retreat to the north to regroup for more war. Ingegärd laughed a demon laugh as Warshield trembled from within the forest. Cold blood ran through their veins on the night of the harvest moon as they watched in disbelief. They could not find their companion Tor'Bjorn the cobbler, among the dead. It seemed he had just vanished.

"When they tell the tales of this night, will they remember old men kindly?" asked Svæin. "Not only will they remember us kindly, but also the names of Wolfclaw, Olaf the brave, Tor'Bjorn, and Lady Valorii will ring through the forests as our hammers ring for all eternity. Our names will be one with the gods, and children will sing songs about what has happened here." Svæin smiled.

"…we can only wish," said Valorii.

THE BATTLE OF HARVEST MOON
PART TWO
THE HIGHWAYMAN

Date: Dimension of Frigg 1855 AD
Arizona Territory, Earth

In another part of the world, many years in the future, a desperate man plotted to escape his bondage. The sun was relentless in its assault on the desert sand. The riverbed outside of town was dried up and cracked like a mosaic in a church. Zachariah Boyd was being held in a territorial jail stagecoach traveling from Camp Clark to Prescott. Seated across from him was a territorial ranger named Noble Brannon.

"Boy, you seem like a good kid. I wish we didn't have to do what we gotta do here," said Brannon.

"That drover cheated me in that card game, and everybody knows it," said Boyd.

"Shoulda went and got the sheriff boy. Puttin' a bullet in his skull maybe was not the right thing to do. Anyways ya gotta hang fer it. Ain't nothing I can do fer ya." Brannon had a pistol in his lap with the barrel pointed toward his prisoner. "I did promise yer Mama I would get you there safe-like."

"Why don't you just let me go?"

"You know it don't work like that, boy."

"Driver! Driver! You know you hear me... you sodbuster! Stop ignoring me. I want me some water!" bellowed Boyd.

"Shut up down there. I ain't stopping until we reach Prescott. I bet you would love to try to get out of there. You don't need no water because you are fixing to die anyway," said the driver as he laughed at his passenger.

"You better hope I don't ever git my hands around his mangy neck!" said Boyd.

The stage struggled down a shallow ravine taking each rock and crevice one wheel at a time. A huge, jagged stone split one of the wheels, splintering it beyond repair. The coach lurched to the side, throwing all the men to the ground. The horses scattered and ran into the desert. Boyd remained in the jail portion of the coach. He looked amazed and disoriented but noticed the coach was cracked open like an eggshell. He crawled out to greet his freedom. Both the driver and Brannon were dead under the weight of the coach. Surely, there was intervention from above, thought Boyd. He rifled through the objects strewn about on the ground. As luck or providence would have it, there was a gun and a fair amount of cash on the ground. Two thousand dollars were lying on the ground. He stuffed the bills into his pockets until they bulged.

The desert was hotter than usual, and no water was in sight. Luckily, Boyd had on a hip canteen. His boots were getting heavy, and seemed like they were filling with sweat. The vultures were starting to circle above. He had seen that happen with a dead horse or possum. Held the pistol close to his heart in the shoulder holster he found amongst the object from the coach. It belonged to Brannon. Sweat ran into his face stinging his eyes and making it hard to see. The sun was a *cruel taskmaster,* and there would be no reprieve today. His eyes grew dark, and his head filled with clouds. He disappeared into a smoky dream world and drifted away.

Boyd's eyes opened to a frightening sight. He was in a small jail cell with a small window in the high upper corner, unreachable by the prisoner.

"Bout time you woke up cowboy, hate for you to miss your own hangin'," said the jailer.

"Where am I?" a puzzled Boyd asked.

"You're in Prescott. You probably already knew that. You're due fer hanging at ten this morn'," said the jailer with a chuckle in his voice. "You're finally gonna swing fer all you done."

"How the hell do you know *all* I done?"

"The lawman you shot in Fort Campbell was my brother. My mission in life right now is to see you swing."

"What time is it?" Boyd asked in a panic. I'm serious. What the hell time is it?"

"It's almost ten O'clock," the jailer said, laughing. The laugh was a deep belly laugh that was disturbingly loud. Sorry, my watch is slow. "C'mon, it's time. The gallows is lonely this morning. We need to fill 'er up."

"Bastard," said Boyd. The jailer opened the door and led his prisoner to the jailyard.

"Go on up the stairs, boy, you can do it easy like or hard like. *Please make it hard.* I need a reason to kill you another way," the jailer threatened.

The young man began to weep. The noose was placed on his neck with the hood over his head.

"Any last words, Boyd?"

"Yeah, tell my ma I love her, and I'm sorry. Oh, and you all can kiss my ass."

The trapdoor fell open. *Crack.*

It was over.

Boyd opened his eyes in the pounding surf of a salty body of water. He choked in seawater by accident. He sat in the surf, and his salty eyes focused on a robed figure.

"Who are you? Where am I?"

"I am known as Viktor Vorobyev, and I have come to pick you up."

"I just got hung! I heard a snap, and I felt it too!"

"You just got the reward due to a murderer and a cutthroat. Come with me."

Boyd was confused about the appearance of the stranger. He wore chaps be he was not a cowboy. He was riding a steel "horse" of some kind. "You don't know me, you creepy devil!" said Boyd.

"I know exactly who you are, and I have been asked to bring you into your future with me."

"I don't get it... I just got hanged... or hung...hung-ded."

"Stop jacking your jaw, and come with me."

"Were gonna ride your steel horse?"

The motorcycle roared to life as the pair sped away into timelessness.

CHAPTER TWENTY-FOUR

THE WITCH QUEEN'S ABOMINATION

———c℘———

Date: Dimension of Odin (126 AD)

"Evil follows us all of our days."

Warshield was still reeling from the events of the battle of Harvest Moon as they slogged on through the frozen mud and pine tree needles on the forest floor. As night drew closer and daylight started to fade, the forest began to rumble. At first, it sounded like wind, but it grew more robust and terrifying. The thunder roared, and the wind started to blow with tempest force. There were the sounds of small bells ringing through the forest, and then it happened. It was the distinctive sound of the North Hundren's foghorn. The ship became visible over the fellowship. The sails were fully bellowed, and the sound of Captain Old-Turas barking orders could be heard.

"Batten down the hatches and bear ye down! Shake the grog out of yer head and drop the lines!" Svæin and Olaf drew swords in preparation for the battle to come.

Svæin screamed at the ship, "Old Turas, stand and deliver. I mean to run you through to the hilt!"

The fellowship drew swords, axes, and bows and waited for the North Hundrun to make her move. A figure appeared through the darkness. He was lowered from a rope over the side of the massive ship in the air.

"Hold your fire and stand fast!" ordered Svæin. "Wait until you see his face!" The figure was lowered slowly, and it was not easy to see him. As he drew closer, the fellowship saw a long white beard and a bear fur coat. The men began to laugh as they recognized the countenance of Wolfclaw.

Svæin welcomed him back into the fellowship. "We missed you, my friend," he said.

Wolfclaw laughed and embraced his men. "Not only do we have the Warshield, but today we have become one with the North Hundrun!" Wolfclaw recalled the events of his time with Captain Old Turas. "We now have the support of five hundred and fifty of the most unruly, filthy, and untrustworthy scoundrels that were fit to call themselves pirates. They are sorely needed for our quest, and they will deserve the same chair in the halls of Valhalla when all is done."

"I am afraid we are about to meet far worse evil than we have already. We must find Tor'Bjorn. We could not locate him dead or alive after the ambush at the cave. I fear they have taken him," said Svæin. I fear the terrifying evil to come."

Wolfclaw thought for a moment and replied, "We will find him and bear his shield on his way to Valhalla. I hope we can sit and tell tales with him again."

"I fear the terrifying evil to come," said Olaf.

Evil is genius, my friend. The genius of evil knows our plans and deters them. Evil knows what we love and destroys it," said Wolfclaw. "Evil knows what we owe, and he doubles it and comes for bloody collection. Evil knows whom we love, and it kills them. Evil knows what we find beautiful and makes it hideous. Most of all, evil knows who we are and then makes us lose ourselves. The genius of evil rolls over all of us."

Svæin asked, "The path we need to travel is filled with monsters and giants. Do you not care? Are you not afraid of what is to come?"

"Yes, the realm is full of terrifying monsters that rip flesh and crunch bones. All the kings' men cannot prevent the fall of the realm of King Tin'Old if we, the defenders, are unwilling to give all we have in the name of the realm," said Wolfclaw.

"Why do we care about King Tin'Old? He does not care a thing about us. Why should we face these monsters for the likes of him?" asked Olaf.

"It is not the King we will fight and die for. It is the realm. We will fight and win for the realm of man and the freedom of the enslaved. We will not die for the king but for what he is supposed to stand for," reasoned Wolfclaw. "We will not rest until we are dancing in the ruins of Drak-North's evil city."

As the men marched toward the Throne of Bones, they were comforted that their leader was among them again. Wolfclaw was ready to fight alongside them. The North Hundrun floated above Warshield as they moved across the forest.

The next day, the North Hundrun was moored, and most of the crew had disembarked. The pirates were regaling the ancients with stories of pillage and plundering victory. The camp thundered with laughter and boisterous stories. One of the ancients, Sir Gareth, seemed to object to the nature of the pirate stories.

The pirate sailor laughed about their conquest of a city and the spoils of their victories there. "There was weepin' and cryin', and they handed over the goods as they stood shakin' in their boots. You should have seen them; it was too easy. It was like taking candy from a baby –hundreds of babies!"

Gareth challenged the braggart. "You have a ship and money and a crew, but there is one thing you do not have: honor. You are a cutthroat and a thief. I would do well to cut you off at your knees and leave you for the buzzards!"

The pirate drew his sword, and Gareth grabbed his ax with both hands. "Stand forth, you scum, and do something honest for the first time in your life. Die!" The men circled each other staring with deadly intent.

"We see you Ancients in your hall in your great chairs, looking down your noses at us and the rest of the world. You think you are so much better than everyone else. The realm protects you, but who protects you *today?* Who will stop me from spilling your haughty guts *today?*" Gareth swung the ax with a mighty groan aiming for the head of the pirate and missing his mark completely. The pirate sword swung mightily with the same result. The weapons clashed with the sound of crashing steel, and the blade sliced through a leather strap on Gareth's tunic. The pirates and the ancients stood by and watched the two men square off. The pirate was smaller and much younger, much to his advantage. Gareth was nearly one hundred years of age and very large and slow. He was powerful and had seen many battles in his lifetime. He boasted, "I will wear your scalp as a trophy of my honor and my metal!"

"I see," said the pirate. "You accuse me of having no honor, but you would take my scalp and murder me for your proof of metal and your honor. It seems you have a problem with your way of thinkin'. We are alike more than you would admit ancient one. Take my scalp."

The steel collided with fury as the pirate and the ancient swung weapons to see who would own the day, but just as Gareth raised his ax for a death blow, Valorii stopped him by thrusting her sword under his ax.

"Save this anger and fury for the Hrothgorn, you two fools! There is no honor or glory if we kill each other. Let one of you fools try to beat me and my sword, and one of us will visit their own grave today!"

Wolfclaw had finished making his way through the noisy crowd when the pirate and Gareth dropped their weapons. "What is happening here? Speak now! I have already been tested too much today," he said with little patience.

"These men were comparing stories of their bravery in battle. They were distracted by description and demonstration of swordcraft," Valorii lied.

Wolfclaw smiled and slapped the men on their shoulders. "We should all enjoy our stories of old as much as you have! Do not enjoy them long as we have much to do and much distance before we are through." The pirate and Gareth parted ways after looking each other up and down.

"I fear Gareth would not have fared well today. He needed to be rescued," said Valorii.

Behind the trees beyond a hill lurked two Hrothgorn soldiers. "We must return to report this location," they said as they slunk into the night.

The spirit of the Witch Queen was seething with anger and rained fireballs of red-hot lightning fire upon the realm, and seething blue pain struck the skull of the dead serpent from the battle of the Harvest Moon. The massive mountain-sized skull received direct hits from the heavenly realm of the Witch Queen Ingegärd. What looked like a great cavern began to move, groan and crumble. The tired, dried bone of the great skull started to rumble in a terrifying low groan. The blue fire engulfed the white bone. The teeth, like that of stalagmites and stalactites, began to vibrate and shatter, sending bone and tooth into the forest floor. The fire flowed throughout the serpent, forming scales and skin on the century-old dead bone. The mouth of the great snake opened and began to hiss an evil and angry hiss. The eyes opened to show their green glow and two sets of lids. The deflated body ceased to be stone long since dead and became a living, breathing thing. The massive snake coiled as if ready to strike and chewed the treetops between screams. Ingegärd began to laugh, and the mountains trembled with fear. An ancient monster had been unleashed from its grave where the old gods had buried it.

She smiled at her creation." I will give you your ancient name as it was in the time of the great kings. Your name will be forever *Ghidorwrath*. You shall be the lord of my bloody vengeance!"

Valorii was cleaning her sword in a clearing when Wolfclaw approached her. "I have a gift for you," he announced. "It is an ancient shield used in the battle of Rilyn many years before your birth."

Valorii seemed astonished at such an almost unexplainable action.

"Why do I deserve such a thing?" she inquired in great confusion.

"I carried this shield when the enemy of the North was driven from the gates of the city of Rilyn by the ancient forces of good King Harweldon. I kept the shield with me throughout my life. For the most part, it occupied my seat at the Great Hall of the Ancients when I was not present. The shield was given a vote in all matters in my absence from the Great Hall. It was assumed the shield would always vote in matters to move the realm in a positive direction. I was just too lazy to show up for the vote,"

"I do not deserve your shield-"

"The shield reminds me of all that is good about you and your bravery," Wolfclaw replied.

"I do not understand, I am greatly honored, but I do not understand," Valorii answered.

"It is simple." He replied. "You have shown great honor and more passion than I have seen in most men I have fought beside. I believe you and the shield should be together for that reason."

Valorii bowed to Wolfclaw in the pine grove. "You do me great honor, Sir, and I will fight with my life to be worthy of this shield."

"You already have Lady Thuireld. You already have." He turned and walked back into the forest.

"He is right and does you great honor," spoke the sword. "There will come a time, I promise you; knees will bend to you. I feel it in my spirit."

"You flatter me too much, but I will always be in your service." She picked up the shield, which stood nearly waist-high. It was decorated with gold borders and the outline of a serpent with a sword in his mouth. She held her sword and shield and walked through the woods to join Warshield. One of the pirate crew saw her approaching the rest of the men. "Ay, what do we have here?" Would we be in the company of something soft and curvy? This piece of fluff cannot be serious about holding a sword and a shield.'

One of the higher-ranking pirates approached her. "Woman, this is not your place. Your place is in the cook's hall making grub and chow for the men."

The men began to laugh at her. Kilmister began to vibrate with anger in her hands. "Let me at them! I will tear this scoundrel a new porthole!"

Valorii answered, "Be calm, my friend. I have this matter in hand." She addressed the men as she laid down the shield and sword. "I dare you, salty sea dregs that feel my place is in the Captain's mess or in any of your beds, to gird up your weak loins and stand in front of me right now!" The men laughed at the bold woman in front of them. A Pirate named K'Gar stepped up to Valorii.

"Ay, I would make you my woman anytime I choose."

Valorii answered with a smile. "I will cook for you, and I will be your woman if you can come here and take me," she said slyly. Come to me, little *baby* man."

This infuriated K'Gar he drew his pirate dagger and lunged toward Valorii. She grabbed his arm and flipped him over on his back in the dirt as he reached her.

"Get up, little man."

K'Gar stood up and lunged forward again, only to be met with Valorii's boot in his midsection. He fell to the ground like a tree falling in the forest.

"Is that all you have?" she asked.

K'Gar stood up and gathered his clothing about him. He raised the dagger over his head above Valorii and brought it down with all his might. She caught his arm by the wrist and twisted it, causing him to drop the dagger as she flipped him over her shoulder like a flour sack. He landed in the dust to the laughing of the rest of the pirates. They hooted and howled, scoffing at their companion, who had been bested. They began to sense that they might have been wrong.

"Hear me! I am *not* to be trifled with. I have fought at the ambush of the Hrothgorn, and I will continue to fight. Those who would fight beside me are my brothers, and I will die for each of you. I will always have your back, and to this, I give my promise and my vow that you are my brethren today. If there are any among you who wish to insult me or doubt my metal, I promise you will eat my steel."

There was a sparse silence, and the Pirates erupted in applause and laughter.

"This brave one has spoken the truth," said Svæin. "I feel sorry for any of you sea dogs that cross her."

Wolfclaw stood from the crowd's edge and marveled at what he had witnessed. *Indeed this was no ordinary person.*

The fellowship marched on, followed by the floating ship over their heads. They were getting closer to the realm of Drak-North. Wolfclaw could feel the darkness falling over his spirit. He could feel that lonely road become more dark and lonely. The spirit of hate and fear was almost too much to bear.

"The shadows are falling, but we will journey on and rise to meet the day," he said to Olaf.

Olaf came from a large family in the south of the realm. He had never been involved in anything out of the ordinary. His life was tending bar at the Great Hall of the Ancients. "What will we do when we reach the realm?" he asked.

"We will rescue the captives and mete out punishment for those responsible. We will show no mercy to those who have wronged us!"

"I am confused. Why would you keep the Hrothgorn soldier as a prisoner? Is that not mercy?"

Wolfclaw was at a loss for an explanation. They were met with a familiar sight as they rounded the next corner. There in their path was *Wormouth.*

"Continue down this path no longer, and to your fellowship, be aware of the peril that awaits you." The men noticed Wormouth had changed in appearance from the last time he was encountered. He was covered with scars and appeared to have one of his eyes gouged out. He was frail, and the once ominous hiss and rumble were reduced to barely a whisper.

"What has happened to you, wise old friend?" asked Wolfclaw.

"Torture and pain ... I would not tell the intruders in my forest who you are or where you had gone. The Hrothgorn plucked my eye and tortured me with the pain of the sword. I told them nothing!"

"They sought us?" asked Svæin. "You suffered this to save us?"

"You showed me you had honor when your companion gave me his Copple fish knife as a tribute, and you asked me to join your fellowship. No one has ever shown me kindness like that in my whole life. No one… I am dying of my wounds. Go quickly; they cannot be far from here as we speak."

"Good Wormouth, we are indebted to you with our lives, and we will avenge you," promised Wolfclaw.

The massive snake hung his head, and tears fell, "My life has been wasted in pain, fear, and hate toward other beings. I have done no good with my time in the realm of men. I have hunted and killed those who were in my path. This thing I do for you is the only good I have done, and it is well with me." The poor creature rested his head on a large rock in front of the men and closed his eyes forever.

"Rest well, Wormouth, the realm of men will hear and know what you have done," promised Wolfclaw.

CHAPTER TWENTY-FIVE

ESGARTH PASSAGE

❧

Date: Dimension of Odin (126 AD)

As Warshield traveled and grew, they approached the forbidding Esgarth Mountain in their path. The North Hundrun floated above effortlessly and gracefully disappeared over the mountain into the clouds. She disappeared into the gray sky and left no trail. The fellowship had grown to two thousand men, Lady Valorii, one very brave talking sword, and a reluctant Hrothgorn. His name was unpronounceable, and four soldiers led him with ropes tied to a metal ring on his neck. He groaned loud grunts and sounded as he was dragged along the path to the North. He was nearly four meters tall and smelled of burnt tar, so the men leading him were changing places to escape downwind. As they approached the mountain, the Hrothgorn became restless and agitated.

"Tell us what lies beyond the mountain, Hrothgorn?" ordered Svæin.

With a growl, he answered, "Death for you and your stinking herd."

They noticed a small passage through the mountain where no light was seen.

"What is in there?" Wolfclaw asked curiously. "If we do not go through it, we must go over it."

"You and your band of fools must go over the mountain to get to the realm of Drak-North," snorted the Hrothgorn.

"Now I know we must go *through* Esgarth! Surely the Hrothgorn lies!" deduced Wolfclaw.

"We will lead the men through the passage! Fashion torches and muster all the men for a march through a mountain!"

As they attempted to enter the narrow passage, the Hrothgorn soldier broke the bonds on his massive hands and grasped the metal ring around his neck, splintering it with a tremendous cracking sound. He was free, much to the surprise of the men who held him. They reared back in fear as they drew their swords. With his massive strength, the Hrothgorn swept his oaken arm and threw four men a great distance. With his right arm, he swept again, causing two men to slam to death on a tree. The sound of splintering bones and broken bodies echoed through the forest. The bloody ground was littered with corpses in a matter of seconds.

The Hrothgorn turned and faced Wolfclaw with his arms raised and bellowed a hoary scream into the air with his head raised.

"Now I will crush your head like an apple in my hand, filthy human trash!" He grabbed Wolfclaw by his head and lifted him several feet in the air. "Now, you will die like the rest of your fellowship as they reach King Drak-North!" Wolfclaw screamed as a man living his last seconds on earth and has seen Hades in a vision. The old warrior kicked his feet and flailed his body as he hung by only his head. As the Hrothgorn began to press his huge tar-like hands together to squash the life out of Wolfclaw, the Hroth warrior looked down at his chest. Something got his attention in the very center of his chest. It was the tip of a sword. He wondered why the tip of a blade would be coming out of his chest from the rear. Valorii thrust Kilmister entirely through from the back.

"Release him and die!" she ordered. The Hrothgorn screamed a throaty shriek heard throughout the forest. He immediately dropped Wolfclaw to the dust and turned to face Valorii. His expression was *anger-filled* and pain distorted. Maybe Valorii just made him angry.

"A *woman* has done this deed to me?" he screamed. As he reached forward to grasp her neck, she drove Kilmister under his chin with a mighty thrust and ran the sword through his face and out the top of his skull. The giant Hrothgorn fell like a great tree in the forest, smacking the dirt with a hearty thud and crunch.

Svæin helped the uninjured but embarrassed Wolfclaw to his feet. He brushed himself off and straightened his clothing and armor. He knew the blood of the eight men killed by the Hrothgorn was on his hands. Had he not kept the Hrothgorn for a prisoner, his men would not have died. How would he explain this to the families of the dead men?

"Lady Thuireld, I owe you my very life, and I now belong to you and am in your service forever." He laid his sword across his arms and stretched them toward her.

"Good Wolfclaw," she replied, "Take your sword and lead on. I was looking for a reason to kill him anyway. That was as good as any."

Warshield began venturing into the passage through Esgarth Mountain.

The passage was narrow so that only one man could walk through at a time. The light gave no solace in such a dark place. Some men started to moan low cries of fear as they walked through the tight passage.

Wolfclaw spoke in a loud voice to the fellowship. "Fear not, hearty friends, we will pass through and gain our prize at the end!"

The walls of the passage were slick with moss and water that formed a cold slime that ran to the cave's ground. The walls seemed to be moving, but it was difficult to see by torchlight. After several hundred men marched through the passage, they, unfortunately, discovered why. At first, the men squinted to see, but then it became known to them. The wall was covered with *bats*. They were restless because of the movement of the men through the passage.

Olaf spoke in a reserved but loud voice. "The walls have bats! Do not touch them because they will all fly at the same time."

Warshield began to stir and murmur. "Bats!" they screamed.

"They are too close, and we are trapped!" cried a panicked Olaf. The men started to scramble through the passage. The discovery of the bats startled the animals and caused panic in the passage. The bats rose like a giant unit in flight, causing the men to flee.

"They are biting us!" screamed a terrified Fältskog.

"Fight the little bastards then! You're not afraid of some flyin' rat, are you?" bellowed Svæin.

The bats shrieked a thousand shrieks of high-pitched violence in flight. The men were trapped as the bats flew into their faces and tore flesh. The sound of swords, hammers, and ax slamming into the walls rung through the cavern passage. All this mixed with the sounds of terrified men and shrieking bats. The fellowship struggled through the path as it grew wider and wider.

At last, they arrived at an opening into a sizeable cathedral-like cavern. The bats dispersed into the cavern and flew to the grand atrium above. All the men had arrived at the passage opening terrified but only a little worse for the wear. They dressed their wounds and prepared for the trip through Esgarth.

As they thrust their torches into the atrium, they saw the ornate decorations on the walls. They were pastoral scenes painted in pesto. Scenes of farm life and peaceful meadows in faded color. There were shepherds in the fields, livestock, and little cabins. As they turned to the other side of the cavern, the pastoral scenes became dark and terrifying. There were scenes of Hrothgorn soldiers burning the fields and cabins and snatching the peaceful inhabitants of this unknown land from their homes. Wolfclaw did not know who these people were who had painted these scenes, but they suffered at the hands of Drak-North, and this fight would be for them also. Where were the survivors of this massacre, they wondered? Had this become their tomb, or was it a temporary hiding place? As they approached the broader area of the cavern, the scene turned into a macabre carnival of bones and death. There before them was a mound of human bones stacked as if it was so much cordwood. The Hrothgorn had done their murderous deeds and left destruction in their wake. They had massacred peasant farmers and sheepherders as they hid in the caverns. The blood that covered the floor had long since dried, and the screams that echoed through the mountains faded away. The bones, ash, and silence were all that remained.

"I vow that these innocents would not have died in vain, and I promise to avenge them," said Wolfclaw. "I hope the gods would smile again on the peasants in the cathedral of the dead." He prayed to the old and new gods that he would keep his promises. "We will move the fellowship through the mountain pass and stop there for the night!" ordered Wolfclaw. He knew the men were full of fear of Hrothgorn strength as they passed the gigantic mound of bones.

"Have no fear men," said Svæin. "The Hrothgorn have much more of a fight on their hands when they battle with someone their size! Let them bite off a big chunk of the Warshield!"

After Warshield neared the cavern's exit and the other side of Esgarth, Tor'Vold, the King's guard, met Wolfclaw as he marched out.

"Stand fast, ye scoundrel, by order of the king!" bellowed Tor'Vold. He had located the very man King Tin'Old had ordered him to find. He was relieved. "I know that you have an army, Thur'Gold! But we have one also, and I mean to bring you to justice by order of the King!"

Wolfclaw thought for a moment, "I promised someone I love a very long time ago that I would not kill anyone, and now I have to break that promise today," he said in jest to Tor'Volds' men. "You have an army, but I have pirates. Do you have pirates?" he asked as he pointed above his head. "They're not very nice, and by this point in the day, they are quite hungry. Did I mention that they are also cannibals? Should I call them down?" he asked in a quasi-threatening manner.

"They are not cannibals. You lie," said Tor'Vold.

"Maybe they are, or maybe they are not. But you do not know for sure. Do you want to take a chance?"

"You insolent fool! I should take off your head for speaking to the leader of the King's guard this way!" Tor'Vold spewed. "Seize him!" As the King's guard stepped forward to do their duty, Svæin and Valorii drew swords and raised the points to Tor'Vold.

"If I were you, I would not move," Svæin said, warning the guard.

Olaf spoke for the fellowship in a loud voice. "We all would be better off dying in the company of such a man as Wolfclaw Thur'Gold. To serve in the Kingdom of a coward like King Tin'Old, the Younger would be disgraceful. We would march into Valhalla holding our heads in our hands than keep them on our shoulders in the company of a coward."

Wolfclaw thought carefully about what his next move would be. "Tor'Vold, I know you to be a man of honor and courage. What happened to you? Surely you cannot support such cowardly behavior?"

"I care nothing for the King. I only do his good will," answered Tor'Vold cleverly.

"There is a time to act, and there is a time to stand fast. Empires have been lost because even wise men often cannot tell the difference. King Tin'Old is not a wise man. This is what I know of the King, my dear Tor'Vold." said Wolfclaw.

"King Drak-North has captured our family members and has killed just as many. He must pay for his deeds, and the captives set free. The King has pacified Drak-North with the blood of the Southern people, and today it must cease!" said Svæin passionately.

"It is almost time for the tribute season again, and there must never be even one more. We all have one choice at this moment. I can have my men fall upon you and see how many of you can be killed. We will inflict the wounds of death upon you," said Wolfclaw.

"You see how my men, my pirates, will live and die at my word," said Captain Old-Turas.

"Tell him what his other choice is, Turas," said Wolfclaw.

"The other choice we have for you is better. Join us, and together we will destroy the Hrothgorn and their reign of terror for the last time. Should we have our bloodbath with your blood, or should we invite the Hrothgorn and bathe in theirs? My men are hungry," threatened Old-Turas.

"You got no bloody choice, you outnumbered bastard!" chuckled Svæin.

"Together, we will spill the blood of the Hrothgorn until vengeance rains down from the sky," promised Wolfclaw. "The spirits of the entire Hall of the Ancients are with us."

Tor'Vold stood motionless and then signaled for his guards to join him. "I am sorry to tell you this, Wolfclaw, but King Tin'Old beheaded Arkule' and the remaining Elders from the Hall of the Ancients...they are no more. I am sorry. Our swords are yours, do with them as you please, for we are in your hands," surrendered Tor'Vold.

Wolfclaw staggered a bit and hung his head. He screamed and grabbed Tor'Vold by his Tunic with both hands choking him. He let him go and staggered back two steps.

"Why?" pleaded Wolfclaw as he stared at the ground. "They did nothing to you or the King!"

"The King ordered it so!" answered Tor'Vold. "It was them or me. We serve at the King's pleasure. He is a coward, and I hate him with all my being, but I am in his service for life."

Wolfclaw put his hand on the swords. "Keep these for today; you will need them to fight. We will fight the Hrothgorn on their land and return to tell King Tin'Old we have saved the kingdom. I will then kill him for my brothers in the hall of the Ancients. You are not my prisoners. You are my brothers today as we fight to victory or fight to a glorious death."

The Warshield of Wolfclaw now numbered nearly four thousand, including the King's guard. They marched toward the north with the North Hundrun overhead with billowed sails and clanging ship bells. In macabre synchronicity, the massive head of Ghidorwrath loomed over the forest floor, slithering a path as the fellowship marched on, unknowingly leaving Esgarth as a distant memory.

The army came to a hill known as the Mound of the People of the Sun. The People of the Sun lived on the surface of the earth above the underforest. A shrine to their god was built in the ancient days at the site of the mound. At the top of the hill was one lone Hrothgorn soldier standing with his arms reaching upward. The soldier dropped his sword to show he was unarmed.

Wolfclaw thought," *what in the name of Rothl'Orca is this?"*

The Hroth soldier dressed in armor and helmet bellowed across the distance.

"King Drak-North sends his wishes for a safe return to the kingdom of the South. I am only a messenger who happens to speak your human language well, and I mean you no harm. I am calling to the one who calls himself *Wolfclaw*. You will be safe to speak with me on the hill."

Wolfclaw replied, "What makes you so sure *you* would be safe in my presence? You may know I could cut you down where you stand as soon as I reach the top of the hill." Fältskog and Svæin chuckled along with Wolfclaw.

"Think you scared him, Wolf?" asked Svæin.

"Somehow, I doubt he scares that easily."

The Hroth soldier spoke again from atop the hill.

"Lord Drak-North desires that you should name your price and take it and return home. He desires that you should not come against him ever again. His Majesty wishes to make this the only opportunity to live to see another day. Name your price!"

"My price is ten feet of ground in the Kingdom of the North so I can bury his stinking corpse."

"You want to answer the emperor of the North with such insolence? You are courageous but more likely, you are just a fool. The next time we meet Wolfclaw Thur'Gold, I will carry you on a spit like a hog. I will report to my King."

"Tell him to keep that one good eye left open because we will be coming for him soon," warned Wolfclaw.

The Hrothgorn soldier growled, snorted, and replied, "It will be a pleasure to see you impaled at the city gate as a warning to all who dare to stand against King Drak-North!" He bent down to pick up his sword, looked down at the fellowship, and paused for a moment. "I shall not come this way again."

Wolfclaw looked to the sky and discovered what he heard in fables and stories from the Ancients in the hall. He was beholding the Northside of the sky. It seemed to have *ominous* and *sinister* attached to it in some way. It was difficult to perceive the danger and evil under the sky's north side. He was seeing it for the first time.

Wolfclaw ordered the army to proceed over the Mound of the People of the Sun. Suddenly there was a whistling sound like something was cutting through the air. The sounds became more frantic and more frequent as the army moved forward.

An arrow buried itself in Fältskog's shoulder, causing him to scream, "An ambush! We are caught in a trap! We're doomed!"

Wolfclaw ordered the bowmen to fire in the direction of the tree line where the Hrothgorn had planted a nest of archers.

"I cannot believe I got caught with my britches down like this!" Wolfclaw said. "I must be getting too old for this! " Fire at will!" he ordered.

Hrothgorn began pouring out of the forest at the base of the mound. Their eyes were on fire, blazing in the direction of the fellowship. The army raised their shields only to have them splintered with the heavy steel of the Hroth hammers and axes. The Hrothgorn screamed a bloody war cry that would ring in the ears of the soldiers for many years to come.

Valorii stood facing the onslaught of several Hrothgorn bearing down on her location. She stood firm with Kilmister in one hand and a heavy ax in the other.

"Come to us and taste my steel Hrothgorn ghouls!" Valorii taunted. "Your blood will oil my sword today." Valorii thrust the horn of an ax into the throat of an advancing Hrothgorn killing him instantly. She hooked a Hrothgorn shield with the same ax and threw it to the ground. This enabled her to thrust her sword to the hilt in the Hrothgorn chest. There was a loop on the handle, which she drew over her hand and let the sword hang there. She took up a Hroth spear in her hand and rushed towards the Hrothgorn line. She jumped over an incoming spear and threw her spear at the same time, landing it in the face of a Hrothgorn. The army advanced from behind Valorii and gave her relief from the attack. She had killed five Hroth soldiers single-handedly. The searing noise of the weapons slicing the air filled the battlefield.

"How in the name of Hades can she do this?" said Wolfclaw.

"Surely she can't be mortal. There is more to her than we know," said Fältskog.

Svæin carried an ax in each hand and advanced to the Hrothgorn line. He spun them with skill and was indeed a remarkable sight.

Wolfclaw had two swords. He knew how to wield sword edges; however, he fought equally well with both hands. He raised one sword with his left hand and swung the right one at a Hrothgorn soldier, taking off one of his legs above the knee.

The archers filled the air with arrows and littered the ground with Hrothgorn dead. The few Hroth soldiers that were left made a hasty retreat to the forest line where they could hide.

"I cannot believe I fell for that trap!" announced Wolfclaw. "If you see that messenger bastard, I want his head. I wonder what made those foolhardy creatures think that could vanquish an entire army."

Svæin answered matter-of-factly, "They thought we were smaller than we are Wolf."

"Let us make them keep on thinking that. Take a detail into the forest and kill all those Hroth cowards before they get too far!"

CHAPTER TWENTY-SIX

FIRE-FANG

~

Date: Dimension of Odin 126 AD

I n the Palace of Bones, deep in the mountain of Asparth, laid the lair of the dread King Drak-North. The guards surrounded him, and he sat on the throne made of several skeletons, primarily human, some Hrothgornian, and some Rhandobeast femurs. The chamber had an acrid, foul smell that seemed to hang in the air like so many clouds.

"Send for my meal. I would have my meal now," the King ordered with a temper tantrum like a small child.

A more diminutive Hrothgorn servant stumbled into the chamber carrying the afternoon meal for his King. "Sire, I beg your forgiveness. I lost track of the time of day it was."

Drak-North hissed, "Put it down and get out of my sight. Let it be late one more time, and I will wipe you and your family from the kingdom's memories." The small Hrothgorn scrambled to get away from the chamber of the dark lord for fear he would suffer the King's overreaction.

"Fire-Fang!" bellowed Drak-North ordering the presence of his advisor. He was the only trusted confidant to King Drak-North and possibly more terrifying in his reputation. He was not of Hroth descent, but instead, he was Rathgarian. The Rathgar were an ancient civilization that warred itself into extinction. There were very few left, and Fire-Fang was proud of that distinction. He was a bloodthirsty ghoul giant. He sustained himself by drinking the blood of the young. He had killed and drunk the blood of several of the young ones in North Sheepshead Village outside of Arom. The town has been in mourning for several months after his ghoulish attack. The townspeople believed Fire-Fang to be a ghost that came upon them for some sin committed by the town fathers. This led to a fanatic religious uprising that almost destroyed the village's good people.

Drak-North had very little control over the actions of the brutal Fire-Fang, and he was given the freedom to torture and destroy at will. He became an extension of the killing machine of the Drak-North kingdom. He did his bloody errands almost nightly, and his ghoulish bloodlust was satisfied, leaving mourning in its path.

"Fire-Fang," bellowed Drak-North.

"Sire, you wish to see me?"

"Tell me of the prisoner that you have brought me today," insisted Drak-North impatiently.

"He was captured during the battle of Harvest Moon. His name is Tor'Bjorn, and he refused to give information about the whereabouts of his fellows. We have inflicted more pain than I have ever seen a human endure, yet he will not yield. I want to kill him with everything within me. I want to make him suffer and bend. He puts me to task, and I want him to die. I do not wish to disobey your order, sire, but I yearn for the death of this filthy human."

"He is no good to us dead, you fool. Keep him alive so that we might find out the plans of Warshield. When we have finished with him, you may drink of his blood and do as you wish with the rest of him. Make him talk. If you do not make him talk, I will show you the definition of torture. You will feel me raking through your sinews and joints before you die. You will become well acquainted with pain."

"Yes, your Majesty, I will serve your purposes, "said Fang as he skulked away into the darkness. As his advisor disappeared from the throne room, King Drak-North tilted his head to the ceiling and began to smile until his grin was as wide as his face. His eyes remained fixed and unmoved. Evil spilled from his face onto the throne room floor as he began to laugh.

Tor'Bjorn was exhausted, bloody, and beaten. He sat bound in a chair made of the bones of dead slaves. He was seated on the bones of a poor soul dead nearly a century ago. No doubt, he was tortured in the same manner. He drifted off from time to time as he was in and out of consciousness. He dreamed of home and his family. He was having a dinner of Copple fish and potatoes. It made him smile to think his beautiful red-haired wife had made him such a good dinner. She was so kind and lovely. His home seemed more comfortable than he remembered and was warm and dimly lit by a single lamp. The fish tasted better than he remembered. What magic had she done with it? She eased the day away with her sweet hands on his shoulders. She rubbed softly, removing all of the day's tensions away... then crack! A large hand struck him on the side of his face taking him away from his Copple fish and his lovely bride. He realized where he was.

"You will know pain as you would know a lover, you foul-smelling wretch. Tell me where the Warshield treads and how many dare to challenge the King," he said, delivering another blow to the head of Tor'Bjorn.

"Your Hrothgorn soldiers who were killed at the battle of Harvest Moon saw Warshield and the Fellowship of Wolfclaw. You should ask them," said Tor'Bjorn attempting sarcasm.

Fire- Fang screamed in anger. "Do you wish to die today? There are things I can do that will make you wish for death."

Through his crimson mask that covered his face with blood, Tor'Bjorn answered with resolve.

"A death is all I have to give to my brothers in this fight. I would rather eat pastries and drink tea in another place, but that is not my lot today."

Fire-Fang sent another hard fist to his side, causing Tor'Bjorn to double over in pain. "The only thing keeping you alive today is the *goodness* of King Drak-North. Do not put him to the test."

"Goodness? He has none. The only thing I have left you cannot take from me."

"What do you have that I have not already taken from you by force?"

"I have my prized possession, honor, and loyalty to my brothers, which you do not possess."

This infuriated Fire-Fang and sent him into a flurry of fists and kicks to the body of Tor'Bjorn.

"I want this insolent pig blinded by red-hot iron pincers, and I want his entrails removed and burned in front of him before he dies. Bring me a hot iron at once," bellowed the torturer. He held a red-orange glowing hot iron in his giant hands as he approached his victim. "I will pierce your eyes with this and continue pushing until I have reached its hilt."

As he moved closer and closer to the eye, Tor'Bjorn could feel the searing heat of the poker on his face. He began to scream out not for mercy but in anger that he could do nothing to stop what was happening to him.

"I will tell you nothing, you demon. Do what you want to me, but I will not betray my fellowship." As he uttered those words, he faded into a dream state. He was on the shore of Lake Shem. The Copple fish were biting, and his creel was packed to the brim. He was smiling at the sun. *That is so odd…the only other time I saw silver on the lake that shone so bright was on my wedding day. It seems an eternity ago and so far away from this unholy pit of despair. I can still hear her voice, but I fear it has been so long that I scarcely can recall her face. I tried so hard, but I could not remember it.* He awoke with a jolt to see he had been alone in the dungeon room. *Where had his tormenter gone? What was in store for him?*

+ + + + + +

Warshield moved on into the land of the North. A blizzard had moved in during the night, causing the North Hundrun to moor near the border, entering the land of the Hrothgorn and the Dark lord Drak-North. The army took cover under the canopy of giant and majestic pines. The ground under the forest was lush with pines and firs, and there was more than enough for good protection from the wind and snow. Captain Old-Turas could be heard from the deck of the mighty clipper ship, his voice booming throughout the forest realm. "Don't worry, you greedy sea-rats, that gold is not going anywhere, and there be plenty for us in time. Hunker, ye down and ride out the storm. Ye men are greater than any blizzard. Ye men are bigger than an army of Hrothgorn and twice as smelly."

His hearty men could be heard laughing with their leader and Captain. One man proclaimed, "We would follow yer stout and brave heart anywhere, Captain."

Old-Turas explained to his crew, "I will take my first mate and five crew members to the forest below to talk with Old Wolfclaw about our battle plans. I leave you in charge of the North Hundrun while I am gone. Take good care of her. Make sure she gets as much care as would yer own mothers." The men then lowered Captain Old-Turas and the six men in a lifeboat to the surface.

The fellowship warmed next to a roaring campfire in a clearing. The orange flames licked the sky and melted the snowdrifts. The sounds of the great army moving about could be heard above the crackle of the fire. The fellowship was ready but apprehensive about the battle to come. Odious-Forge approached the fire rather gingerly to light his night torch.

Valorii broke the silence of the moment. "Odious- Forge, please tell us of the land beyond. Use your magic seer stone to tell us what you see ahead."

"I can foretell the future or read the thoughts or feelings of another. I can only see it if it is written in this stone," Forge said.

"I thought you were an alchemist and astronomer?" asked Svæin. "You can wield your magic in any manner you wish."

"It does not operate like that. I used my knowledge of chemicals and fire to enchant the seer stone-."

"Valorii interrupted him. "What do you see in your stone? I do not fear death, but I worry that which I cannot see."

The alchemist peered into the stone that fits comfortably in the palm of his hand. He began to tremble as the words came to his mouth.

"There is nothing to fear... there is simply a journey to a place where we can rest and walk in a greater forest, to feel the pine needles on our bare feet. There will be joy in being in a place where fear has no home. There is no end to life… There is no end to joy.… There is no end to love or justice. All who fight with the sword and hammer will follow us into Valhalla. There will be a great and glorious feast in our honor when we arrive."

"I have seen the things in a dream," said Wolfclaw." My eyes are tired, as is my soul, but even though my eyes are aged, my spirit sees clearly. I will tell you of the vision as best as I can remember it," recalled Wolfclaw. "The night was cold and icy, my hands white from frost as I trudged through the snow. It was much like this night. I returned to my home after one of the many battles I had fought for the realm nearly a century ago. As I walked through a snow-covered field, my steps were getting slower and shorter. I could hear the howling breeze as it blew me side to side. The snow was soft to walk on, yet my feet were numb. A gush of snowy wind pushed me back, and I fell. I could see the moon hiding behind the gray clouds. As I stared at the gray moon, it stared back as an enemy in battle. I struggled to get up, my hands sinking in the cold snow. I stood up, my legs shaking and stumbling. I heard a whisper behind me."

"Come with me," said the voice. "I have much to show unto you."

"I reached a tree and used it for balance. I could still hear the voice. Perhaps it was the wind. I looked into the sky to see the Winterhawk circling above. I felt I could almost reach him… I fell once again into the snow. All became dark, and I was sure I was freezing to death. The shroud of death covered me as I shivered violently in the snowdrift. I felt warm at last as I settled into my bed of snow. I surrounded myself with more snow like a goose-down blanket. My eyes grew dark, but I saw things that night that was more real than any battle I fought in up to that time."

"How do you know the things you saw were real?" asked Svæin." You could have been mad with the cold and almost dead. I believe we go into the funeral pyre or the hard ground to rot when we die. Fate swings like a sinister pendulum, and we all must face its inevitable swing in our direction."

"I also felt that way all those years ago as I lay dead in the snow. I saw a vision of life as a journey. When the night was over, we would rise to find ourselves in that great land that I had a glimpse of that night. There was a great feast," Wolfclaw's voice quivered as he told the story. "The feast was at a long table covered with every food one could imagine. There was a duck under the glass and a pheasant on silver platters. Cheese and wine were flowing freely. Desserts of all kinds finished the bounty of the table. This was the feast to welcome and begin our celebration and homecoming to Valhalla. All those who had gone before me were there. My father and my grandfather were there in all of their armor and carried their swords by their sides. As I looked out the windows of the great hall, I could see the sandy shores and the endless water of the unknown sea. I woke up in a traveler's cabin warming next to the fire. The travelers found me in the snow and revived me. I was angry with them for taking me away from the halls of Valhalla before I was ready."

"I look forward to returning someday. I am sure this was real and not a dream as I am Warwok Thur'Gold!" he proudly proclaimed.

Valorii Thuireld smiled a comforting smile.

Fire-Fang returned to Tor'Bjorn in the dungeon chamber at the Palace of Bones. He screamed in the face of the prisoner.

"By the mighty power of my god Roth'l Orca the god of Warriors and kings of the sea, you will tell me of all I need to know. Where are your fellows now? What do they have in store for the realm of Drak-North?"

He held a red-hot branding iron in his hand to mark the Rhandobeast herd kept by the Hrothgorn for meat. He tore open Tor'Bjorn's' shirt exposing his chest. The letter in Hrothgorn's language was as red as fire lighting the cavernous chamber of torture. The ghoul pressed the branding iron deeply into the trunk of his prisoner. A piercing scream filled the room with terror. Drak-North smiled from his Throne of Bones as this was music to his ears. He enjoyed terror and reveled in pain. He thought *Fear was the fuel that feeds the fires of victory. Let it burn on. Let the fires sear and scorch on to defeat all enemies!*

CHAPTER TWENTY-SEVEN

THE RESURRECTION OF GHIDORWRATH

———⚬ɴ⚬———

Date: Dimension of Odin (126 AD)

You cannot explain away a wanton act of immorality and
brutality just to suit your idea of a higher cause- The Destiny

A s the determined Warshield approached, the realm of Drak-North and the evil ones prepared themselves for the inevitable onslaught to come. The fires of Ingegärd wrought their power upon the earth below. Ghidorwrath dragged his massive form from the battleground of the Harvest Moon to the North. His enormous head appeared as a stone in a light gray. On top of his head were six eyes pointed in all directions. He could focus on all sides simultaneously, making him a formidable adversary. There were two cavernous holes on the side of his head. One might suppose they were probably ears of some kind. His height was dizzying. His head would rise over most of the mountains in his path.

The Witch Queen laughed a most satisfied laugh." I am the sum of all evil!" she shrieked. I am sure they still worship me as a god on some distant planet!"

The colossal serpent was covered in scales running in a large path from under his chin down to his belly. Where once were stalactites and stalagmites as a former cavern were now large jagged formidable teeth capable of catastrophic destruction. What once was a hiding place for an ambush was now the murderous mouth of an ancient dragon.

Ingegärd kissed Ghidorwrath's head with her divine wind giving her the blessing of doom. In his destructive path, he laid waste to trees and hills, leaving a swath of bare ground in his wake. Nothing that got in his way was spared. The Witch Queen laughed in anticipation of Ghidorwrath's pure destruction and path of death. The huge dragon-serpent heaved his white underbelly over buildings that dared stand in his way. The ground trembled, and the earth shook as Ghidorwrath ran his race to the north on his deadly errand. The evil Witch Queen directed Ghidorwrath's deadly path as he pushed forth behind Warshield. The army stood a fortnight to the north, and the smell of the Hrothgorn filled the air. The encampment was made at Shimmoorath, or "the place of the hole."

The North Hundrun was moored above the army, and Captain Old- Turas was lowered to the earth with his closest advisors to meet with Wolfclaw to discuss strategy.

"Not long before we see the gold we were promised, boys," bragged a confident Old-Turas. "After that, we make way for other adventures, and maybe we will even buy another ship. Maybe some of you could even be Captain of yer' own ship. Watch me and learn from the best boys."

"How are we going to get the gold away from Wolfclaw, Cap?" inquired his first mate.

"You let me worry about old Wolfclaw. Gold is not his motivator. He is a fool; his motivation is heroism, *love*, or some damn'ed thing… but it is not gold. Remember that I said this, young man. Love is a bad dream that keeps us awake at night and makes us hold ourselves as weaklings and cowards, and it makes us feeble in the knees."

"What about the Hrothgorn, Captain?" asked one of the toothless sailors?" "I mean, they are three meters tall. How can we fight something like that? I just have to say something about this Cap, I do not mean any disrespect, but it does not seem like it is a good idea to get an army of giants angry with us. I think we do not need that kind of attention."

"That is why this is my ship and not yours! Slack-jaw!" He took a deep breath and collected himself. "Do you know how much gold there is just for the taking? If you do not have the intestines for the fight, you can go home by way of the plank. Any of you other cutthroats got anything else to say?" said Old-Turas." I am not afraid of them bastards… are you? They bleed just as good as any other man."

His men voiced appreciation for their Captain and nodded in agreement with him as they reached the floor beneath the forest.

The earth quaked, and the sun was drowned out by the shadow of Ghidorwrath as he approached Warshield. Wolfclaw and Old-Turas sat in the tent with the leaders of the Warshield army. They felt the roar and rumble of the ground behind them. Old- Turas was thrown to the ground by the explosive sound of thunder Ghidorwrath left in his path. The men ran outside to witness a dreaded sight. The army stood to their feet and drew weapons at the horror they all beheld. Ghidorwrath screamed a bloody and terrifying shriek that bounced from the mountains and echoed throughout the realm. A stream of orange fire flew from the snake's massive jaws into the sky above him. An evil hiss slid over his tongue like a boulder rolling from a mountain. His forked tongue flipped about, feeling all that was in the path. The beast slid over the massive pine trees and flattened them.

"Retreat, men! Sound the all retreat and head to the forest. "Archers! Fire a volley at his underbelly!" ordered Wolfclaw. "Aim for the white parts!"

The archers aimed and fired as each one was well equipped. The quiver is made from hide and is to be worn around the archer's belt. The outer side has been decorated with metal emblems and good luck charms. Each archer carries thirty arrows.

"Fire at will!" ordered Wolfclaw.

The arrows landed deeply in the beast's flesh. They did not affect Ghidorwrath's ominous approach. The sound of crushing and splintering lumber beneath the giant abomination drowned out the sound of screaming soldiers. Again, fire spewed forth from the beast burning the forest around him. The army of nearly four thousand continued to run as quickly as they could. Olaf ran toward the huge beast *instead of retreating* as ordered.

"I will slice his underbelly and spill his damn'ed guts right here!" he bellowed.

He had never shown fear since Valorii and Kilmister reassured him that the fellowship would be victorious. They made him believe it could be done. Olaf stood before Ghidorwrath and the fire of Ingegärd with his sword in both hands, pointing at the snake. "Come for me, you vicious monster. Come and get me. I am waiting for you. I am right here!" Wolfclaw witnessed this scene from across the encampment. He grabbed the battle ax of Artonimous and vaulted toward Olaf and his foolish standoff.

He screamed with all his might. "You blasted fool! Retreat with the rest of us. You cannot wield enough power to destroy the beast." Wolfclaw thought *I gave him too much. I made him believe he was a great warrior, and now he will get himself killed. I do not want to face his mother.* Once again, he screamed while running toward the beast. "Get back here."

The colossal dragon-serpent reared his head back, preparing a stream of dragon fire. As the beast unleashed the orange ball of death toward brave but foolish Olaf, Valorii Thuireld raced from beside the creature and rushed him to the ground, narrowly missing the fire stream. As they stood together, she grabbed the back of his tunic and dragged him away from the action just as Wolfclaw arrived to help.

"Do not ever put me in danger again, or I will kill you myself next time," she threatened as they all ran away from the monster.

"I would have run him through with my sword, and you stopped me!" argued Olaf obstinately.

"You will thank me later," said Valorii.

"All you would have done was to get us all killed and get yourself cooked. You are not experienced, you fool. You are brave... yes, but bravery is not enough. I know I have told you otherwise this entire time...but I was wrong. Promise me you will not try anything that heroic again," reasoned Wolfclaw.

Ghidorwrath imposingly menaced the army with roaring and hissing sounds as he approached the encampment. Above the beast was moored the North Hundrun. She floated gracefully, fully loaded and packed with the crew of Captain Old-Turas. The mammoth monster opened his unhinged jaws and pointed skyward with a shriek from the belly of Hades. He snapped them closed around the hull of the North Hundrun, splintering yardarms and shredding the sails. The crunch and thunderous cracking could be heard throughout the forest as the giant reptile squashed and crushed the great Spanish Gallion in his horrific jaws. Pirates were screaming in fear and leaping from the ship to the forest floor. Bodies were slamming to the floor like many sacks of flour thrown from the boat. Ghidorwrath's jaws continued to crush and mutilate the ship as it was dragged further and further into the snake's jaws. Wood shards and splinters the size of trees fell from the sky. As he destroyed the once majestic ship, the beast shook his head in a demonic dance of death. The dreadful creature dropped the wreckage of the North Hundrun, sending it to its final resting place in the trees. He unleashed a massive fire stream burning all that was left of the ship. Nothing but a flaming skeleton hull in the trees remained.

The Battle-ax of Artonimous was still in Wolfclaw's left hand as he once again came face to face with the powerful and massive Ghidorwrath. The screams of the pirates as they remained in the wreckage of the North Hundrun were fading away into the night air. Their life's blood was quenched in the fires of Hades and the power of Ingegärd and Ghidorwrath. An eerie silence came over the encampment as Wolfclaw faced the fire-breathing snake.

Ghidorwrath spoke his first words in a thundering baritone rumble of a voice.

"You are in my hands. Move from my path so that I may continue to your army,"

"In the name of the god of a victorious war, Artonimous, I defy you and order you to die," said Wolfclaw.

The colossal beast laughed. *"I will inflict death upon you and crush your bones to show your men what will happen to those who defy the Witch*

Queen and Ghidorwrath. Move from my path, highwayman… or are you just a cutthroat pirate?"

"I would take the wounds of all my men so they would not have to. I would die all of the deaths of those in the fellowship so they would not have to. I would lay down my life"-

"Are you quite done with your speech yet?" asked the Witch Queen. "You certainly do more than the army's share of monologue!"

"As I was saying…so that none would have to suffer. I would give my life so that you.….evil serpent, would kill no more. Does that sound like a pirate or a highwayman to you? Can a highwayman do this?" he asked as he raised the battle ax over his head and hurled it end over end toward the great beast. It landed three paces in front of Ghidorwrath.

Wolfclaw was unable to wield the battle-ax of Artonimous. He picked it up once again and hurled it toward its mark. "I order you to die in the name of Artonimous!" Once again, it landed three paces in front of the snake. He drew his sword and slashed at the great belly of the monster. It caught its mark, and the dragon shrieked and reared its head up and back, landing with a crash in the branches behind him.

"Scoundrel!" the beast screamed. "You villain, you cheat, you rogue! I will see you pay for this!"

A large gash opened in the front of the snake, and copious amounts of blood poured from his wounded belly. No one was more surprised than Wolfclaw.

"Sometimes I just get the luck of the gods with me," he said.

The great snake turned and limped back into the forest, leaving a trail of blood and entrails behind him.

Indeed, he was mortally wounded, but Wolfclaw could not take a chance. "Archers… Fire a volley at this heinous blob of flesh and bring him to his death!" he ordered.

Arrows flew and darkened the sky even further. They buried in the fat flesh of Ghidorwrath, the horrible causing him to flee into the darkness until he was a distant rumble in the dark. He screamed into the deep of the forest.

Wolfclaw ordered the army to take up camp and move to the safety of the caverns of Ko'Dor, where a people called *the Børger* once lived. "We will be safe there. Ingegärd will be angry at the defeat of Ghidorwrath, and she will rain fire down into the realm of men.

While the army set up camp, Ghidorwrath slid to the river regions while licking his wounds. Captain Old-Turas hung his head in the fog of sadness. "I am a Captain without a sea or a ship. I am at the end of my world. There will be ghosts in the fog whenever I sail. I fear I will see their faces for all eternity in my dreams."

Wolfclaw put his hand on the old Captain's shoulder. "We can't save your men now, Turas, but we can damn well make sure we make that slimy son of a bitch pay with his hide. What do you say?"

"If it were not for your Warshield and your mutiny, my crew and I would be plundering in some faraway land. We would be far away from giant killer serpents and giant Hrothgorn. I am a pirate, not a soldier. I should take your head off where you stand. I will be haunted by the scent of the sea in the twilight of the morning just before waking. I will forever hear the bells of the North Hundrun."

Wolfclaw looked intently at Old-Turas. "Do not forget your thirst for the gold trinkets of King Drak-North. I did not force that upon you or your men!"

"Do not ever suppose I have forgotten that gold, you villainous cutthroat. I will have it, and I will have my vengeance on the Hrothgorn. I will also make you pay! From this day forward, you are a dead man to me." Captain Old-Turas grasped the handle of his sword and stormed away from Wolfclaw.

⸺⸺ ✦✦✦ ⸺⸺

In the caves of Ko'Dor, the company came upon a man living in the caverns. He had taken refuge in the place of his people. Wolfclaw approached him in curiosity. "Stand fast and show me you have no weapon of war," he ordered as the man stood up from his bear pelt bed. "We mean you no harm, and you may be some help to us. Have you seen any Hrothgorn in the area, my good man?"

"No...none. In truth, I have not seen a soul for many years. I am what remains of the Børger and wish to live where my family lived. I mourn the loss of my people. We were once proud and free but hunted and killed by the Hrothgorn and King Armagorn. Why do you and your companions invade my family home?"

"It just so happens…I have an army of ancients, pirates, the King's guard, and an assorted rogues gallery. I am Warwok Wolfclaw Thur'Gold of the hall of the Ancients. I mean to avenge my brothers and. we aim to hunt and kill as many Hrothgorn as possible. We will then rake for and kill King Drak-North himself. We would be sure to help you avenge your people… if you are so disposed to such a thing," Wolfclaw said in an inquiring yet hopeful tone.

"I would like that on behalf of my people. They scream from their graves to be redeemed. They linger in the thousands between two worlds and wait for the time to be set free from bondage."

"How did this come to be?" asked Wolfclaw.

"They were murdered as they slept and as they fled. Men, women, and children. Fire-Fang and the Hrothgorn showed no remorse for their killing. All of my people screamed for mercy from the evil King Armagorn, but there was none to have. The power of hatred trapped them in between worlds, and their souls have been unable to rest in peace," the man lamented as he spoke.

"How did you come to survive the massacre?"

"For reasons, I do not know, I alone was spared to be a slave to the King. I waited. I planned and plotted with a Hrothgorn soldier to assassinate the King. His name was Drak-North. He was no better, and my mistake in helping him will forever haunt me. After he killed the king, he turned his sights on me, but I escaped and have been here ever since in hiding in my family's home. I always feel their spirits here, and it comforts me. The blood that surges through me will always be Børger. My name is BáulfR."

So will you come with us? Svæin, my second in command, will fit you with weapons," said Wolfclaw.

"Yes, I will," promised BáulfR.

Later that night, Wolfclaw retired to a quiet corner of the cavern to rest for the evening. As he settled down, a horseman appeared to him.

"I have come again to speak with the brave Wolfclaw in his quest. Have you yet decided what there is to be gained by your journey?"

"I want *justice,* you unnerving and mysterious phantom, but I also want revenge...revenge. *Bloody terrible revenge.* I want all who have wronged us to scream in pain and searing bloodletting. I want to *remove* the heads of Drak-North and his hosts of demons."

The Horseman paused a moment. "Many have died already in your search for something that is not yours to have. If you want to rescue captives, that is heroic and honorable. If all you seek is vengeance.... What role do you play in this nightmare?"

Wolfclaw became enraged to the point of screaming. "I will kill Hrothgorn men, women, and animals to get to King Drak-North. It matters not. They are all animals!" he screamed as his face reddened with rage.

The horseman raised his arms above his hooded head while speaking. His body and the horse became nearly three times their size. In anger, he said. "Hear me now, Wolfclaw! You are not as terrifying as you think you are! You cannot explain away a wanton act of immorality and brutality just to suit your idea of a higher cause or to justify a good end. You must keep yourself at a higher plane and never lower to a level equal to the demons you purport to hate. Doing otherwise does not make you appear courageous, just cowardly."

"Be gone with you. This is my quest and battle; I will do it as I see fit. Do not attempt to tell me how I should make war," bellowed Wolfclaw.

Light is shown brightly from under the Horseman's cloak.

"This battle belongs to us all now. You know in your heart that we speak the truth. Do not challenge us. You cannot win this fight alone, and you will need the truth we give you to defeat your foe. Most of all, you will need the help of your friends."

Wolfclaw spoke as the Horseman faded into the darkness. "I have no friends! Wait... I did not mean *be gone with you.* I have more questions for you... damn you!" *I can never get them to stand long enough to reason with them.*

Valorii walked among the men of the fellowship, looking at each man's weapons of war and giving swordplay pointers wherever she could. The sword/man Kilmister was a teacher to the men in the fellowship army as he had taught Valorii in the past. The army was made up of the Ancients from the remainder of the hall. They needed the skills to match their bravery. The cowardly had already taken to the forest to return home, hanging their heads in sorrow. As Valorii worked with the men, she met BáulfR. He had difficulty looking into her face as he might have been ashamed of what he had done to put the Hrothgorn in the position to haunt and torture the good people of old Turknorse. He could not face her after she told him of losing her mother and sister to the Hrothgorn work camps.

"I can in no way justify my treachery, my good lady," BáulfR explained with remorse in his voice. "I know I must pay with my life for helping the evil Drak-North climb to his seat of power on the throne of bones. Please… forgive me. I will not blame you if you do not. I would not forgive *me* either."

Valorii reflected on the situation and remembered something. "There is someone you should know, good sir. I would like you to meet my sword."

BáulfR took three quick steps back, expecting her to run him through with her sword.

"Do what you will with me! I deserve death by the sword for my treachery," he said as he bravely stood fast now with his chest uncovered and his arms to the side, completely expecting to die.

"No, my friend, you do not have to fear me. My sword is…a man. His name is Kilmister."

The sword began to vibrate and hum as the voice of the dead slave moved BáulfR to tears.

"I am a lost soul trapped in a lonely place… I am only here today because I was able to move good Lady Thuireld to take me up and wield me. You are also a lost soul who feels he has done wrong. I *know* of your struggle. You were captured and forced to watch your people die and serve a harsh and brutal master. I, too, did this. You blame yourself for the deaths of many. I have also killed at the behest of my masters as a sword of the Hrothgorn. I had no choice, and neither did you. You and I are the same. I do not blame you, and you should not torture yourself with doubt."

BáulfR hung his head and began to weep.

Valorii put her hands on the shoulders of the weeping man and looked into his eyes. "Stay with us, and you will make right what is wrong. You can be set free and be a captive no more to your guilt. Trust me. Within the week, we will assault the Throne of Bones, and you must be a part of it. Do you think you can take the palace with us by force, brave BáulfR?"

"I will do everything I can to undo what I have done. I am at your service Lady."

"I am at your service, good BáulfR ... fear not," said Valorii.

CHAPTER TWENTY-EIGHT

THE MOONLIT KNIGHT

———— ∾ ————

Date: Dimension of Odin 126 AD

After the Hrothgorn resurrection at the hands of Ingegärd at the battle of Harvest Moon, the Hroth soldiers regrouped for an assault. The attack on the city of Arom was sudden and violent. The Witch Queen was rancorous and livid at her defeat at the Battle. Her wrath was particularly raw because of her defeat at the hands of Wolfclaw Thur'Gold and Svæin, the Elder, in the Dragon battle at The Holy Forest of Er'osque.

Now the city of Arom was on fire. The Hrothgorn clawed through the very heart of a small village outside Arom to wring the people of information about the coming uprising of Warshield on the dominion of King Drak-North. The Hrothgorn wielded giant swords and curved daggers to separate bones, sinew, and cartilage from the joint in a frenzy of torture to the people of Arom. Flamethrowers spewed fire at every corner of the city. Shrieks of mercy and screams of pain in the air hung there like foul fruit clinging to the trees. Chants of "Howrah, O'Rah Ama Gorn" filled the air with a terrifying cadence.

A close translation is "bleed for the god of Hroth."

The people of this once great city told the Hrothgorn all they knew but were tortured nonetheless. King Tin'Old the Younger, in an attempt to stop the Fellowship of Wolfclaw, had sent most of the king's guard away to the North. The city was at the mercy of the resurrected Hrothgorn.

The ghouls filled their back- nets with new prisoners from the city

"This will please the master," they growled with sick satisfaction as they trundled away in their iron bulls crushing everything in their path.

Cries of "Help us, King Tin'Old." echoed throughout the streets of Arom, but they were ignored because of the cowardice of the King. The king continued the tradition of his father by hiding during attacks on the city. The ghoulish monsters stomped through the city streets and caused the ground to shake at their approach. The sound was much like an approaching squall and gathering tempest. The Hrothgorn carried torches to light the night and set fire to the humble storefronts on the city's main street.

A group of several Hrothgorn soldiers set fire to the Hall of the Ancients to watch it light the night as it burned. The flames licked and jumped into the sky as an offering to the old and new gods. The leader of this Hrothgornian Company was a particularly heinous specimen of ghastly proportions named Mo'Rog. He led an attachment to the Palace of Stone in search of King Tin'Old the Younger. The Palace was guarded heavily by the remnants of the King's guard. As the Hrothgorn approached on stomping feet, arrows and bolts flew into their faces stopping many of the beasts in their tracks.

"Move forward, you dogs!" ordered Mo'Rog. "I will have the head of any Hroth whose face does not run with blood on this day. Breach the Palace and eat your fill."

The Hrothgorn ground soldiers toppled a tree to use as a battering ram and crashed it into the palace doors. With several mighty plunges and stabs, the door to the palace splintered and cracked, allowing the entrance of most of the Hrothgorn. They scattered throughout the court, throwing statues and priceless items to the floor. The King's guard rushed from the corridors to confront the Hrothgorn invaders. Mo'Rog reached down, grabbed two King's guards by the neck, and threw them against the wall violently, causing them to fall to the ground quivering in the throes of death.

"Where is your King?" demanded Mo'Rog. I will spare your lives if you tell me where I can find him." Mo'Rog reached down and picked a King's guard up by his head. "Tell me, weak and tiny man person, where is your King hiding? Tell me, and I will not kill you!" The man shivered with fear and shook from his toes to his head.

"He is... hiding... in the main dining hall... at the end of the corridor. Please let me down...."

Mo'Rog dropped his temporary prisoner to the floor, leaving him uninjured. "Tell all who you know that Mo'Rog kept his word today. Tell all who will listen to what you have seen today. We cannot be defeated and will roll over the realm like a great stone crushing all in our path. This land belongs to King Drak-North."

MoRog and his Hrothgorn crept to the end of the corridor and opened the great door to the Palace of Stone dining hall. In the corner next to a winged back chair was the figure of the fat crouching King Tin'Old the Younger.

"Guards! Guards! Attend me at once... I order you to attend to me at once. I warn you, do not hurt the King," he said as he scrambled on all fours behind the furniture. "I have arrangements with King Drak-North... I have paid the tribute for this season...please." He began to quiver and rose to his knees, begging.

Mo'Rog smiled at the sight of the pitiful, fat, cowardly King hiding behind something smaller than him as if he could not be seen. "Come to me, you vile pig-man. Do not hide from me."

The King peered from around the chair to look at his invader. "Leave the Palace and leave me unharmed and I will make you rich beyond your wishes," bargained the King. "I will shower you with gold and trinkets, and you will never want a thing... I promise."

Mo'Rog laughed. "You think I want riches? Do you think I can be bought with your useless trinkets? I am taking those from you anyway after I kill you. Tell me...am I one of your court whores to be bought and sold? Do you think that will save you? Come to me, and I will be quick and merciful with your death. Make me come to get you, and you will *regret the manner of your doom*."

The King quivered and hid behind the chair with even more intent on not being retrieved from his hiding place. Mo'Rog had lost his patience with the King. He walked to the chair and threw it against the wall revealing a crouching whimpering King Tin'Old.

"Please, no!" he begged. "My people need me to lead them!"

"You wish to lead your people from behind a chair? It will be my pleasure to kill such a coward today and to rid the realm of the likes of you." Mo'Rog raised his massive Hrothgorn-made sword, two meters long and too heavy for a man to wield. He grasped it with both hands and raised the sword handle first in the air with the point down. With all the force of his Hrothgornian strength, he drove the sword through the chest of the King. "Now I have skewered you like the fat hog that you are. The King quivered in death as he tried to speak.

"My kingdom... my kingdom..."

"That is *your* problem ... *King*...you thought it was *your* kingdom," Mo'Rog said in the voice of Odious- Forge the Magician. The King and the wizard's eyes met for several seconds.

"Do not forget the curse of the Kings. Payment must be rendered!" demanded the Wizard

He became deathly still and closed his eyes forever.

The wizard's countenance faded, and Mo'Rog then bellowed to his soldiers. "Kill all who reside in the palace and leave none alive. Kill them all." The Hrothgorn performed their evil work to completion until there were none left alive in the Palace of Stone.

The invaders left the city of Arom in ashes as they stomped through the scorched earth and the burnt skeletons of their victims. The sound of crushing scorched bones could be heard as the horrible creatures marched out of the city. Some on foot and some in tanks, their prisoners screaming from the back-nets.

The meadows where the children played were now scorched earth. The forest shrieked in pain as the trees that had been there for centuries burned to the stumps. The Palace of Stone wept and smoldered.

In the Holy forest of Er'Osque, Wolfclaw rested leaning against a large rock with his helmet over his eyes. He fell asleep for the first time in many days. His sleep was restless and uncomfortable. So many questions had to be answered. *What have I done to these people? My decisions had already cost so many lives… How can I live with this? Is my hunger for revenge costing people their lives? The Horsemen frustrate me."*

As he opened his eyes, he could see the form of the Alchemist, Odious- Forge, standing over him. "You startled me. Has no one ever told you not to sneak up on a military man?"

"I am sorry for the intrusion, but I think you need to know something before we go further to the Northlands. I have read in the stars that *fire* is rushing to us in waves like the sea. There has been a tremendous loss of life, according to my Alchemy. The planets are positioned for war, and many have already died. I fear we are going into an ambush, Si

"What do you think this fire represents?" We cannot abandon our mission now. Too many people depend on us. Every moment is a race against time," said Wolfclaw.

Odious- Forge thought for a moment. "I do not know what the fire in the sky holds for us. We do not know what is on the other side and what awaits us as we pass through. It is a gamble, and we depend on the turn of a friendly card. Do not doubt this…fire burns brightly and very soon."

"We shall play the game then. We will wait for the payout, and we will not leave our cards undrawn!" said Wolfclaw, who seemed more sure awake than asleep.

"What if you can never locate your wife? I am not saying that I believe something has happened to her, but- "said Odious- Forge. It seems too much to gamble with that. My father, Eldon Void, told me that one who gambles is a diseased savage who is temporarily refined until he loses and becomes a beast again. I pray for the turn of a friendly card and that I may never host that beast in my game again."

Wolfclaw became determined and slightly enraged. "If he harms one hair on her head, I will find who he loves, and I will kill them! I do not care if it is his Queen, mother, or children. I will kill them all! Call me a diseased savage again, and feel my steel! Get the hell away from me."

Forge took three steps back and excused himself in silence. He was surprised by Wolfclaw's sudden declaration of brutality. He walked away swiftly.

"Does this surprise you, Alchemist? Do you think that for one moment I would not do that? Do you not hear me?" bellowed Wolfclaw as he was left standing alone

Wolfclaw laid his head back on the rock and closed his eyes, searching for sleep that was not to come. The morning arose too early, and the time to leave the Holy forest of Er'osque had come. The army was on the move. The sound of marching feet on the move and swords clanging was heard as the army moved on. They chanted a marching song of victory as they marched.

Victory will be ours, and blood will spill.
The hammer will ring as the sword will."

Later as Valorii and Kilmister reached the base of a great hill, she saw a figure walking toward her. She drew her sword quickly.

"Stop in your tracks and tell me your forename. I mean to cut you down if you are my foe."

The figure came into view. He was wearing a dark cloak from head to foot, and it shone like the brightness of the stars at night. There was a luminosity coming from under the cloak. The figure's face was not to be seen.

"Stand fast. Tell me who you are at once!" Valorii ordered sharply.

The figure spoke softly as he dropped his cloak, revealing a complete set of silver armor much like what was used in the Renaissance.

"I am The Moonlit Knight, the Steward of the Horseman. I have been sent by those who are greater than I am. I am at your disposal in your pursuit."

"Where did you get this armor? Are you a god?"

"I am afraid not, m'lady. I am a simple servant."

Find another one of the soldiers who need help. I can take care of myself. I need no *squire*. What do you think you know about me…?."

"I am *not* a squire, m'lady, I am an empty silhouette, and I have been sent by good friends to serve only you."

"I am not a *lady*. I am a warrior! How did you know where to find me or what I am called? Speak, or I will cut your throat!"

"Then I must die, for I am sworn to keep the secret of my master who sent me."

Valorii lowered her sword. "How can I trust a shadow? I must see your face."

"I have none. If you lift my helmet, you will only see darkness."

"I am to trust... a ghost?" puzzled Valorii.

"I am no ghost. I am genuine. I exist only to serve you."

"Why? That makes no sense at all! I must call you a name of some kind... what would you have me call you?"

"Call me nothing... that is all I am. The light from within me comes from those who have sent me. I live now only to serve you. If you look into the sky, you will see the moonlight not to shine on you, Valorii Thuireld, but it is there for *you* to shine upon *it*. The moon lives *only* to serve you."

Valorii was puzzled over this for a time. "I am a simple peasant girl. You must have me greatly confused with someone who deserves this more than I do. I assure you there is nothing special about me. Just stay out of my way as we advance to the north. I will carry my sword and shield, and I need no help. You may follow me but do not fall behind."

The army and the fellowship came to the crest of a great hill. They went to a ledge with a massive drop to the forest floor. There they saw a horrible sight. Below on the forest floor were hundreds of Hrothgorn. Gathered in their ghastly array, they carried lit torches and raised weapons. They chanted war songs and practiced war formations in their camp. The Hrothgorn were gathered around a smoldering cauldron containing some meat. Some would raise their arms with their hands full of the meat still on the bone as it dripped with liquid from the boiler. They ate heartily and brawled with each other challenging their strength in combat. The sound of swords clashing could be heard across the valley.

"Stand fast and be silent!" ordered Wolfclaw to his men behind him. "We can watch them prepare. I do not wish to disconcert them. I wish to catch them unaware!"

Valorii worked her way to the front of the flank, stooping as she walked to the top of the hill, where she took her place next to Wolfclaw.

From their vantage point, Svæin, Olaf, and Fältskog could see the Hrothgorn in their horrible display.

"Ugly bastards, are they not?" observed Svæin.

Olaf observed, "I can almost smell them from here."

The army remained behind the fellowship in silent waiting as they remained low to the ground.

Two Hrothgorn started to shriek at each other in Hroth's language.

"They are livid with one another over something," said Valorii.

They both raised their swords and dropped them with mighty blows. The strikes were blocked, and the fight commenced. Hrothgorn gathered around the two warriors, and coins were tossed about as the conflict began. Screaming and cheering rattled the valley floor as the fellowship witnessed the Hrothgorn battle below. The challengers clashed swords. Blood flew from the mouth of one of the Hrothgorn soldiers from an unknown injury. Spit flew from the mouths of the fighters as the swords found their marks on the adversaries. One Hrothgorn fell to the earth, and his opponent stabbed him to death with his sword by running him through the chest. Cheering erupted for the victor in this demonic battle. The remaining Hroth soldiers tore their fellows to pieces and ate them in a gory celebration of victory.

Valorii turned her head, covering her face as the ghouls ate their companion. "They are just animals... how could they do that?" she asked.

Wolfclaw replied, "It will be easier to kill them when they are fat and slow."

Valorii appeared confused and wondered about the plan of her mentor. "What is our plan now that we are faced with these Hrothgorn?"

Captain old- Turas made his way through the army to the front of the formation. "Let me at those slimy sons of bitches. I will have my vengeance for the North Hundrun. I will kill them myself."

"We will have our chances... all of us. We must wait for nightfall," replied Wolfclaw." I have a plan."

The Moonlit knight stood quietly to the side of Valorii Thuireld and spoke not a word.

"Who in my uncle's name is this?" asked Wolfclaw. "Take off your helmet so we can see you," he said surprisedly. Who are you, and from where did you come?"

"He said he was sent to protect me, and I do not know by whom, and he said he does not have a face," Valorii answered.

"Well," said Wolfclaw addressing the Knight, "If you knew her at all, you mysterious son of Hades, you would know that you are the one that needs to be protected. The Knight remained silent. "This will not do at all, but keep an eye on him and don't let him get in the way," warned Wolfclaw. "It's going to be a long night while we wait."

Valorii sat diligently, awaiting the movement of the Hrothgorn on the valley floor below.

----------◆◆◆◆◆----------

At this very moment, Tor'Bjorn was deep in the dungeons of King Drak-North. He had been tortured and branded by the vicious Fire-Fang. He said nothing to the evil torturer that could be used against Warshield. The lack of results sent Fire-Fang into a murderous rage. His eyes were the color of raw meat, and his teeth were bared in anger. The giant screamed aloud and ran from the dungeon. In haste, Fire-Fang left something essential behind on the cold, hard cell floor. He dropped his dagger. The light glinted from the surface of the deadly blade as if it was beckoning to be picked up.

As he ran from the dungeon, Fire-Fang screamed, "Curse you. Curse you *filthy human trash*. You will rot in this place and soon become food for the rats."

The heavy door slammed behind him, closing off the light except for a small hole where the tiny window threw a small beam. Tor'Bjorn could hear the rats scurrying about the cell floor. He felt a sharp bite on his leg as he slung the animal to the wall causing it to scream in pain. He was tied to a wooden pole and was seated on the floor. His hands were bound at the wrist behind him. He had been busily scraping the ropes on the rough wooden surface for days and had almost worn through them. Just a few more times, and they would be loosed. Another bite on his leg sent him into a panic.

He thought, *is this where I am to die? One day I am fishing, and the next, I am being bitten by rats as a prisoner of the North. Surely I have angered the gods in some way!* The ropes snapped open as he thought his arms would not move further. His hands were free. Tor'Bjorn reached down, grabbed the dagger on the floor, and cut his legs free. He then tucked it gently into his belt in the back of his trousers. He stood and crept foot by foot to the door. He waited to the right of the door on a four-step ladder and tried to control his heavy breathing to not give himself away to his captor. He waited for what seemed like hours in the dark and silence. After some time, the door swung open, and Fire-Fang walked in with a flaming torch in his hands.

"Perhaps fire will burn some truth from you. I will set fire to you and listen to all you have to say through your screams of mercy-." He noticed the pole where Tor'Bjorn had been was now absent of its former occupant. He turned to face him in the dark. Tor'Bjorn, the once peaceful village shoemaker, screamed and brought the dagger down in one movement into the neck of the ghoul. He drew the blade out, causing a copious spray of cherry red blood, and struck another blow to the other side of his captor's neck. The giant could not make a sound except for the gurgling of drowning in his blood. His lifeless body collapsed to the floor of the cell. Tor'Bjorn stood over the body and breathed heavily. *What would he do now,* he thought?

CHAPTER TWENTY-NINE

THE CLIFFS OF ATHGOR

᠅

Date: Dimension of Odin 126 AD
The Palace of Bones

Tor'Bjorn seized the torch from the wall and ventured into the corridor of the Palace of Bones. He could see the faces of long-since-dead soldiers, heroes, and villains. They were all the same in death. Their works in life made no difference, as now they were just so much decoration on the wall. Their sad faces gaped from the corridors as if wishing for some kind of rescue from their predicament. Their hollow eyes pleaded for mercy from an eternity of staring into nothingness.

Whoever they were, there was no rest for their torment. I wonder who they were. Why were they here? Hundreds of these gaping skulls in the walls were staring back at him. Tor'Bjorn heard the words of Wolfclaw echo through his mind,

"This is your fight from which you cannot run. This fight will follow you like a hungry wolf for all of your days. Your guilt will only be surpassed by the pain of knowing you did nothing."

A chill covered his back as he hurried down the corridor. He crept further down and away from the dungeon to a supply area full of oaken barrels. Tor'Bjorn smelled a strong odor of oil. This was a supply of oil for the catapults set near the palace's walls. There were at least one hundred barrels in the catacombs standing before him like so many soldiers at battle-ready attention. He turned to leave the area and walked stealthily up the corridor to a large oaken door. Oak timbers lined the arch above and a single file along the walls. He quietly opened the door with a slight creaking sound. He thrust his head in and saw a grand meeting hall with dozens of Hrothgorn elite seated at a table. King Drak-North was at the end of the table at the far end of the hall. He seemed to be surrounded by darkness on all sides. A faint red light came from the table's far end. Tor'Bjorn closed the door just far enough for him to peer through the tiny crack at what was going on in the hall. He controlled his breathing so as not to give himself away. He was genuinely afraid his heartbeat would alert the Hrothgorn that he was there. He touched his hand to his chest and felt the searing burn of the brand of Drak-North. He had been branded just as a Rhandobeast in the service of the King of darkness. He continued to watch and hear what was happening.

They were chanting a call to war in unison. "Horth'gorn, ama gorth." It was a war chant. Tor'Bjorn recognized from his village where he left tears behind on the ground so long ago.

The Hrothgorn were preparing for war, and cries of certain victory echoed throughout the palace. Tor'Bjorn was stealthy and full of care that he must not be seen. He looked too small to be wearing the Armor of Fire-Fang and certainly would not pass for a Hrothgorn soldier if he were caught. He entered the stairwell that led to the entrance of the Palace of Bones. Once out in the open, he thought he might make a run for it into the forest. As he turned the corner of the grand stairwell, he saw two Hrothgorn soldiers at the top of the stairs.

They were laughing and boasting to each other. "Human flesh has a taste like no other. We will know its taste tonight as we conquer the tiny human army!

The companion of the Hrothgorn boasted, "I have tasted the flesh. It is sweet to the taste and tender. Before we leave, I will pick some meat from the worker's pit tonight."

Tor'Bjorn turned and hurried to the bottom of the stairwell once again and thought,

The prisoners are not in the Palace. There must be a way to tell Wolfclaw. He felt desperate pain as he thought about his family in the pit. He wondered if they were alive and safe. His mind wandered to horrible thoughts concerning the fate of his loved ones and the others in captivity.

At the Cliffs of Athgor, rain began to fall in a graceful dance that too soon turned into a violent torrential downpour. Ingegärd added her lightning bolts to the deluge, causing a terrifying crashing of the heavens. The army stood silently in the storm and waited for the order of Wolfclaw to begin. The soldiers started to shiver as icy water ran down their armor's inside, turning frost on their skin. Thick ice formed on the men's long beards, causing the hair to crunch with movement as the soldiers turned their heads. Lightning pirouetted about them as demons in a hellish ballet of destruction.

Wolfclaw drew his long broadsword and held it high into the night. "Now is the time," he roared to Warshield and the fellowship of Wolfclaw. "As the Winterhawk hunts rabbits from on high, so will we hunt and rain death from above. Let their dripping blood tell the tale of our victory today. Archers fire at will! Crossbows rain your bolts down upon them!"

From the cliffs of Athgor, a wall of arrows and bolts flew into the night to find their fleshy targets. The startled Hrothgorn below fell like dead trees in a winter storm as arrows and bolts pierced their heads and hearts.

"They shrieked in disbelief as the ambush from above continued.

As the Hrothgorn gathered their senses, they returned fire to the cliff above. Several large Hroth soldiers pushed a wheeled tower to the precipice.

"Climb to meet them, you worms!" ordered the Hroth leader. "The more you kill, the more you eat." The bowmen could not stop them as the Hroth was protected by the tower. A dozen or more Hroth soldiers carried ladders to the cliffs. They had brought them in hopes that they would breach the walls of the Palace of Stone later in the kingdom to the South. They were unaware that a previous rank of Hrothgorn had already attacked the city of Arom.

The Hrothgorn started to scale the cliffs by the dozens, and soon many more breached the cliffs. Their enormous size made it easier to reach the cliffs faster. The archers were unable to return fire quickly enough. As the hideous beasts reached the top of the towers and ladders, they were met with swords and axes. Bodies collided in combat as sounds of the throes of battle rose through the cliff of Athgor.

Sweat stung Wolfclaw's eyes; all around him was a hurricane of disorder and bloody chaos.

"How long can we hold 'em, Wolf?" asked a panicked Svæin as he struggled to fight his way through the melee.

"Make those dirty bastards bring the fight to us. We will wait and cut them down as they climb the cliff. We have the high ground!" replied Wolfclaw as he lost his footing and fell face to the ground. A Hrothgorn warrior saw an opportunity to strike and raised his sword over his head, preparing for the death blow to Wolfclaw. As the Hroth was bellowing a death cry celebrating victory, he felt a searing pain in his side followed by flowing blood. He reached down to find a dagger sticking from his ribs. He turned to see the Alchemist Odious-Forge holding another dagger in his other hand.

"Come to me, you greasy pile of shite! I will spill your guts like a Rhandobeast," threatened Forge.

The Hroth warrior reached down to grab the dagger, which gave Svæin enough time to run the monster through with his sword.

"Good work, Sorcerer!" said Svæin. "What manner of magic was that?"

"There was none. I am too afraid to use my magic."

"That was all you. You can be fearsome when you want to be, "said Svæin.

Wolfclaw recovered in time to rejoin the fight at the cliff. "Below us is a large flank of Hrothgorn. We will wound them there," said Wolfclaw.

"How will we get to them?" asked Valorii. We would be seen for sure."

"We will drop the Hammer and ax of Artonimous right in their midst," explained Wolfclaw as he hacked away at approaching Hroth Warriors. Svæin and Wolfclaw hurled the ancient tools of war to the forest floor below. They landed in the middle of the most extensive section of Hroth Warriors and obliterated them all. Almost like an explosion, Hrothgorn body parts, flesh and bone flew through the forest air.

"That turned out better than I thought," said Svæin in a surprised manner.

The battle continued to rage, and sadly, the tide began to turn. The Hrothgorn blades were enormous and forged in the blood of slaves. The swords of the kingdom of the North were no match for the Hrothgorn blades. They pierced flesh and separated sinew and joint even through chainmail and armor. The Northern warriors fell like trees as the Hrothgorn army mowed them down.

"Kill them all. Litter the ground with their flesh," ordered the Hrothgorn Captain. "Leave no one alive."

The air was filled with men shrieking and swords crashing. Warshield was being destroyed before his very eyes. Valorii Thuireld and her sword were slashing and hacking with as much fury as she could muster.

"In the name of Artonimous, the ancient god of victory, we claim the dead bodies of the soldiers of King Drak-North as spoils of victory!"

Nevertheless, the bodies of the army of Wolfclaw fell in glorious defeat. The warriors danced in death like marionettes in the vengeance of Drak-North.

Wolfclaw struggled to see what was before him. His face was a crimson mask, and his eyes filled with tears. Sweat stung his face, and all about him was disorder and confusion. The sound of men's screams and the metal sounds of swords clashing were all around him. Valorii could feel her fear pounding on the inside of her helmet. She could feel it like a clock racing through time. She peered through the melee and caught the eye of Wolfclaw as he fought and slashed his way through the crowd of flesh and bone. Their eyes met for a moment in silent agreement. They both knew Warshield had failed in the final battle.

The Hrothgorn chanted their battle cry, "Horth'gorn, Ama gorth." It was a final taunt to the vanquished under their gigantic feet. The cliffs of Athgor were bathed in blood and tears on that day.

———————— ⁘⁘⁘ ————————

Tor'Bjorn crept through the halls of the Palace of Bones. There was no way out for him. He knew all the exits were guarded by mammoth Hrothgorn. He felt trapped in a maze from which there was no escape. His mind wandered to home. He felt the presence of a lake where he was fishing for Copple fish. He could feel and smell the leather with which he made shoes for the townspeople. His sweet wife made cakes and bread for him and rubbed the day's tension away from his shoulders. He sighed. He could see the city lights from his fishing spot. He always felt lucky he could live away from the confusion of the city.

An idea came to him and his eyes filled with tears. *He* thought *would I trade one life for over three thousand? No one is so exalted that he should not make that choice himself. I must not wait for the gods to decide. I would do what is right! Fear is the fuel that feeds the fires of victory. Let it burn on.*

Tor'Bjorn dropped the armor and helmet and ran to the dungeon basement where the barrels of oil stood. He grabbed a bone-covered ax from the corridor wall and ran to the oil barrels. Two Hrothgorn guards spotted him at the end of the long corridor, and they began the long run to capture him.

"There is a human in the Palace! We smell his filthy flesh!"

When he reached the oil barrels, he swung with all the might an angler could gather. He hacked the side of one barrel after another, spilling the oil on the floor of the Palace of Bones. The Hrothgorn reached the entrance of the catacombs and fell to the bottom on the oil slick created by Tor'Bjorn's ax.

He held the torch with both hands high in the air and screamed to the sky," Odin and Rothl'Orca, give me the strength I need to die with these Hrothgorn!" He touched the torch to the oil on the floor, and it flamed up like lightning from the depths of Hades. The two Hrothgorn were consumed in flames within seconds. The shrieking and burning Hrothgorn was an alarm to the demons that resided in the Palace of Bones. The remaining barrels caught fire quickly and began spreading through the catacombs under the palace. The fires consumed the Hrothgorn in the catacombs and quickly overcame brave Tor'Bjorn.

As his final act the Cobbler took his place in the halls of the heroes along with Kings and the souls of the brave. The fire raced through the bottom floors of the Palace, catching curtains, hearthrugs, furs, and timbers in the wildfire, consuming all in its wake. The Hrothgorn on the top floors of the palace were unaware of the hellish blaze below. The oil reserve in the barrels below caught fire and exploded in an orange bomb of violent rage, bursting through the upper floors and killing all who were there. Flames filled the sky of the kingdom of the North. Wolfclaw and the fellowship could see the blaze from the battle of Athgor.

Through the confusion of the destruction of the Palace of Bones, King Drak-North was spirited through the woods by some advisors and moved safely from the devastation.

He hissed at his advisor, "I will drink mead from the skull of the one who has done this to my palace. He will suffer at my hands, I swear it."

The palace burned like a torch in the night. Ingegärd peered down from her heavenly carriage and voiced her anger by heaving lightning bolts and thunder to the ground.

She shrieked from the skies, "Wolfclaw will soon see the day when he will burn as the Palace of Bones has burned."

As the palace burned, the battle raged on. The Hrothgorn wandered the battlefield, destroying and killing all in their path. The fellowship and the remaining soldiers numbering nearly two thousand were all faced to the North, watching the onslaught of a wall of Hrothgorn monster soldiers. There seemed to be thousands of filthy beasts all approaching and surrounding the remainder of the fellowship.

Fältskog screamed, "In the name of Rothl'Orca, we were comfortable in our mead hall, and now we are appointed to die."

"Not without a fight, we are not. Come and get us, you gruesome bastards!" bellowed Wolfclaw.

Valorii proclaimed, "We will die on our feet. We will never kneel to your King." The Hrothgorn chanted their war chant as a taunt to the fellowship.

Svæin raised both hands filled with his hammer and ax. "If ye are thirsty for a bit of steel, come and drink from my sword, you beasties!"

Olaf stood behind Svæin and quivered but bravely held his sword high. Svæin assured him, "Stay near me, my boy, and come with me to the halls of Valhalla!"

The Hrothgorn circled the remainder of the army of Wolfclaw, closed the circle tighter, and sealed the doom of the heroes. The air seemed removed from the ring as the giants closed in. Wolfclaw raised his head to the sky, breathing in all he could as if it was his last breath. The sky turned blood red as Ingegärd danced in vengeance. She laughed a maniac's laugh from the sky as the lightning struck the trees and lit the night in a demonic display of terror and fire.

Valorii cried from her position in the center of the crush. "This is not how this will end. We have not come this far to die!"

Her sword vibrated in a battle cry. "We will not be defeated. Wield me. I will dispatch as many Hrothgorn as I can. Strike me in glory, and I will sing your praises."

A broadsword blow caught Wolfclaw in the forehead crushing the front of his helmet. Blood rushed down the front of his face into his nose and mouth. The blood stung his eyes and clogged his breathing through his nose. He struggled to see what was in front of him. He wiped the gushing blood with his glove but could not staunch the flow with the leather backing of his glove.

First, a rumble-like thunder was heard, and then the ground started to shake. Wolfclaw turned to look over the crowd of fighting and dead bodies to see a terrifying sight. Ghidorwrath had slithered a return to the battleground. The terrible and mammoth snake had returned for vengeance.

Ingegärd laughed with a satisfied laugh.

Ghidorwrath rolled over trees, Hrothgorn and men alike. The horrible crunching of wood and bones echoed through the forest. An orange fire flew from his jaws as he burned his way to the battle.

The Witch Queen shrieked. "Feel the wrath of Ghidorwrath. Die writhing in his teeth! He will light up this world's end, and tears will fall for generations!"

The sky grew darker, and the thunder grew louder. Clouds swirled above like angry demons dancing in Hades. Wolfclaw could no longer see because of the blood running into his eyes. He could see a tiny bit of light in his right eye if he kept the blood staunched with his glove. He saw several orbs of light on the horizon through his right eye. They looked shapeless and without form, and he struggled to see them. They grew larger and seemed to be surrounding them.

Svæin thundered from the center of the melee, "Ghosts are surrounding us." The forms grew in size and perspective as Ghidorwrath approached, spraying fire on the area. The ghostly apparitions took shape and increased in number. Now there were hundreds, perhaps thousands, of the specters on horseback.

Valorii recognized them first. "It is the Horsemen... thousands of them." The apparitions became clear. They blazed hot white under the cloaks, and their faces shone white under the cloaked hoods. They were armed with swords, hammers, and crossbows. The attack was swift, ferocious, and violent. The Horsemen slew the Hrothgorn removing their heads and limbs with broad strokes of the swords. Hammers crushed Hroth's skulls, and crossbow bolts found their way into many Hrothgorn hearts. Bodies fell and littered the battlefield. The pile of dead was as massive as a mountain. They slew any that moved and took no prisoners. In a few minutes, the Hrothgorn armies lie dead in heaps at the Cliffs of Athgor.

Ghidorwrath raised his fierce head and sprayed fire on the Horsemen below. The fire did not affect the specters, and they swarmed Ghidorwrath and stabbed the beast with a thousand sword wounds. He shook from side to side and danced in death and fire as flames shot from his neck. He shrieked as he collapsed to the forest floor, rolling and writhing in pain. Ghidorwrath moved to the cliff's edge and pitched himself to the rocks below, where his corpse was to lay forever.

The battlefield became deathly quiet. Thousands of Horsemen lowered their weapons and stood silent. Wolfclaw removed his helmet and gloves and cleared his eyes.

Valorii stood holding her sword and looked bewildered at the array before her. Svæin and Olaf looked to Wolfclaw for an explanation, which was not to come from him.

"What in the name of Hades happened here?" asked Svæin.

Wolfclaw answered in bewilderment, "a damn'ed miracle, elder. A damn'ed miracle." He turned to the equestrian nearest to the fellowship. "Why...I do not... thank you... for... you saved us... why?"

"We have followed you since you began this quest in the Hall of the Ancients, and we have not left your side. You were never alone. Your fellowship must be preserved," said the Horseman.

"Why... What do you see that I do not? I must know," pleaded Wolfclaw.

"We can only say we are but a speck of dust from the past, a blade of grass from the field of memories. *Know that we have done this thing for a reason.*"

"What reason could there be for your vast army to save us this way?"

The Horse masters all receded into the forest as quickly as they came, much to the annoyance of Wolfclaw. "No... No...not until you stand and speak. Do not leave this way." They remained silent once again as they faded away into oblivion.

"Next time, I will grab one of them for you, Wolf," promised Svæin.

"Tell me what happened here today because I do not understand?" asked Olaf. "I will petition the gods to explain the meaning of this. The entire army that was about to kill us all and probably eat us in revenge was killed by ghosts on horseback. I must know what the gods are trying to tell us."

Wolfclaw looked to the sky, "We might as well let the flowers and trees tell the tale. If you search the clouds for the truth, it is not there. Truth is written in the stars and long forgotten. There is truth at the world's end, and we may know it someday, but I fear the gods mean to keep it a secret."

Olaf shook his head in astonishment.

The wounded were bandaged, splinted, and carried to makeshift shelters in the forest near the cliffs. Svæin ordered a funeral pyre to be built for the dead of the fellowship, and he spoke these words over them.

"These the brave will hear the hammers ring in the halls of Valhalla. Valhalla, this is where you belong. You will drink and rejoice this day in the halls of the kings and the courts of the queens. Mourn not for these brave people, but mourn for yourselves that you were not with them today in Valhalla. The Longboats will arrive to take these men of steel and iron to their place of reward."

The remaining soldiers of Warshield trudged over the dead bodies of the enemy and started the trek to the Palace of Bones.

Wolfclaw exclaimed, "Now we seek the head of Drak-North. We must first find where our *dear ones* have been taken. They are not ghosts in the fog; they must be where we can find them. They have not been left behind. We will find them!"

Chapter Thirty

WINTERSITE

———ᶜᵛᵒ———

Date: Dimension of Odin 126 AD
Camp Winter at the Underforest

"You are the only scholar Warshield has concerning the stars and all things in the supernatural realm," said Wolfclaw.

"I have a gnawing in my heart that I feel somehow I know that these horsemen are from across the universe and have great tales to tell. They are the spirits of heroes and the brave who have heard the hammers ring in the courts of Kings and the halls of the Queens. They have seen battle bloody and great," observed Odious-Forge.

"In the Cathedral of the Gods, I felt their presence and was overwhelmed by their power, but I was unsure until Athgor. I felt they must have been waiting for something... or someone," said Wolfclaw.

"So that they might return to their rest, I am to presume," answered the Wizard.

"We can in no way begin to repay them for what they have done at the Battle of the Cliffs of Athgor," said Wolfclaw. "They turned our certain defeat at the hands of the Hrothgorn into victory. We can now march on to the Palace of Bones. We might be bloodied and pained, but we will march on nonetheless and liberate our dear ones from the jaws of King Drak-North. May the gods guide the souls of these great heroes to their rest at last."

Wolfclaw said in a subdued tone. "May the empty sky be filled with valor and the sounds of swords ringing." He took his leave of Odious-Forge and began to wander among his men.

Ice began to fall like stars from the sky. It started as flakes of frost and increased in size as time progressed. Soon heavy icicles were dropping from the sky like spears and arrows, causing the men to seek cover under trees and beneath their shields. The snow crunched in a crisp icy, snapping sound throughout the forest. They were the mighty footsteps of an ice giant who had discovered the fellowship and the army.

"Who is it that enters Wigmir's forest?" the ice giant demanded an answer. "You have disturbed his slumber. Wigmir owns this forest, and you unworthy beings have sullied his domain."

Valorii answered the giant with a question, "Who is Wigmir? We did not mean to disturb him."

"Wigmir is I and I am Wigmir. You have disturbed his domain, and he is furious." The giant towered over them at the height of nearly ten men. Ice fell from his coat in large icicles and sheets of frost as he spoke. His beard was forked and braided to the middle of his chest. His hair was long, flowing nearly to his waist, and completely white. He was covered with a long fur coat made of bearskins and raccoon pelts." I could stomp all of you and smear you, measly humans, into the snow for the disrespect you have shown Wigmir in his home!"

"If it is all the same with you, worthy Wigmir, please… I would rather you did not. We are on an errand to rescue our loved ones from the clutches of King Drak-North and the Hrothgorn."

"I smell a human lie; I do. You mean to steal from me. I know a thief when we see one!" said Wigmir.

"We are not thieves. We have defeated a Hrothgorn army and are now marching to the Palace of Bones. We could not have known this was your home, and we will pay any tribute you ask to pass through," Wolfclaw bargained with the ice giant.

The mighty Wigmir hung his head in thought, almost like a prayer. His eyes filled with icy water, and a smile filled his colossal face. The ground shook with his booming voice even though he was trying to speak softly. "Wigmir knows where your loved ones are being kept."

"Wolfclaw answered, "What have you seen… are you sure?"

The giant answered to the best of his recollection. "Wigmir knows there is a work camp not far from his region, as he has seen it during some of his walks through the mountains of Doran. The people work under the lash of the Hrothgorn, making steel weapons in the fiery forges. Wigmir will take you there if you wish."

Wolfclaw offered a tribute for Wigmir once again. "We will give you a tribute fit for a King if you would take us to them, I swear."

"Wigmir has been alone here in this forest for thousands of years. He needs no tribute. When he spied your army approaching, he became faint and dizzy with excitement at the sight of other beings in his realm. He does not need to squash you now. He only needed to know of your quest and if it is one of righteousness," assured the ice giant.

"How did you come to be alone here for so long?" asked Valorii.

"Wigmir was banished here long ago by Ingegärd because of his loyalty to the humans of the forest realm. She killed innocent villagers… with lightning because she thought they stole tribute from her. Wigmir obstructed her inferno and saved many other villagers with his size and strength. She was furious and banished him here."

Wolfclaw fell to one knee before the great ice giant and pointed his sword to the snow. "We are your servants, great Wigmir," vowed Wolfclaw. "We will do what you require of us."

"Wigmir requires nothing but your fellowship. Let him come with you on the march to the Palace of Bones.

"Drak-North has Hrothgorn, but he does not have an ice giant!" boasted Wolfclaw. You will lead the army to the North good Wigmir?"

"Tell me what you wish of me."

The mountain of Doran lies ahead. What was easy for an ice giant would be an arduous task for a man. They would have to go through the mountain, over it, or around it. Svæin had much climbing experience in his battles to the north. He decided he would lead all of the fellowship and the army over the mountain to the work camp. Wigmir would help those who could not climb well to get over the peak as he had walked over it many times in leisurely walks in the evening.

"Wigmir will carry you, tiny humans, over the mountains of Doran to the other side. Do not be afraid."

Later as the fellowship topped the mountain of Doran, they saw the camp in the distance. Hundreds of men, women, and children were pounding molten swords with heavy iron hammers as sparks flew from the sides of the newly forged weapons. The anvils rang by the hundreds as the Hrothgorn growled orders over the din of the forgery. The fires roared, and the people cried and wailed in agony under the lash of the Hrothgorn.

"We need a diversion so they will take their attention away from the prisoners," suggested Svæin, already thinking of battle strategies.

"I will lead the charge to the camp after the diversion. Do my men have any ideas?" asked Wolfclaw.

"Well, I cannot help to think that our new friend Wigmir may be a good diversion all by himself," Svæin said laughingly. "Let us see those vicious dogs try to overcome him. I would pay one hundred Gromels to see that!"

"We will march behind Wigmir and take the heads of any Hrothgorn that cross our path to victory. Let us remember our dear friends we left behind at The Hall of the Ancients. We thank our friends, the Horsemen, for the Battle of The Cliffs of Athgor. We show gratitude to Wormouth, the serpent in the Forest of Shem, for giving us the time needed to approach the Northlands. We will not forget our friend Tor'Bjorn for his bravery in the Battle of Harvest Moon, wherever he may be. We cannot and will not forget those who were in our fellowship and who gave their lives in battle so bravely. All hail the young Halfdan, who was taken from the fellowship too soon. We go with them to the Halls of Valhalla. We will always be in debt to the crew of The North Hundrun and their heroic sacrifice at the hands of the dreaded Ghidorwrath. Raise your swords to all who got us here that we might be ever mindful that they have earned this victory for us!"

Wolfclaw wiped the snow from his Helmet and shook the ice from his beard. "It is the time! Come with me, Svæin."

"I will as sure as I am the Hall of the Ancients arm wrestling champion. Let us give these buggers something to die for!" He turned to young Olaf and said," follow me, and we will lead the charge together."

Olaf stood tall and bravely charged into battle. He felt he had earned his place among the warriors.

The charge was sounded, and the ice giant Wigmir trudged slowly toward the encampment.

The warriors ran at top speed to keep up with his slow pace. Ice fell from the giant as he bounded through the snow-covered hills. The Moonlit Knight stayed close to Valorii and remained silent on their way to the camp.

Kilmister spoke only to Valorii. "Wield me skillfully, my lady, and we will own the day. Countless Hrothgorn will feel death by day's end."

The Hrothgorn saw Warshield approaching and started to rain arrows down at the company.

Warshield approached the camp and startled the Hrothgorn on the wall who were standing guard. They sounded the alarm.

Wigmir was the first to walk up to the giant doors of the slave encampment known as *Winter Site.* This was where the yearly tributes had been kept since the pact forged between King Tin'Old the Elder and King Drak-North.

The archers were positioned behind the ice giant, and the Pike men were at the rear. The sharpened pikes were poised for action and at the ready. With one mighty kick, Wigmir crushed the door to Winter Site into splinters the size of small trees. The Hrothgorn on the walls were swept away and fell to their deaths. The army swiftly moved in and took defensive positions behind the walls. Wigmir kicked and crushed Hrothgorn under his ice-giant feet. He scooped Hrothgorn in his ice hands and threw them against the walls and the trees like bags of wet sand. The prisoners within the camp scurried to find hiding places and escape the fire of the forges. The archers found their targets striking Hrothgorn as the beasts ran away. Valorii and her sword earned their glory as they dispatched one Hrothgorn after another.

Valorii came face to face with a nameless Hrothgorn. He raised his newly forged sword and let it fall from right to left in a massive blow. The sword's blade missed Valorii by inches and nicked her cheek as it flew by. Blood flowed from her face to the white snow below in large crimson droplets. The Hrothgorn kicked her in the center of her breastplate, sending her backward into a tree knocking her unconscious. The Hrothgorn approached her lifeless body, slumped against the tree, took his hammer from his belt, and raised it over her head to deal the death blow. Just as he raised his arms, the Moonlit Knight appeared from the shadows and buried a battle ax in the Hrothgorn's skull. The monster continued to walk forward toward his prey. The Knight stood between the beast and Valorii and stabbed the Hrothgorn with a dagger. The Knight ripped the blade from left to right across the belly of the Hrothgorn, opening up and spilling his entrails in the snow. The massive monster fell like timber to the snow-covered floor of Winter Site. Valorii had opened her eyes to see the Moonlit Knight deliver the death blow to her adversary. The knight approached her and asked," Are you still with us today, my lady?"

Valorii jumped to her feet, still dazed but puzzled by the very existence of the Moonlit knight. "Who sent you to me and why? I must know this."

He replied, "I was sent to be of service to you."

"Is someone here thinking I cannot wield a sword or fight my battles? Let him show himself. Imagine the nerve one would have to think I need a caretaker to do the same brave job everyone else is doing. If I was marked to die... then *let me* die. It was my time to die in battle and not your place to rescue me, as if I was a poor maiden in distress. You stole my glory from me." Valorii blustered in the face of the Knight. "You will let me fight my battles and die my death. Do you wish to disobey me?"

"No, my Lady... I only wish to serve you. Your life belongs to others and not your own."

"What are you spewing? I am mine! I belong to no other! Do you hear me? Serve me by doing as I wish," she ordered.

The battle began to rage around them, causing Valorii to raise her sword again and begin to fight.

Svæin and Olaf took turns covering each other as they brought down one clumsy Hrothgorn after another.

Svæin bellowed, "They are large, scary, and damned ugly, and they cannot fight. They are just too slow. It is like shooting fish with an arrow in a bucket! They are greasy and disgusting, and there are too many of them. Reminds me of some of the meals we had in the forest. Ha-ha!"

Wigmir began reaching down from his high position, grabbing Hrothgorn, and throwing them over the wall to the trees. The remainder was crushed under his feet. A few Hrothgorn were now the prisoners of the king's guard. The only sounds that were heard now were children crying and clapping hands in celebration. A woman rushed from the crowd shouting in celebration and said," I knew the King would send someone. I just knew it!"

"We were sent by the King to stop and kill Wolfclaw in his quest, but we wish to join Warshield instead," said Sir Tor'Vold. King Tin'Old is a coward and a tyrant and had no intention of saving any of you."

The fellowship moved quickly throughout Winter Site Camp looking for loved ones. Some prisoners had only been there a short time and told the sad tale of the destruction of Arom and the death of King Tin'Old the Younger.

As Wolfclaw searched through the sea of people, he heard her voice. "Aspeth Thur'Gold! Aspeth Thur'Gold! Where are you? I hear your voice. Come to me. He could contain himself no longer. "Where are you?"

"His eyes met the eyes of an old woman surrounded by dozens of younger women standing around an oversized chair where she was seated.

"I would know that voice anywhere. It is the voice of one whom I knew would come to find me. It is the voice of one whom I knew would never let me down and leave me to doom," the old woman told the others.

"Your beauty shines through the ages as a shining band of gold. You were simply never alone. I would have clawed through a mountain of dirt and stone to bring you back to me," said Wolfclaw.

Wolfclaw held his forehead against the forehead of his lost bride and held her head in his hands as the soldiers of Warshield began to applaud with shouts of victory and joy.

As the time in Winter Site grew short, she explained what happened in Arom as it was told to her by newer prisoners.

"Arkule' and all of the men in the hall of the Ancients... were all killed. Murdered because they refused to tell where you had gone. They died saving you."

Wolfclaw's eyes filled with tears. He remained silent for what seemed like an eternity.

Valorii wandered with passion and purpose through the camp. She learned from an old woman at the forge that Valorii's mother, Ek'roin, is among them. After a frantic search, Valorii found her. An emotional reunion took place as the camp watched and hoped for their loved ones to come. Ek'roin explained that she and Valorii's sister were cooking for the Hroth warriors as soon as they reached the Winter Site. She said that Ine'Ath was murdered some years before by Hrothgon soldiers trying to steal bread so we would not starve. "I am so sorry, my little one," Ek'roin began to weep. "There is so much I must tell you that I was never able to put into words." The two women held each other close and wept.

"You are free now, and I will see that nothing ever hurts you again."

"You will do that and more, my precious gem... gather your friends around you. I must tell you more," said Ek'roin in a mysterious tone. Please...hurry.

The Fellowship of Wolfclaw and Warshield members gathered in a large opened area used for a pen for housing Rhandobeasts but had long since been abandoned. Wigmir did not want to miss these glorious family reunions, so he leaned over the walls and listened. Ek'roin spoke with the eloquence of her age.

"My dear one Valorii, I have told you that your father was killed by an Oxen cart in Old Turknorse shortly after we were married. The truth is that you were born one year after he was killed. He was… not your father. I am not ashamed to admit that. I must tell you something…."

Valorii seemed agitated by her mother's confession. "Why must these people hear of this? Surely, we could have done this in private. Why tell me this now?"

Ek'roin replied, "It is the reason I have brought everyone here. When the man I told you was your father was home…he was not home. Only his body was present. He was drunk and angry. He beat me daily, gambled our money away, and stayed away for long periods."

"Mother, I fail to see-"

"I was angry and hurt, so I begged King Tin'Old the Elder to help me. I just wanted him to *make* my husband act kindly to me. He visited our home when my husband was gone, and we became very close. As his mistress, he visited me for many years, and you resulted from that love affair." Valorii dropped to her knees upon hearing this.

"Did King Tin'Old know this, Mother? Why did you not tell me?" she asked angrily.

"Yes, he did, and that was why he wanted you in the Palace with him to help take care of him until he died. We could *not tell* anyone of this, especially after King Tin'Old the Younger grew of age, because he would have had you killed. He was evil. We had to stay quiet to save you."

"I held my father's head in my arms at his death?"

"Yes, but there is also something you should know. Please prepare yourself, young one. King Tin'Old the Younger was just murdered by the Hrothgorn, and Arom was nearly destroyed with the hall of the Ancients."

"Why should I care about that fat swine of a King? He would never protect the kingdom without a thought for himself first."

"That is just the point, my dear one… *you* are the rightful heir and Queen of the lands to the South. You are to be seated in the Palace of Stone." Ek'roin sank to one knee and bowed her head as Valorii rose to her feet. "My precious young one…you *are* our Queen."

Svæin bellowed from somewhere in the crowd," how do we know if this old woman does not lie? This sounds like a gold grab to me!"

Valorii had to be steadied on her feet by Wolfclaw. "Move back, all of you! She deserves as much respect as the rest of you. She has fought bravely and has never backed down from a fight. We will determine if this is true."

The Moonlit Knight, who had been silent all this time, stepped forward and raised his sword over his head, pointing to the sky. "I have much to say to this fellowship concerning this matter."

"He does not even show his face, and *he has much to say*," said Svæin in a mocking tone. It is just dark in his helmet. He is a specter. Why should he be trusted?"

"I am to be trusted because you have been given no choice. It is true. The young woman you see before you is your Queen. I have been sent by the spirits of those in the hall of the Ancients and the Horsemen. They are heroes, Kings, and Queens of the past and have bestowed a precious gift upon you. The ancients give unto you... Valorii Thuireld, daughter of King Tin'Old, the Elder."

The Knight opened the front of his chest piece and reached inside. There, in the palm of his hand, was *a live hummingbird.*

"What are you trying to do? What kind of trickery is this?" asked Valorii.

"This is not me.... trust me, my Lady. It is about being prepared to lose what you have for what you might receive or what you are... for what you might be. It is time to let go." He placed the hummingbird in her hands. The Moonlit Knight turned to dust before everyone's eyes and fell scattered to the ground like so much sand. Stillness overcame the crowd, and they could not believe what they had seen.

Valorii closed her hands gently around the hummingbird and felt the beating wings in her palm. Wolfclaw's eyes were intently on Valorii as he watched the tiny bird. There was almost silence in the yard as this occurred. Valorii's body took on a glow, a powerful yellow-white brightness as the sun's rays. She grew in stature and became taller and larger than a human form. Her armor burst off and fell to the ground at her feet. A clap of thunder burst from the clouds to announce the coming of something beyond description. Within the blink of an eye, a divine being had appeared before the crowd. Their gazes turned to the visitor for a moment. The creature was an angel. Wolfclaw and the men of the hall of the ancients had been told of the existence.

"In the name of all that is holy, tell us why you are here, good spirit…if that is what you truly are?" asked Wolfclaw.

Tattered, feathery wings made the angel look far more imposing. A surprisingly agile body moves as if every move is calculated. His robes were covered in religious markings. He carried a gold-trimmed book, which was already open to the book's center.

"Hear ye all here gathered. I am a messenger sent from the heavenly realm above to announce the coming of your Queen," said the angel.

The crowd gasped in panic.

"What manner of demon is this?" Save us," pleaded Olaf.

"No, you misjudge me. We are quite the opposite. Hear my decree! Your Queen is in your midst."

In the distance came a low rumble and a cloud of dust. The sound of hooves appeared in seconds.

The four Horsemen appeared from the tree line and knelt before the new Queen. The horses bent one leg and thrust the other forward so they might kneel.

"She is *your* Queen. She is *our* Queen! Let the voices of the heroes and Kings ring in your ears," said one horseman. She has been ordained from her birth to be your Queen. She was brought here for this time."

Suddenly two feathered wings rose majestically from either side of Valorii's rib cage. They were the span of four or five men laid end to end. She raised her arms to the sky in a form as majestic as the great pines in the forest.

"Wait... we are moving too fast. I do not know what is happening! I am no queen," said Valorii.

"All hail Queen Thuireld the Winged Queen," repeated the horsemen as they knelt before their new Queen.

"Are you not listening to me? I do not wish to be a queen!" she loudly insisted. "Stop this at once." The glorious wings retracted, and Valorii, Queen of Arom, returned to her original physical form.

The angel in attendance faded from view and ascended into the heavenly realm. He bade farewell to the new queen, "May all the powers of good be at your back as the wind blows."

"This must end! I do not wish to be a queen. I am a warrior."

"It is as they say," said Odious-Forge. My Alchemy tells me so and is written in the stars."

Sir Tor'Vold knelt before the Queen and said," Your Majesty, in your honor, we will now execute all of the Hrothgorn prisoners we are holding."

"No, you must not do that." she answered sharply to the former king's guard.

"What will we do with our captured prisoners, your majesty?"

Valorii thoughtfully considered her first order as Queen. First, stop calling me your majesty. Then set them free. Let them know it was I that gave them their lives. If we do otherwise... we are no better than the enemy we seek to destroy."

Kilmister spoke to the Queen from his scabbard. "Your Majesty, I will serve you all the days of my life."

"Not you also. Please-

"I will always be at your side. With me here, you will be the warrior Queen. I am at your service forever!"

She held the sword close to her side as if to say, *"You will always be with me!"*

Wolfclaw knelt before Valorii and attempted to speak even though his voice was shaking. "I have no words to describe… your Grace… Majesty…my Queen. I am a foolish old man… please have mercy on my foolishness."

"How could I thank or reward the greatest warrior of our time?" Valorii asked Wolfclaw. "You require no mercy from me."

"Let me serve your highness, and that would be the greatest reward," replied Wolfclaw.

"You serve no one. You will sit at my side as my advisor for all time."

"I am not who you think I am, your Grace. I do not think I am capable of such a position. I am a *villain* and a *thief*. There would be no joy in having such a scoundrel in your service."

"You have been those things in the mirror of the past dear Wolfclaw, but you are something more important. You are my *friend* and my mentor. You have come face to face with your mortality on our quest. You have had many visitations with death and stared them down like many pitiful enemies. Most importantly, you have protected others with your life. You have laid down your life for your friends. How much longer must you pay for your past life, brave Wolfclaw? As far as I am concerned, you are redeemed. We must stay the course, dear Wolfclaw. We must not lose sight of what we are to accomplish here. The Throne of Bones awaits our deadly visit. We will rain death over the throne."

"Your Majesty … you are now in charge of what is the remainder of my army. What are your orders?"

"No…, this is the fellowship of Wolfclaw and his Warshield and always will be so. Take your army to the Throne of Bones. Enough of the 'Queen' talk. Let us move out!"

"Very well, men, let us move out. May we count on you for help at the Palace of Bones?" Wolfclaw asked the ice giant, who had been wide-eyed while watching all that had unfolded before him.

Wigmir looked down upon the fellowship with deep concern in his eyes. "Wigmir will be there for Wolfclaw and his new Queen." He knelt as well as an ice giant could and spoke with all the sincerity his heart could muster, "Wigmir will do what Valorii wishes."

"Thank you for your bravery. You are the greatest ice giant I have ever known." The Queen did not have the heart to tell Wigmir that he was the only ice giant she had ever known.

The army passed through the valley on the Northside Mountain of Doran and pushed to the Palace of Bones. The fellowship marched on, protected by Wigmir, the ice giant.

All was well tonight except Odious-Forge. He fell on his face in the dirt, knowing what he must do according to his curse. If he did not kill the Queen, someone else would be set in motion. He knew there was something he must do now.

"I call upon the old and new gods to help me break this curse!" said Forge loudly. "It is too much a weight to bear to be forced to kill my friend. Rothl'Orca, save me from this destiny," he said, sobbing

CHAPTER THIRTY-ONE

THE BEAR-CLAN

—cɲɔ—

Date: Dimension of Odin 126 AD

We've paid in hell since Moscow burned
As Cossacks tear us piece by piece
Our dead are strewn a hundred leagues
Though death would be a sweet release- Mark Knopfler

Time traveled on the path for Wolfclaw and his soldiers. Warshield could see the lights of the cities to the North, and they were getting very close to the Palace of Bones. Wolfclaw would not admit to the terrible churning inside his gut. He was sure all his soldiers would think he was a coward for admitting something like this.

Perhaps it was just some rotten Rhando meat, he thought intently as he marched. He started this quest with revenge in mind. He wanted blood so severely but was now reunited, and sure she was safe. The warriors had freed the captives, and they were safe. *I have seen so much blood. So many good men gave their lives for the quest.* He thought he might be able to find Tor'Bjorn somewhere near the palace. Most of all, Wolfclaw was just tired. He was tired in his very soul and thought he would just lie down on the ground and take a long sleep if no one would say anything to him about it.

The Queen noticed Wolfclaw in his quiet state.

"What is the matter? The look on your face gives me some concern.

"What is wrong with my face…aside from the obvious?"

"Most of all, you are never this quiet."

"I wish I could tell you how I feel. I think my age is affecting me. You are the Queen, and the torch has been passed to you. You are more worthy than I ever have been. The pupil has surpassed the teacher."

"You think too deeply," the Queen observed." When we return to our kingdom, I will see to it there is an oversized bear pelt chair for you in the palace. We will have hot drinks brought to you and make a footrest for your feet. The only thing we both need right now is the old *ferocity* of Wolfclaw, the pirate, the highwayman, and the soldier of old."

Captain Old-Turas had been eavesdropping and spoke his piece," We will carry your carcass to the Palace of Bones if we need to. Svæin and Olaf would help to carry you if you were not strong enough. King Drak-North will be dancing the hempen jig." It was an ancient description of an official pirate hanging. "To see him twistin' at the end of a rope would let my men rest in peace. I will not let anyone stand in the way of seeing that sight, so move your old lazy pirate arse."

"You once told me that I was not a warrior and that I was just brave enough to get myself killed. You were right. I am not a warrior, but I am someone who has honor, bravery, and a sense of what is right. You have taught me these things. I will carry you into battle if I must," said Olaf.

"That is enough from all of you," bellowed Wolfclaw. "I did not realize a private conversation would turn so public. I can carry myself. I am not so old that I need to be carried. Drak-North should quake in his boots as we approach."

The fellowship laughed with Wolfclaw as he continued to threaten King Drak-North verbally.

"There is no place for him to hide. I will use his skull as an ashtray for my pipe." The men laughed more heartily as he went on. "I will dance in the ruins of his palace!"

King Drak-North and a small detachment of Hroth soldiers retreated into the forest, fleeing the ruins of the Palace of Bones. Spit flew from his face as he screamed for the head of the person responsible for the palace's destruction.

"Fire-Fang, where is Fire-Fang? Bring my *armies* to me at once. Gather them from all corners of the kingdom. Wolfclaw will pay for this… I know they have destroyed my Palace, and they will pay… Wolfclaw will pay. There is a seat in my parliament for the Hroth, who brings me the head of Wolfclaw. I want his bloody head. I want to mount it next to my throne to remind all who would dare to challenge me."

A trusted Hrothgorn soldier assigned to his King spoke in terrified tones and a trembling voice. "Your grace… there is a word from our forward scouts, I mean from our spies…Wolfclaw has liberated…I mean, disrupted the camps."

"Speak Hrothgorn fool, or I will tear your words from you."

"Wolfclaw has set the workers free from the camps." The Hroth soldier had also been told of a new queen, but he would not be the one who would report such a thing to King Drak-North.

"Take a detachment and make haste to the work camp. Redirect the army to the camp and find Wolfclaw and Warshield. Find them! Take the iron horses!" Drak-North screamed at his soldiers as they scattered in all directions. Not since he was captured and tortured by Wormouth had he felt so helpless and without power. He had always been able to control all the situations thrown in his path with fast, decisive action and aggressive violence. "I will not let some old man and his dusty skeletons deter me from my destiny," Drak'North told an advisor. "It is time to awaken those who are in the cult of the bear."

The Fellowship of Wolfclaw moved quickly to the Palace of Bones. As they approached the edge of the tree line of the Kingdom, they saw the smoldering ruins of the once-great Palace of Bones and a few scant soldiers guarding the ruins.

"Someone beat us to it, brave men. It appears we are not alone in our search for Drak-North. I think I spoke too soon. I am going to *dance in the ruins* sooner than I had thought. Let us hope his corpse is in there smoldering," said Wolfclaw.

He signaled to the archers to dispatch the remaining Hrothgorn soldiers standing watch.

"One Hrothgorn down like a tree... two down where they stood... the third arrow cut down another. This is not even good sport at this point," said Svæin.

Warshield scouts walked through the ruins of the Palace. Piles of black tar and blackened bones were covered with ash and powder.

"It looks like corpses of Hrothgorn soldiers were stacked like refuse outside the entrance and exits of the palace as if they had been caught unaware in the fire," said Olaf.

"Most of the dead had their armor and were prepared for a battle that was not there. There were no enemy soldiers. There was no King's guard sent from King Tin'Old that might have done this. There is just no reason for this resounding defeat of the Palace of Bones," observed the Queen.

This puzzled all the brave ones as they looked at the ruins.

Svæin asked, "You do not suppose this was an act of the gods, do you?"

"I do not feel his presence here," said Wolfclaw. "What are your wishes, your majesty?"

Valorii thought intently before she answered. "I agree we must search for him amid the forest." As she spoke, she bent down to find a metallic object on the ground in front of her. The object was covered with the soot of the Palace but still had its shine. The shape was recognizable at once. The Queen held the object before her to show Svæin and Olaf. *It was a Copple Fish knife.* There was no reason why a Copple Fish knife should be within hundreds of kilometers of the Palace of Bones. Tor'Bjorn, the cobbler, was among the ashes. The Queen hung her head in silence at this revelation.

"Odious- Forge bent and scooped ashes in his hands. "There was a struggle, a fight to the death. Fire-Fang is dead. He is among the ashes of the palace. The cobbler burned the palace with himself in it. I see this in a vision." There was an uneasy silence in the fellowship while they thought of their friend. Fältskog looked over his shoulder to Wolfclaw with an icy stare.

"What a brave and selfless sacrifice was made at the Palace of the Bones by our friend," said Valorii.

The Army of Drak-North had circled back behind the Army of Warshield and gained speed quickly. They had followed the path of Warshield and traced them back to the Palace of Bones. Drak-North had awakened a long-since sleeping band of mercenaries called the "cult of the bear." They were an army of Northern berserkers who could put themselves in a trance-like state at will and were nearly invincible in battle. A large band of these warriors, *almost* running on all fours, dressed in furs only and armed with shields and axes, were approaching with great speed from the hills. They held shields made of wood with steel inlays and borders. Some had chewed through their shields, awaiting battle at the command of King Drak-North. Their cries of war were cries for blood and were terrifying to behold.

"I thought the cult of the bear was a myth," said Olaf. "They even run like bears."

"They have used some kind of magic to become actual bears!" observed Odious-Forge.

"Prepare to let them run... onto your swords and spears. Tonight we dine on bear meat," Wolfclaw ordered. He knew these would not be an easily defeated foe.

Wigmir ran toward the onslaught of Hrothgorn and Bears. Queen Thuireld spread her entire wingspan and rose several meters from the ground, raising her sword and shield to the ready.

"Come to me and meet your sure defeat. We do not fear you, and I will surely show you to your deaths," she motioned to the forest line.

The roar of the bear clan was as loud as a herd of Rhandobeasts. What seemed like thunder was the roaring of their throats in unison. Olaf swallowed as hard as he had done the entire time with the fellowship.

"Now is the time to meet the foe face to face. Show the bears we *are real* also," ordered Wolfclaw. "Let us draw our swords and make it so.

Wigmir ran into the fray, kicked, and grabbed the bears by the mighty handful. Archers buried their arrows in the first two ranks and dropped the bear beasts where they stood. The pines roared from above their approval, and the winds blew their voice of victory for the fellowship. The elongated pikes clashed in crashing, snapping, and splintering sounds of battle.

The Queen could levitate above the battle and swing her sword into the enemy. Some bear clans had broken through the battle lines and engaged the archers. The archers were unable to fend off the ruthless killers.

The Berserkers ripped flesh with their teeth and bare hands as they screamed vengeance for a purpose they did not know. They only wished for chaos. The archers and soldiers of Warshield were being massacred by the bear clan. Wigmir turned to run to the back of the battle to rescue the archers. In their screaming ferocity and insanity, the berserkers bit and ripped at the feet of the ice giant. He stomped and crushed them under his gigantic ice feet.

Svæin met one of the bears face to face. He traded mighty blows with the beast. The berserker screamed in the face of Svæin as they battled one another. He was continuous in his verbal assault of Svæin.

"You are much older than your Warshield companions! I am sure your taste is tough and grisly, but I will eat you anyway. Lie down and die!"

"Oh shut up, you infernal beast. Your scream is no more impressive than your fighting skills," shouted. Svæin. He saw he was making no progress. He threw away his sword, slipped under the beast's waist, picked him off his feet, and threw him to the ground. He retrieved and buried his sword deep in the beast's belly. "Scream from your grave now, ye devil."

Olaf fought with stones picked up from where he stood. He let them fly one by one. Two bears were dead when he had used up his stones. He thought, *It cannot be that simple.*

A colossal bear lifted Svæin above his head and threw him down with a thundering crash. The beast lost his grip on his sword, trying to retrieve it. Svæin took up the fumbled sword and cut off the Bear's head without a word. The stone attack by Olaf infuriated the remaining warriors. Olaf had a spear in one hand and a sword in the other but no shield. He was able to jump over an incoming spear thrust to deliver an attack. He lunged at the beast-man, aiming for his middle. The Berserker leaped in the air, and the spear passed between his legs. He struck Olaf with his sword, and the blow landed on his neck armor and made a loud metallic noise. The impact sent Olaf to the dirt, gasping for air. Wolfclaw picked up an ax and lifted it quickly up above his head, intending to bring it down on an enemy head, but when the man-bear heard the whistling sound of the weapon through the air, he ducked under the blow. Wolfclaw sprang up to meet him, throwing his cloak on the sword and instantly twisting towards him. Wolfclaw grasped the bottom of the shield with his other hand and drove it into the bear's head so that he was killed at once.

Svæin ran to the enemy with a raised ax, struck him in the head, and split it below his shoulders.

Olaf grabbed a spear and thrust it at another member of the bear clan, and it hit his shield. The ghoul jerked his shield to the side - otherwise, the spear would have gone through him. He swung his sword and turned on his heel so the blade missed Olaf. Wolfclaw stepped in, and immediately his shield took a blow from the unbelievably strong warrior. His shield was split right, and he tossed it away. He took his sword in both hands and hacked away with all his might.

Wolfclaw kicked the bottom of the shield into the Berserker's mouth so hard that his face ripped open, and his jaws fell open in death. Fältskog sprang up, lept at a beast, and struck him between the shoulder blades with his hammer so that he fell flat on his face in the dirt.

"Good place for ya' to take a nap, laddie!"

The Witch Queen's anger rained down from the sky. "The Fellowship cannot defeat my bear warriors. You cannot defeat the Hrothgorn. You will join them in unity to do my will. As we speak, the shadow of war creeps over the land of Arom, and innocent lambs go to the slaughter."

Wolfclaw stood straight and pointed toward the sky. "Take me, damn you! Do not harm the women and children who have already suffered enough."

"What do they know of suffering? Suffering is disobedience and rebelliousness to your god. I only require your hearts and your minds to be turned to me. I will end their suffering. For your insolence, I will hear the sound of the crunching of skulls and the sound of crashing blades. Fire will burn all that defy me. An army of Hrothgorn has amassed from the South and is marching upon them. It does not matter what you say or do at this point," said Ingegärd in a voice filled with hate and terror.

Wolfclaw spoke in a subdued tone to Svæin. "Take a large number of the Warshield and stop the attack on Arom."

Svæin gathered the men around him. "You... and you... come with me." The detachment disappeared into the forest.

The Witch Queen warned loudly, "Do not waste your time. You forget yourself. You seek to save what is already lost... fool. Death calls to you, Wolfclaw. How do you answer?"

"I answer by spitting in the face of death."

"Your Queen cannot save you. Your ice giant cannot save you."

Queen Thuireld stepped in front of Wolfclaw, opened her wingspan, and looked into the sky. It was time for Valorii to take her rightful place as Queen. She was righteously indignant.

"I believe I can keep my kingdom safe from an old witch," she said, taunting the Witch Queen. "Who do you think you are that you torture mortals so? Who do you think you are that you should cause such fear upon the world?"

"I am the bringer of war and death unto all who defy me...*your majesty*. Who are you to defy a *god*?"

"I will do all in my power to stop you in your quest to fill the world with pain and tears," swore Queen Valorii. "You and I are enemies. My kingdom will fix its gaze upon causing suffering to you and those who would serve you. I will do all in my power to block you and destroy you."

"Insolent child! You were nothing more than a lowly maidservant to a cowardly King. You have fooled yourself into thinking you are the heir to the crown. You are nothing more than the result of fornication and cowardice. You are nothing more than a bastard child! Surrender now, and I will spare *some* of your people."

Wolfclaw raised his voice for all to hear. "I came here to collect what is due from Drak-North. The payment is due. He cannot hide from me today. I want Drak-North to *die twice* for everyone he has killed and miserably *once* for himself. Show him to me ... and we will return home."

"You are not in the position to bargain, old man. Perhaps I should kill you in front of your men as we speak. Drak-North is my creation and my masterpiece. He was a stroke of genius in his evil... but... I am not unreasonable. I *will* bargain with you if you wish. How much are you willing to give for the head of Drak-North?

"I wish to do as my Queen wishes. I will give you *your death* as payment," said Wolfclaw.

"Shut your insolent mouth. I can offer you anything you desire. I offer the head of Drak-North... for your soul. I will deliver his bloody head to you on a spike before nightfall. I will make no offer such as this again. Submit to your destiny."

"My soul belongs to me, and I do not share."

"Accept your fate and the fate of your Warshield... fools." She waved her great hand and knocked Wolfclaw from his feet. We will meet again soon... *highwayman.* "As Warshield walked among the ruins of the palace of Bones, one soldier noticed a breathing Hrothgorn soldier.

"This one lives and breathes. What am I to do with him?"

"Bring him to me," ordered Queen Thuireld.

The soldiers helped the gigantic Hroth soldier to his feet and brought him to the queen despite his reluctance. The Hrothgorn soldier looked upon the glorious wingspan of Queen Thuireld and began to tremble in fear. The winged queen drew her massive sword from its scabbard and held it over the Hrothgorn soldier.

"Help our cause or accept your death instead."

"I am sworn to serve my King. There is no other above King Drak-North... I also have no wish to die tonight, dread queen." He trembled at the sight of the levitating, glowing apparition before him. He was used to the ghouls in the Palace of Bones. He had seen the cruel torture of the meek. He witnessed so many abominations but had never seen such a vision. Queen Thurield's armor was gold with silver inlay. She wore a half-crown upon her head, which was covered with long red locks almost to her waist. Her stare was enough to burn a hole in the recipient.

"Make your choice Hrothgorn. You cannot have it both ways."

"Who...are... you?" the Hrothgorn asked in a quivering voice. "I am terrified of you and have never been fearful of any being before."

"I am your Queen. Bend the knee before me," she demanded once again. "Kneel, and I will spare you. You will serve me and become part of Warshield. Help us put an end to the tyrannical reign of King Drak-North."

The Hrothgorn soldier dropped his sword to the dirt.

"No tricks, Hrothgorn! We will drop you where you stand," threatened the Queen.

Tears began to stream down the Hrothgorn's face, and he realized he did not know he was capable of crying. Embarrassed, he stood before his Queen. "I...am not weak. You will never see a tear from me again, your majesty. I am Asgorn, son of Ramshorn, the executioner. I was taught to show no mercy, but you have spared me. I am at your service...." He slowly and thoughtfully bowed to his queen."I want no more war and no more death. I am finished with it."

"Asgorn, arise and meet your new life. Together we will forge ahead and bring peace and freedom to all. Follow Svæin. He is a freedom fighter and a brave soul. Stay with him and learn the ways of Warshield," said the Queen.

"Our new Queen seems to be accepting her new role rather well," said Wolfclaw.

"Yes indeed," said Odious-Forge as he contemplated another course of action. He had murdered King Geir'wolf Tin'Old, King Falstuf Tin'Old, the lost prince, and King Falstuf Tin'Old the younger. Queen Thuireld must be next according to his curse. A single tear rolled down his face for the first time.

Chapter Thirty-Two

THE FLIGHT OF THE WINTERHAWK

Date: Dimension of Odin 126 AD

"Pack your things. I've come to take you home"-Peter Gabriel

"I must know this. Are we fighting for honor? There is no honor in death...only darkness and the deafening sound of silence," he said.

"Long ago, I took an oath to fight for peace and peace alone. I broke that oath in my thirst for vengeance. I could have turned back at any time and let this journey fail. It would have been easier," lamented Wolfclaw.

"You could have returned to the Hall of the Ancients and regaled the old ones with stories of the road," said Fältskog.

"That would have been much easier to tell stories," he said in an elevated voice. "I could have saved the lives of all those who have died serving the Fellowship that bears my name. That also would have been easier. I could have turned back... but I kept thinking of what we told Tor'Bjorn when we persuaded him to come with us...."

"I know of the things that persuaded Tor'Bjorn, but I remain... doubtful. All those in the great hall would still be with us, "said

Fältskog. They were our eldest friends, and they are *dead*. As if we had killed them. Our hands remain stained with their blood."

Wolfclaw grabbed the old man by his tunic and pulled him close enough to his face that he could count every whisker. He spoke in a barely audible voice as Fältskog struggled to break free. "Everyone involved had to search their soul to discover what was inside them and what manner of man or woman they were. Each was to make a decision. You...had a choice to make, even you... *Fältskog*. This was your own choice and no one else. What has happened here belongs to me. It belongs to you and Svæin, Olaf, and Queen Valorii!" Do not excuse yourself." Wolfclaw released Fältskog and threw him to the ground.

The two men locked eyes for a moment, and Wolfclaw abruptly turned. "Captain Old-Turas lost his entire crew and the North Hundrun, and yet he continues to fight," added Wolfclaw as he walked away.

The morning sun rose like an emperor over all it ruled. Warshield and the Fellowship of Wolfclaw gathered in the ruins of the Palace of Bones. The Queen emerged from her tent in full armor, shining like gold. She turned to face her people.

"There are things worth dying for and things for which we would be willing to kill. If we cannot stand as men...as humans, and fight for what is right, then we are *not* truly alive. Fight for the woman and children," spoke the Queen in a voice she did not recognize.

Warshield raised their swords, hammers, and axes, and a battle cry erupted."

"Fight for the dead of the Hall of the Ancients. Fight for the heroes gone before. Fight for our friend Tor'Bjorn the Cobbler. Most of all, friends, I fight for you. I say to you this day. At this precise moment, King Drak-North retreats further to the north. Thane Wolfclaw will continue to lead the offense to destroy Drak-North and his Hrothgorn demons. Follow him as always. Wolfclaw the brave, you have my word I will find Drak-North," promised the Queen.

The Winged Queen Valorii Thuireld stood in the middle of the fellowship, opened her new wings, and rose from the ground surrounded by a glowing light.

SALVATORE' DeBella

She rose into the sky where she could have a vantage point to watch King Drak-North's movements. She took flight, she surveyed all below her and realized…. She could hear the sounds of birds in the air and flutes and pipes from a minstrel's band, and… *she could fly*. Meanwhile, Odious-Forge knew what he must do but fell on his face in agony. He loved Valorii Thuireld as much as all the others.

Asgorn the Hroth continued to march with Warshield and serve his new Queen. It was said of him there was no better subject to be had in the entire realm. He marched next to Svæin in the move to the North.

"I may know where Drak-North is hiding…," offered Asgorn.

"Why had you not mentioned this before?" said Svæin.

"I had to be sure you would not kill me after you found out what you needed to know," he admitted.

"You have my word as an ancient and as a warrior. Our Queen trusts you, so in turn, I also do."

"I believe he is in the hidden caves of War'mouth. There may be soldiers there with him in great numbers. I had often heard of training grounds there. It would seem a suitable place to hide for a scoundrel."

"You may have just helped to even the scales of the war," said Wolfclaw.

"If you ask me… the first chance that dirty bastard gets, he will split your head with an ax," added Fältskog aside. "I mean, after all, he is a Hrothgorn. Have you forgotten who they are?"

"We will trust him and believe him until he gives us a reason not to…do you understand? This is not a suggestion but a direct order," said Wolfclaw sternly.

Fältskog walked away with a sour look. "I wonder when all of us will have enough of your shite for one lifetime?" he said, mumbling under his breath.

"Keep an eye on the Hrothgorn until we get further north," Wolfclaw said aside to Svæin, ignoring the curse from Fältskog. No sooner had he spoken than an arrow flew past his helmet. He could smell the acrid stench in the air of the Clan of the bear. Wolfclaw and the company took cover behind a group of trees as the arrows continued to fly. Above the ridge, almost out of view, was a line of Hrothgorn bowmen supporting the Bear Clan. Wolfclaw remained quiet in his position. Sweat ran into his eyes and down his beard into his mouth. He could taste his fear as the smell in the air became more pungent. The bear-men were close now. Wolfclaw signaled to the soldiers on his left flank to move closer to the ridge to gain an advantage. The Hroth bowmen rained arrows upon their position as Warshield took cover. Ingegärd, the Witch Queen of war, was making her presence felt again.

"Give us your prisoner, filthy human trash, and we will not torture you before we kill you. Turn Asgorn over to us now, and we will be merciful with your deaths," said the lead Hroth soldier.

"We have no such prisoner here," replied Wolfclaw.

"Keep up the lie; it will be worse for you and your men when we get to you."

"I only require one thing from you. Give me this, and I will *let you* live," said Wolfclaw turning the tables on his enemies.

"There is no bargain to be had today, Warshield. I smell man fear. It has a stench like none other. It smells sweet to Hrothgorn."

"Bring me the head of your king... mounted on the handle of your battle-ax."

"Enough talk! It is now time to die."

Asgorn stood up before the soldiers of Warshield. "I am not a prisoner. I remain with Warshield of my own free will. I serve Queen Thuireld, and I am no longer a subject to the tyrant Hrothgorn Drak-North."

"Die with the traitors. Drak-North will hear of your treason, and torture will await you for your reward."

Wolfclaw pulled Asgorn down with the rest of Warshield. "Are ya trying to get killed, ya beastie?" he asked. We will need your help later, no doubt, and you cannot just go and get yourself killed."

"I did not want them to destroy you because of me. I have done too many bad things already in my life. I care not to add to them."

"Just keep down, laddie, and stay close to us," said Svæin.

A charge signaled from above the ridge, causing the Hroth soldier to fire several rounds of arrows in the direction of Warshield. The Bear-Clan spilled over the hill in a sea of beasts on all fours. They were large and black and held shields of wood and short swords. They roared a terrifying war cry as if possessed as they ran down the hill to the waiting Warshield. Wigmir stepped over Warshield and squashed several of the bears under his giant feet while raining down ice from above. The Hrothgorn arrows bounced from his icy skin and fell broken to the earth.

"Come to us, you beasts! Die under Wigmir's feet," he bellowed.

Asgorn seemed to have no fear as he ran into the skirmish. The sound of clashing steel and war cries broke the forest's silence. Blood pounded inside Wolfclaw's helmet. *I must move the men up the hill,* he thought. He barked out orders as he ran. " Prepare to follow me up the hill as I lead...."

"No... we need you here to be a symbol to Warshield for our fight," reasoned Svæin.

Wolfclaw appeared to be angered by this. "A leader that does not lead the charge upon the enemy is no leader but a true coward and thief among men... charge up the hill! Let us give these bastards a mouthful of Warshield."

The army ascended to the rushing bears and clashed powerful steel with them. Many of them lie dead in the path of Warshield. Several soldiers lie dead in the clash after being bitten and having their throats ripped out by the berserkers.

"They are just men. They only look like bears. Be not fooled by *their* delusions," bellowed Svæin. "Slaughter them all."

Steel clashed with steel, and flesh clashed with flesh. The sound of men and the roaring bear men caused a frightening wave of noise echoing through the mountains. Shields were splintered, and armor was pierced. When it was all over, Warshield managed to slay all of the approaching bear clan and left the carcasses for the buzzards.

Wolfclaw and some of his men approached the top of the knoll and spotted an incredible sight in the clearing. Drak-North and his remaining Hrothgorn had fashioned a makeshift throne in the forest. They had fallen trees and a throne chair from logs and grass. Drak-North sat on the throne as if nothing had happened to his palace or army. He was flanked by at least a rank of Hrothgorn soldiers.

"Here, we will raise a new Palace of Bones! We will use the bones of Warshield and their leaders. I want the skull of their leader, what is his name…Eagle-claw, Bear-Claw, or something Claw?"

"Wolfclaw, my liege," answered a Hroth soldier.

"Yes, I want his skull. Bring it to me at once. I want to drink mead from it. If you do not bring it to me, substitute your worthless skull for his. They have destroyed the Palace of Bones. Quench the fire the peasants set with their blood and do not stop until it is extinguished. We will see their brazen bravery now!"

Warshield and the Fellowship of Wolfclaw waited at the top of the knoll to take action. Each member desired a part in the victory over Drak-North.

"Let us crush them under our feet?" asked Wigmir.

"Let us meet them face to face!" said Svæin.

"I will run them through with my sword," boasted Olaf. "There are too many of them. I might need some help to defeat them."

"Stand fast, everyone and wait for orders from our Queen," said Wolfclaw.

"Together, we will fall upon them and slay them all," ordered the Queen.

The remainder of Warshield, Queen Thuireld, Wigmir, and a handful of pirates charged the hill. The Hrothgorn were caught unaware and tried to scatter into the forest while drawing their greasy black and dirty broadswords.

"This one is for Wigmir," said the ice giant as he crushed several Hrothgorn under his feet.

Several Hrothgorn were felled by cross-bolts as they rushed down the hill. The sound of the banging of the firesticks came from behind the throne. Hrothgorn soldiers threw their bodies on King Drak-North.

"Damn it to Hades! One of those fire rocks just got me on my shoulder, boy," Svæin said to Olaf. "Look out for 'em. They will get ya!"

Asgorn the Hroth charged at his former companions in the name of Queen Thuireld. "I will defeat the Hrothgorn and make my promise to the queen come true!"

"Just keep that big head of yours down, beastie," warned Svæin. "Yer too big of a target, my boy!"

A fire –rock cut through Asgorn's chest, and then one flew through his head. He fell to the ground like a huge pine tree in the forest. Svæin came to his side and knelt over the dying Hrothgorn. "I am sorry, my boy…," said Svæin. "If there would be anything I could do to save you, I would."

"It is no matter. I have already been saved. Tell my queen… no matter… she knows," said Asgorn as he slipped away.

"Queen Thuireld stood in the middle of the fray witnessing this, stood straight, and opened her entire wingspan. The site was unsettling for the Hrothgorn soldiers who had never seen her before, and several of them ran heads down into the forest to escape. As she was bathed in bright white light, she brushed a wing roughly in the direction of the enemy. It threw five soldiers against the trees in the background, knocking them out as they fell to the ground quivering in death.

One remained. As the fellowship of Wolfclaw stood staring at the one lone survivor huddled in a ball behind the throne, Wolfclaw ordered him to come out. "Hrothgorn! Come and show yourself to us at once!"

As the Hrothgorn rose from behind the throne, his identity became known. It was King Drak-North himself. He stood and faced his enemies with the defiance he was known for.

"You have a wolf claw in your face!" said Drak-North. You have a wolf claw in your face…," he increased in volume and anger.

"What of it? That should be the least of your problems right now," said Wolfclaw.

"You have a wolf claw in your face!" he screamed and fought while spit flew from his mouth. He was being held by several Warshield soldiers as he was straining every sinew to get to Wolfclaw. Drak-North screamed unintelligibly through tears and fluids running from his face. Wolf-claw, wolf-claw…"

"Wait…That is all you can say to your executioner?" said Wolfclaw. Why are you concerned with my face?"

Drak-North breathed heavily through his screams and the shock of recognition and spoke. "On the day my mother died, the leader of the soldiers was a man who had a claw in his face."

"What difference does it make who it was?" bellowed Wolfclaw as he drew his dagger and put it to the throat of Drak-North. "In the name of Queen Valorii Thuireld, ruler of the realm, I execute you for crimes against the kingdom and its' people.

"Warwok," said Drak-North softly. "Warwok… is your name."

"How do you know that?" asked Wolfclaw. Did you hear one of my men call me that? Prepare to die." As Wolfclaw drew back for the final blow of death, Drak-North cried out in a voice of pain and suffering.

"You killed my mother. You murdered her. You killed her with a crossbow while aiming for me."

Wolfclaw dropped the dagger to his waist and grew deathly pale.

"She was peaceful and beautiful, and you destroyed her!" The King shrieked with a raw voice. He struggled to break free from his bonds. "I want to kill you with my bare hands. I want to squeeze your neck until you are no more! Talk! Talk you, treacherous rogue! Talk! What do you have your say for yourself?"

Wolfclaw was too stunned to form a response.

"I ran far away and was wounded and maimed by Wormouth the terrible," said the King.

"Do you not see what you have done, Wolfclaw?" asked Fältskog. "You made him what he is! This is your fault!"

"Enough of that talk. I am tired of your mouth! I will run you through. Wolfclaw is no more at fault than you," said Svæin to Fältskog.

Wolfclaw hung his head in front of the trembling King Drak-North. He trembled not from fear but pure anger as he gnashed his teeth and clenched his fists.

"I cannot kill you. I cannot justify this as revenge for your deeds, as horrible as they may be," said Wolfclaw. I have wanted nothing more than to remove your head as soon as I laid eyes on you… and now I can do nothing."

"Do what you must! You began destroying my life when I was young, and you should finish your ghoulish work. You killed my mother in front of me. You call me a monster, but you are a monster, also. You cannot justify this! I lost an arm, a leg, and one of my eyes because my mother was not there! You destroyed my palace and killed my Hrothgorn soldiers. Kill me now! You must finish!"

"This whole campaign has been a mistake that cost many men their lives! I warned you it was a mistake! We have rescued our people, execute him and let us go home," Fältskog pleaded.

"We have already pledged loyalty to our leader and our Queen," said Olaf.

"We will do as she wishes."

The Queen appeared to freeze and could not give an order as she was not accustomed to such power. A vibrating metallic-sounding voice emitted from her scabbard.

"Your Grace, my dear queen Thuireld, Drak-North has done terrible things to the kingdom and its people. He must pay a dearer price. I would never question you or your authority, I owe my life to you, but he must pay with his life," pleaded Kilmister.

Drak-North struggled beneath his bonds and managed to shake loose and escape the soldiers holding him. He rushed forward and knocked two men and Wolfclaw from their feet. He bent over Wolfclaw and grasped him around his neck, sinking his claws into flesh.

"Now you will pay for your crimes, and my mother-"

Before he could get the words out, Kilmister flew from the Queen's scabbard and drove his blade through the chest of the mighty Hrothgorn.

"Villains!" spoke Drak-North as he fell into eternal sleep. Svæin helped Wolf to his feet, and Olaf returned Kilmister to the Queen.

"Your sword has more guts than all of you put together!" said Fältskog.

The group stood silent at what had happened.

"Bury him, "ordered the Queen.

"Let the birds pick his carcass. I will not bury this ghoul," said insolent Fältskog.

"You will do as the Queen has decreed or face my steel. He deserves the dignity of a burial," said Svæin.

Fältskog began the process while muttering.

"Let us begin our march to the North. Let us go home. We have given all we have to give. Valorii placed her hand on the sword. "You are brave, and when we arrive in Arom, I will Knight you."

It was said that if a sword could smile, Kilmister had done it.

Later that night, Fältskog was discovered running by himself to the tree line to the left of the flanks. He had dropped his ax and was running full force away from Warshield.

"Stop at once and return to your post," ordered Svæin. As Fältskog reached the tree line, Svæin drew an arrow and pulled it into his bow, aiming it at the fleeing Fältskog.

"Too many of us have died already. No more death," said Wolfclaw as he grabbed the arrow before it could fly. "Let me deal with him later. We have far to travel."

As the soldiers reached the crest of the ridge, the Hrothgorn bowmen retreated to the forest below. Warshield was able to slay some of them in their retreat.

A lone bolt from a crossbow came from the tree line where Fältskog had retreated. It traveled the long distance and found its mark sinking into the unprotected area under the back of Wolfclaw's helmet. It exploded deep into his neck, causing him to fall forward to the forest floor. Svæin and Olaf ran to his side while the others tried to see from where the arrow had flown.

"This is a Warshield bolt! Damn him... the treacherous pig! Bring me the traitor Fältskog who hides in the tree line!" cried Svæin. "Bring him to me alive so I might make him regret the last few moments of his treacherous life."

They rolled Wolfclaw over as he opened his eyes to what was above him in the sky. The Winterhawk circled above in wide majestic circles. Wolfclaw seemed to recognize him.

"Wolf... hold fast. We called for Odious- Forge ... he will know what to do," said Svæin as he knelt beside his dying friend.

The Winterhawk tightened his circles as he descended to earth. He approached Wolfclaw, became much larger, and stood as tall as a Hrothgorn when he landed gently. He spoke with a calm voice.

"Good Wolfclaw, it is time," the giant bird said.

"I had supposed so. It seems I knew it all along. I am not completed with my work here. This cannot be how it all ends. Must I go now?"

Svæin, Olaf, and the rest of the fellowship stared in disbelief as the Winterhawk spoke.

"I have followed you all of your days. You have seen me. You must have known this. I know of your bravery."

"I am not brave… I am a scoundrel… and a rogue. My thirst for revenge shrouded my judgment," Wolfclaw said in a broken, painful voice." I killed a boy's mother and created a monster."

"If you are not brave, then there is no such thing as bravery," said Svæin." If you are a scoundrel, then all of us are scoundrels. We would be proud to be so. Let my spirit possess all that it means to be a rogue if it means to be like you. You have restored me, my friend."

"I am here to bring you to the forests of valor, where you have much work to do. Some souls await your company, good Wolfclaw. We have come to take you home," spoke the Winterhawk. "You will be in most excellent company."

"Am I going to Valhalla?"

"Valhalla is later. There is much to do first," promised the Winterhawk.

"Listen to your Queen, my fellowship and brave men of Warshield. Would that I could join you on the rest of this quest, but it is not to be. You must hold to our purpose… no matter the cost. We must recover what was lost from our Kingdom."

The Winterhawk grasped Wolfclaw in his talons and rose into the sky and soon out of sight. All of the bravery, valor, and ancient wisdom Wolfclaw had imparted unto the fellowship, and Warshield stayed with them as he soared high above.

His voice rang through their memories and ears, *"I have grave counsel today, brave warriors of Arom. There will come a time in our realm when men have no honor, for it has escaped them. There will come a time when men have no bravery, honesty, or integrity. All of these things will have been left in the past. It is entrusted to our fellowship and us to see this does not come to pass."*

CHAPTER THIRTY-THREE

THE FOREST OF VALOR

———— ⚭ ————

Date: Dimension of Thor (2229 AD)

"I speak to you through the corridors of time...."

The flight of the Winterhawk took the dying Warwok Wolfclaw Thur'Gold deep into the forests of the land of the North. They flew through the valleys, and the mountain passes, soaring ever higher over the desolation caused by the Hrothgorn of Drak-North. They flew far across the sea of darkness. What was below the murky waters of the sea was only known in the realm of the travelers and the dead heroes in their valiant battle cries. That was no concern from the Winterhawk because he was on an errand. The dying old man in the Winterhawk's talons brought remembrance to his ancient mind. Wolfclaw had visions of the bravery of his past. His imagination-filled memory slipped back into the pockets of time reserved in the old man's memory. He fell into a dream...

"Today, the people of the villages are safe from the monster's bloodthirsty lust for death," Thur'Gold announced as he pulled his sword from the beast's lifeless body.

"All hail the bravery of good Wolfclaw Thur'Gold, " the people chanted. "Our village has been spared the wrath of the dragon Killowrath."

Wolfclaw remembered another battle and what he told the villagers after he clashed with the sea serpent…. "I am afraid I failed you, good people of the Southlands. Killowrath has made his horrible destruction on the land and your people before I could stop him. I regret my dire failure. I have failed in my quest to protect you," lamented Wolfclaw as he faced a crowd of townsfolk. A man eagerly spoke from the group, "My Lord Thur'Gold, our hearts are with you in your quest to save us from the wrath of this beast. We have traveled far beyond the cities of the south, pleading for help. None came. My family is safe tonight because of you and your sword."

Brave Wolfclaw's dying eyes filled with tears as he remembered the words of the good people of the Southlands who needed him so.

His mind drifted to the sight of Valorii flying to take her place among the great Queens of the past and present. *How could I have known?* He imagined doing battle with the Hrothgorn as they confronted the despot Drak-North. He imagined the Hrothgorn ordering his men to "Lay down your weapons of war!

"Come and pry them from us as we hold fast even as we die," replied Warshield in their resolve. Wolfclaw smiled at such a thing.

As he continued to soar over the land and sea in the talons of the Winterhawk, Wolfclaw Thur'Gold reviewed what he saw on the ground below. Just as one would watch a play, all of the events of his life came alive before him. The North Hundrun roared to life, led by her fearless and ruthless Captain Old-Turas. *"We will have the gold of the Hrothgorn, and we will swim in it like a river!"* promised Old-Turas.

He saw Tor'Bjorn the Cobbler laughing in the destruction of the Palace of Bones. *"There was metal in this meek maker of shoes. The bravest among us…he did the job that was set before an entire army by himself. We will never see his like again."*

Fältskog screamed through Wolfclaw's old ears. "I see thousands of men fighting and dying for one man's revenge!"

"No… treacherous Fältskog, they fight for their families and farms. They fight for what is right and good without considering my revenge. It matters not to those who fight. They fight for their own."

The Harvester of Eyes screamed from the Isle of Kelda as the Albatross left her shores. Wolfclaw could still see and hear the howling of the old man as he was left exiled in his own spiritual and physical blindness. *"I know that you require payment, old man. Your death is your pay.*

Ghidorwrath the horrible raised his ugly head again and slithered to the south. *Queen Thuireld must hold fast!"*

The Bear-Clan and Hrothgorn soldiers regrouped to the North and trudged their way to the south. Wolfclaw looked to the ground below from the sky and saw the Witch Queens' seething anger and revenge, throwing lightning to the ground. Amid the torrential downpour and thunder, the dirty faces of new Hrothgorn rose from the ground as if the earth gave birth to new savages to horrify the land.

Wolfclaw peered down from his lofty vantage point and witnessed Odious-Forge the Alchemist as he hurled himself from the cliffs and crashed to the rocks below. Wolfclaw had no warning that Forge would do such a thing and had no way to stop him. He was gone.

Svæin the Elder, young Olaf, and the Hall of the Ancients stood together, looking to the North and the battle to come. *Warshield is ready in its resolve.*

Wolfclaw's eyes closed and dimmed to the light, and all was blackness. Eternal sleep overtook the old warrior. The sound of the great horn echoed throughout the sky. Men of iron and men of steel blow the ram's horn called the "Bukkehorn." It played for the souls of the dead heroes.

The Winterhawk placed the body of the dying Wolfclaw on the deck of a great Longship and turned to fly away forever.

"Sleep well... while these brave souls attend you, brave Wolfclaw. I have attended you all these many years. Now the mantle will fall to another," said the Winterhawk as he rose into the sky.

A crew appeared on the deck of the massive longboat to carry the warrior to the Forest of valor. The souls of all those who had gone before escorted the solemn procession. The destination was the final resting place until Wolfclaw could be received unto Valhalla.

The ship's deck, named *Father Pine*, smacked the waves of the sea before it. It swallowed water like a drowning sailor after a swell. The crew attended to her as a child to an aging mother. As holes appeared in the deck, they were just as quickly nailed over with old doors and boards that had left their posts many years before. The storm was enormous and punishing and beat against the steel sides of Father Pine. The ship had brought other heroes to Valhalla to kneel before Odin for many centuries but had never encountered a storm likened to this. The keel master held on with all his might with the help of five other brave men of the sea. Ordering the oarsman to drop oar was useless, for the swell was covering the oar ports. Old Wolfclaw rested. The water crashed against the hull as if smashing against mighty cliffs.

As the men stared into the blackness of the sea of the night, a form began to appear. The helmsmen screamed in a raw voice, "Jörmungandr!" The sea serpent had been spotted on the sea many times. Most knew to avoid the solemn procession out of respect for the hero. This Jörmungandr knew no such consideration. The sea monster had eight heads fanged in a toothy array, and the heads were covered in horns and scales. The Jörmungandr shrieked angrily that such a trespass had been done unto him. He slammed his massive tentacles against the ship smashing the hull to bits. The sailors dove into the sea to save them or were swept off by the monster.

Wolfclaw's lifeless body was swept into the sea as the ship sank to her eternal death on the bottom of the sea of the Forests of Valor. The Jörmungandr slunk into the depths, never to be seen again. *Father Pine* rested eternally on the bottom, never returning another warrior to his reward to kneel before his god.

With each lap of the sea, his body was pushed further into the sand and became covered over at the sea bottom. The spiral tide flowed along with the corpse of Wolfclaw, washing it ashore. The sea bells tolled as his corpse came to rest in the surf, covered with sea plants and urchins. His dead eyes stared up into the nothingness of the sky. A storm raged on the island. Lightning flashed all about, and the thunder of the gods made their presence known. As the torrent of rain pounded the dead face of Wolfclaw Thur'Gold, seven phantoms rose from the surf further out from the breakers and approached the body. They were clad in old armor and carried mace, ax, and hammer. They marched through the waves until they reached the shore and the corpse of Wolfclaw.

One of the figures reached into the surf and lightly touched the face of the dead man. "Wolfclaw Warwok Thur'Gold, I command you in the name of Odin and Rothl'Orca to open your eyes and see me where I stand," he said in a whisper. The rain continued to pound on Wolfclaw's face, and he did not move. A moment passed as the armor-clad apparitions watched over the body. The corpse began to jerk and twitch in violent contractions. Life ran through the body as if it had been overcome by fire and lightning. He started to cough and spit water from his lungs as he struggled to clear his eyes to see what was before him. Wolfclaw sat in the surf and struggled to open his eyes to see the apparitions before him.

What is this? How can it be that I have been interrupted in my journey to Valhalla? Wolfclaw thought. "Who are you? What do you want with me?"

The ghost raised his hand, and the storm became instantly silent.

"Who are you that you can silence the storm? I feel like I have met you somewhere."

"I am part of a great chorus of voices that have been with you from the beginning of your quest."

"Are you the Horsemen?" Wolfclaw asked as the apparitions helped him stand and walk further up the beach to a grassy area under a large tree, where he sat down.

"We are what you have believed us to be and were sent into the world to fulfill the will of our god. We were nailed to trees by the Hrothgorn in the Holy Forest along with our horses.

"I blamed the wizard Odious-Forge for that," said Wolfclaw. "It seemed logical."

"No, it was nothing more than a sport for the Hrothgorn. However, in life, we were the *dragon masters* of the Realm of Arom. When the dragons ceased to be, we rode horses. We are now part of the *Destiny of Tyr*, the gods of war, justice, and order. We have an offer from Tyr directly for you, Warwok Thur'Gold," said the ghost.

"I am no good to you or the effort of the war gods of Tyr! I am certainly not worthy of being in the presence of the dragon masters of Arom. I am a dead man bound for Valhalla. I took a bolt from a crossbow in the neck from one of my men. I am dead! Let me rest. I have done enough. Now it is time for my sleep," said Wolfclaw.

"You speak well, dead man. Here is your offer-"

"No- let me attend to Valhalla! I have earned the view of the shores of gold. Let me be. I have spent the better part of my life earning this honor. I have spent my life as a thief and a rogue only to gain this honor. Do not steal this from me!"

"Do not let the tales with which you pacify yourself get in the way of the truth Warwok Thur'Gold. Do you not see that the entirety of your life has been presented as a stage play to bring you to this exact place and the precise moment in time? This is your choice. Live as an immortal being with us, and serve or become a corpse again and rot on this island. The seabirds will pick you to pieces until there is nothing left but bones. What is your wish? Come with us and *live forever* or *die forever?*"

"I am of no greatness or consequence...I do not understand."

"You were always looking for greatness in others, but it has always been within your soul. Tyr awaits your answer."

"Why have you chosen me?" Wolfclaw asked.

"You are a descendant of the Destiny of Tyr. That is why you had to walk through the test of time with us. We never left you. Your valiant battle with the Jörmungandr showed us that we were not dealing with just any mortal man. No man alive has fought a Jörmungandr and returned to tell the tale. We were sent to follow you all of your days until your death."

"That seems a little ghoulish to wait until I died to ask me to serve Tyr," observed Wolfclaw. You could have killed me a long time ago and in a less painful manner than I just died. The arrow in the neck was very painful."

"We cannot cause a death unless it is in mortal combat," replied Tyr.

"I know it had to be so. It just figures there would be rules."

"We are here, and you are now set with an offer, and you will be at our call and command. You will fulfill all of the wishes of the Destiny of Tyr."

Wolfclaw paused for just a moment and accepted the offer of the apparitions. Power and life flowed through his body. He was quite startled to see his hands and arms were free of scars and looked much younger. "My hands. My scars...where are they?"

"Look for the scars no more. Your face is young as it was in the days of old. Do not fear... all have been renewed. All of your muscles and sinews are renewed. Your bones will no longer ache in battle. Your hair is its original red, along with your beard. Grasp your sword. Wield it as in the days of old."

Wolfclaw began to tremble as he drew his sword, and it burst into a full flame before his eyes. He was wide-eyed in fear and apprehensive joy as the flame followed the length of the blade. "What does this mean?" he asked.

"You have a portal of flame to your heart's desire. Your sword will light your way. Let it burn bright for all to see, and let it burn deeply for your enemies!"

"I will use it well." His countenance turned once again to his friends. "I must return and assist my queen and her army! Had I known Valorii Thuireld was *the chosen one,* I would have protected her, and I would have seen to her well-being-?"

The Destiny interrupted Wolfclaw. "She was *not* the chosen one. She is merely the queen. Being the chosen one is a fairy tale. There was never such a thing. If there ever was a chosen one, that would be you."

Wolfclaw hung his head in thought as tears filled his eyes. "I cannot leave," he said in a resolved tone. "I am at your service but owe my comrades and Queen so much."

"We did not lead you this far to abandon you. Your people will be safe and far from harm. From this day forward, you are an immortal resurrected being and part of the Destiny of Tyr. Your name shall be *Dreki-Vargr* or Dragonwülf! Show all who care to see...your heart of courage!"

He began to feel faint, and his eyes grew dark. A veil was placed over them, and he fell again into a deep sleep.

Chapter Thirty-Four

THE OLD GODS RETURN

————— ✦ —————

Date: Dimension of Hod 2296 AD
Miles Above the Earth and the UnderForest

The old gods had returned. They decided in a council the cities would be swept into the sea and be subjected to death and destruction. The ancient god Tyr was one of the oldest gods known to man, and now he had returned when the people least expected it. The old gods hated the presence of Tyr, the god of weapons and war.

"Even as ye are carried as dead upon your shield, the fight will be yours. If ye fought with bravery with all the goodness in your chest, you would die a happy death. Ye will die a good death... still... peace is a better alternative." These are the words of Tyr.

While he tried to seek peace with the giant wolf Fenrir, Tyr put his hand in the mouth of the wolf/creature as a show of treaty or truce. The old gods, jealous of Tyr's attempt at reconciliation with enemies, decided to capture Fenrir and tie him while Tyr had his hand in the wolf's mouth. Fenrir bit off Tyr's hand, leaving him the one-armed god.

From that moment in time, Tyr formed a council and enlisted their help to direct the conduct of war throughout the earth. He called this council the Destiny of Tyr. Then the mantle of each time dimension was placed on each council member.

The founding council members were seven great gods: Frigg, Odin, Loki, Thor, Hod, Heimdall, and Dragnon Shadowland.

Dragnon Shadowland, as he was known, was different from the other members of the council and the Destiny of Tyr. He seemed unconcerned with the concepts of Tyr but was obsessed with competition and victory at all costs. He would have all the glory for himself. He would soon be known by another name known only to the Destiny of Tyr.

The Long Ship cut through the air like a sword through the snowdrift. The ship's bells rang throughout the darkness of night and space. The stars hung in the sky and lit the way for the giant wooden boat. The rowers pulled in unison. There were twenty-five each on the port and starboard sides. "Pull! Pull! Pull!" The Captain barked his orders like a military man with decades of experience. A Winterhawk was perched on the ship's bow to lead the way.

The south side of the sky shone like a lighthouse in the distance leading the ship to its destination. Dragonwülf opened his eyes from a long, tumultuous sleep. He was sleeping in his new quarters on a ship he did not know. He had just awoken from the dreams of his last days in the Kingdom of Arom. He worried about his friends and his Queen and that he had left them to face Drak-North and the Hrothgorn alone. He sat up on the edge of the bunk just in time to see the Captain enter his quarters. The familiar man laughed when they met eyes.

"Not exactly what I thought you would look like, you broken down old dog!" the Captain said while clenching a pipe between his teeth.

"They did not help your appearance, Old-Turas," answered Dragonwülf. Why are you here? How did you get here?"

"Let us just say The Destiny needed someone to pilot their wood pile, and I got here the same way you did. Now I am the Captain of this bucket of splintered wood. They call it "The Shadow," answered Old Turas. "I got my stupid ass killed in a fight with Fältskog after Svæin captured him. It was not much of a fight. He waited until I was distracted and stabbed me in the neck. I suppose Fältskog has a thing for necks," said Old-Turas.

"He killed you also?" Dragonwülf asked as if he could not believe what he was hearing.

"The rotten bastard killed both of us," said Old-Turas. "If it helps you to feel better, Svæin took his head after they sent me to sea. That is what those Destiny fellows told me anyway. Hope he felt that in *his* neck for a little while."

"I very much misjudged him. I thought he had character and honor," said Dragonwülf.

"Never mind him. Now we have much work to do."

"What? What do we have to do? I have not been told," answered Dragonwülf.

"All I know is that they gave me a choice between staying dead and being Captain of this ship. Not much of a choice."

"I am to be called Dragonwülf now."

Old Turas shrugged. "I suppose it fits you."

"Where are we? Everything is so dark, and I feel like shite," said Dragonwülf.

"Yes, you *look* like shite also. I do not know our location. I was told we are in outer darkness. We are not in the Kingdom of Arom any longer. We are above the world instead of in it," explained Turas. The men were in awe of the wonders of the black sky.

"Are we in the realm of the gods? It is so cold out here. Why is it so cold?" asked Dragonwülf. "If you look down, you can see that round rock floating in the black sky. What is it?"

"I do not know the answers to your questions. I am just as surprised as you are. I must get topside now and mind the crew."

The Destiny brought those robed ghosts or whatever they are to hoist the mainsails. I have to keep them busy. What am I talking about anyway? They are going to work until the end of time if they are told to," said Old- Turas with a chuckle. "I feel like I am wasting my time when I am up there."

"Do you still want to kill me?" asked Dragonwülf.

"I gave up trying for that a long time ago. Everyone keeps trying to do it for me. Besides, you are already dead, but I still *want* to kill you anyway, just for folly," said Old-Turas.

"Just warn me before you do. I am not as young as I used to be. Where are we going?" asked Dragonwülf.

"The Destiny of Tyr has many things for us to do. What those things are, I do not know. I have been told that I am to assist you, but I am not sure what makes you so special to the Destiny."

"Perhaps it is my humble personality."

"I do not suppose I could pay you back for that punch in the face on the North Hundrun."

"You had that coming, ya daft bastard."

"I can see how this is not going to go well for me," said Turas.

Dragonwülf began to explore the new ship and gain his bearings. He walked to the aft portion of the Longboat, where he saw an old man sitting facing the water, smoking a pipe, and visiting with a haggard-looking chap clad in black leather. They were both dressed in odd clothing Dragonwülf had never seen before. He approached the old man and tapped his shoulder. The man turned abruptly.

"Oh, you startled me. I did not mean to jump. I have just had bad experiences on ships," said the man.

"I am Sir Robert Winterfall, and I am not sure how I got here. These Destiny chaps are calling me *Winterhawk*. I am not sure about that name. My new friend here is named…let me try to get this right, my good man. Vik-tor Voro-by-EV… Viktor Vorobyev. He is one of the Tsar's men, I presume."

"That was about 60 years ago. You're way off, old man," said Viktor as he was increasingly panicked.

As the men conversed and tried to gain their bearings, one of the Tyr leaders appeared on the water outside the ship startling everyone. They were accompanied by a younger man in a sailor's uniform, the wizard Odious-Forge, and a holy man named Jarvis Nightwish in very odd temple robes.

"Forge! I saw you break apart on the cliffs of Athgor! You could not have survived that," said Dragonwülf in amazement.

"Indeed, I did not survive. The Destiny of Tyr brought me into their service. How could I say no? Tyr removed a personal curse that has plagued me. The curse that I created was lifted from me. Now I must seek forgiveness from Queen Thuireld. I am afraid that might be impossible given what I have done in the name of revenge."

"See here, you cutthroat! Stand, and I shall give you a good thrashing," ordered the sailor, J.W. Smithson. The moment he recognized Sir Robert Winterfall, he became enraged. "I cannot believe I am staring into a face I never thought I would see again. I refuse to sit back and let you lose another ship." Pointing to Sir Robert, J.W. loudly proclaimed, "I want all of you here to know that this man who was the captain of our ship *ate my body* after I died. He's a bloody cannibal!" said Smithson. "He ate me! My only regret is that I did not kill *him* first!"

"See here, old boy. We are in a different place and a different time, and it is time to release our hold on the past," said Sir Robert.

"If I get my hands round your neck, I am not likely to release my *hold* on you!" threatened Smithson.

"I have not survived this many years just to die *again* on this ship of all places," complained Odious-Forge. "I refuse to be seen in the company of such buffoons as you!"

"What in the hell are you dressed as?" asked a confused Viktor Vorobyev staring directly at the Wizard. Are you one of these Destiny dudes?

"I am here the same way you came," Odious replied. "I serve the Destiny. We are all dead. Do you not know that?"

The robed figure spoke. "Hear me but remain in your silence!" "I am Avat'or of Tyr! We must think as one if we will succeed in our quest." He spoke as a god speaks through the clouds. His voice was deep and booming as thunder but with a touch of age breaking through. He seemed to draw the stars and the moon into his speech as celestial audience members.

Another member of Tyr appeared through the fog.

"Let the seasons hear me tonight. Let the celestial bodies and all near and far hear me tonight. May the darkness fall, the light feast on the night, and my voice be heard. May it be that the shadows must journey a fortnight to join us and rise to hear the truth! Our quest is right, and the eternal gods are to our backs."

"That is the issue," argued Dragonwülf. We do not know where we are bound or what our quest should be."

"Yes, good sir! I was an old man reading in my private *library* when everything around me went black, and I found myself wrapped in seaweed and lying in the breakers. The next thing I know, these chaps from Tyr put me on this bloody ship," said Sir Robert in an indignant tone.

"What is a Lie-bare-e?" asked the Captain. "Do you keep your gold there or other valuables?"

This drew a stare from Sir Robert and Dragonwülf.

Viktor said," I was trying to find four other dudes that crashed their *motorcycles*. Then these beings showed up and brought me to a thousand places, all on the same day! What day is this? It is October 31, 1969... Is it?" He reached into his vest, produced a switchblade knife, and pointed it at his shipmates. "I will stick you like pigs! I got no problem with killing any of you," threatened Viktor. "I gotta get out of here! This whole thing is freaking me out, man!"

Dragonwülf pulled his sword from the sheath on his back and lifted the broad sword in the general direction of the biker. "I can run you through with this, and then I can take your head off with one swipe. You do not have a knife; you have an old lady's knitting needle." With one swipe, Dragonwülf hit the back of the biker's hand with a flat side of the sword, causing the switchblade to fall to the ground. Just leave it there; it will do you no service here."

"I'm just scared, man. I was just looking down a dark hole in Memphis, Tennessee, and *poof*, I'm in the sea," said Viktor.

The holy man Jarvis Nightwish broke his silence and approached the biker with a weapon called a disruptor and pointed it at his head. Avat'or kicked Nightwish's arm and caused him to drop the disruptor. "Put that down, fool! There is no need for killing here," he said.

"That is all quite impossible, gentlemen, because I was in my study in London, it seems like minutes ago," asserted Sir Robert.

"What is a mo-tor-cycle?" asked a confused Captain Turas.

"It's my hog, man. Are you that far behind our conversation?" inquired Viktor.

"I see no swine here," said a more confused Old-Turas.

The answer drew a blank stare from Viktor. "I tell you, I was stalked by dark hooded figures on horseback and couldn't get away. The faster I rode, the faster the horses charged behind me. It was these Destiny people!" said Viktor. "Nothing surprises me anymore."

Out of the waves walked several figures covered in black robes with the same decorations as the messenger of Tyr and stepped into the ship.

"Dragonwülf, I present to you your rogues' gallery of the Destiny of Tyr," said the messenger. "You will command them in your quest."

"I await your direction. I am your servant," said Dragonwulf

"What if I don't want to do this??" asked Viktor. "What if we don't? I don't think I want to go on a 'quest,'"

"You all will remain dead for eternity!"

"We have no choice then. Our only other choice is… *or* be dead? Some choice," complained Sir Robert.

"! This is Jarvis Nightwish from the Jupiter moon colony."

"Is that another world or realm?" asked Dragonwülf. "What is that pointed thing you have?"

"It is called a Disruptor. It kills better and faster than any other method," said Nightwish. "All I have to do is touch it to someone, so do not touch this."

"I also present to you Luciano Cantore," said the messenger. "He belonged to an organization early in Earth's twentieth century. He will be perfect for what we are about to embark upon."

What is that we are going to do? You keep talking about it, but… what," said Viktor.

"I wouldn't be here if my brother and friend hadn't killed me," said Luciano. "I'm not sure *why* I am here either."

"In time, you will know…in time," said the messenger.

Another figure rose from the surf in the same manner.

"I am Hansel Gru'el. They call me The Harvester of Eyes. I can feel the thoughts and emotions of those whose eyeballs I snatch out of their heads."

"Oh my God...how?" asked a flustered Viktor."

The last figure emerged from the surf.

"This is Highwayman Zachariah Boyd from 19th-century earth. We saved him from the hangman," said Destiny.

"Yeah, after I hung...thanks," he said sarcastically.

"So...*Everyone is a time traveler*?" asked Sir Robert. "Who knew that H.G. Welles was right all along?"

"You and they are here for a reason," said the Tyr. "Soon, you will know."

"I don't see how a guy that kills people with a stick, a gangster, an old man who plucks people's eyes out, and a cowboy is going to be useful for anything," said Viktor. "All I know how to do is ride a motorcycle. Oh yeah, that eye-plucking thing is gross, man."

Nonetheless, we will await our orders," said the Avat'or. "You will all be redeemed in time. We speak for the *souls* of those you all have murdered," said Avat'or in a low rumbling voice. "We lament for those you have thrown into early graves."

Viktor was shaking inside from cold and fear. The memories of *murder* crept into his brain. He could still smell the blood and hear the pleading of his last victim.

"He shouldn't have been shootin' off his damn mouth," he thought. "He would still be alive." He tried to calm himself and find a reason for this visitation.

"The Destiny of Tyr represents the god of weapons of war and justice. Many among us remain in chains and have for what seems an eternity. We wait for justice. I say to you that there is no reasoning with evil. We have all seen the monsters in the forests that come to destroy the lives of the kind and meek and sink their fangs into flesh. That is why the Destiny of Tyr exists. I have heard a cry from another realm, and we will answer it," said the third member. We toll the bells under the sea to welcome the age of the Destiny of Tyr. The bells announce our new era and the beginning of our search."

"A search for what?" asked Old Turas.

"A search for what we have lost and for what we must find."

"Damn you creepy bastards and your riddles," said Boyd. "I ain't been able to figure you boys out since I got hung."

Yes...my good man! That is all very well, but I've done nothing wrong. I only wish to return home to England with proof of all this to repair my name. So see here, good fellow, let us just turn around and head for the shore," demanded Sir Robert.

"Not until I find another clipper ship to commandeer or... borrow or... pirate," said Captain Turas.

"Listen to me as I explain," said Avat'or. "Our task has been to bring you all into the fold of the sea. The Destiny of Tyr is to make a reckoning of the universe," explained Avat'or. "This is the nature of things. Dragonwülf fought his battle against the evil in *his* world," said Avat'or. "Good must be balanced with evil, and evil must be matched with the same amount of good. It is the *law* of the Universe. If this law is broken, the universe is out of balance that will set a cataclysmic event in motion that cannot be undone."

"How is that possible? You speak with lies on your tongue... fool," said Dragonwülf.

"We have gathered you together for a certain purpose. We have traveled through time and space to follow and capture one *of our own* who has escaped the Destiny of Tyr. We must stop him as he sweeps evil throughout the universe. He is responsible for the deaths of millions in the Saturn Moon colonies. He destroyed the civilization disguised as an ice giant."

Jarvis Nightwish became enraged upon hearing this. "How will we find him?" asked Jarvis." I will kill him with my bare hands! He will pay for what he has done to my world and people. What is this cutthroat's name?"

"His name is *Dragnon Shadowland,* and his mercy and compassion have been lost in the battlefields of time. He is now known as *Temerator Animarum* or the *Defiler of Souls.* Finding him is the task set before you. We are on our way to the kingdom of Arom, where we will meet with Queen Valorii Thuireld. Her Majesty will go with us as we seek the Defiler. We must find an ice giant name Wigmir. He will hold some answers."

"I have heard that name somewhere in my past," said Jarvis.

"I am sure I know where we can find him," said Dragonwülf. "He is most certainly with the Queen."

CHAPTER THIRTY-FIVE

RETURN TO AROM/ EPILOGUE

———

Date: Dimension of Odin 126 AD

Heroes of the Harvest Moon

"I am the sister of your late King and the Daughter of King Tin'Old, the lost prince," said the Queen.

The crowd had gathered around the palace of stone at the arrival of the winged queen. Many people gasped in audible surprise at her appearance. The King's former guard who escorted the Queen confirmed this fact for the people of Arom.

"Good citizens of Arom! We must move quickly toward the coronation of our new Queen. It will speak to the rest of the world of our resolve for peace," said the royal guard. Bring forth the crown from its lazy resting place on the floor of the palace. Let it rest upon the head of one worthy to bear it."

As the crown was being retrieved, the new Queen spoke to Arom.

"My good people...I am afraid I know very little about being a queen. The truth is that it was thrust upon me. My living sword Kilmister and I are touched by your willingness to support me. I must let him speak as well."

The Queen drew her sword from the scabbard and held it with both hands over her head. Much to the surprise of the people gathered there, Kilmister began to vibrate and speak in a metallic tone.

"I am the Queen's sword, and my name is Kilmister. I am the spirit of a man whose soul the sword possesses. Give our Lady Thuireld, Queen of Arom, all your support and love as much as I do. I would go to the ends of the realm for my Queen, and I wish the same for you."

You flatter me much as I have not yet done anything to earn this," said the Queen.

"You are humble, but the people here should know you are a hero. You destroyed King Drak'North. You saved the lives of many at the battles of Harvest Moon and the Bear Clan. You fought heroically while some more experienced warriors ran to the forest in shame," said Kilmister.

"Before these witnesses in this palace today, I confer upon you, Kilmister, the brave, the title of Knight of the realm. Today you are Sir Kilmister the brave, and you hold the title of the hand of the Queen."

"Thank you, your majesty. I am humbled," said Sir Kilmister.

"Do not be too happy about it. You may be sorry; you are so thankful. From this day forward to the end of days, we will have peace in our time. We will rebuild this city and appoint new elders for the Hall of the Ancients. We ache for the loss of our elders at the hands of Drak'North. We will form an army of willing souls to defend our good city from evil," said the Queen. "Most of all, we will be an oasis for the thirsty and a place of rest for the weary."

The crowd stared in amazement as they fell to their knees individually and in groups until all were on bended knees. It was a new day for Arom, and the realm as Queen Thuireld entered the Palace of Stone and took her place in history.

"I promise the good people of Arom that our history of royal cowardice has come to an end with the death of a quivering fool inside the throne of stone," said the Queen.

The royal guard spoke loudly so he might be heard. "Hear all present so we may present the realm's heroes to you."

One by one, they presented themselves to the Queen on bended knee.

Bless you, Svæin of Warshield. Your service to the Crown is close to my heart. Your bravery in battle has no equal. I confer upon you the title of Knight of the first order. Arise, Sir Svæin the mighty.

For the first time in his life, Svæin was speechless at seeing an ice giant approaching the palace door.

"Welcome, good Wigmir!" said the Queen. You are just in time for your reward! "Kneel, mighty one. Your service to the Crown is close to my heart. Your bravery in battle has no equal. I confer upon you the title of Knight of the first order. Arise, Sir Wigmir!"

Bless you, Olaf, Son of Gandor. Your service to the Crown is close to my heart. Your bravery in battle has no equal. I confer upon you the title of Knight of the first order. Arise, Sir Olaf Son of Gandor." The Queen became strangely silent as if to fight back the tears. "This is a joyous time but also a time to mourn our lost comrades in arms. We can never forget the sacrifice of Sir Tor'Bjorn, the cobbler. He singlehandedly burnt down the Palace of Bones!" The crowd applauds thunderously.

"Let us not forget the loss of brave Halfdan the younger. He was taken from Warshield too soon by a serpent of the sea. The sacrifice of the many brave warriors of Warshield will be remembered as we hear their hammers ring forever from the halls of Valhalla!"

More thunderous applause happened spontaneously at the very thought of these brave souls.

"Lastly, we must never forget why we are here as free people. That reason has a name, which is Wolfclaw Thur'Gold. He will rest in the Halls of Valhalla forever. I will miss Wolf's wisdom, courage, and friendship, as I know, many of you will. It is now my solemn honor to confer upon our friend and brave soul the title of *Sir Knight of the silent realm.*"

"Let us all make our way to the hall of Mead so that we might all celebrate and be merry," said Kilmister. Join our Queen in victory."

As Queen Thuireld walked to the Mead hall surrounded by her kingdom subjects, The Destiny of Tyr arrived on horseback.

"Your majesty, we must speak with you," said Avat'or of the Tyr. "We have news from the fellowship of Dragonwülf. He humbly requests to see your Grace."

· "Dragonwülf who?" asked the Queen. "I know no Dragonwülf."

Soon the entire kingdom would know of the legend of the old warrior.

Acknowledgments

The author would like to thank all the individuals who directly or indirectly helped me to undertake writing epic fantasy for my debut novel. Without their help and inspiration, it would not have been possible.

Douglas James "Dutch" Mann for believing in me since 1978.

Angela Ort, for her beautiful illustrations

Andrew DeBella for advice as a fellow writer.

Anthony DeBella for a plane ride that was used for inspiration.

Cecelia DeBella, for reading the rough draft and naming the toad in the Smithson letter, and Salvatore DeBella Sr.for moral support.

Thanks to Mindy Wilkinson for her portrait of Sebastian the Toad.

Also:

Eric Bloom and Donald Roeser and the music of *Blue Oyster Cult*

Floor Jansen and Nightwish

Joakim Brodén and his band Sabaton

Antii Martikainen for his music/ ToVallhalla

Thomas Bergersen and Two Steps from Hell

Ian Grimm and his excellent medieval music catalog

R.A Salvatore for his advice and encouragement through Facebook

JRR Tolkien for being my inspiration for virtually everything.

Author Page (E-mail etc.)

saldebella@gmail.com

Webpage
https://saldebella.wixsite.com/website

Facebook Page
https://www.facebook.com/sal.debella.7

Twitter
https://twitter.com/sal_debella

Sebastian the Toad by Mindy Wilkinson (1894).
As drawn from the Smithson letter.

Printed in the United States
by Baker & Taylor Publisher Services